diviner

Other books by Bryan Davis

Dragons of Starlight series:

Starlighter

Warrior

Echoes from the Edge series:

Beyond the Reflection's Edge

Eternity's Edge

Nightmare's Edge

Dragons in Our Midst series:

Raising Dragons

The Candlestone

Circles of Seven

Tears of a Dragon

Oracles of Fire series:

Eye of the Oracle

Enoch's Ghost

Last of the Nephilim

The Bones of Makaidos

dragons of starlight

diviner

Bryan Davis

ZONDERVAN®

ZONDERVAN.com/
AUTHORTRACKER
follow your favorite authors

We want to hear from you. Please send your comments about this book to us in care of zreview@zondervan.com. Thank you.

ZONDERVAN

Diviner
Copyright © 2011 by Bryan Davis

This title is also available as a Zondervan ebook. Visit www.zondervan.com/ebooks.

Requests for information should be addressed to:

Zondervan, *Grand Rapids, Michigan 49530*

ISBN 978-0-310-71838-3

Any Internet addresses (websites, blogs, etc.) and telephone numbers in this book are offered as a resource. They are not intended in any way to be or imply an endorsement by Zondervan, nor does Zondervan vouch for the content of these sites and numbers for the life of this book.

Cover design: Jeff Gifford
Cover illustration: Cliff Nielson
Interior design: Carlos Eluterio Estrada
Interior composition: Greg Johnson, Textbook Perfect

Printed in the United States of America

11 12 13 14 15 16 17 18 19 20 21 22 /DCI/ 24 23 22 21 20 19 18 17 16 15 14 13 12 11 10 9 8 7 6 5 4 3 2 1

diviner

one

Koren stood at the brink of a precipice and stared into the darkness below. Only inches in front of her black boots, a stairway descended sharply into the seemingly endless void. The rocky steps appeared to be hundreds of years old—narrow, crumbling, without rails or even walls—the bare, sculpted stone jutting downward into the chasm before being swallowed by the eerie darkness.

Floating a few feet above the stairs, globules of vaporous light streamed toward her, each one stretching out like a comet—a shining head of shimmering radiance followed by a glowing tail. Wiggling like tadpoles, they seemed to swim in the air, and as the first one passed by, it orbited her face, brushing her skin with a tickly buzz.

A soft voice emanated from the tadpole's radiant head, like a whisper from afar. "Has Exodus caused our pain? Will it ever return?" Then, after a final brush against her

cheek, the stream flew toward the wall behind her, a sliding barrier that someone had left open, as if anticipating
her arrival at the Northlands castle.

The parade of elongated globules flowed through
the opening, some pausing at Koren's spot at the top of
the stairway before joining the escaping herd. The rush
sounded like a crowd of people hurrying by, with only
snippets of their private conversations reaching her ears
as they passed.

"If the genetics are pure, we can force the recessive to
survive."

"I will take the eggs to Darksphere. The children will
have a dragon for a father."

"Find the escapees. No one will leave Starlight alive."

Clutching the stardrop she had taken from Cassabrie's
sanctum, Koren raised the hood of her Starlighter vest-
ment, shielding her ears from the barrage of splintered
sentences. She stepped down and shifted her weight
forward. Although the stony material crackled under her
boot, the stair held firm. Then, fanning out her cloak, she
walked slowly down the stairwell. Ahead lay the darkness of the unknown, a dizzying descent into a river of
visible voices.

Koren pressed on. She had no choice. Somewhere in
the castle lay the fallen star, Exodus, and Taushin, the
new dragon king, had compelled her to locate it — without detection. He waited outside, leaving her to pass
through the empty foyer and explore the castle as if she
were a burglar.

Her mind's eye drifted beyond Taushin, across the
Northlands' snow-covered landscape, southward to the

lush, fertile valley where she had left Jason Masters, her
new friend from the world of humans, a young man her
own age who had tried to rescue her. So much had happened since she had allowed herself to be captured in
order to save him from Taushin's sorceress, Zena, and her
pack of wolves. Where was he now? Dead? Captured? Had
he returned to his own planet and forgotten all about her?

Koren heaved a deep sigh. She had to push away these
dark thoughts. Jason was a warrior. Somehow he would
have found a way to survive, to continue his quest to free
the slaves, even if he had to retreat to the south. One
way or the other, he didn't appear to be anywhere in the
Northlands vicinity.

As light from the world outside faded behind her,
Koren slowed her pace. The never-ending streams of
light illuminated the area just enough to allow a view of
the dangers—a deep plunge into nothingness on each
side and crumbling, narrow steps ahead, seemingly more
fragile in the dimness. The slightest misstep could send
her tumbling into a bone-breaking crash or hurtling over
the precipice.

The stairs went on and on. Doubt stirred with each
careful step. How could a star have burrowed into a castle's cellar? Yet the whispering streams had to come from
somewhere, making the chasm a likely place to search, if
not the safest. The whispers continued, quieter now but
still audible in spite of her hood.

"The Starlighter is alone and forsaken. She wants to
die."

"Fear not the loss of life. Fear the loss of the eternal.
For life can be restored. Once lost, the eternal can never
be found again."

Koren kept her stare on the steps in front of her, marching to the beat of an inner rhythm. The fleeting statements seemed to beg to be put together, like puzzle pieces or perhaps threads in a mysterious mosaic. If she concentrated, maybe she could weave them into a coherent story, but so far the big picture seemed elusive.

Her tired feet plodded on and on. With each stair she passed, another appeared in the distance, creating a hypnotizing monotony, darkness giving way to light only to reveal yet another obstacle for her trembling muscles to overcome. Finally, a solid foundation came into view, an expanse that looked like the floor of a cave. A few paces in front of the final stair, a solid wall blocked forward progress. The chamber appeared to be wide open to the left, but it was too dark in that direction to see what might lie in wait. To the right, the whispering streams flowed from a cave opening in another wall.

Koren smacked her lips. Bitterness laced the air and coated her tongue with an acrid film. Taking a deep breath, she strode to the right, her gaze fixed on the cave. The pulsing lights funneled through the entrance, thick and frenzied, like radiant bats fleeing their daytime abode. She lowered her head and pushed through the barrage, trying to ignore the flurry of chaotic whispers.

Light appeared, growing brighter and brighter until she reached a massive chamber where a glowing sphere hovered a foot or so above the floor. As she crossed the threshold, the whispers stopped. All was quiet. Ahead, about twice the span of outstretched dragon wings, the nearly transparent ball of light trembled as if shaking in fear.

A flow of radiance erupted from a point on the surface and shaped into new streams before swimming into the tunnel behind her. At the sphere's lower extremity, liquid dripped to the floor, sizzling on contact. Vapor rose briefly before being sucked into narrow crevices zigzagging across the stone surface.

Koren eyed the vapor-producing liquid seeping into the ground. Pheterone. The miners back home found it in veins that likely originated from this spot.

She peered through the star's curved wall. Inside, a smaller ball of light, about half the size of the entrance to a dragon's cave, floated at eye level. Images flashed on the surface, changing every second—a red dragon, a cattle child, a stone worker with a cart. Each image acted as a layer on the sphere that peeled off in a pulse of light before shooting out as one of the vapors.

Koren touched the edge of the streams' exit point, a jagged hole nearly as big as her hand. As a new stream poured out, the flow warmed her skin. The light filtered through the gaps between her fingers and gathered behind her into yet another tadpole-like projectile.

Mentally, she ran over what little she knew about this star that wasn't a star. Taushin had called it "a celestial angel," referring to the sphere as a guide given to this planet by the Creator. Unbidden, his words rose in her mind. *The citizens of the planet labeled it a star, even though they knew that the twinkling dots in the heavens were very different. Although it was somewhat hot centuries ago, Exodus sustained a wound in its outer membrane, and it lost its heat.*

As another trickle of warmth leaked from the wound, Koren uncurled the fingers of her other hand, revealing the stardrop. The size of a large knuckle, the sphere glowed with white light.

Her mission was to enter Exodus through the hole and tell Starlight's stories from within. The light energy from her tales should cause Exodus to inflate and rise again. It would then release pheterone, infusing the atmosphere with the gas the dragons required to survive, thereby eliminating the need for human slaves. Her people could finally shake off their chains and return to their home world, Jason's world.

She stared at the pulsing stardrop in her hand. One problem spoiled this scenario. If the hole remained in Exodus, it would eventually sink as it did before, and what they had gained would be lost. Only one alternative seemed to be foolproof—she could enter the star and use the stardrop to seal the hole from the inside. She would become the guiding angel of Starlight—her destiny as a Starlighter, according to Taushin.

Again his words returned to her mind: *You may take your place as a star in the sky, a watchful angel who forever tells the Creator's stories to every soul in the world, dragon and human alike ... if they will listen.*

If. And if they did not, her sacrifice would be for nothing. For there would be no way out ... ever.

As if waging war in her mind, Taushin's counter-argument reverberated.

Why sacrifice? Why risk harm to yourself when it is possible to gain what you long for without it? With your power, I am sure you can keep the star aloft long enough for me to

*get the slaves out. To be eternally trapped while your liber-
ated friends celebrate their freedom without you would be
the greatest of tortures. Yes, you would feel some joy . . . temporarily. But what about after a hundred years? A thousand
years? Ten thousand? After every rejoicing slave is dead,
you will be hovering over a thankless land, forever and ever.
Your sorrow will never end.*

Koren shook her head, trying to sling the competing
thoughts away. No matter what she decided to do later,
she could do nothing from outside the star. Maybe when
she entered, a new secret would be revealed that would
make her decision an easier one.

She pushed the edge of the hole to one side. It
stretched easily. As if in response, a low wail sounded
from the inner sphere. She pulled again, stretching the
gap and pushing her head and torso inside. Another wail,
longer and louder, echoed throughout the sphere's inner
cavity.

She slid all the way in and allowed the pliable membrane to ease back into place, leaving a slightly larger
hole than before. This time a gentle sigh drifted from wall
to wall.

Koren stood on the curved floor, angling her body to
keep her balance. "Is someone in here?" she called.

Her own words bounced back at her, repeating her
question several times before fading.

A voice emanated from the small inner sphere. "Who
are you?"

Koren let her boots slide down to the bottom of the
floor. As she approached the source of the voice, she
spoke in a soothing tone. "My name is Koren."

"Koren?" The images on the sphere's surface stopped, freezing at a portrait of Koren pulling a cart filled with honeycombs. "Koren, the Starlighter who works for Arxad?"

"Yes." She reached a hand toward the sphere, feeling the energy flowing from the speaking ball. "What is your name?"

The flow diminished. Then, as if deflating, the sphere contracted, growing taller in proportion to its width. It formed into the shape of a girl, and the colors in the portrait spread across her body—red into her flowing hair, green into her eyes, and blue into a cloak that matched Koren's. Only her dress remained white. Finally, every detail crystallized. She seemed as human as any young woman on Starlight. It was like looking at a mirror ... with one exception.

Koren looked down at her own clothes. Although she wore the Starlighter's cloak, the black dress Zena had forced upon her covered her body from neck to knees, and the equally black boots adorned her feet, tied at the back to mid-calf.

The girl stared, her expression curious, yet sad. With her hood raised, she tilted her head to the side and spoke softly. "Why are you here, Koren?"

Koren glanced back at the hole. The question felt like a challenge, a rebuke. It would be easy to retreat and slide out, run away from this responsibility ... too easy. "I'm here to try to resurrect Exodus."

"It is impossible," the girl said with an ache in her voice. "I have tried for many years, but the star will not rise. No matter how many tales I tell, Exodus remains here, trapped in the grasp of Starlight itself."

Koren swallowed. Whoever this girl was, she had obviously suffered greatly. "What's your name?"

Blinking, the girl tilted her head to the other side. "My name?"

"Yes. I'm Koren, and you're …" She nodded, hoping to prompt the girl for an answer.

The girl averted her eyes and stared blankly at the wound in the sphere's surface. Her cheeks changed hue, though not with normal red tones. It seemed that the colors from the flashing images bled into the surface of her skin. "My name," she repeated in a whisper. "That is a thought that has not entered my mind in a very long time."

"You mean, you don't remember your own name?"

"A name from long ago is returning. I know not whether it is mine or another's." She returned her gaze to Koren, her face still infused with multicolored splotches. "Does Brinella suit me?"

"Brinella," Koren repeated. "It's lovely."

"Good. Then I will—" Brinella stiffened. Her eyes shot wide open. As if seized by convulsions, her body heaved. Words poured from her mouth, a river of competing voices, yet none matching her own.

"I am from another world. I have come to request help against the forces of corruption."

"But you're a dragon. You captured our people and enslaved them."

"Don't worry. He's with us."

"But how can you trust one of them?"

As the words continued to spew, they became garbled, unintelligible. They collected into streams and shot out the hole, and once outside, they formed into glowing whisperers and swam through the tunnel.

After nearly a minute of disgorging, Brinella finally stopped. Holding a hand against her stomach, she looked at Koren, her face now pale. "I apologize for that outburst. When the tales of Starlight fill me, they must eventually come out."

"It's all right. Feel free to … uh … empty yourself whenever you need to." Koren suppressed a grimace. Brinella's role as a guiding angel of Starlight surely had many drawbacks. She nodded toward the wound in the surface. "Have you tried to escape through that hole?"

"I cannot escape, Koren. Exodus must have a Star-lighter dwelling within, or it will collapse and no longer feed the air with sustenance. Because of my love for this world and our Creator, I made a vow to stay here. If I were to leave my post untended and break my vow, I would become a disembodied spirit, trapped between the worlds of the living and the dead. I would have no path to paradise. My best hope is to die here. Since I am bound to Exodus, its destruction by the hand of another will bring about my death. Then I will fly to the Creator and live with him forever."

"But no one would want to destroy Exodus. It's the only hope for dragons and humans."

"I know," Brinella said. "If I could make Exodus fly and once again fill the atmosphere with life-giving sustenance, I would. But I cannot."

Koren slanted her head upward. Directly above, a channel at least as wide as Exodus led to a faraway light, apparently an exit to the outside, perhaps at the top of one of the mountains that rose behind the castle. "I don't understand. The dragon king said I could inflate Exodus and make it rise again."

Brinella looked away. "If the dragon king said so, then you are able."

"Really?" Koren slid to the side to catch her gaze again. As she studied Brinella, more of Taushin's instructions came to mind. *I alone know how a Starlighter can resurrect the star, and now I reveal the secret, a prophecy hidden from other dragons, even Tamminy. Once your will is set to raise Exodus, a crown of light will appear within the star. Take it. Wear it. Only then will you have the ability you need to accomplish this task. It is the crown that gives you the ability to hear Starlight's tales, a spiritual receiver that collects the planet's joys and woes.*

Yet Brinella wore no visible crown. "If I am able, then why aren't you?"

Brinella pushed her cloak to the side, revealing a gap in her dress just under her rib cage. The length of a hand, the rip in the material appeared to be stained red. "Like Exodus, I am wounded. Because a spear pierced its skin, it also pierced me. I have not the power that I possessed before. I am still able to collect and tell Starlight's tales, but I do so now without providing the wisdom that follows the words."

"Oh, yes. A guiding angel. You provided lessons behind the stories."

Brinella nodded. "For a long time, many enjoyed my tales and my commentary, but as humankind grew wicked, they also became intolerant. In fact, it seemed that they no longer even heard me. They merely felt heat and did not comprehend the infusion of wisdom. What was meant to provide discernment and a light to their paths became to them nothing more than an irritant. A few still heard my tales, but even they questioned my purpose. Some demanded that I come down from the sky and speak to them as a friend, to not be so self-righteous, but, of course, I could not."

"Because you couldn't get out of the star?"

"Because of dire warnings to keep Exodus out of reach of the people. The star is holy, and humans with impure hearts endanger their lives if they draw too near. Close interaction with humans is likely to be disastrous."

Koren imagined the sight, a flaming sphere descending toward a group of people who either fled or cast stones to send it away. "So they tried to get rid of you."

Nodding again, Brinella pulled the cloak back in place, hiding the gash. "I want to die. If this world cares not for a guiding light, then it would be better for Exodus to be destroyed, but I cannot do this myself and still keep my vow. It is true that if someone dared to do this deed, Starlight would become another Darksphere, but that would matter little. The light our planet once had fled long ago. The people make a show of honoring the Code. The words flow like poetry from their lips, but they rarely let the wisdom penetrate their hearts. This is darkness, indeed."

Koren pointed at herself. "What would happen to you if *I* were to resurrect Exodus?"

Brinella's eyes seemed to brighten. "I dared not mention that option. It would be selfish of me to suggest it."

"Go on. I'm listening."

"If another Starlighter were to take my place, I would no longer be bound to Exodus. I could go to my Lord without the star's destruction." Brinella shook her head sadly. "But I could never ask you to do that. The world would lash out against you as it did me, and you could easily face the same fate, either centuries trapped beneath a ceiling of rock or, should you escape the star's embrace, an eternity of lonely wandering."

Koren gazed into Brinella's weary eyes. The poor girl was so sad, so tired. She just wanted to go home to her Creator. She knew nothing about Taushin's alternative idea, to temporarily resurrect Exodus without sealing the hole. What would happen to Brinella then?

Reaching out, Koren took Brinella's hand. A buzz ran up Koren's arm, warming her skin. "Are you sure there aren't any other possibilities? Could you sit against the hole and block it with your body?"

"I have tried, but Starlight's tales don't come to me unless I am at the center."

Koren tapped her chin. "Then maybe I could block it while you tell tales from the center. Then it would rise, wouldn't it?"

"With both of us weighing it down?" Brinella shook her head. "I doubt it."

"Maybe I can find the king of the Northlands. He can tell us if Exodus can carry that much weight."

"Find him?" Brinella asked. "You said the king of the dragons told you to inflate Exodus and make it rise."

"Yes. That was Taushin, king of the dragons in the south."

Brinella's tone sharpened. "There is only one king of the dragons, and his name is Alaph, the lord of this castle."

"Alaph?" Koren repeated. "I don't know that name."

"How is it that a Starlighter does not know the white dragon's name?" Brinella squinted. "Are you sure you are a Starlighter?"

Koren withdrew her hand. "I ... I'm pretty sure. When I tell stories, they come to life around me. Everyone can see them."

"Do your listeners lose their focus on the world?"

Koren nodded. "It's like they're hypnotized. I have used their loss of senses to escape from danger more than once."

"You left them in that state?" Brinella backed away a step, new color filling her cheeks. "I think I am beginning to understand."

Koren tried to close the gap with a step of her own, but Brinella slid farther away. "What's wrong?" Koren asked.

"You wear the vestments of a sorceress. You do not know Alaph. When your listeners are prepared to hear your teaching, you leave without filling their minds with wisdom. Under your influence, they are open, vulnerable, easily enslaved. A Starlighter must never leave her listeners in that state. If they come out of a trance on their own, they are susceptible to any influence that enters their minds. The Starlighter must command her visions to flee so her hearers can return to normal and decide whether or not to accept the wisdom she has provided. Otherwise, they are nothing more than—" Spasms rocked Brinella's body. As before, a barrage of words surged from her mouth in a series of altered voices.

"You cannot understand her words, because you are dull of hearing."

"What a fool you are! There are no sounds. It is merely a star."

"She provides wisdom. She warns of disaster. The star is a gift from the Creator."

"The star is a curse. The sooner we are rid of it, the better."

The flood of words ceased. Panting, Brinella backed farther away, waving a hand as she spoke in halting gasps. "Leave me now … You cannot replace me … You have the power … the power of a Starlighter … but you lack the spirit or the wisdom of one."

Koren stepped closer again, displaying the stardrop in her palm. "Do you want this? You can seal the hole and—"

"I want nothing from your hand!" Brinella thrust a finger toward the wound. "Leave me! It is better that I suffer alone than allow a pretender to take my place!"

A wave of heat flashed across Koren's skin, and tears welled in her eyes. Brinella's pain-twisted expression tore a hole in her heart. As she slid her boots backwards, she closed her fingers around the stardrop. "I'll find the white dragon and ask him what to do to get you out of here. I won't forsake you."

"As you did not forsake those you hypnotized?" Brinella turned her back. "Speak to Alaph if you wish. If you search the castle, you might be able to find him. But leave my presence. I will not be deceived by a sorceress in a Starlighter's body."

Brinella's head sank into her torso, and her legs drew upward. Seconds later, only a floating ball remained, again covered with an array of images and again emitting streams of multicolored light.

The streams zoomed toward Koren, pelting her body with their buzzing impulses, though they carried no momentum and left no mark. As if driven back, she turned toward the star's wound and scaled the slick incline, her boots providing traction. After glancing at Brinella once more, she stretched the hole and slid through. A new cry of pain sounded from within, but it quickly silenced.

Now on the outside, Koren clenched her fists. Her ears flamed. A pretender? A sorceress? How could Brinella say such things?

Glaring at her clothes, Koren pinched a sleeve. This black dress wasn't really hers. Zena forced her to wear it. It wasn't fair to be judged based on what she did under compulsion. And how could she have learned the white dragon's name? How could she have known she shouldn't leave people hypnotized? There was nothing in the Code about how to be a Starlighter.

She turned toward the tunnel leading to the long stairway. The answers to her questions lay elsewhere. Taushin waited outside the castle, and the white dragon abided somewhere within. Since Taushin was able to see through her eyes due to the connection he'd forged with her, he had likely watched everything that happened within the star, but without the transmission of sound, he couldn't know what Brinella had said. Still, he probably had read the girl's facial expressions and figured out that something went wrong. Yet, no matter what Taushin thought about Koren's actions, he couldn't do anything to stop her, at least not right now.

Koren turned back to the sphere and, keeping the stardrop in her grip, pulled the sides of the wound together. Brinella moaned. Koren flinched. This would be like performing surgery without anesthesia. She squeezed the stardrop, then opened her hand. The once spherical shape had flattened and spread out. Pinching the gap closed with one hand, she pressed the stardrop against the wound with the other and rubbed it across the narrow opening as if applying a salve.

While Brinella continued whimpering softly, the glowing material drizzled over the gap but dripped to the floor. It didn't appear to be sticking at all. Even as she rubbed, fresh material from the star's membrane gathered in her palm. Her hand acted like a scoop, digging out stardrop-like radiance without leaving a divot in the surface.

She spread out her fingers and looked at the handful of radiance. Taushin had said she could seal the wound from inside, so maybe she should give it a try. After releasing her pinching hold, she reached through the wound and applied her newly gathered salve on the inner wall. The top of the wound sealed instantly, but, of course, with her arm in the way, she couldn't possibly seal the rest of it.

She withdrew her arm and scooped out another handful. Then, after compressing it into a new stardrop, she pushed it through the hole and rolled it toward Brinella.

"You can use this to seal the wound and rise again," she called. "It's up to you."

As the stardrop rolled toward the center of Exodus, two eyes appeared in Brinella's floating ball, blinking. Her voice returned, weak and lamenting. "If you think Exodus's rising is up to me, Koren, you have much to learn."

The stardrop rested near Brinella's hovering sphere, but she seemed to pay it no further mind. The eyes vanished, and the flashing images continued—more tales to be communicated, stories of Starlight emanating from the bosom of the planet for the sake of anyone who cared to listen.

Heaving a sigh, Koren walked into the tunnel, her legs wobbly. The swimming lights streamed from behind, breezing by without pausing to deliver their whispered messages.

Koren shuffled her feet. There was no need to hurry. The climb would take a long time anyway. When she reached the stairs, she looked beyond them and scanned the path leading in the opposite direction from the one that had taken her to Exodus. A glowing whisperer broke off from the stream and swam that way.

After glancing at the stairs, Koren followed the floating voice. It swam slowly into a new tunnel, allowing her to catch up. Its glow illuminated the area, making a spherical halo large enough to envelop her body as she walked at its pace.

Soon the tunnel opened into another chamber, and the glow, wiggling as it floated, continued. Koren stopped and slid her foot along the floor. It seemed solid. In fact, it felt smooth, more like marble than unfinished stone. A few objects lay scattered about, books and stacks of papers, but with the whisperer's light farther away now, shadows kept their details hidden.

At the far side of the chamber, maybe five steps away, the elongated orb stopped at a wall of rock. It turned to the left and inched along the barrier, as if searching for a hole that would let it escape.

Glancing down at the floor to avoid stacks of books, Koren caught up with the whisperer and listened as its voice grew clear.

"Store them, Arxad. The research and relics might be useful later."

Then, as the globule of light continued its slow, futile crawl, it repeated the sentence again and again.

Koren picked up a hefty book and blew a coat of dust from the cover. In bold handwritten letters, the title read *Disease Progression — Observation Book #3*. She opened to the first page, but the small handwriting prevented her from reading anything beyond the title at the top. *Day Seventeen — Account Recorded by Orson of Masters Lake University.*

"Orson," Koren whispered. "How odd." Her father was named Orson, but there wasn't any place on Starlight called Masters Lake University. Yet Jason's last name was Masters, so two familiar names in the same old book had to be more than mere coincidence.

She laid the book on top of its stack. Since she couldn't possibly haul one of these all the way up the stairs, the mystery would have to remain a mystery, at least for now.

Koren shifted her attention back to the whisperer. It lit up the wall's gray, stony surface all the way to the floor, where a wooden pole lay a few inches in front of her boots. She stooped and looked it over. About twice the width of a broom handle, it appeared to be as long as she was tall.

She grasped it and slowly lifted. It was heavier than she expected, more so to one side than the other. She raised it closer to the floating spheroid and examined the heavier end. There the wood changed over to metal and widened to the barbed point of a spear, similar to the weapon the hunter dragons used at times. A leather band encircled the spear's neck, securing a cylinder wrapped in paper. The cylinder appeared to be as big around as her forearm and about half as long.

She squinted at a series of letters printed on the side—*DANGER. EXPLOSIVE*. Easing the spear away, she leaned it against the wall and studied it from two steps back. She set a hand on her hip and let *explosive* roll around in her thoughts. The miners had created explosive devices from effervescent minerals, allowing the gasses in a sealed compartment to build up until they exploded, but the force was great enough only to dislodge small, stubborn rocks they couldn't reach with a hammer and chisel. Surely it couldn't be considered dangerous or be used as an enhancement to a weapon. What could a small pop like that do to an enemy that the point of a spear couldn't?

Koren grasped the spear again and drew it close to her nose. The odor was unfamiliar, nothing like the minerals the miners used. It smelled like sulfur, charcoal, and ... and something else.

She touched the paper. It seemed fully intact. If this device was meant to explode, it obviously failed or perhaps was never used.

After taking a step to the left to move back into the glow, she drew the spear close again and studied the words. The lettering was perfectly straight without a hint of change in width or darkness. Who could have written this message so flawlessly, and why? Someone stored it here for a reason—a relic that might be useful someday. But what was its purpose?

Her thoughts snapped back to Exodus and its hole. This spear could have easily ripped a gash that size. But with an explosive attached, someone meant to do more damage than merely deflate the star. Whoever threw that spear meant to destroy Exodus and the guiding angel within.

The whisperer passed by a wooden slat nailed into the rock. More slats ran up the wall until they disappeared in the darkness. Just like in the Exodus chamber, a tiny light shone far above, another opening to the outside, though this one seemed even farther away.

Koren touched the closest slat. Together, these slats could act as a ladder, another way to leave the castle's underground, but it would take hours to scale, and the danger would be even greater than climbing the staircase.

She looked at the floor again. More oddities met her gaze, but—except for papers and books—nothing looked familiar. It would be fascinating to sit here and search through everything, deciphering what the objects might be.

As her eyes followed the globule's path, one item caught her attention, a black rectangular box no bigger than her hand. She picked it up and studied a series of white letters near the edge of one surface. Printed next to a raised circle, they spelled out an unfamiliar word— *DETONATE*.

She formed the word silently with her mouth, then, shrugging, she laid the box back where she had found it. More mysteries. More unanswered questions.

The whisperer finally reached the entry tunnel and, breaking away from the wall, headed back to the stair- case, taking the halo of light with it. Koren let her shoul- ders sag. Learning about the other relics here would have to wait, but at least she could take the spear into brighter light and get a better look at it.

After following the whisperer back to the stream, she stopped at the bottom of the stairs and studied the spear again. The off-white paper had charred edges, and a sooty smear underlined the word *DANGER*. Why would a spear have been exposed to fire and then only partially burned?

Koren gazed up the stairs. Taking this to Taushin would be foolhardy. Though he had likely already seen it through her eyes, she couldn't allow him to use it for evil purposes.

With great care, she laid the spear on the floor near the base of the wall opposite the bottom step. Then she walked into the flow of whispering lights and began climbing the stairs, listening to the disjointed murmur- ings. It might take an hour to get to the top, but trying to piece together the jumbled sentences would keep her mind occupied.

When she reached the top, she would find the white dragon, as she had promised Brinella she would. Taushin might protest in any number of ways, but she had to learn the truth, and if the white dragon could be found, she would find him.

two

ason stood in the midst of the forest and listened to the eerie quiet. No birds flitted. The leaves gave no hint of a breeze. His father, Edison Masters, waited close behind, only a heartbeat away, breathing not a word.

His sword drawn, Jason scanned the dark sky through an opening in the canopy. A moon peeked between cloudbanks: Pariah, the smallest of the trio that rose and set together. Until now, lack of light proved to be a benefit. After leaving the abandoned dragon village, he and his father had been able to cross miles of open land without detection, even though two dragons had flown overhead during the journey. Now deep in a thick forest, they had reached a concealed area, but it seemed that the real danger lurked here rather than out in the open.

A breeze passed through the branches and filtered down to their level. Jason took in the sensation, searching the wind for telltale odors and gaps that might indicate a close presence. About twenty paces to his left, something stood between two trees.

Edison leaned close and whispered, "I smell a familiar odor, but I can't place it."

Nodding, Jason pointed with his sword at the suspected hiding place. His father's sense of smell was keen, and something familiar could mean good news. Recognizable odors would likely originate from Major Four, so the lurker might well be human, but whoever it was could be combative. Coming upon two strangers in a dark forest had to be a frightening experience, especially for a runaway slave.

When Jason drew in a breath, hoping to call with a reassuring word, a sharp voice broke in.

"It's you!" The undergrowth rustled, and a human form burst into the open. As it closed in, Jason lifted his sword, but when the form took on a feminine shape, he lowered it again. She leaped, wrapping her arms around him. "Oh, Jason! You're alive! Praise the Creator!"

Jason pushed her back gently and sheathed his sword. "Elyssa?"

Dim moonlight illuminated her smiling face. "Of course it's me! Who else on this planet would hug you like that?"

"Uh ..." He glanced at her waist. A sword belt hung loosely at her hips, and the hilt protruded from a scabbard at her side. "You look ... different."

She touched her sword. "You didn't expect a girl to wander around here without a weapon, did you?" Reaching out, she lifted his necklace chain, pulling a pendant from under his shirt and letting it dangle from her fingers. "You found it!"

"Yeah. It's been a good reminder. That's why I'm here, actually. I was searching for you."

Her smile wavering, she kept her gaze on the pendant. "What happened to Koren?"

"Exchange stories later," Edison said. "I detect another odor. This one isn't human."

Jason pulled away from Elyssa and moved to his father's side. A new rustling disturbed the silence, maybe fifty paces away. This creature didn't seem to care to hide its presence.

Elyssa touched Jason's back and whispered into his ear. "It's intelligent. It's searching for something. I sense determination … and malice."

Drawing his sword, Jason waved for Elyssa to move back. She stayed put, withdrawing her own sword. Now all three stood in the dark with weapons brandished, Edison a step or two in front. The rustling grew closer and closer. Thirty paces. Twenty paces. A snuffling sound blended in, then a growl.

Barely visible in the moonlight, Edison glanced between Elyssa and the source of the noise. He raised a hand and whispered sternly, "Son, stay here with Elyssa. That's an order." Then, starting with a quick leap, he hustled toward the creature.

"No!" Jason took a hard step but halted. Father gave an order. How could he disobey?

A draconic scream erupted from the darkness. Elyssa charged. Jason leaped to catch her but missed. He dashed after her, following the sounds—crunching footfalls, splintering wood, and horrific squeals and growls. He stopped at a gap in the forest. Elyssa stood there, her sword drooping at her side as she looked up at the sky. Pariah shone through, giving light to the battlefield. With broken branches strewn about, a second sword lay at her feet.

Her body quaking, Elyssa's quiet voice shook. "A dragon took him."

"Took him?" Jason picked up the sword, Father's sword, wet with blood. His head swimming, he scanned the sky. A dragon flew across the purple canopy carrying a limp body in its claws. Pain stabbed Jason's gut. Bile rose in his throat, bitter and burning, and a bare whisper leaked out. "Father!"

"Oh, Jason!" Elyssa dropped her sword and embraced him. "I'm so sorry! It's all my fault. If I hadn't come, your father wouldn't have tried to face the dragon alone."

Jason blinked. His arms felt like stiff logs. He couldn't lift them even to return the embrace. A tragedy. As his mind threatened to become numb as well, one of his father's teachings broke though. *Allow for grief, but a warrior must not give in to despair.*

He pushed her back. "We have to follow that dragon."

"We can't possibly keep up with a flying—"

"We have to try." Jason shoved his sword back into its sheath. "Let's go. Stay as close behind me as you can."

He jogged through the forest, ducking under branches that seemed to reach out just as he approached. Twice he stumbled over tree roots before regaining his balance. Elyssa kept pace without a mishap, taking advantage of his trail blazing or maybe her Diviner's gift. He glanced at the sky as often as he dared. The dragon shrank in the distance and finally dropped out of view.

"He's going to the dragon village," Elyssa said from behind.

Jason kept his focus straight ahead, speaking in short bursts as he marched on. "I see that … I was there a few hours ago … The place was deserted."

After several minutes, he stepped into the open. To his right, the ground sloped upward into a range of mountains. To his left, a plateau stretched out for miles, leading north to the dragon village. A few lights glimmered in that direction, probably lanterns. Maybe dragons and humans had returned to the streets.

Elyssa joined him, taking in deep breaths. "It's a long way."

"I know. Father and I just crossed this area." Jason took in a deep breath of his own and let it out slowly. Every muscle ached. It seemed that energy drained from his body and spilled into the ground, as if stopping had caused his determination to spring a leak. Everything he carried seemed to double its weight—his sword, his scabbard, even the pouch in which he transported the stardrop, still attached to his belt.

He touched the dangling pouch with a finger. He and his father had come to find Elyssa. Job number one was complete. Now he had to get the stardrop to Koren. For some reason, she needed to swallow it. At least that's what Petra had indicated before he and his father had left Alaph's castle. Yet now with his father in danger, how could he go on with job number two?

"You must be exhausted," Elyssa said. "I know I am."

"I have to go!" Jason bit his lip. That came out far too harshly. Taking another breath, he reached his hand toward hers and softened his tone. "If you can come, that would be great. Your gifts would be helpful. If not, I think you'll be safe hiding in the forest. But no matter what you decide, I have to go. You understand that, right?"

"Of course I do." She took his hand. "And I am coming with you. I don't want to let you out of my sight again. It was hard enough finding you this time."

He looked into her eyes, more visible now that they stood in the open. They were tired but determined. With her sword again in hand, her body straight, and her legs firmly set, she was the portrait of the ready warrior.

Giving her a smile, he nodded. "I was hoping you'd come," was all he could manage. He turned and marched toward the distant lanterns. With so little light to guide their way, and with his leg muscles threatening to lock in spasms, he had to keep a slower pace than his passion demanded. Father was out there, probably badly wounded, maybe dead. Getting to him as quickly as possible was all that mattered.

⋙⋘

Standing in the cave's kitchen area, Constance turned the mill's arm-length handle one last time. There. The final bone had gone through. That was one hard job finished, one of many chores Koren used to do. When she and the other two girls were around to help, getting to bed at a reasonable hour was commonplace, but not tonight. The list of things to do would last well past midnight.

Bracing one hand on the kitchen's central oak table, she mopped her brow with the fringe of her apron. It took a lot of strength to grind sheep bones, but Arxad always insisted on wasting nothing. Of course, he and his family crunched the larger bones with their powerful jaws, but the lower legs often splintered, and thus were saved for grinding. According to Arxad, the powder made an excellent flavoring for his morning brew of cactus tea.

She pulled the catch bin from the bottom of the grinder, using both hands to slide the wooden bowl to the edge of the table. With light from a wall lantern flickering behind her, her head cast a shadow over the bowl, making it difficult to tell how finely the mill had ground the bones. She could always use a sifter to —

"Hello? Madam Orley? Are you in there?"

Constance wiped her hands on her apron. "Yeager? Is that you?"

"Yes, Madam. May I come in?"

"You may. Do you have your ... uh ... valuables with you?"

"Of course." Yeager, a tall man with a muscular build, dark curly hair, and at least a three-day's beard, ambled into the lantern light, holding a chain that led into the darkness behind him. "And they are valuable, indeed. I heard you need help, so I brought what little I have available."

He stopped and rattled the chain. A boy wearing a leather collar limped into the light, using a walking stick to compensate for a missing lower leg. Another boy followed, his collar linked to the other boy's by the chain. He held a withered forearm close to his waist. Finally, a girl joined them. The chain ended at a hook attached to her collar.

Constance stepped out of the lantern's way. The flickering light danced on the boys' clean bare chests and illuminated their glassy eyes. Standing no taller than her own five feet and two inches and wearing only short trousers, they appeared to be about twelve years old. The girl was slightly taller, but her sunken cheeks and eyes spoke of severe malnutrition. If not for her clean tunic and skirt, anyone would have thought her to be a cattle child.

"Where did you get them?" Constance asked. "The cattle camp is empty."

"I took these and a few others from the camp before the escape. I cleaned them up a bit. Gave the girl some clothes."

"But we're in lockdown. Why are you trading at all?"

"I asked the Separators for an exception. I can't afford to feed my inventory, so they said I could sell them to whoever would take them. Actually, it was easy to place them. When there is short supply, there are willing buyers."

Constance pointed at the closer boy. "But you had no buyers for these."

His eyes shifted, blinking, then a confident smile emerged. "I saved them for you. I heard that Koren, Natalla, and Petra are all missing, so I guessed you would need at least one new servant."

"This is true. I suppose everyone knows about that by now." She studied the eyes of each child in turn, all glazed and faraway. Yeager had obviously drugged them. "What are their names?"

Yeager stared at her for a moment, then coughed. "Well, as you can imagine, I don't ask them their names. A man in my line of work can't afford to get emotionally attached."

"Yes, I can imagine." Constance glared at him. If greed could walk and talk, his name would be Yeager. "The reality is that you brought these three because you couldn't place them anywhere else."

"Nonsense. As I said, I saved them for—"

"Do you think me a fool?" She touched the first boy's shoulder. "They're handicapped. They need to work with the accountant or with the nursery maid."

"Those positions have been filled." He nodded toward the kitchen table. "I understand your dilemma. With household labors you need boys with strong arms and legs."

"It's not that I don't want to care for these boys, it's just that there is hard work—"

"Say no more. I said I understand." Yeager touched the girl's head. "This one is not handicapped. She is malnourished, to be sure, but that is easily remedied. Everyone knows Arxad feeds his servants well."

Constance took off her apron and folded it, keeping her eyes on her hands. "I would gladly take her, but Arxad is not here. Nor is Fellina. I cannot get authorization."

"When will they return?"

"Neither gave me word." She laid the apron on the table and smoothed it with both hands. "Arxad has been known to leave for days or even weeks. When he is gone, Fellina sometimes leaves for quite a while as well. They trust me to keep their home in order."

"Then surely they would trust you to acquire new help."

"You know as well as I do that only a dragon can approve a placement. Even Arxad would get angry over such a breach in protocol."

Yeager stroked his chin. "The Separators said I have to place them today. Since the girl is obviously too malnourished, the breeders didn't want her. You know what will happen to them tomorrow."

Constance glanced at the grinding mill on the table, then lowered her head, unable to look the girl in the eyes. "Yes, I know."

"Then take her," Yeager said. "Hide her. Feed her. Have some compassion."

"Compassion? How dare you speak to me about compassion!" Constance aimed a shaking finger at him, her voice rising. "You're the one who drags these poor children from place to place, drugging them out of their minds and auctioning them off like property."

"They *are* property. Every cattle child belongs to Magnar, or rather Taushin, I suppose. I get to keep the bare scrapings of the purchase price, and the rest goes to whoever sits his scaly backside on the Basilica throne." He pointed a finger of his own. "You are property, too. Arxad's property. Even though you wear no chain or collar, you are every bit as shackled as these children are. You just refuse to admit it. You were born a slave, and you will die a slave."

She lowered her finger and cooled her tone. "I know. I have said the same myself, but I am beginning to doubt it."

"What is there to doubt? Do you doubt the cattle camp? The barrier wall?"

Constance shook her head. "Those are undeniable. I doubt only that I came from my mother's womb in chains. Slaves are made, not born. Dragons keep me here against my will. The barrier wall is proof enough that every one of us would run to freedom if not for the wall and the guardians who patrol it. If I had wings, I would fly to the Northlands and be with my daughter."

Yeager laughed. "Do you still believe that story? There is no king of the Northlands. Promoted slaves are eaten by Magnar and his closest friends."

"You are the one who believes the myths." She reached into her tunic pocket and withdrew a folded parchment. "My daughter wrote to me from the Northlands. I recognize her handwriting."

Closing his eyes, Yeager took in a deep breath. Then, leaning close, he whispered, "I risk my life in telling you this, but I do so for the sake of this little girl and for pity's sake, pity for your loss of a husband and a daughter within the span of three years." He glanced around the kitchen. "I have witnessed part of a Promotion myself. Do you remember when the dragons extended the barrier wall on the western boundary?"

"I remember. They had men chiseling stone night and day."

Yeager nodded. "During those months, I worked with the stone movers. When that Assignment ended, the Separators were trying to decide whether or not to return me to slave trading. I was in the Basilica—drugged, of course—but they didn't give me enough, so it wore off early. Arxad brought your daughter in to Magnar. He said, 'I chose this one for promotion from my own household. She is proficient in medicine.' Then Magnar said, 'Are you certain her medical background is your primary motivation?'

"Arxad put on a show of surprise, but even I could see through it. He said, 'What other reason would I have?' So Magnar gave him a scowl and said, 'A pretext to obtain the redhead from the cattle camp. You should forget her. It would be better for us all if she dies there.' After they argued for a while, Magnar finally gave in."

Constance felt her mouth drop open. With her throat tightening, she couldn't utter a word. Koren had replaced her daughter in Arxad's household. Everyone knew that. But who could have guessed that Arxad had planned the exchange all along?

"Then," Yeager continued, "Magnar asked if Arxad had completed the preparations." He tapped a finger on the parchment in Constance's hand. "That's when Arxad showed him this very letter."

She rattled the parchment at him. "I don't believe a word of it! How could you know it's the same letter?"

"Because Arxad read the first part out loud, and they both got a good laugh out of it. Then Magnar led her away. I assume he intended to eat her, because he said something about preparing a banquet."

Constance shook her head hard. "Arxad would never laugh at our pain. He is good to us. Everyone knows that."

Yeager snatched the parchment from her hand and, leaving it folded, set it close to her eyes. "Do you need to open it to see what it says? I don't." He looked in the opposite direction. "Dear Mother, I am happy in the Northlands with the great dragon king. Arxad told me I would learn more about medicine here, so I am looking forward to that. Papa will be proud of me when—"

"Stop!" Constance grabbed the letter and spun away. As she pressed it against her lips, spasms rocked her body. "Leave now. Just leave."

"And what of the girl? I'll give her to you at no charge. You can't let her go to the stone."

Staying turned, Constance glanced over her shoulder at the girl. With hair cut into four different lengths and her face so sunken her eyes seemed ready to roll out of their sockets, she was truly a pitiful sight. Could she hide the girl here without getting permission, at least for a few nights? Fellina might return with Xenith at any moment, so getting food for the girl secretly might be impossible. And what of Arxad? He laughed with Magnar! Laughed about poor, sweet Agatha! And then ... Constance bit her lip hard. And then Magnar ate her? Could that part really be true? Yeager didn't see it happen, but if Agatha had really gone to the Northlands, why would Magnar have taken her away? Shouldn't Arxad have prepared her for the journey?

Constance hid her face and sobbed. Arxad wasn't the kind master he pretended to be. He was just as heartless and cruel as all the others. She couldn't hide this poor girl. No, she would be leaving this household herself. As soon as possible. But where would she go? The wilderness? Yes, the wilderness. Even though no one had ever returned from there, that didn't mean they died. After all, since they were trying to escape, why would they return?

Taking in a deep breath, Constance wiped her eyes and turned back to Yeager. "I'm sorry, but I cannot take this girl in. I understand what will happen to her, but there isn't anything I can do about it."

"So be it." Yeager shook the chain and walked toward the cave's entrance. The three children followed, ignorant lambs being led to slaughter. As the shadows enveloped him, Yeager called back, "Just don't preach to me again about being a slave trader, Madam Orley. You have just traded this girl to the mill for the sake of your loyalty to dragons, and some of those dragons ate your daughter."

When Yeager's voice faded to silence, Constance looked at Agatha's letter again, opening it with shaking hands. With her back to the cave wall, she slid to her bottom and read the precious words for the thousandth time. Yeager had quoted them fairly well, closely enough to prove he had heard them spoken. Just this morning she had read the letter, and the sweet prose had been a blessing, an uplifting start to her day: *Somewhere in the North, Agatha served the great king, perhaps as a doctor to the other promoted slaves ...*

But now?

Now Agatha's dream had been shattered, along with her body and bones. The many months of hope had been a lie, a heartbreaking lie. The poor girl had been eaten by a vile monster, likely ripped to shreds and shared with other vile monsters.

Sobbing again, Constance clenched a fist. The beasts! The villains! Somehow she would find a way to get revenge. First, she had to escape, get help and weapons, but how?

She leaned her head against the wall and looked up at the dark ceiling. The cave's boundaries never seemed so black before, so heavy, so crushing. Arxad and Fellina had always been kind, but now their kindness seemed a pretense, a way to get her to work harder, a mask to hide their real intent. Even if Arxad didn't eat the slaves himself, he didn't stop the barbaric practice. He didn't speak up. His closed mouth was just as guilty as the open ones that had chewed Agatha's body.

Brushing away new tears, Constance looked past the ceiling and let her mind fly to the North. It was time to plan a way to escape, but it would be impossible without help, especially with everyone in lockdown. Yet there was one slave who seemed to enjoy more freedom than any other. Even though she had given in to Taushin's tortures, maybe her heart had not yet been enslaved.

"Creator," she said out loud. "Help me find Koren. Maybe together we can figure out how to end this madness."

The sound of flapping wings echoed throughout the cave—two dragons, probably Fellina and Xenith. Constance shot to her feet and brushed off her apron. She would have to pretend to be an obedient servant, at least until she could learn where Koren might be.

three

Koren lifted her leg and scaled the final step. Tremors rippled through her muscles. On the landing, she halted and mopped her brow with the edge of her hood. Hunger and thirst gnawed at her stomach, and exhaustion threatened to overwhelm her, yet she had to press on. The worst part of the journey might still lie ahead. Taking a deep breath, she stepped up to the sliding door that led into the castle's massive foyer, every sense on alert for a sign of Taushin.

Although he had often spoken in her mind before they reached the Northlands, he had been silent ever since. Maybe the castle provided some sort of protection from his probing presence. Could he see through her eyes anymore? If he could, there would be no getting by him. He would have seen all and would know her location. If not, though, there was some chance she could slip by, or at least pass off her new direction as a continued search for Exodus. There was only one way to find out.

Pressing her hard-soled boots down lightly, she passed by the open wall and glided through the castle's entry room. Light poured in from the wide doorway, casting a ray of sunshine across the marred wooden floor. Without daring to peek outside, she lifted her hood over her head, turned to the right, and scooted toward a huge corridor.

Where are you going?

Taushin's voice.

Koren halted, her heart sinking. She leaned back and looked. He stood at the bottom of the portico stairs, his eyebeams locked on her. This was her only chance to learn what he could and couldn't see. "To search the rest of the castle," she called. "Haven't you followed my progress?"

She waited through Taushin's pause, her heart pounding as she forced herself to breathe evenly.

Continue your exploration, he finally said. *Just remember that haste is essential.*

Koren walked into the corridor. "Why?" The word echoed through the cavernous space.

Because I hold ... His voice died away.

She kept walking. So, being near the door allowed Taushin access to her mind, and now he couldn't finish his reply. Why *was* haste essential? Learning what he held might be helpful, but going back into his zone of influence wasn't exactly her first choice. The farther away from Taushin she wandered, the better she felt.

As she walked, her footfalls echoed in the massive hallway. For some strange reason, it seemed that a bubble of light surrounded her. Crystals embedded in the walls sparkled in an array of colors, briefly highlighting a portion of a long mural. With each step, a new portion shone. As she moved, it seemed that the mural on the right moved with her, a white dragon with shining blue eyes repositioning its wings with each new appearance as if it were flying at her pace. From mouth and nostrils, it blew a river of white crystals that sparkled like sunlit ice.

She looked to the left. Another dragon flew on that side, a black one with red eyes. It breathed a torrent of flames with specks of orange and yellow almost too bright to behold.

When she neared the end of the corridor, a huge, arching entryway came into view straight ahead, leading into another chamber. She stopped at the boundary and peered inside. A network of roots and vines covered the floor, or perhaps they were the floor itself.

Her surrounding aura dimmed, but a lantern on each inner wall provided enough light to illuminate a few details. Beds lined the walls to the left and right, maybe four on each side. They appeared to be neatly made and empty. Two ragged holes interrupted the floor's woody network, one large and one small. Apparently this floor was too fragile to walk upon, though a dragon might fly in without a problem and perhaps deposit a human on one of the beds.

To her right, another corridor, not quite as large as the first, stretched out into darkness. With a solid marble floor, it seemed to be the safer option. Letting her boots strike the hard surface noisily, she marched that way. If anyone came out to check on the noise, she could ask to see the white dragon. Maybe calling would be even better.

Still walking, she lifted her voice enough to compete with her footfalls. "Hello? Is anyone here?"

"I am here," a feminine voice replied from behind her.

Koren halted and spun around. No one was there. "Who said that?"

"I did." A wisp of light shaped like a girl curtsied. "I am Deference." As soon as she straightened, she vanished.

Koren slid a step closer and tried to find her in the dimness. "Have you been following me all this time?"

"Only since you came out of the star chamber."

"Why didn't you say something?"

"The king said I was to remain quiet until you called. He knew you wouldn't be able to see me while I was behind you, and whenever you stopped, I stopped. You can't see me unless I move." She swayed back and forth, appearing again and creating a new aura all around. She looked to be about fifteen years old, her hair and eye color impossible to discern.

Koren pointed at her. "So you made the light while I walked."

"I did, but the light works only in these corridors. It has something to do with the jewels in the walls." Deference spread out her hands, a sheepish expression evident in her glowing face. "But I have no idea how it works."

"That's okay. I wouldn't expect you to know every mystery in this strange castle." While the glow remained, Koren looked at one of the walls in the new corridor. The design resembled a girl inside a sphere. With red hair, green eyes, and a blue cloak, she had to be a Starlighter.

Koren pointed at the wall. "Is that Brinella?"

"Brinella?" Deference turned toward the mural, brightening the aura again. She gave a light shrug. "I don't know her name, and I've never heard of Brinella."

Koren pressed her lips together. This interrogation might not provide many answers. She pointed down the hall. "Is the white dragon in that direction?"

"He is, but you'll never find him without a guide."

"Will you be my guide?"

Sweeping her arm out in front, Deference bowed low. "It would be an honor."

"Then lead the way. The last thing I want is to get lost."

Deference ambled down the hall, her light illuminating the murals lining the corridor.

Lowering her hood, Koren followed. To the right, the Starlighter in the sphere floated alongside. She changed positions at times, from sitting to standing to walking. She certainly looked like Brinella, perhaps a little younger.

To the left, another mural appeared, this one a reflection of herself, a redhead dressed in black—the same dress and boots, but no Starlighter cloak.

As Koren glanced between the two, they seemed to emerge from the walls, taking on minute details and vibrant colors. Brinella's eyes shone green, and her hair looked pomegranate red. The girl in black had eyes of ebony, Zena's blank eyes, barren and lost.

Koren shuddered. Was her Starlighter gift doing this? Was she making the images animate? What other explanation could there be?

As if brought to life, Brinella called out from the painting, "Starlighter, why have you used your gift to seize the minds of those who lack your vision without providing sustenance for their starving spirits?"

The girl in black replied, her tone sour. "You have no idea what I've been through. They enslaved me. They put me in chains." She lifted her arms, showing reddened abrasions on her wrists. "Then that foul dragon master tortured me with painful jolts that nearly killed me."

"I know," Brinella said. "Starlight showed me every cringe and cry, but your protest does not provide an answer to my question. When your listeners withdrew from the world and awaited your wisdom, why did you forsake them by running away? Why did you not impart your wisdom?"

"Because I was in trouble. I had to run. And I didn't know I was supposed to say anything to them. Even if I did know, I had no idea what to say. I have no wisdom to impart."

"Ah! Now there is a faithful answer. But did you ever consider the fact that you have an extraordinary gift, a talent too wonderful to fully comprehend? When you realized that you had control over the dragons, why did you choose to flee rather than to persuade them to join your cause? And this power is merely one of many gifts you possess. You will learn that even the scrapings of the skin of Exodus can provide healing. Did you not know that such gifts must carry with them a responsibility to use them wisely? Or did you take them in stride and not seek the counsel of the Creator who fashioned you for greatness?"

"Why didn't Arxad tell me what to do?"

"Arxad?" Brinella said. "How is a dragon, even a good and noble one, to know what the Creator wishes for you to do? How can he discern your path? Only the Creator can provide that knowledge."

"If the Creator knows my path, then how can I do anything but walk on it?"

"Oh, my dear Starlighter, you always have the choice to depart from the path. It is set there so that you may fulfill your part in the Creator's purposes, but you are free to step away. The Creator is able to find another to take your place."

Koren stared at the girl in black. It was like looking in a mirror and seeing the twisted face of a demonic twin. Was she transforming into this phantasm? A dark reflection of herself who answered every challenge with an excuse?

Shuddering, she shook her head. No. It couldn't be. At least it *wouldn't* be. She would stay on the path and battle Taushin and Zena. Somehow she would free her people.

Deference stopped. She and her aura dimmed, and the visions evaporated.

"We're here," Deference said.

Double doors, white and reflective, stood closed before them. A pair of black wooden handles protruded near the center, each one carved into the shape of a dragon's head. As large as the Zodiac's entry doors, these could easily have allowed a dragon to pass through, but the handles appeared to be too small for a dragon to grasp.

Deference waved a hand toward the entrance. "This is as far as I can take you."

"Thank you for being my guide," Koren said. "I suppose I could have found it myself, though."

Deference shook her glowing head. "You would not have found it. Everyone needs a guide." She turned and walked away, skipping at times as she hurried down the hall. Soon her aura turned down a branching passageway and disappeared, leaving only a dim light that seemed to radiate from the walls.

Koren pivoted back to the doors. She reached out and touched an ear on one of the dragon heads. With all the strangeness in this castle, she half expected the dragon to snap at her, but it remained still and silent. She slowly spread her fingers over the handle and pulled, but the door didn't budge. She tried to turn the handle, but it wouldn't move, not even an inch.

The dragon within her palm grew warm, then hot. She jerked away. The dragon head had turned white, or at least the part she had touched was white. She grasped the other handle and pushed and twisted to no avail. It, too, turned hot and white.

Koren set her palms on the massive door. She braced her boots on the tiles, lowered her body, and pushed again, grunting with the effort. Nothing. She might as well have been a black mouse shoving a white elephant. At least then a squeak might get his attention.

She halted. A squeak? Well, it was worth a try.

"Hello?" she called. "Is anyone there?"

No one answered.

She set her knuckles against the door. Might a knock be appropriate? Her fellow humans knocked on doors, but this was the domain of a dragon. He might not appreciate such a vulgar way of gaining attention.

Shrugging, she rapped on the door. Again, no one answered. She rapped a second time, but the doors stood in motionless silence.

She let out a huff. Why would Deference lead her here if there was no way to get in? It just didn't make sense.

As she turned away, a low, masculine voice drifted by. "Whom do you seek?"

Koren searched for a source, but it seemed as if the voice permeated the air. "I wish to see the white dragon."

"A wish? As a child hopes for sweetbread? Many human children cast their wishes to the stars, but their prospects for a response are the same as yours."

Koren glanced around. The corridor remained empty. "You mean my wish won't be fulfilled?"

"Answer for yourself. How well did the star respond to your wish when you cast it?"

"If you mean my wish to help her resurrect the star, it was more of a suggestion, and it didn't work out very well. Brinella didn't believe me. She thinks I'm a sorceress."

"A fair assumption, considering your choice of dress. She has seen a sorceress dress in a similar manner."

Koren resisted the urge to look at her clothing. It probably wouldn't do any good to protest his use of *choice*. Grinding her teeth, she glared at the door. "Does that mean I won't be able to see the white dragon?"

"That depends."

She waited for him to continue, but he apparently wanted her to ask the obvious question. "Depends on what?"

"You are a Starlighter. Will you tell me a tale?"

"Uh … sure. I can do that." She tapped a foot on the floor. "Do you have a preference? Something true? Or something I make up?"

"Oh, definitely something true. I *wish* for you to relate a very old tale. Show me your origins, how you came to this world."

Focusing on one of the dragon heads, she pointed at herself. "Do you mean me, personally, or humans in general?"

"It makes no difference. Either will suffice."

Koren spread out her cloak. "I will see what I can do." She turned toward the star chamber. Although it was nowhere in sight and far below her level, it seemed easy to locate in her mind. After seeing Brinella, her own abilities made much more sense. Brinella collected the tales of Starlight and sent them out for gifted listeners to gather, streams of whispered tales that spread throughout the atmosphere, ready to be plucked and spoken again.

Taking in a breath, Koren gathered the invisible stories. Then she stooped and set a finger on the floor. A form took shape under her touch, growing as she raised her hand. The form expanded into a dragon with scales of red. She touched another spot on the floor, raising a second dragon, this one with tawny hues. She then lifted her arms, and called out, "In the midst of turmoil, death, and despair, two young dragons emerged from their hiding places, escapees from slavery who faced decisions of enormous import, decisions that could drastically alter their world."

Around the dragons, scenery appeared—a gravel path winding through a field of lush grass, leading to a cluster of low buildings in the distance. A white picket fence demarked a border for several grazing sheep that seemed to be unconcerned with the presence of dragons. A lone human male knelt in front of the dragons, his hands clasped as if in entreaty.

With every detail painted throughout the corridor, it seemed to Koren that she stood in the midst of it. She crouched and felt the grass, soft and supple. A sheep bleated, only to be interrupted by the man's pleading voice.

"I beg of you, Magnar. You and Arxad are our only hopes." Dressed in a clean white smock and gray trousers, the man looked ready for inside work rather than for the labors of a farm. "My two sons have already perished," he continued, "but my daughter shows no signs of the disease. Can you save her? Can you take her to Darksphere?"

Magnar glanced at Arxad before extending a wing to help the man rise. "Orson, you know this disease better than any of us do. Can you say with all honesty that your daughter cannot carry the disease to Darksphere even if she has not yet contracted it?"

With terror in his eyes, Orson shifted his gaze from Magnar to Arxad and back to Magnar. His entire body quaked. "I ... I don't know. It's possible for her to be a clean vessel if we—"

"Possible?" Magnar said. "If you want the human race to survive, we have no room for *possible*. We must deal only with certainty. If your daughter dies along with the

countless thousands of others, what price is that for ultimate survival? She will be just another human who succumbed to the disease you brought upon yourselves."

"Magnar," Arxad said, "she is not just another human
to Orson. I suggest that you offer a bit more compassion."

"Compassion?" Smoke spewed from Magnar's nostrils.
"Was it compassion that drove humans to enslave our
race? Was it compassion that compelled them to plunge a
spear into the heart of our guiding star? No! They have no
knowledge of compassion. They seek only comfort, freedom from labors, selfish satisfaction. They prefer to heap
misery upon others, refusing to listen to the warnings
provided from above. Instead of heeding, they attacked.
Such fools deserve no compassion."

Arxad waved a wing at Orson. "You know he is not one
of the fools. He has never owned a dragon, and he has
often spoken against our enslavement."

"Yes, yes, I know." His eyes glowing red, Magnar
clawed the ground. "But did he not continue friendship
with the taskmasters? While he imbibed with the intoxi-
cated in comfort, our kind continued to toil in chains. He
who numbers himself with the guilty, even if not partici-
pating in their deeds, will find himself washed away in the
flood of righteous retribution."

Orson extended his clasped hands again. "Forgive me,
Magnar! I was a fool! I did seek my own comfort. I listened to my fears. I desired the favor of other fools rather
than the approval of the Almighty. I should have done
much more. But why should my daughter be punished
for my folly? She is only an infant and bears no guilt in
my affairs."

Magnar turned his head away. "How many other infants have already perished because of the foolishness of adults? Why should your daughter be exempt from—"

"Magnar!" Arxad extended his neck and whispered in Magnar's ear. "Let us speak in private."

The two shuffled several paces away. Still whispering, Arxad continued. "We must appease Orson to some extent. His genetic keys are essential to our plan, and he has yet to deliver the final sequence."

Magnar's brow rose as he whispered in response, "Is this a scheme to manipulate us? We cannot risk saving his daughter. You know this."

"Yes, I know, but we can speak hope to him. His wife died giving birth to the girl, so he is a desperately grieving man. Allow me to find the words."

"Very well, but take care. You have trapped yourself in vows too many times."

When the two dragons returned to Orson, Arxad set a wing on his back. "You are the genetics expert, and we are relying on you for accurate information. The survival of your race depends on your complete honesty. When you deliver the final sequence, we will examine your daughter thoroughly. If you are able to convince me that she has no trace of the disease, you may place her in the clean room. I will include her in the transport."

"Arxad!" Magnar shouted. "You promise too much!"

Arxad looked down and dug a claw mark in the turf. "What I have promised, I have promised."

Orson leaped to his feet. "Oh, thank you, good dragon! Thank you! You will not regret this. I will have the final sequence ready by tomorrow. I will not fail you."

He turned and ran along the path toward the distant buildings.

When Orson was out of earshot, Magnar growled. "Do you really believe Orson's examination will yield any hint of that disease? He will falsify the data to save his daughter."

"I have researched this disease thoroughly. I will not be easily duped."

"Not easily, but Orson is a genius. He will find a way to convince you."

Arxad watched Orson as he shrank in the distance. "I realize that a father's love is a great motivator. I will be careful."

The farm setting vanished, as did Magnar, but Arxad remained. A new scene painted itself around him, a large room with no windows. The walls appeared to be made of smooth wood, dark and polished to a sheen. A long table sat at the center of the wooden floor, and two eggs the size of hefty pumpkins perched at one end, nestled in a large wicker basket. Oddly shaped glassware stood at the center of the table, partially filled with liquids of various colors, some with tubes rising from their narrowed tops.

Arxad studied an object lying on the opposite end of the table, something that had not yet fully formed in Koren's vision. His head swayed over it, and a growling yet sweet melody arose from his throat, the sound of a dragon humming.

The object began to clarify, a bassinet of woven straw. Orson materialized in front of the table, sitting cross-legged on the floor. With his head drooping near his chest, he seemed to be weary or sick.

Koren walked to the table and looked into the bassinet. A girl lay inside. Thick red hair covered her head, but closed lids concealed the color of her eyes. She breathed sporadically, fitfully, her little brow wrinkling.

"The end is close," Arxad said. "She will not survive the night."

Orson pushed against the floor, struggled to his feet, and staggered toward Arxad. With his hands bracing his body on the side of the table, he peered into the bassinet. "All is lost for my family. Justice is served, the penalty carried out. I prayed for mercy, though I deserved none. I asked the Creator to forgive me of my foolishness, my selfishness, and my pathetic excuses, but he has rightfully denied my pleas. I have done nothing to deserve anything but death. Yet I don't understand why my daughter must suffer. She has done nothing to warrant such pain."

"She will not suffer long. She will be in the Creator's arms in mere moments."

"I hope beyond hope that I will join her." Orson leaned over the bassinet and kissed the girl on the cheek. "I love you little K," he whispered.

Koren gasped. Did he really say that? Those were the same words she whispered to herself night after night, the only memory she had of her own father. What could this mean?

A loud bang sounded. Koren spun toward the noise. A door in this tale's vision had slammed open, allowing dim moonlight to spill through an entryway, a cave-like arch much bigger than necessary for a human abode. In a flurry of wings and scratching claws, a white dragon burst through and settled on the floor. Carrying a sphere of clear crystal in his clawed hands, he shuffled closer.

Orson trembled. "Why are you here? Are we already..." He swallowed hard. "Already dead?"

Arxad bowed low. When he lifted his head again, he looked at the white dragon, his ears perking straight up. "Has the time come?"

"Soon. The portal is forming even as we speak." He stretched his neck toward the bassinet. A network of thin red lines appeared on his white scales. "Is the girl dead?"

"Very close," Arxad said. "Mere moments."

"Then I will take the time to explain." The white dragon lifted the sphere. "This is a—"

"What?" Orson shouted. "If you're who I think you are, then you can heal her, but if you take time to explain, she might die."

The white dragon spoke in an even tone. "You prayed for mercy. Is it up to your discretion how that mercy is delivered or the manner or timing the deliverer chooses to employ?"

"No." Orson wobbled in place. "Not at all. I didn't mean to offend you. I just—"

"Lack understanding. I know." The white dragon's voice carried neither anger nor sympathy. "If you will stay silent for a moment, you will gain that which you lack."

Orson raised shaking fingers to his lips and spoke between them. "I will be quiet. Please forgive my haste."

"Forgive?" The white dragon's eyes pulsed blue. "In a moment, you will see for yourself whether or not forgiveness has been granted." He placed the crystalline sphere on the table. With dozens of smooth facets making up its clear surface, it was able to sit without rolling. "I call this a Reflections Crystal. When you learn its properties, you will see that it is an appropriate name, but for now I must demonstrate an ability that you would think is beyond reason unless you see it for yourself."

Arxad drew his head closer to the sphere. "If I may ask, King Alaph, what is the purpose of this demonstration?"

"To ensure that your plan succeeds. You are transporting an embryo in each of those eggs, which will result in life, but long-term human survival depends on another factor."

"We verified that the human younglings within are free from the disease," Arxad said, "and the virus cannot penetrate the shells. They are male and female with a wide genetic pool, so they should procreate efficiently for multiple generations, and I will care for them until they are of age. What aspect have I missed?"

"You have done well, but there remains a danger that you were unable to detect." Alaph set a foreclaw above the sphere. It rose a few inches and hovered in place over the table's surface. "The fate of humankind hangs from a bare thread. The younglings will likely survive and breed, but our world still needs a Starlighter."

"To replace the one within the star?" Arxad asked. "What happened to her? Where is she now?"

"Leave her fate to me. For now you must collect genetic material from Orson and his daughter."

Arxad turned toward Orson. His body lay slumped over the table. The girl's tight forehead was now slack, and her chest heaved no more.

Alaph pressed both foreclaws against the sphere. It flashed with brilliant light, casting a white glow around the room. A pair of misty forms appeared in the light, somewhat human in shape yet without substance. They stretched out and, as if funneling through a tube, streamed into the sphere. Alaph guided the crystal back down to the table. As soon as it touched the surface, the light blinked out. "Those bodies are but shells now, but Orson and his daughter are safe inside the crystal. Collect the genetic material. You will need it in order to restore them at the proper time, and I will show you how to reconstitute them, both their bodies and their spirits."

"I will do as you say, good king, but whatever I collect will be infected. Is that a concern?"

Alaph gave Arxad a slow nod. "A grave concern. If the virus reactivates, they could spread it to their fellow humans, and we would face a new pandemic."

"Then why take such a risk?"

"Because without another Starlighter, humans and dragons alike will be doomed."

Arxad laid a clawed hand on one of the eggs. "Can a Starlighter arise from the two younglings we are saving?"

"The possibility exists, but we cannot count on chance. We must preserve what we know and have available." Alaph touched the top of the crystal, his expression anxious. "This little one has the potential to do what she must to save all of Starlight. Still, since she is extraordinarily gifted, if she decides to follow a darker path, the damage could be catastrophic."

"The risk seems greater with every word you speak." Arxad shook his head, a look of resignation on his face.

"As you said, we cannot count on chance. Perhaps we should simply force her to obey."

A low growl rumbled in the white dragon's throat. "She must act freely, from a heart of love, without chains or compulsion. Chains will lead her to destruction. Chains never lead to love."

The scene vanished, leaving Koren alone in the silent corridor.

Gasping for breath, she rapped on the door. "Are you there?"

No one answered. She drew back and stared at the white doors. They seemed to glower at her, annoyed at her pounding knuckles. "Are you the white dragon?" she called.

Silence.

"Answer me!"

Her words echoed, fading until silence again ensued, bringing with it a sense of lostness, loneliness, abandonment.

As tears welled, she hugged herself. What had she seen? Who was that little girl? Herself as an infant? Her father's name was Orson, but was this Orson her real father?

She repeated his words in a whisper. "I love you, little K."

Koren dragged her teeth across her bottom lip. Tears dripped to her cheeks. He *was* her father. He had to be. But how could her mother have died giving birth? Memories of Mother were real, nothing that a newborn infant could have remembered.

Turning slowly in place, she cried out, "Why did you want me to tell this tale? What do you want me to do?"

The white dragon's final words echoed in the air, as if recalled by her plea. "Chains never lead to love."

Koren looked at her wrists. The abrasions had almost faded, but the memory of the manacles had not. How many times had she reminded herself that love doesn't need chains? Yet here she was, following Taushin's orders as if the manacles were still clamped in place.

The air, now quiet, seemed empty, void of any guidance. Nothing more could be done here. It was time to return to Taushin. What choice did she have?

She shuffled along the hall, retracing her steps. More than ever it seemed as if chains dragged against her ankles. She was still a slave, still in bonds. But what could she do to break free? The white dragon wouldn't allow her to come in. Brinella had spurned her. Taushin watched her every move through her own traitorous eyes. It was hopeless.

After finding her way back to the entry room, Koren stopped and looked outside. Taushin stood there, still waiting, his eyes alive with blue sparkling light. Was she really his slave, hopelessly bound in chains forever? Would her chosen path lead to catastrophe? Somehow she had to prevent it, halt the progress of events she had set in motion.

She studied Taushin's expression—puzzled, impatient, perhaps wondering why she stood there staring for so long. Maybe it would be best to pry for more information, make a pretense of obedience. If he really believed chains would bring about love, perhaps a display of love would get him to reveal his ultimate plans.

She straightened her black dress and marched down the stairs. When she reached the bottom, she offered a curtsy and smiled. "I found Exodus."

four

ason lay on his stomach, his head raised just enough to watch the dragon village. About a hundred paces ahead and to the left, the Zodiac's spires towered into the black sky, glowing with an eerie silver radiance. A spear's throw to the right, the Basilica sat in shadows, nearly invisible except for its telltale bell tower jutting upward into the Zodiac's glow.

As he stared at the eerie sight, chills crawled along his skin. Up to this point, his journey with Elyssa to the village had been peaceful. With no dragons in sight, it was more like a casual stroll, giving him a chance to tell her about some of his adventures, including rescuing Koren from the cooking stake and carrying the stardrop that healed his father. Elyssa related a tale about unchaining Arxad from the same stake and another about her and Wallace rescuing the cattle children from the camp.

Sharing thoughts and feelings with her was peaceful and joyous. Now, the peace seemed to melt away. Reality returned. The casual stroll had become a foreboding surveillance of deadly abodes.

Elyssa scooted up to Jason's side and copied his pose. Pariah's dim light drew an outline of her profile against the dark backdrop, just enough to discern the tightness in her jaw, yet the night shadows couldn't hide the intensity of her gaze as she probed the blackness with her Diviner's vision.

About halfway between them and the buildings, a single dragon flew along what appeared to be a village boundary, a hedge of stones that rose to the height of a human's chest, apparently a way to funnel slave foot traffic to a gate not far to the left.

Flapping his wings furiously, the dragon zoomed from right to left, low enough to snatch a human from the top of the wall if any dared to attempt the climb. After every few wing beats, he blew a blast of fire at the ground, lighting up the search area. On Jason's side of the wall, grass ignited, creating a new obstacle, a knee-high line of fire.

As the flames crackled, Elyssa whispered, "He's completely focused on what's ahead of him. He has a one-track mind."

When the dragon neared a cliff face far to the left, he reversed course and returned, this time closer to Jason and Elyssa, again blowing fire in rhythmic bursts.

"One track could be right," Jason said, also whispering, "but that track is shifting this way. If we stay here, we'll be caught."

Elyssa nodded. "Or cooked."

"Any ideas?"

"Follow me." She jumped to her feet, but Jason grabbed her and pulled her back down.

"Don't start skipping steps again. What's your plan?"

She pointed toward the cliff face, a hint of impatience in her tone. "Some of the caves are on this side of the dragon's path. We can make a run for it. Then, if that dragon finishes his search without spotting us, we can go to the gate and see if it's unlocked."

"And if it's locked?"

She shrugged. "We climb."

"Maybe." Jason eyed the dragon as he swept again from right to left, his path now thirty paces in front of them. "We'll go on his next pass."

"But when we get to the caves, let me probe inside first." Elyssa lifted both hands. "The fingers on my left hand will tell you how many dragons I think are inside, and the other hand will be for the count of humans."

Jason nodded.

After another turn at the left-hand extremity of his path, the dragon flew by again, this time so close, the heat from his fire blasts warmed Jason's skin. When the swinging tail whipped past, Jason waved for Elyssa to follow and dashed toward the cliff, running as silently as possible while holding his scabbard against his hip.

When they reached the cliff, Jason stooped at the edge of a cave entrance and peered inside. Elyssa knelt behind him and peeked over his shoulder, taking deep breaths as she slowed her respiration. Then, crawling on hands and knees, she inched toward the dark opening.

Jason looked back. The dragon approached from a distance, still pumping fireballs at the ground. Apparently he hadn't seen them, but when he came within range, those flames would light them up like a campfire.

Elyssa straightened her torso and twisted toward him, raising two fingers on her left hand and one on her right—two dragons and one human. She then dropped to all fours again and crawled in.

Jason did the same. Elyssa likely had gauged how far within the cave the dragons were and judged it safe to enter—at least safer than risking a blast of flames. Once inside, darkness shrouded his vision. A hand gripped his wrist, and a whisper tickled his ear.

"I think one of the dragons is awake."

A rumbling growl permeated the air, but it seemed more tortured than menacing, like a wail of lament. Jason began withdrawing his sword, but Elyssa's grip tightened and pushed it back in place. "There is no danger."

A woman's voice drifted their way, calm and reassuring. "He will return. He always has before. The length of this absence is nothing compared to other times he has gone on a journey."

"How little you know," a female dragon said, her voice trembling. "How little all you humans know. We are reaching a prophetic climax, and death stalks in shadows, death for all of us if we sit on our haunches and do nothing. Evil holds sway over too many of my people. We must act."

"What do you propose to do?" the woman asked.

In the silence of a pause, Jason reached for Elyssa. "Sounds safe. Let's follow the voices."

"I was hoping you'd say that," she said as she shifted her grip to his hand. "Lead the way, warrior."

Extending an arm to feel for obstacles, he walked toward the sounds of draconic breathing. Elyssa kept a grip on his hand, looser now. A dim light appeared in the distance, revealing their surroundings—a high, wide tunnel, encompassed by rocky walls and ceiling. Ahead and to the right, a flickering glow emerged from a gaping hole at one side, casting a shaft of light against the opposite wall.

"I will ..." The dragon's voice choked for a moment before continuing. "I will appeal to my people, try to break through to their sense of reason. We will rise up against this dark pretender, this scourge from the black egg. He cannot withstand a united front."

Jason halted at the opening and sneaked a look around the edge. A dragon sat in the center of a relatively small room, her head low at the end of her drooping neck. A woman dressed in a long skirt and apron held a lantern while stroking the dragon's flank. "How can you rise up?" the woman asked. "Will they listen to a female without the affirmation of Arxad or Magnar?"

"I will appeal to Tamminy. He has long voiced his concern. He will affirm my plan. Magnar ignores him, but many dragons still respect his views."

The woman's voice lowered, barely audible. "Mistress Fellina, Tamminy is missing as well."

"Missing?" Fellina's head tilted to the side. "Explain."

"Only an hour ago his cave keeper told me of his absence. No one has heard from him in quite some time."

As Fellina's neck sagged lower, her chin touched the floor. "The night gets ever darker, Madam Orley. In this world of cowards, it seems that every courageous male has abdicated his protective station. Where can we find someone who is bold enough to rally our cause, a masculine voice who can break through the callused ears of those too foolish to heed the words of a wise female?"

Elyssa gave Jason a nudge. "If you want a better cue, you will have to come up with it yourself."

"Right. But that doesn't make it any easier." After swallowing through his tightened throat, Jason strode in, steeling his body to keep from trembling. With a hand on the hilt of his sword, he planted his feet in front of Fellina. "I'll be that voice."

Fellina lifted her neck and drew her head back, blinking. "Who are you?"

"Jason Masters." He gave her a quick bow. "I am from Darksphere. I have come to liberate the slaves. You said you needed a masculine voice to break through, so I thought—"

"You thought?" Fellina glanced at Madam Orley before returning her gaze to Jason. "Are you suggesting that my stubborn dragon friends will respect you, a human, more than they would respect me, one of their own kind?"

"Well ..." Jason shifted his weight from foot to foot. "When you put it that way ..."

"And if you think you can free your people with that primitive weapon, you are as foolish as you are bold. Before you could bare the blade, any dragon could roast you where you stand."

"There are more of us," Jason said, bowing again. "And I don't expect that we could do it with only humans. Like you said, with a united front, humans and dragons who are friendly to our cause, we can do whatever needs to be done. But first, I need to find my—"

"*Our* cause?" Fellina repeated. "And what exactly would our cause be?"

Jason spread out his arms. "To free the slaves, of course."

She snorted. "You are as ignorant as the rest. You think freeing the slaves is the ultimate purpose, but you are too shortsighted to see the larger picture."

"I'll be glad to hear about the picture, but first, I need to find my father. A dragon captured him. Do you know where they might have taken him?"

Fellina looked again at Madam Orley. "The mill?"

She nodded. "Since we are in lockdown, most likely."

"Summon Xenith and ask her to meet me at the cave entrance. I will speak to these humans in private."

"As you wish." Madam Orley gave a shallow bow and scurried from the room.

As Fellina extended her neck, her head glided to within inches of Jason's face. "I am sympathetic. Losing a father is a tragic event. Yet this is also a lesson as to how easily your numbers will be trimmed. You would need a thousand seasoned warriors if you hope to liberate the slaves."

Jason firmed his jaw. Breathing deeply, he tried to keep his voice calm. "If you will just tell me how to get to this mill you're talking about, when I return with my father, we can talk about the larger picture. He is a brilliant soldier and a cunning strategist. If we work together, we can find a solution."

"Perhaps," Fellina said, "but you make it sound as if rescuing your father from the mill is as easy as lighting a torch. The pair of dragons who operate the mill are the wickedest sisters you will ever meet. They enjoy grinding the flesh and bones of humans, and they have firepower equal to most of the male warriors. It will require much more than cunning to rescue your father."

"Ahem." Elyssa stepped out of the shadows and slid her hand around Jason's arm. She pulled him close to her side and spoke with passion. "Against all odds, this warrior rescued me from a dungeon. He traveled to the Northlands, marched into the bowels of Starlight, and scooped a handful of fire from Exodus in order to heal his father. He even rescued Koren the Starlighter from the cooking stake while Magnar himself stood guard. He has cunning, to be sure, but his real weapons are his courage, his resolve, and his love."

Fellina glanced between them, her eyes wide and searching. After a few seconds, she drew her head back and nodded. "We will take you to the mill."

❈

Koren stood still, in spite of the biting cold. As Taushin's blue beams penetrated her eyes, her legs felt stiff, immobile. It seemed that his control over her had strengthened, at least whenever he came close.

"Did you see the hole in Exodus?" he asked.

"Yes." She stopped herself before saying more. For now, simply answering his question seemed to be the best strategy. It didn't make sense to offer more information than he demanded.

"Were you able to enter?"

She nodded. "The hole stretched quite well." She kept her voice flat. No need to mention Brinella and the pain she felt. Maybe Taushin didn't think a Starlighter still lived within. After so many years, he probably assumed she had died.

His head swayed from side to side, his eyebeams staying locked on her. "Did you try to seal the breach?"

"Yes, but it didn't work. The stardrop's particles just dripped down the surface."

"Interesting." Taushin's beams intensified. "I perceive that you are telling the truth, but you are concealing something."

Shivering, Koren didn't bother hiding a nervous swallow, though she kept her voice level. "I see no reason to deceive you. I came back, didn't I? I could have hidden in the castle."

"As if the white dragon would let you stay."

While Taushin closed his eyes, apparently thinking, Koren breathed deeply, trying not to let the truth of his words scratch a new wound in her soul. It did seem that the lord of the castle didn't want her around.

Taushin touched her shoulder with a wing. "I will be more honest with you than you have been with me. While you were in the castle beyond the entry room, I could no longer see through your eyes, so I am unable to verify your story. Your return to me is, indeed, a sign of obedience, for which I applaud you." The claw at the end of his wing slowly dug into her skin. "You see, even that relatively minor act of acquiescence has further bonded us. More than ever before, I am able to detect your trail. Every place you enter, I am able to follow. Even now I could track the steps you took inside that castle, feel what you felt, hear what you heard, smell what you smelled. If you ever try to free yourself from me, I will be able to learn what you have done and eventually find you. Do you understand?"

Koren nodded once again, cringing at the sting in her shoulder. Any sudden movement, any sign of rebellion, could result in a cruel slash down her back.

"Now," Taushin continued, withdrawing the wing, "look up at the sky. Show me the land's profile again."

Koren scanned the castle. The wide entrance lay open, as if inviting her to come in and warm her frozen fingers and toes, but the impression was a lie. She was an unwelcome intruder. She then shifted her gaze to the mountains behind the castle, guessing at the location of the hole out of which Exodus would have to rise.

"At least now your decision is an easy one," Taushin said. "If you cannot seal the wound, you will resurrect Exodus then exit after the slaves are liberated."

She continued sweeping her gaze across the mountaintops, stopping briefly at a snow-covered, truncated cone with a flat top. "How long do you think I'll be in there?"

"Impossible to determine. We will not know until you make the attempt. Guide Exodus to the South, and I will tell you what to do when you arrive."

"How will you get there?" Koren asked. "Since you're blind without me, I mean."

"As I said, I can detect every place you have been, so I will follow your trail backwards as well as utilize other scent landmarks. The guardian dragons will guide me from the barrier wall, and once I arrive at the Basilica I will use Zena as my vision host. She will be adequate for the time being."

"I understand." Koren imagined the staircase leading to the chamber. Of course she could go back to Exodus, but what would Brinella say? Would the original Star-lighter even let her back in?

She lowered her eyes to Taushin's face again. His expression gave away worry, as if he wasn't sure of his plan. A wave of sympathy rose in her heart. She lifted a hand to stroke his cheek but quickly jerked it back. *No! He's a cruel monster! Don't let him have complete control.*

Taushin spread out his wings. "Let us proceed."

He lifted off and flew into the sky. Soon he became a black splotch in the midst of a beautiful blue canopy.

Koren frowned at the sight. Taushin was the spill of a pen, an artist's mistake. His wickedness made him the scourge of Starlight. For generations the dragons waited for him to rise to power, selfishly hoping for a paradise— no labors, no lack of pheterone, and no pesky humans to provide for.

Letting out a sigh, she turned toward the castle. Yes, evil had awaited a greater evil, and now she had to do its bidding, or at least feign to do so. Taushin had left her here unguarded, trusting that the invisible chains she wore would keep her in line.

And he was right. She wouldn't leave. The mysteries here were too great to abandon, and the opportunity to free her fellow slaves would be her chains. If she could keep Exodus aloft long enough, maybe Taushin really would fulfill his promise. Wasn't it worth a try? If only the slightest chance existed, shouldn't she make the attempt? What harm could come?

She looked again at the sky. Taushin was nowhere in sight. It felt so good to be away from him, relatively free from his influence. His hold on her had become too strong. She had very nearly shown him sympathy—that longing to touch him with tenderness had risen without a thought. Somehow she had to break loose. She had to avoid becoming a dark-hearted, fawning servant like Zena.

As she imagined the dark-eyed sorceress, a violent shudder ran through her body. She would *not* become like her! She would die first.

Koren scooped up some snow and quenched her thirst before facing the castle. With new determination firming her lips, she ascended the stairs leading to the entryway. Every step felt like walking on broken pottery. Obeying that monster grated her conscience. She would rather chew rocks, but the pain-streaked cries of her fellow slaves urged her onward.

After entering, she headed straight for the stairway and began the descent toward the star chamber. Again the whisperers assaulted her ears.

"How much gunpowder did you put in? We need enough to blow that scourge out of the sky."

"Arxad, when you teach the new generation, do not pass on the secrets of human weaponry. They need genetics and the principles of light. Nothing more."

"Beware. If you try to manufacture a Starlighter from the genetic code, the result could be disastrous. Allow the Creator to bring her to us at the right time."

Koren drank in the words. Now they seemed more coherent, as if they had aligned in order to grant her knowledge. Was this Brinella's doing? Probably not. She didn't seem to have much control over the messages she provided. The only other option seemed to be the white dragon, but how could he send messages to Exodus?

When Koren arrived at the star chamber, she leaned over and massaged her legs. Could she take much more of this? Muscle cramps and fatigue might do her in before Taushin could.

Inside the chamber, Brinella sat in her human form, her head hanging low. An aura surrounded her, dim but noticeable. Various colors flashed across her face, new tales building up within the imprisoned Starlighter.

"I knew you would come back," she said without looking up.

Koren stepped over to the wound and spoke into it. "How did you know?"

Brinella raised her head and aimed her stare through the hole. "I know stubbornness when I see it. You didn't get what you wanted, so you have returned with a new scheme to obtain it."

"Maybe I'm stubborn," Koren said, allowing her tone to grow firm, "but maybe someone else is, too. If you would just listen to me for a minute, I could—"

"Listen to a sorceress?" Brinella straightened and crossed her arms over her chest. Indistinct images painted her face with splotches of green, purple, and red.

"I should say not. If I learned anything from Alaph, it's not to listen to a charmer's guile."

Koren cringed. The label hurt, but how could she protest? She really was a charmer. Still, this girl must know she was one herself. It seemed that she held out bait for Koren to take, daring her to object.

Lowering her voice to a whisper, Koren gave in, hoping her gentle tone would calm Brinella's ire. "Why do you call me a charmer? Don't *your* gifts charm people?"

New colors, deeper and richer, turned Brinella's face into a tapestry of royal splendor. "A charmer enthralls, hypnotizes, or distracts to get what she wants. I am a prophetess who draws people into a net of love in order to give them what they need."

"A net?" Koren imagined Taushin casting a net over her head and dragging her away. "That sounds like just another form of slavery."

"A Starlighter's net draws those who already want to serve the Creator, but since they are enslaved to another master, a powerful force is necessary if they are to sever their bonds. The net bypasses all others—those who wish to stay enslaved. And there are many, though they may outwardly deny it, because it is easier to be led along by chains than it is to love and sacrifice in freedom."

Koren cast a furtive glance at her wrists. The manacle abrasions seemed darker once again, though it might have been because of the star's brilliant light. For some reason, Brinella's words stung, as if they were tiny arrows aimed at Koren's heart. "Maybe I am in chains, Brinella, and maybe my garment proves it. If that's so, shouldn't you help me? I want to serve the Creator, so please listen to what's happening outside this chamber. Maybe you can tell me what to do to sever my bonds, and I will gladly submit to the net."

Brinella kept her stare on Koren and gave her a slight nod. "Go on."

Backing away from the hole, Koren spread out her cloak and began her story. Although Brinella, a Starlighter who distributed these tales, likely knew many of the facts, she couldn't know Koren's interpretation of them. At least now she might understand.

As Koren spoke, every character in her story appeared in the star chamber, fading into and out of existence as they were needed. In each scene, she played herself, taking on the pose of a slave during her labors and a prisoner during her captivity. Manacles appeared on her wrists, and chains weighed down her arms, feeling so real she could barely believe they were merely phantasms from her mind.

Finally, when she replayed the scene in which Taushin tortured her with electric shocks, the pain again shot through her body, stiffening her limbs and arching her back. Koren wailed. The agony seemed as awful as reality, like hot claws digging through to her heart and scratching her soul out of her body.

"I couldn't escape!" Koren's throat narrowed, pitching her voice higher as she lifted her chains and made the links jingle. "Taushin assaulted me with jolt after jolt, racking my body with unbearable pain. I couldn't breathe. I couldn't—"

"Stop!"

The sudden call jerked Koren out of her story. The pain eased. The chains and manacles faded away. As she shook out her stiff limbs, she turned toward the sphere and peered inside.

Brinella rose to her feet. "Your tale rings true. This vivid picture of slavery surely pierced my heart. As a Starlighter, I often show people images of realities they cannot comprehend because they have never witnessed them, so I should have known that rendering judgment against you without witnessing your trials was too harsh. I apologize."

Koren bowed her head. "I accept without reservation. I understand your concern about my appearance and lack of knowledge."

"Perhaps you can learn from my mistake and show the slaves images of freedom so they can witness what living in liberty looks like. This could inspire them to do more to counter their oppressors than merely licking their whip wounds."

"What images?" Koren asked. "We've never been free."

"Well ..." Brinella glanced up, hiding her green eyes for a moment. "You could draw from days long ago when humans roamed the planet free of chains, but that might not be very effective. The people of that time will be foreign to them—dressed in odd fashions, acting in odd ways. To the humans of today, the humans of yesterday will be a different species."

Koren tapped her chin with a finger. "But if I can show them the slaves who escaped to Darksphere—"

"Ah! Now that would be a trick!" Brinella paced in a tight circle, her fingers intertwined behind her back.

"Starlight has not seen their freedom, so you would have to draw from a different source, someone who has witnessed the events you wish to portray." She stopped and pointed at Koren. "If you are a true Starlighter, you have that power, especially if you call for the images while standing within Exodus. If the people believe your words, their faith will bridge the gap between you and them."

Koren imagined Jason walking straight and tall with his sword in hand. No slave on Starlight could ever display such confidence, such liberty of mind and body. Surely he could be a source for tales of freedom. "I think I understand."

Brinella gestured toward the hole. "You may enter again, and we will see what we can do to resurrect Exodus."

five

His back bent and his head low, Tibalt skulked through the dead flowers in the meadow leading to the portal. Fortunately, they hadn't recovered from the poison he and Randall applied earlier, so he could trample them safely without raising their sleep-inducing aroma. A weight at each hip kept him balanced: a pouch the size of a small gourd hung from his belt at one side and a sword and scabbard at the other.

As he passed by the bottomless pit, he grasped the hilt of his sword and sneaked a glance down into the darkness. No snatchers ... yet. Those smoky ghosts were nowhere in sight. Picking up his pace, he chanted a poem Pappy had taught a long time ago:

Snatchers, catchers, keep away.
You can eat another day.

Bones I am, no juice or meat.
Eat my sister, she's a treat.

When he neared the hole in the ground he and Randall had cut to free the dragons from the portal chamber, he leaned over the edge and peered in. Again, no snatchers.

Kneeling, he grasped a rope Randall had tied to a hook embedded in the ground and reeled up an attached ladder. After leaning the top of the ladder against the side of the hole, he climbed down and stepped off the lowest rung to the portal room floor. Drawing his sword, he glanced around and called out in a loud whisper. "Anyone here?"

The river rushed by on one side of the chamber, drowning out his voice. The portal wall stood on the other side. Sunlight filtered in from the opening, illuminating the horizontal row of holes in the wall.

Grinning, Tibalt flexed his fingers. "This will be as easy as playing a fiddle." As he stepped closer to the holes, he mumbled, "Not that I ever had a fiddle, but I bet I could play one."

He pushed the fingers of his free hand into the left-most four holes. Then, after leaning his sword against the wall, he inserted his other fingers into the remaining holes. The wall vanished, and his sword toppled into the mining chamber on Starlight. About ten paces ahead, a stone stairway led upward, but, unlike the last time he came, no light poured in from the outside. Solarus's rays from his own world provided only enough illumination to let him know that the front part of the mining chamber—the only part he could see from Major Four—was empty.

Tibalt sniffed, then licked his lips, grimacing. No obvious odors, but extane coated his tongue with a bitter film. That stuff tasted worse than hair tonic, though why he ever tried drinking that stuff as a child he couldn't remember.

Using his foot, he pushed the sword the rest of the way in, then jerked out his fingers and leaped into the world of Starlight. One second later, the river disappeared, replaced by three tunnels leading deeper into the mine.

After snatching up his sword, Tibalt marched toward the stairway. "I knew I could play a fiddle."

When he reached the top, he halted and stooped low. Ahead and above the tree line, the first hint of dawn tinted the edge of the black sky with a purplish hue. The flat ground in between stretched across the gap like a tattered black cloak, dark and lumpy with protruding trees of one kind or another.

"Well," Tibalt muttered, "if I can't see anyone on the ground, I'll have to watch for those flying lizards in the sky. They should be easy enough to spot."

He loosened his pouch's drawstring. Digging inside, he felt around for his glow stick, whispering the names of each object his fingers came across. "Apple, vial of knock-out juice, sneezing powder … Ah!" He withdrew a small cylinder the size of a finger and clutched it in his fist, ready to shake it. Then he frowned. "If I carried this beacon out there, I'd be a fool lightning bug, flashing my light like an idiot. I'd get plucked like a chicken in a hurry."

He put the glow stick back in the bag and gazed at the dawning sky. After a few minutes, the purple edges near the horizon expanded, and a dragon flew from right to left just above the treetops. Tibalt shot to his feet. That critter was fast, but if he could figure out where it landed, he would catch up in time. If not, maybe another one would come around, and he could follow it. Even though chasing dragons wasn't exactly a good idea for someone who wanted to keep his skin intact, it was the only option available.

Keeping his eyes fixed on the dragon, Tibalt slid his sword into his scabbard and marched forward. He tripped on a protruding stone and nearly fell headlong, but, scrambling forward, he regained his balance and stopped. As he tried to catch his breath, he shook his head. "I'll catch up, if I don't kill myself first."

Then, squaring his shoulders, Tibalt strode into the darkness. Somewhere out there, Jason and Elyssa needed him, and maybe a dragon would lead the way.

⇥⇤

Jason rode low on Fellina's back, holding his scabbard close to his thigh while gripping a spine in front. Their approach required ultimate stealth. If the wicked dragon sisters detected a human passenger, the rescue mission would end before it began. At each side, Fellina's wings beat in a consistent rhythm, steady and strong, even as a hefty breeze from the right buffeted her body.

Sneaking a peek back, Jason watched the dragon trailing them—Xenith, a smaller female dragon who flew with the same grace and power her mother displayed. Elyssa rode low as well, nearly invisible in the darkness.

A gust knocked Fellina to the side, forcing Jason to regrip the spine. The breeze seemed cooler now, and a slight glow at the horizon signaled dawn's approach. Fellina had provided a filling meal of bread and sweet potato paste and then insisted on waiting until morning before embarking on this journey. She explained that the dragon sisters had locked the mill's victims in an inaccessible cage during the night and would march them to their execution shortly after dawn. Only then would it make sense to attempt a rescue. No matter the hour of the night, one of the sisters would be awake and standing guard.

In spite of his anxiety, Jason had slept a few hours on a mat in one of the cave's tunnels while Elyssa and Madam Orley passed the night hours in the slaves' quarters. The food and nap helped. He felt stronger than he had in a long time.

He looked back at Elyssa. In place of the lumberjack ensemble, she now wore a red vest over a white, flowing shirt with frilled cuffs at her wrists. Fellina had retrieved it from her own sleeping quarters, explaining that Arxad once brought it home from a Promotions ceremony. In earlier days, the dragons dressed up slaves for the ceremony, and this was one of the vestments.

Fellina slowed and began a descending orbit. Between wing beats, a small flame appeared on the ground, maybe a torch or a campfire. It seemed to burn at the floor of a basin, but with only the barest of light illuminating the area, the topography remained indistinct. The basin appeared to be a sinkhole in the otherwise flat terrain, with steep drops from the circular precipice.

As quiet as an owl, Fellina settled near the precipice, her left flank toward the edge. Xenith did the same at the rear, her wings lifted to hide her rider.

"Dismount immediately," Fellina whispered, "and conceal yourself on my right."

Jason slid off her back and dropped to the ground, touching first with his toes and bending his knees to absorb the impact. Without so much as a sound, Elyssa copied his move and hid under Xenith's right wing. She clutched her own sword, keeping it close to her body.

"As we move toward the edge of the basin," Fellina continued, "move with us. Mallerin and Julaz have keen eyesight and hearing, so you will have to peer around our bodies with great stealth if you wish to view the obstacles you are about to encounter."

Fellina and Xenith shuffled to the edge and sat on their haunches, their faces toward the basin, with Xenith on the left and Fellina on the right. Jason dropped to his stomach and motioned for Elyssa to do the same. They crawled over a blend of prickly heather and pebbles until they settled against the dragons' scaly sides, Elyssa between them, and Jason to Fellina's right.

Once in position, Jason gazed over the rim. The dawning sun provided misty light, giving shape and depth to the basin. It appeared to be about thirty feet deep and three hundred feet in diameter. A monolith stood at the center, its top nearly as high as the basin's rim, but lack of light kept any details from clarifying. Still, the form of a dragon stalking near the monolith's base was clear enough. Her wings stretched out, and her mouth opened wide, as if she were yawning. As she passed by a flaming torch mounted in a bracket at the monolith's side, her size became obvious. She was considerably larger than Fellina, at least in girth.

Jason looked to his left. Elyssa lay there with her chin propped on her folded hands, her stare locked on the scene. She would be the first to know if the dragon sisters noticed their human audience.

A shout sounded from the basin, a dragon's voice speaking in the draconic tongue. Fellina whispered to Jason. "This is Mallerin, the older sister. She wants to know who we are and why we are here." She then answered in a series of deep grunts and a variety of shrill whistles.

Xenith lowered her head and provided the translation. "I am Fellina, mate of Arxad. My daughter, Xenith, is here. With Taushin's rise to power now a reality, I wish for Xenith to witness the consequences of human rebellion so that she can employ the appropriate passion when warning the slaves in our domain."

"We grind rebels, to be sure," Mallerin replied, "but will she be able to tolerate the disposal of useless slaves?"

"Warning slaves to be industrious should carry the same passion," Fellina said. "This is reality, and Xenith is of age."

"So be it." Flapping her wings and carrying a whip, Mallerin skittered to the right along the basin floor until she reached the wall, where, with sunlight now streaming in, a large hole had become apparent. Blocked by a gate made up of a matrix of slats, it appeared to be a prison cell.

Mallerin blew a jet of fire at the side of the gate until it popped ajar. Then, using her wing, she swung it outward. "Come forth!" she called, this time speaking the human language. "Or you will be cooked where you stand."

Jason shifted his gaze back to the monolith, now clearer in the brighter light. A ladder in front led to the top where a hole lay open, wide enough for humans to enter. Near the base of the monolith, a wheel was mounted against the left side, similar to a sailing vessel's steering wheel, though only a single handle protruded outward.

"The grinding wheel," Jason whispered.

Elyssa glanced his way. With her brow furrowed deeply, she needed no words. The details were all too clear. The victims had to climb to the top of the monolith and drop into the hole. Then the dragon would turn the wheel and grind their bodies.

A loud crack sounded. Jason jerked around. With another crack, Mallerin snapped her whip across a muscular man's bare shoulders. Dressed only in short trousers, the man led a procession of humans. A girl followed, her long hair tied in a rope in the back and her ribs clearly visible on her narrow frame. Dressed in the same manner as the man, she lowered her head as she inched along, her hands wringing.

"The girl is a slave from the cattle camp," Fellina whispered. "She was likely too weak to fight for the morsels, so she became malnourished and failed to enter puberty. Now too old to remain in the camp, she went unclaimed by the Breeders. The only option is to grind her into bait, which the guardian dragons use to lure dangerous beasts into traps. We cannot afford to lose the stronger slaves to the jaws of wild animals."

Jason kept his stare on the line, hoping Fellina's voice was low enough to prevent the dragon sisters from hearing her explanation in the human tongue.

Two adolescent boys trailed in the procession, walking with a fully clothed man between them. One of the boys appeared to lack a lower leg and used a hefty stick to keep from falling. The other boy crossed a withered arm over his stomach, while the man walked with a slight limp.

Jason rose up a little, squinting. Could it be?

"Your father," Elyssa whispered. "No doubt about it."

A growl erupted unbidden, spicing his low reply. "I can't wait any longer. I have to rescue my father."

"Patience," Fellina warned. "Our only chance will come when he is atop the grinding tower. You will ride on my back, and we will pluck him from the top. With enough speed and with the advantage of surprise, we should be able to avoid an attack from the sisters."

Jason nodded at Mallerin. "But there is only one of them and two of you. Can't we try to rescue all the humans?"

"Julaz will come. She would never miss a grinding." Fellina let out a sigh. "Look to the left. Even now she emerges."

A second dragon appeared from a cave on the opposite side, batting her wings just enough to scoot her hefty body toward the stone. When she arrived, she stood close to the wheel and waited, using a wing to stroke her shimmering scales, reddish in the rising sun.

"If we attack at their level," Fellina continued, "the two of them will easily defeat us, and I will not subject Xenith to such a battle."

"I am not afraid of them," Xenith said, her own growl emphatic. "I can—"

"Silence!" Fellina cleared her throat and lowered her voice again. "When I fly with Jason to pick up his father, it will be your duty to distract them. Stay out of fire range. If they give chase, hurry with Elyssa to our refuge. I know for certain that you are faster than they, even with a passenger."

A proud tone flavored Xenith's reply. "Neither one of those fat hens can keep me in view."

"Remember humility," Fellina said, though her chastisement carried the same proud tone. "Your speed will serve you well as long as the Creator is pleased with your spirit."

As the slaves approached the grinding stone, Jason tried to calm his heart. If they had to wait for his father to climb to the top before launching into the basin to pluck him from the stone, their timing had to be perfect.

The victims continued a slow march. The girl behind the lead man dragged her feet. Edison Masters, as well as his escorts, faced straight ahead, marching like mindless animals.

"Elyssa," Jason whispered. "Something's changed. Can you pick up anything?"

"Their minds are being affected by something. They were vibrant when they first came out of the cage, but, except for the man in front, their signals are fading."

"Mallerin gave them a drug as they left their prison," Fellina said. "Not only does it ease the pain of the grinding, it is the only way to get them to voluntarily climb the ladder. Forcing them is a messy business."

"A messy business," Jason repeated, growling again. These monsters viewed humans as slaughterhouse animals, beasts worth nothing more than the prey they feasted upon at meals. Even Fellina's tone seemed mechanical. Obviously she knew that this butchering occurred frequently, humans with souls being mercilessly pulverized into a bloody mass day after day. Their screams didn't bother her. No, the shredding and grinding took place out of sight, within the darkness of a stone enclosure into which no one could see except for the victims and their killers. And Fellina did nothing about it.

Taking in a deep breath, Jason clenched a fist. Well, *he* would do something about it. At least one of their victims would escape the grinder, and any ugly sister who tried to stop them would meet the point of his sword.

The lead man circled the grinding stone and gripped the wheel's handle. The girl, her expression stoic and faraway, began climbing the ladder, methodically setting hand and foot in place.

Jason swallowed. His father wasn't first! For some reason, this scenario had never crossed his mind. A jittery "Fellina?" spilled from his lips.

"Yes?" she replied.

"The girl is going first." He slowly rose to hands and knees. "What are we going to do?"

"Wait for your father to climb. He will go after the girl is killed. Mallerin chose the first man to perform the grinding. He will likely be spared until tomorrow."

"But ..." Jason looked at Elyssa. With her mouth hanging open, she stared at him, fear in her eyes. "But the girl. We have to rescue her."

"We have the opportunity to rescue only one," Fellina said. "When the sisters give up pursuit, they will grind the others. Girls such as she go to the grinding mill regularly, and she is of no value to our ultimate goal."

As the girl neared the top of the stone, Jason repeated Fellina's words in his mind. *No value. Ultimate goal.* But what *was* their ultimate goal?

Jason looked again. Edison reached a hand up to the girl, his expression confused. He took a step toward the stone but faltered and staggered backwards, his eyes wide as if lost in a dream.

The futile struggle resurrected a memory in Jason's mind — his father's spasms as he tried to breathe while lying on the Northlands healing bed. Jason had saved him then, but he would have to do otherwise now.

"No," Jason said as he rose to his feet.

"No?" Fellina bent her neck, bringing her head close to his eyes. "Hide yourself, or your father is doomed."

Fighting to keep his voice steady, he met her stare. "We have to save the girl."

"Nonsense, Jason. Do not lose sight of your ultimate goal."

He growled once again. "She *is* our ultimate goal!"

"Why? What is that little girl to you?"

"A little girl." Jason climbed onto Fellina's back and drew his sword. "And that's enough for me."

Elyssa leaped to her feet. With her fist tight around her sword's hilt, she gave him a thumbs-up.

"I did not agree to rescue the girl," Fellina said as she spread out her wings, "but it seems that you are forcing my compliance with your rash behavior."

The she-dragon flew into the air. Jason tried to see in front, but with her body angling upward, only bare sky lay ahead. Then she leveled out. Hanging on to a spine and using his legs as a vise, he gripped her body. With her angle leveling, the bottom of the basin came into view. Edison grasped the ladder and tried to climb, but the man at the grinding wheel wrestled him to the ground and held him there. The girl, now standing atop the stone, advanced a foot toward the hole.

"Remove your clothes first," Mallerin called, "and throw them down to us."

As the girl reached for the button at the front of her trousers, Jason fumed. These foul dragons would strip every shred of decency from their victims. And for what? To save clothing? To keep their precious mill from clogging? He patted Fellina's scales. They were only a moment away. They had to rescue her in time.

Mallerin suddenly launched from the ground. Blasting fire, she stormed toward them. Jason drew back his sword. Fellina ducked under Mallerin's flames, and as the bigger dragon flew over, Jason slashed at her belly, making a gouge in her soft spot.

Screaming, Mallerin wheeled around and surged toward them again. Fellina dove toward the stone, but she couldn't possibly avoid Mallerin this time. The larger dragon was closing in too quickly. From near the base of the monolith, Julaz spewed a torrent of flames. They splashed against Fellina's chest and arced over Jason, singeing his hair. With Mallerin bombing toward them from above, and flames erupting from below, a cataclysmic collision lay only seconds away.

Then, out of nowhere, Xenith zoomed in, Elyssa brandishing her sword. The younger dragon sideswiped Mallerin, and Elyssa whacked at Mallerin's flank, but as Fellina steepened her dive, a river of flames blocked Jason's view.

Fellina suddenly shot upward, beating her wings furiously. Jason whipped around and looked back. Xenith flew toward the opposite edge of the basin, Elyssa still riding and Mallerin in pursuit. Although Xenith began with a sizeable head start, Mallerin was catching up. Xenith flew erratically, as if she had injured a wing in the collision.

Jason scanned the ground. The girl was gone. Had she fallen in? Or had Fellina snatched her away in time? The dragon's wings blocked his view of her claws, making his hope impossible to confirm. Julaz sat next to the stone, eyeing Fellina but apparently unwilling to give chase. Edison sat on the ground while the other man stood behind him, his posture indicating victory in their struggle.

"Father!" Jason shouted. "It's me! I'll be back for you!"

Edison raised a hand, but Fellina's flight angle shifted, moving him out of sight.

Jason strangled the hilt of his sword. His father was wounded and drugged, yet he still tried to rescue the girl, in spite of two dragons and a muscular slave standing nearby, ready to make sure the execution commenced. But what would they do with him now?

"Did you pick up the girl?" Jason shouted forward.

"I did, but I will have to deposit both of you immediately. I must help my daughter."

"Yes," Jason said. "Set us down anywhere. We'll be all right."

"So you think." Fellina dove again and landed in a trot.

Jason slid down her flank and patted her scales. "Go!"

Fellina launched back into the air, her wings raising a wave of sand and grit. Squinting to protect his eyes, he ran into Fellina's wake. The girl sat cross-legged, her head hanging low. When he reached her, he dropped to his knees and laid a hand on her bony, welt-covered back. Blood oozed from a claw mark at one shoulder blade where Fellina had dug in. "Are you all right?" he asked.

The girl swiveled her head toward him, making her eyes visible behind a curtain of scattered bangs. Her dry lips pursed, forming a whisper that came out slurred. "Who are you?"

"Jason Masters." Straightening as he slid the sword to its place, he searched the area. The basin was perhaps five hundred paces away, and only bare, heather-covered ground spread out in between. In the opposite direction, however, a refuge lay in sight. Fellina had deposited them near a stand of trees, close enough to reach within seconds. He checked the stardrop pouch. It was still there, safe and sound.

Jason scooped the girl into his arms and lifted her as he rose. As light as an eight-year-old, she felt like a heap of bones wrapped in damp skin. She laid her arms loosely around his neck, staring at him with glazed eyes. As he hurried toward the trees, her head bobbed in time with his gait.

After passing several narrow trunks with low-hanging limbs, he turned and looked back. Although not densely packed, the trees and branches shielded them well enough. Anyone standing in the heather field wouldn't be able to see them.

Jason set the girl down. As she crossed her legs again, he knelt at her side and spoke in a soothing tone. "Stay here, and stay quiet. I'll be back as soon as I can."

She grasped his sleeve and called out with a stronger voice, her eyes suddenly filled with panic. "Don't leave me."

He wrapped his fingers around her thin hand. It trembled in his grip. "You'll be all right, at least long enough for me to rescue my father. The dragons can't see you."

She squinted at the sunlight above. "Not so."

Jason looked up at the sparse canopy overhead and frowned. "I see what you mean."

She slung her arms around his neck and pressed her cheek against his chest. "Don't let them get me. They want to crush my bones and grind me into bait." With a quaking sob, she added, "One of the men said I would be all right. It would hurt a lot, but as soon as I died, an angel would sweep me up to heaven where I would never have pain again. But ... but ..."

"But what?" Jason prompted gently.

"I don't want to die." She buried her face in his chest and cried, her sobs muffled by his shirt.

Jason embraced her fully and laid a hand on the back of her head. "Go ahead and cry. I'll be here as long as you need me. I promise." He ached to run back to the basin and help his father, but how could he leave this poor girl without a protector? Unlike the man Cassabrie had fabricated in the Northlands as a test, this girl was flesh and blood, as real as love and pain. He had failed his earlier test badly, not even bothering to ask the man his name after giving up on bringing the healing stardrop.

A breeze filtered down from above, cooling his skin. He was drenched with sweat, but the girl didn't seem to mind. She kneaded his back, shaking gently as she wept. Somehow he had to comfort her, settle her down enough so that he could sneak back to the basin.

He pushed away and ran a hand over her dark hair, dirty and tangled. Her sunken cheeks told of starvation, and her probing gaze hinted of a longing for love that had never been fulfilled. Jason sighed. Yes, she was real, tragically real. He wouldn't miss his opportunity, not this time. "What's your name?"

She sniffed and swallowed. "Acknod."

"Acknod? I have never heard that name before."

Her voice slowly steadied. "It sounds like the dragon word for spittle. When I was born in the breeding stable, they saw how weak I was, and the Trader spat on the ground and said *Acknod*. The name has stuck ever since."

Jason rolled his eyes upward. "Maybe we should give you a different name, something that—"

A shriek sounded from the basin, sharp and clear. Then, as abruptly as it began, it ceased.

Acknod threw her arms around him again. "The kind man," she cried.

"Shhh ..." Jason's shushing died on his lips. He added his own swallow. Acknod was right. The scream was too deep to be from one of the boys, too human to be a dragon's bellow. It had to be his father's cry.

Jason bit his lip hard. Father was dead. But he couldn't lose control, not now. He had to keep his wits sharp and his perception skills active. Who could tell when one of those dragons might fly over and ...

His thought melted away. The horrid phrase trickled from his lips. "Father is dead."

As his body began to shake, Acknod rubbed his sleeve. "Your father? The kind man was your father?"

Looking at her through a wash of tears, Jason nodded, but he couldn't speak. His throat had clamped shut.

Acknod rose to her feet and wrapped her arms around him, her chest now level with his. She set her hand behind his head and drew his cheek to her shoulder. "Go ahead and cry, Jason. I'll be here. I promise." She hummed, then whispered softly in his ear. "An angel came and took him to heaven. His pain is over."

As Jason wept, her gentle voice brought back a memory — Elyssa, when the two of them were both eleven years old. She crooned a song she had written herself, a gift for Jason when his grandfather died.

Allow your tears to fall on me;
I'll catch them all, and you will see
That friends who love are friends for life,
Together walking paths of strife.

Jason cried on, trying to imagine Elyssa holding him close, but Acknod's bare shoulder and moist skin brought him back to reality. He gently pried her arms loose and slid back on his knees. After wiping one sleeve across his eyes and the other under his nose, he gazed at her sincere face. She blinked her sunken brown eyes.

"Thank you," he said as he laid a hand on her cheek. "You are truly an angel of comfort."

A slight smile bent her lips. "Did you think of a new name for me?"

As he studied her expectant countenance, a dozen common names flew through his mind—Madeline, Elaine, and others. Then the girls from the Northlands entered his thoughts. Their lovely names matched their personalities—Deference and Resolute. Why not give this girl a name that matched her gifts?

"How about Solace?" he said, using his thumb to brush a tear from her cheek. "It means comfort."

She dipped her head and repeated his words slowly. "Solace. It means comfort." Then, looking at him again, she smiled and nodded. "I like it."

"Then Solace it is." His hands trembling, Jason unbuttoned his outer tunic, stripped it off, and helped her put it on. "It's so big it will be like a dress, but it's better than nothing."

"It's beautiful," she said as she rolled up a sleeve. "I have never worn anything so lovely. The slave trader let me borrow a nice tunic for a while, but this is much softer."

Once she had fastened the buttons, Jason laid a hand on her shoulder. "Can you be brave for me?"

"I think so."

"I want you to hide next to one of the tree trunks and bury yourself in that tunic as much as you can. I will be back soon. I promise."

"Where are you going?"

"Back to the grinding stone."

"Why?" Solace asked, her voice quavering again. "Your father is dead."

"I didn't hear any other screams. Maybe I can help those two boys."

"The dragons said the fall into the stone sometimes is enough to kill a human, so we wouldn't have heard them scream. They might already be dead."

Jason shook his head. The dragons probably told the victims that story to settle them down, make them believe they wouldn't suffer. "I have to check. It's the least I can do. And I'm not going to let them use my father's remains as bait for wild beasts."

Solace pressed her lips together as if firming her resolve. "I'll be brave, but I hope you'll hurry. If you don't come back, I won't have anywhere to go."

"Don't be afraid," Jason said, slipping his arm around her shoulders and giving her a gentle hug. "No matter what happens to me, I'm sure Fellina will return for you."

"The dragon?" Solace pulled away and touched her shoulder. "I hope not."

"She didn't mean to hurt you," Jason said reaching toward the wound. "She was just—"

Solace swiveled away from his touch. "Dragons always mean to hurt. They do nothing but hurt. They are cruel and heartless."

Jason drew back his hand. What could he say? Solace had experienced nothing but cruelty, and even Fellina considered her an expendable beast. Not only that, dragons had killed his own father. Truly they were murderers—evil, villainous cowards who drained every drop of sweat and blood from their captives before disposing of them in the most horrific way imaginable.

"You're right, but I don't have any choice." Jason rose and squared his shoulders. "I will be back. If Fellina comes first, that's fine. Just tell her where I went. We'll get together again somehow."

"I'll trust you, then." Solace got up and sat next to the nearest tree. She pulled the tunic's shoulders over her head and sank into the roomy material. Then she drew her legs in, making them disappear as well. "Hurry back," she called, her voice muffled.

Jason let a smile emerge. "I will." But the smile quickly wilted. The pain was too heavy, too deep. The wound in his heart wouldn't allow more than a split second of relief.

Blinking away new tears, he took a deep breath and marched ahead. As he drew near the edge of the trees, the basin came into view. His father's scream echoed in his mind—loud, pain-streaked, abrupt. His final living moment was one of torture, a crushing of body and bones that squeezed out a desperate cry and then silenced him forever.

He stopped at the tree line and looked out over the arid terrain. In the distance, the Zodiac's spires rose above the rocks and scant trees, and the Basilica's belfry stood nearby, symbols of dragon authority and rule over Starlight.

Jason spat on the ground. This planet wasn't Starlight. It was the darkest place in the universe. If any planet deserved to be called Darksphere, this was it.

He checked the sky. No dragons flew anywhere in sight. With a quick swing, he hacked a branch from a fallen tree. Although the leaves had turned brown, they were dense enough to conceal him if necessary.

Regripping his sword, he marched ahead. Someone had to bring light to this dark world, and rescuing two innocent boys from the grindstone would be the first step.

six

Inside Exodus, Koren alternately walked and slid closer to Brinella, who stood beside the untouched stardrop at the lowest point of the sloping floor. Although regal in expression and dress, Brinella still wore no crown, contrary to Taushin's expectations. Yet, crown or no crown, they had to resurrect this star so the slaves could be freed.

When she reached Brinella, Koren turned and surveyed the breach in the wall. "At the rate the star deflates, we'll have to work together to have any hope of success." She glanced at the red stain on Brinella's dress. "Especially since you're wounded."

Her expression softer now, Brinella touched her side. "I thought it would eventually heal. It hurts, but it doesn't bleed. It simply makes me feel weak all the time."

"That's why we have to work together." Koren compressed Brinella's hand. "Since Starlight gives you all the stories, it's up to you to let them flow to me. I'll see if I can absorb them and retell them with more power. If I direct them away from the hole, maybe we can fill the sphere before they exit."

"It's worth a try." With her face again displaying a rainbow of flashing colors, Brinella took a deep breath. "I have been holding them in for several minutes, so prepare yourself."

Koren walked across the curved floor and settled back against the hole, blocking it with her body. "Okay. Let's see what happens."

Brinella's face, now dark purple, swelled. Her chest expanded, and her back bent inward. Then, like a striking viper, her body snapped forward, her mouth opening as her head whipped. Colorful light roared from her throat and streamed toward Koren, splashing against her waist. The colors washed over her body and filtered through her clothing, soaking her with multihued radiance. Like a confused mob, a thousand voices spoke at once, some angry, some lamenting, some as quiet as a whisper. Yet none seemed clear enough to distinguish.

With the influx, it seemed as if Koren's own thoughts were pushed to the side while the competing voices took control. A stream of light, blue and glittering, spewed forth from her lips, and a frightened tone spiced her voice. "She has the plague! There is no hope!"

As the blue flow headed toward the sphere's ceiling, a radiant magenta stream followed, this one with a calmer, soothing voice. "We are paying a severe penalty for our foolishness. Our only hope is to heed Magnar's advice."

Then, like a sporadic fountain, gush after gush erupted from Koren's mouth, displaying more colors than she had ever seen. With each one, she provided a louder voice, but they came so quickly, it seemed impossible to tell where the statements began and ended.

"The plague will devour your body until it's a useless relic, perishable unless you consume the substance of the cause ..." And the words rambled on. Streams of radiance continued to shoot toward the ceiling, collecting there as if drawn by the light in the opening above. The transparent wall vibrated. Rocks surrounding the sphere crumbled, striking the outer surface before falling to the chamber floor. Then, as if buoyed by an unseen cushion of air, Exodus began to rise.

Finally, Brinella's eruption ceased. Now without a source, Koren's flow ebbed until a final globule of light flew from her lips, followed by a whisper. "Now we will learn the nature of this fruit. Is it borne of faith or of fear?"

As she looked up at the mass of shimmering blobs, Koren let her arms and legs go limp. She took in a deep breath and exhaled heavily. Sweat trickled down her cheek and dampened the shirt under her dress. "It's—" She coughed, clearing her voice. "It's working."

"Probably not for long," Brinella said. "Even without the hole, the light always escapes. It just takes a little longer for it to push through the membrane."

As Brinella predicted, the globules of light began sifting through the sphere's skin, popping out as swimming whisperers before climbing through the air toward the opening above.

Koren checked her position. Her body still fully blocked the wound. "How did you control the star's movement when you floated through the sky?"

"When Exodus was airborne, I was able to will its movements with my mind. I also used to control the tales more easily and tell them whenever I wished, but it has been so long, and I am so weak, I no longer feel the power."

"Once we get it airborne, you can try. For now, just keep feeding me tales of Starlight, and I'll keep filling the sphere."

"Very well." Grimacing, Brinella laid a hand on her side. "I will do what I can."

Koren kept her limbs splayed. "I'll magnify whatever you're able to deliver."

Lowering herself to her knees, Brinella folded her hands and looked toward the sky. She closed her eyes and spoke in a rhythmic cadence.

Creator,
The bringer of life, singer of songs,
The breaker of strife, righter of wrongs,
Regard my estate, humble and low;
Remove this dread weight, let my light flow.

As light, white and pulsing, flowed from Brinella's face, Koren felt her mouth drop open. What was happening? Her own prayers hadn't done this before, even when she sang them.

Brinella continued, her countenance becoming more dazzling with each word.

You gave me this vow, chains of pure love,
Accepting I bowed, shackled above;
So do what you must, be who you are;
Produce from the dust, make a new star.

The light emanating from her face continued to pulse, growing brighter and gaining substance. With every throb, a layer of Brinella's body peeled away, each layer attached to the previous one and spiraling upward as if she were unraveling. The lead end of the coil of light rose to the apex of the sphere and pierced the top. Soon Brinella's body shrank, leaving only a floating ball with bright green eyes.

Still attached to the rising coil, it floated to Koren and brushed against her cheek. A whisper passed into her ears. "Good-bye, Starlighter. Thank you for taking my place." Then the ball unraveled completely, and the stream of light disappeared through the apex.

Koren climbed to her feet, sliding down as she stumbled toward the floor's center. The toe of her boot struck the stardrop, making it roll up the wall. "Taking your place?" she shouted. "I can't take your place!"

Her words bounced, echoing throughout the star's core. The remaining light from Brinella's stories streamed toward the wound. Exodus drifted downward, faster now. The stardrop rolled back and settled near her boots.

As Exodus continued to descend, Koren stared at the contrast, stark-white radiance next to the blackest of leather. Would she be able to do Brinella's job? She knew so little, especially about the Creator. Sealing the hole with the stardrop would make it easier, but that would entrap her forever. Surely no one truly expected her to make such a sacrifice.

When the final globule of light exited, the sphere's walls began to wrinkle. Like a slowly deflating balloon,

Exodus shrank. The ambient light within faded, and the entire chamber grew dim.

"No!" Koren turned in a slow circle. Lifting her hands, she shouted upward. "Creator, don't let this happen! We need Exodus! We need a guiding star!"

Again her words echoed, this time warped, as if bent by the wrinkling wall, but now they appeared as a stream of light that brushed by her ears each time the words repeated. Her own voice crying out, "We need a guiding star!" pierced her mind, feeling like a dagger with every repetition.

Dropping to her knees, she looked up. The ceiling continued to collapse, drawing nearer to her head. "I can't do this!" she shouted. "I am not a Starlighter, at least not one like Brinella. I can't be a guiding angel. I don't know enough about you."

She lowered her head and wept. Visions of slaves entered her mind—Wallace as a boy, still with two eyes, cringing in front of a dragon who carried a hot poker in his clawed hand; Petra struggling against a dragon as it held open her mouth and inserted a knife; Natalla dragging chains into the Basilica theater room just before her trial.

"Koren?"

Natalla stooped in front of her, her wrists still bound by chains. The links suddenly crumbled into dust. She lifted a hand and caressed Koren's cheek. "I am free now, dear sister, because of you. You faced Maximus at the Basilica, helped me escape execution at the trial, and offered your-self as a sacrifice at the mine. Because of love, you risked death for me, and now I live in peace with a new father. I still work, to be sure, but now because I love to serve my new father, and we work together to make a home." She picked up the stardrop and held it in her palm. "You know how to resurrect Exodus, but you cannot do so as long as you allow the chains of slavery to remain. A slave cannot do the work of a daughter of light. A slave works under compulsion. A daughter works for love alone."

Natalla faded away, and the stardrop, bright and shining, appeared on the floor where it had been before.

Koren blinked. How could she have conjured Natalla and given voice to her new experiences? Could those thoughts be wishful thinking, a projection of her hopes? She nudged the stardrop with her finger. Perhaps this piece of Exodus, still radiant in spite of the star's deterioration, had a lot of power. Then again, if Exodus knew only tales of Starlight, it couldn't tell about the happenings on Darksphere. Who could possibly know what was going on in that world?

As the walls warped and wrinkled, the ceiling continued its slow descent, now only ten feet or so above her. She rose to her full height and reached with both hands toward it, hoping to support it when it fell that far.

The stardrop continued shining, sparkling, pulsing. As she concentrated on its radiance, the wrinkled walls faded, and a corridor appeared, the same one she had been in earlier when Deference guided her. The door that no one would answer was now open.

Koren lowered her hands and peeked inside. The room appeared to be empty; an expanse of marble floor stretched as far as she could see. She leaned into the room, then stepped fully inside. Although Deference and her aura weren't there this time, light was plentiful.

She stood on a bare floor of white marble with surrounding white walls, and a white ceiling loomed above. With perfect whiteness all around, it was impossible to guess the distance to the boundaries or to be sure of the room's shape.

A whisper entered her ears, as if spoken by someone within reach. "Close the doors, Starlighter."

Koren reached for the doors, but there were no handles to grab. Gripping the side of each, she pulled them toward herself and jumped back, allowing them to swing. When they met at the center, the gap disappeared. Every line that framed the entry sealed and vanished.

She called out, "The doors are closed. What am I supposed to do next?"

The voice returned, this time louder and clearly masculine. "Prophesy, Starlighter, for such is your purpose."

Looking up, Koren walked backwards, searching for the source. "Prophesy? What do you mean? How can I predict the future?"

"Predicting the future is a narrow definition. To prophesy is to reveal, to uncover, to speak forth that which you see. It is a simple task for a Starlighter."

Koren touched the edge of her cloak. "If you mean that I should tell a tale, then I can do that, but what tale do you wish to hear?"

"Your stage is blank. It is a canvas for your mind. Fill it, Starlighter, with the mysteries you long to solve. Answer the questions that torture you."

Koren looked up. At least that direction seemed to be up. Which questions did he mean? So many had tortured her mind. She looked at her wrists, both still marred by manacle wounds. Chains. This had been the biggest question. Was Taushin right about love requiring chains? So far, he had been proven right about so many things. Yet one mystery still haunted her mind. When she cried out to the Creator during Taushin's chastising jolts, the pain fled, but her manacles remained. What good did it do to provide temporary relief without granting freedom? Any refusal to obey Taushin would have resulted in another jolt. Whatever it meant, it seemed clear that the answers lay so deep in mystery, she would have to start at the beginning.

She lifted her hood over her head and spread out her cloak, giving it a dramatic twirl. "Starlight, a world less bright, forsaking wisdom's call ..." She exhaled. The words in her mind evaporated. Her arms felt heavy, weak.

"What's wrong with me?" she called out. "I don't feel the power."

"Starlighter ..." The voice took on a stern tone. "You cannot prophesy here if you are in an unclean state, for this place is holy."

She looked at her palms, no more soiled than usual. "Unclean? I don't understand."

"You are not such a fool. Your days of claiming ignorance have come to an end."

"Ignorance?"

"Repeating my words makes you a hollow echo. Gird yourself with courage and examine yourself. Although you are better than most, a standing of relative goodness will not provide you with access should you ever reach the Creator's door."

Koren pulled in her bottom lip. No more talk. Her tongue was just digging a deeper hole. Examine herself?

What could that mean? She looked down at her body. The room's pristine whiteness made her clothes look blacker than ever, like a pile of soot on clean sheets. Could that be it? Her clothes? Taushin had forbidden her to remove her symbolic dress, but Taushin couldn't see her now. In this room of white, even his memory seemed foreign and out of place.

After taking off her cloak, she stripped the dress over her head and threw it to the floor. Although she now wore only a pair of knee-length trousers and a short-sleeved white tunic, her exposed skin stayed comfortable, still warmed by her Exodus abode.

As she wrapped the cloak around her body again, her boots came into view, still on her feet and still black. Not long ago, those boots were a hated addition, a sign of Taushin's controlling influence. Now that they had stretched to fit, however, they seemed a part of her, cozy and snug instead of cramped and constricting, perfect for the Northlands climate. They were just footwear, not something that should weigh her down as she told a story.

She lifted her hood again and spread out her arms, but they were still heavy, empty of energy. She let them flop to her sides. "I took off that horrid dress," she called. "Wasn't that enough?"

The voice returned, sharp and angry. "Enough excuses, Starlighter! If you continue with this charade, you will employ your precious boots and trudge home through the snow."

She dropped to her seat and pinched the laces at the back of one boot, tightly tied at the top. The knot was stubborn. It wouldn't budge. She tried the other. No better. For some reason they had swelled, maybe from the drastic change in temperature. Of course she could cut them if she had a blade, but wishing for a knife wouldn't make a real one appear.

"I can't get them loose," she called out.

The answer drifted past her like a soft breeze. "Do you want them off?"

"Don't you want me to take them off? I thought I was supposed to prophesy and—"

"You failed to answer my question."

Koren let out a sigh. "Okay. I'm not trying to claim ignorance, but I am confused. Can you at least give me a hint?"

"You have had more than your share of hints, and the power you need has already been granted. Examine yourself. Why do you have chains? To whom are you enslaved and why? And finally, do you really want your boots to come off?"

As Koren stared at the laces, the final question echoed throughout the room. *Do you really want your boots to come off?* It seemed so simple and the answer so obvious. Of course she wanted the boots to come off. Couldn't the stranger behind the voice see how hard she had been trying to untie them?

The question continued to echo, softer and softer, the tone altering to a pleading lament, as though she wouldn't have another chance if she didn't respond before it faded completely.

Two words seemed to reverberate louder than the others—*really* and *your*. Do you *really* want *your* boots to come off?

Koren scowled, anger rising in hot flashes. Of course she *really* wanted the boots to come off. Why else would she be picking at the knots? How hard would she have to try to prove to this stranger that she really meant it?

Then, as if gasping for a dying breath, a final echo sounded, and *your boots* hung in the air like a foul odor. Koren wrinkled her nose. *Your boots?* She caressed the black leather with a gliding finger. These were *her* boots. Although Zena had ordered her to put them on, she could have refused. Would refusal have meant punishment? Probably. Death? Maybe. Still, no matter the consequences, she had a choice. Her boots, her chains, her acquiescence to Taushin's dominion all were still a choice. She could have chosen pain. She could have chosen death. Either one would have been better than slavery.

Now the easing of the torture made sense. The Creator didn't provide a respite as mere temporary relief; he simply provided her an opportunity to choose. The short pause in the pain had given her a moment of clarity, a chance to examine the options. Would she choose suffering and death instead of obedience to an evil power?

Ever since that moment, she had used pain as an excuse. She had explained away her actions by lifting her chains and bemoaning her slavery. She had given in to a slave's mind-set and assumed that no power could set her free. Her boots had become comfortable, as had her chains.

She glared at the laces. She had tied them herself. And now their tightness relied on her own desire to keep her boots on. What did she really want?

She picked at the knot again. It stayed as tight as ever. As she continued working, the strings seemed to pulse, as if swelling and shrinking in her grasp. Manacles clamped around her wrists. Chains weighed down her arms. It was hard ... so hard!

Taushin's voice whispered within. *You are now mine, and you could not leave me if you tried. You would always come back ... always. And when you learn to love me, the chains will become self-imposed, for you will not ever want to leave.*

"No!" Koren ripped at the laces. The manacles dragged against her skin, peeling away the top layer. As heat roared through her body, she cried out, "I hate you! Boots, chains, slavery, I hate you!"

She jerked on the knot, ripping a nail, but the laces finally broke free. Yanking on the heel, she loosened the boot, then savagely kicked it off. She shifted to the other boot and tore through its knot, breaking its bond more easily. When that boot fell away from her foot, the manacles and chains vanished.

Sucking in shallow breaths, she looked at her bare feet, red and swollen. The swelling receded, and the color slowly faded to normal flesh tone. The boots lay near her dress, dirty smudges amidst the whiteness. There they would stay, even if she had to walk barefoot in the snow.

She climbed to a standing position. With a strong push, she gave her cloak a new spin. It swept around her legs, drawing cool air against her ankles and feet. The sensation felt wonderful, alive, liberating. Her feet danced unbidden, shifting her body into a sway. She lifted her arms, now lightweight and filled with energy.

"Starlight!" she called out. "Hear my command and release your secrets." Her words then slid into a rhythmic cadence.

Starlight, a world less bright,
Forsaking wisdom's call,
Starlight, explain your plight,
Reveal to me your all.

Like a dancer on a stage, Koren glided across the white expanse. As she waved her arms, her hands painted the air dark, whisking away the light in the room. The pristine chamber transformed into an evergreen forest illuminated by a twilight sky. A bright lantern sat in a grassy clearing and spread flickering yellow light all around, making a row of crystalline pegs sparkle on the ground. Several sheep lay close together in a makeshift cage of wood and wire, quiet and still, though their eyes stayed alert.

Not far away, a river bisected a valley, cutting through a verdant meadow. Beyond that, a castle sat nestled against the base of a snow-capped mountain. Three red turrets highlighted an upper floor, and a doorway on ground level stood open.

At the center of the forest clearing, Arxad stood beside two eggs in a wicker basket, apparently the same two eggs he had in the previous tale. Another dragon landed, his wings beating the air as he settled.

With his head low, Arxad caressed the top of an egg with his wing and spoke in the dragon language. "Magnar, I am grateful that you have come. It will be a long time until we see each other again."

122

Magnar scooted close to Arxad but stayed well away from the eggs. "I will never forget your sacrifice. Your willingness to preserve this species has gone beyond what anyone could expect."

"I cannot deny it. To most, I have played the fool by trying to save those who brought destruction upon themselves and untold suffering to our race."

"It is not foolish to invest in our own preservation, but I understand. Many think you actually love these vermin. I would not want to carry the weight of that accusation."

"Love them?" Arxad withdrew his wing from the egg. "I love our race, and I care for these humans out of respect for the Creator who deemed it necessary to use them in this fashion. I spend this time away from Starlight, from my mate, and from my fellow dragons to protect our species, not theirs."

"Well spoken." Magnar laid a wing over Arxad's back. "As many disagreements as we have had, I will never forsake our vow. By the time you return, the Zodiac will be complete. Unlike the Basilica, it will be designed for dragons, and you will be the first high priest."

Arxad bowed his head. "I am grateful."

Magnar refolded his wing and looked at the eggs. "Have you already transported everything you need?"

"With the exception of these sheep. The lenses and the genetic testing equipment are already there. When the children are born, I will apply Orson's tests to ensure that his chromosome sequences are in place, and I will leave updates here in a photo tube so that you can track my progress."

"Excellent. I am sure Fellina will be pleased to check for your messages frequently."

"Yes …" Arxad's head drooped. "Fellina."

"In any case," Magnar continued, "with Tamminy's prophecy looming over us, it will be important to see how the humans progress. They must be ready for when we need them."

"But no gunpowder."

Magnar shook his head. "When the prince is born, we will need their numbers. If they had gunpowder, they would be able to subdue us again."

"Very well." Arxad gently pushed an egg past the row of pegs. It disappeared. He did the same with the second egg. As soon as it faded from view, he took to the sky and circled once around the clearing. He then swooped down, grasped the sheep pen with his back claws, and flew over the portal line, instantly vanishing.

The entire scene faded with him, leaving Koren alone in the white expanse, save for her black dress and boots lying on the floor. She released her cloak and let it settle, then looked around the room.

"What now?" she called. "What do I do about Exodus?"

The room faded from white to various shades of brown, the colors of the rocks in the star chamber. The curved wall within Exodus, now smooth and clear, gave the chamber's boundaries a vibrant sheen, but they seemed to be moving.

Koren looked down. The floor lay a hundred feet below, and the gap widened with every second. Above, the exit point at the top of the mountain grew brighter.

She and Exodus would soon emerge into the sky to begin their journey.

Her dress and boots appeared at the corner of her eye, lying in a heap between her and the star's wound. That wouldn't do, not here in Exodus. Those foul clothes had to go.

She gathered the bundle into her arms and pushed it into the wound. As the sides stretched out, a terrible pain ripped through her arms and legs, like someone had grabbed her skin and tried to tear it loose.

When the clothes finally popped through and fell toward the floor, the hole eased back to its original size, and the pain slowly ebbed. What a relief! Now Exodus could rise unencumbered, powered by a healthy Star-lighter.

As she watched the boots strike the floor, light from the star's upper boundary streamed down and passed through the wound. Exodus's ascent slowed, becoming almost imperceptible.

Koren turned and set her back against the escape hole, blocking the light's exit. Above, the mountain's opening lay only a few feet away. Would she make it? Was there still enough light from her tale to push Exodus past the rim?

Just as the top of the star reached the exit, it stopped and began a slow drift downward.

"No!" Koren shouted. "Not now! We were almost there!"

The star's descent hastened. Its outer membrane bumped against the sides of the passageway, breaking rocks and sand from the walls.

"Starlight!" Koren shouted, lifting her arms from where she sat. "Hear my command and release your secrets!"

As the rough slide continued, it seemed that dragon claws scratched her own skin, digging toward her bones. No words came to mind. Like a spilled pitcher, she felt empty and without hope of being filled.

A light at the center of the sphere came into view, a shining dome with flashing spires floating head high, like a radiant crown waiting for a queen. Sparks drizzled from the dome and rained to the star's floor.

Koren gazed at the dazzling display. Had Taushin been right about a crown after all? Brinella had said that she couldn't relay Starlight's tales from the side of the sphere. She had to be at the center. But could someone tell a tale from that point, inflate the star, and run back to the hole to keep the energy from leaking out? It seemed impossible.

She climbed to her feet and half ran, half skidded to the center. Ducking under the dome, she allowed the sparks to trickle over her head. Immediately hundreds of words flashed through her mind and then poured out her mouth, so quickly she couldn't understand them. Light pulsed with every word, and the energy flowed toward the ceiling.

Exodus slowed its descent until it halted, then, as if pushed by a lazy laborer, began ascending once more, crawling along at a frustratingly slow pace. Yet the star again drew close to the exit—so close that if she were to ride on top, she could easily reach up and grab the rim.

As before, light streams crawled down the sphere's sides and filtered out the wound. The top third of Exodus poked out of the mountain's cone and stopped before easing down once again.

"No!" Koren cried. "I'm doing everything I can!"

Even as she spoke, the stardrop, still shining on the floor, caught her attention. There *was* more she could do. Unless Exodus rose again, there would always be need of pheterone reserves and slaves to drill for them. Even if she could get the star to fly, the remedy it provided wouldn't last, not without constant superhuman effort. There was no way she could keep up this frantic pace. And who could tell if Taushin would honor his word and free the slaves during the short time she could keep Exodus aloft?

Natalla came to mind again, her wrists clamped in manacles. Petra entered next, blood oozing from between her lips as she wept over her severed tongue. Finally, Lattimer appeared in front of her, his mouth agape as she finished telling her very first Starlighter tale. She dropped to her knees and repeated the closing phrase she had uttered not so long ago. "May the Creator of All guide me as I seek the path to enlightenment and the succor that a girl of my age needs in this dark and dangerous world."

Lattimer pinched the stardrop and set it in front of Koren's eyes. "Freedom from chains is not the end of the journey, dear Starlighter. It is only the beginning. Every step from here to eternity has the potential for tears as we sacrifice, as we bleed for others, as we take their burdens upon ourselves. We must be willing to stand in flames for them." He pressed the stardrop closer to her eyes. "As I did for you."

His words echoed through her own lips. "As I did for you."

When Lattimer faded, the stardrop once again sat at the lowest point of the sphere. Below, the chamber's floor drew closer, illuminated by Exodus's light.

A tear trickled down Koren's cheek, then another. A spasm heaved in her chest. Weeping, she picked up the stardrop, stumbled toward the breach, and knelt in front of it. She mashed the stardrop between her palms and made a paste, then dug out a glob with her finger and dabbed the top of the rip, smearing it downward across the wound. Like thick honey, the paste adhered to the sides and stitched them together. Every option had vanished. She was either going to be the world's Starlighter or not a Starlighter at all.

Her vision glazed by tears, she applied glob after glob until she had sewn up the entire hole. She rose and staggered back to the center, lowering her head to get under the radiant dome. As she straightened, she pushed her head up into the cap. When her hair touched the light, the cap snapped down and attached to her scalp.

A shock jolted Koren's spine. She stiffened, crying out as sizzling pain roared to her fingers and toes. Her arms shriveled and withdrew into her shoulders. Her feet dwindled until only stumps remained below her knees. Finally, her entire body shrank into a ball, and she floated in place.

The shock simmered to raging heat, then to soothing warmth. Every muscle ache and every pang of hunger fled away. She floated in the midst of a river. A warm spring of water buoyed her body, keeping her motionless in the current. Yet she stayed dry. The water wasn't wet at all. It was light, pure light. And as the energy washed over her, the light transformed into information, a stream of words that jelled in her mind, pushed to the outer part of her spherical body, and sloughed off into whispering streams as Brinella had once created.

With awareness of her surroundings clarifying, she stretched out her body. Arms protruded at her sides, and legs extended underneath. She stood once again at the center of the star's floor. Below, the chamber rushed away. Above, the mountain exit zipped toward her. Then Exodus shot out of the cone and flew into the open air.

After she and Exodus ascended well above the peak, Koren spread out her arms. "Not so high," she whispered.

As if responding to her command, Exodus leveled out and began a slow descent. The world of Starlight lay before her—the castle with its sun-drenched turrets and columns; the snow-draped hills of the Northlands, dotted with evergreens and striped by the ice-covered river; the flowered meadows that lay south of the white cap, bordered by the south-flowing river.

Beautiful! Magnificent!

Words flowed into her mind, and a tune sewed them into a song.

Exodus arise and shine,
Cast your light about!
Slaves in chains upon this sod
Dance and sing and shout!

Freedom comes adorned with light;
Make the blinded see.
Love arrives encased in fire;
Set the captives free.

As she sang, a gaseous vapor emanated from Exodus's membrane and diffused into the air.

Koren laughed. *Pheterone!* She was doing it! She was spreading pheterone into the atmosphere! Now the slaves wouldn't have to drill for the dragons' precious gas. They wouldn't have to be slaves at all!

Koren looked at the castle. Exodus drifted that way, apparently following her mental cue. "No," she whispered. "We need to go south."

As Exodus began a slow turn, a dark blotch on the snow came into view, slowly climbing the castle's outer stairs. Koren shifted back and hovered about thirty feet above the creature. With wings folded in, Taushin sniffed the stairs, apparently following a trail.

Koren gasped. He hadn't gone back to the Southlands! Had he stayed to learn what she would decide? If he was tracking her, he would find her discarded clothing in the star chamber. He was smart enough to figure out why she would leave it behind, and, even blind, he could detect that Exodus wasn't there.

Taking a deep breath, Koren urged Exodus southward. She was free now. Taushin would trouble her no more. She would spread pheterone throughout the planet and urge the dragons to set her people free. After all, she was a Starlighter, and now she could use her power to persuade even the most stubborn dragons.

seven

As Xenith dove through a gap in the forest canopy, barely missing branches with her wings, Elyssa hung on to her neck and stayed as low as possible. With Fellina's help, they had escaped Mallerin's pursuit. Then, after hiding for a few hours in a remote cave, they flew here to the family's enclave, whatever that was.

As soon as Xenith landed in front of a moss-covered boulder, Elyssa tossed her sword to the ground, jumped from the dragon's back, and ran around to face her. "Is your wing all right?"

Xenith nodded. "I think so."

"I wish I could do something for you." Elyssa shifted to Xenith's side and caressed her wing. A purple bruise covered a double-fist-sized section of the mainstay, the product of her collision with Mallerin in the heat of the battle. Xenith moaned at the touch.

Elyssa grimaced. "Sorry."

"I require no sympathy." Xenith's tone seemed defeated rather than annoyed. "I appreciate your concern."

"Well, let me know if you think of something I can do." Elyssa scanned the area. There was no sign of Fellina.

Xenith, too, looked up, her ears twitching. "I hope Mother arrives soon. I know of this place only because she and Father pointed it out from the air. I do not know where to go from here."

"And I want to find out what happened to Jason and his father. If she wasn't able to rescue them, I'll have to go back." Elyssa pinched a bit of moss from the smooth, dark boulder, a granitelike stone about twice the height of a dragon and sixty feet in circumference. Setting her feet to stay balanced on the sloping terrain, she studied the surrounding flora. A mixture of evergreens and molting deciduous trees surrounded the clearing, dense enough to hide them from ground-level eyes. The arching branches provided an umbrella to keep them from being seen by all but the keenest flying searchers. It seemed to be a good hiding place indeed.

"I think we're safe until she shows up." Elyssa drew the moss to her nose, rubbed it between her thumb and finger, and sniffed. The variety indicated a humid region, and its current moisture content proved that it had rained recently. "I tried to keep track of where we are. We're near the base of the southern mountains, right?"

Xenith nodded. "This is considered the edge of the wilderness. The closest pheterone mine is about five miles to the northeast. In fact, this boulder is the marker where Magnar hoped to extend the western side of the barrier wall, but my father said it was a low-priority goal since slaves fear coming this far, and the wilderness and mountains provide a natural barrier. If you travel farther south, the mountains become too steep and treacherous. Western trails lead to lower elevations, but a traveler will encounter impassable swamps where beasts, snakes, and insects will devour even the heartiest of humans."

"Interesting." Elyssa took in a deep draw of air, studying its flavor as it entered her nostrils and coated her lungs with its wild freshness. The environment felt similar to the place she had left Wallace and the rescued cattle children. Maybe they were close by.

She mentally probed the area for other forms of life. Smells, tastes, and sounds proved that it abounded here—birds in the branches, slugs under fallen logs, small mammals hiding close by, one making a chittering noise that reminded her of the silly call Tibalt made while following a rat through the dungeon maze.

Using her mind, she followed the sound as it drew her deep into the thicket. A presence stalked the forest, far more intelligent than a chittering squirrel. It possessed emotions that reflected those of humans, the clearest one being self-defense, readiness to fight or fly. Yet it appeared to be more frightened than menacing, perhaps wary of a dragon intruder.

"Hello?" Elyssa called as she scanned the ground for her sword. "Don't be scared. We won't hurt you."

Xenith blocked her face with a wing. "Quiet! What do you think you are doing?"

Elyssa pushed the wing out of the way. "Just trust me."

"Trust a human from another world who has spent no more than a few days here?" Xenith wrapped the wing around her, blocking her vision, and dragged her close to the boulder. "You need to consult me before doing something so brash."

"Unhand that girl!" A rustling noise followed the new voice. "Or unwing her, if that's what you dragons understand."

"I will not be commanded by a human," Xenith growled.

"Then be persuaded by this!"

A stinging odor penetrated Xenith's protective wing. Xenith sneezed and staggered back, releasing her captive. Now free, Elyssa squinted at a gray cloud hanging in the air and inhaled the peppery dust, then pinched her nostrils shut to prevent a sneeze.

An old man strode into the clearing, a sword in hand, but his unbalanced gait indicated that he was something less than a warrior. His stringy gray hair and unkempt beard prodded Elyssa's memory. "Tibalt?"

"Yes, of course. How many old coots like me have you met?" He pointed the sword at Xenith and dug into a pouch at his side. "Now if you don't let her go, I will speak the magic words that will turn a dragon into a chicken."

"A chicken?" Xenith snorted the remains of the dust from her nostrils and drew back her head. "Beware, foolish human. You will be a torch before you can part your lips again."

Elyssa eyed Tibalt's fingers. Did he really have something more than sneezing powder in there, or was he bluffing? "Xenith, he's a friend of mine. He's harmless."

"Very well." Xenith drew her wing in. "But I do not trust humans who threaten me."

Elyssa bolted forward and embraced Tibalt. "It's so good to see you again!"

Tibalt patted her on the back. "The feeling is mutual." He drew away, lowering his sword. "So is this dragon on our side?"

Elyssa glanced at Xenith, then lowered her voice to a whisper. "She is loyal to the ideals of her parents, Arxad and Fellina. They are on the side of justice and liberty, but their love for their own species comes before regard for humans."

"Fair enough." Tibalt sheathed his sword. "I feel the same way ... but humans first, of course."

Elyssa took him by the arm and led him closer to the boulder, picking up her sword along the way. "We're waiting for Xenith's mother to join us. Tell me what's going on back home."

As they settled cross-legged on the carpet of grass and leaves, Xenith shuffled to the center of the clearing, her gaze constantly focused on the sky.

"Well," Tibalt began, "Orion would have us believe that he has had a change of heart. He says that he's given up his witch hunting. When you come back, you will abide in peace."

Elyssa rolled her eyes. "The peace of the grave. If you believed him, then you must have contracted dungeon fever."

"Oh, I didn't believe a word of it. You can't fool an old fooler like me."

Elyssa laughed. "Okay, but how did the old fooler find his way here?"

Tibalt touched the side of his nose with a gnarled finger. "I'm a tracker, I am. Better than a palace hound."

"Really? Whose scent did you pick up?"

"Whose scent?" Tibalt pushed his finger into the moist soil and drew a line. "Well …"

"C'mon, Tibalt. You can't fool a Diviner, either."

"Well, the truth is, I didn't have a clue where to start looking for you, so I followed a flying dragon's trail for a while, but I lost sight of him. Then I saw a different dragon fly down into the woods, so I figured that was the best place to start."

Elyssa grasped his arm. "Thank you, Tibalt. I'm glad to have a warrior at my side."

For the next several minutes, the two exchanged stories, Elyssa finishing with their recent rescue attempt at the grinding mill. "So we're waiting for a report, and if Jason and his father are still in trouble, I have to get back to that basin."

Tibalt touched the hilt of his sword. "You mean *we* have to get—"

"She is here." Xenith scooted back toward the boulder. From above, Fellina glided into the clearing, the breeze from her wings tossing damp leaves, plastering one on Elyssa's cheek. A girl in a baggy tunic rode atop Fellina's back, both arms clutching a spine as she trembled.

Elyssa jumped up and reached for the girl. "Slide down. I'll catch you."

The girl looked at Elyssa as she slowly unwrapped her grip. Fellina drew in her wings, clearing the dismount path.

"I could not find Jason." Fellina breathed so heavily, tiny sparks flew from her mouth. "This girl, Solace, said that he has returned to the mill to rescue the others, but I did not see him there."

"The others?" Elyssa asked as she caught Solace and swung her to the ground. "Who is still alive?"

"I do not know. After I eluded Mallerin, I hurried back to find Jason, and although I flew close enough to see that the basin was empty of humans, I could not tell if anyone was in the holding cage. Solace believes Jason's father died in the mill, but I could not verify that."

Solace crouched at Elyssa's feet, nearly buried in the oversized tunic. "Solace is such a lovely name," Elyssa said as she reached down a hand.

"Jason gave it to me." Solace took Elyssa's hand and rose. "He also gave me this shirt."

Elyssa touched the sleeve. Yes, it was Jason's. "Fellina, I know you must be weary, but can you take Tibalt and me back to the mill?"

Fellina extended her neck and set her face in front of Tibalt. Her head swayed slightly as she looked him over. "Not to offend the gentleman's resolve, but he is better suited to stay here with Solace while we return to the mill."

Tibalt gripped the hilt of his sword and thrust out his chest. "I'll have you know, lady dragon, that I, Tibalt Blackstone, was once captain of Mesolantrum's first regiment, a champion swordsman, and the most decorated warrior during the frontier campaign."

"The operative word being *was*," Fellina said. "Your age, while dressing you with boldness, will not help you run from a pursuing dragon."

Tibalt touched his bag. "My age has also made me wily. I have a few tricks you dragons have never seen before."

"Let him come," Elyssa said. "With Xenith's injury, she should stay with Solace."

"What?" Xenith shouted. "I can still fly. I flew all the way here with Elyssa on my—"

"Silence!" Fellina glared at Xenith. "You did well, but now we need you here. If the old man wants to risk his life, that is fine with me, but I will not risk yours any further."

Solace wrung her hands, trembling. "Do I have to stay here alone with a dragon?"

"Don't worry," Elyssa said as she stroked Solace's hair. "She won't hurt you."

"Not intentionally," Xenith muttered.

"Xenith!" Fellina slapped her daughter's flank with a wing. "What is wrong with you? You never spoke to Koren or the other girls this way."

"They were self-sufficient. I am not a nanny for value-less humans."

"We have no time for more impertinence." Fellina spread out her wings. "Stay and protect the girl. Behind the boulder you will find an entrance into an underground hideaway. Just step on the flat stone and the ground will angle downward, allowing entry. When you step off, it will spring back. Below, you will find a rope that will open the door again. The refuge is small and dark, so there is no need to go in unless you detect danger."

Xenith bowed her head. "Yes, Mother."

"Elyssa, you and Tibalt climb on. We should waste no more time."

While Tibalt scaled Fellina's side, Elyssa set a hand on Xenith's neck, whispering. "Sometimes it takes more courage to accept menial tasks than it does to risk our lives in battle."

Xenith opened her mouth to speak again, but after a sharp glare from her mother, she nodded and backed away.

Elyssa climbed up to Fellina's back and settled behind Tibalt, a shoulder-high spine jutting between them. As Fellina rose into the sky, Elyssa watched the ground fall away. Xenith and Solace stood face-to-face, Xenith apparently talking, but the wind swept her words away.

"That was a fine speech, Miss," Tibalt said, looking back at her. "Where did you get all that wisdom?"

"At the school of shame. I learned it the hard way."

Tibalt turned to the front. "Say no more. I understand."

Fellina stayed low, skimming the trees, flying barely high enough to keep her wings from brushing the tops during her down strokes. Elyssa surveyed the land. With the mountains at the rear, the mining mesas ahead and to the right, and the barrier wall coming into sight to the left, they appeared to be flying northward. The village lay nearly due north, and the grinding basin sat to its west between the dragons' grottoes and the river.

Since the basin sat in a treeless area, a stealth approach seemed impossible. If Fellina had a plan, she hadn't mentioned it, so the human passengers had to rely on the dragon's wisdom and experience.

Elyssa fidgeted on her rough seat. This was how it felt to be the ignorant party when someone skipped steps — helpless and dependent, not in control. Literally going along for the ride was foreign and unsettling.

She sighed. Another lesson learned. For now, without a plan simmering in her mind, what could she do? It seemed so wasteful to allow these minutes to pass without doing something to aid their cause.

Inches in front of her, Tibalt clutched a spine and bowed his head. Elyssa bent around to get a look at his face. Was something wrong? Had the flight brought a spell of nausea?

With his eyes tightly closed and a fist clenched, Tibalt moved his lips silently, speaking with passion at a level that only he and his Creator could hear.

Elyssa settled back and slapped herself on her thigh. Of course!

As she closed her eyes and took on Tibalt's pose, a hundred thoughts raced through her mind. The most painful one? Shame. Again that school lashed her with its sharp whip. All this time she had fretted about not being in control and wasting precious minutes, when the option to pray had never crossed her mind.

Slowly letting out a breath, she concentrated, pushing out the stinging thoughts and probing the sky with her mind. As tears welled, she whispered, "Is someone really out there? Are you so intelligent that you can process and understand a thousand simultaneous cries for help? Are you so compassionate that you can dry the tears of countless tortured souls? Are you so patient that you will take time to listen to a bullheaded girl who couldn't remember to talk to the one who is really in control? Why should you listen to someone who obviously believes more in herself and her own abilities than you who bestowed those abilities?"

Her tears flowed freely. "What a fool I am! What a stubborn, self-important fool! I deserve a whip on my back. Let it strike me until I learn my lesson and—"

"Release the whip, Elyssa."

She looked up. "What?"

"Release the whip."

Elyssa scanned the sky, squinting in the midday sunlight. The voice was audible, not something in her mind. Had the Creator decided to respond in a new way? She had never heard such a clear voice before, and this one was feminine. If the Creator was really female, that would be a shock to the clergy back home.

As if ending an eclipse, a bright sphere slid away from the front of Solarus and drifted toward her. With the sky as its backdrop, its size seemed impossible to gauge, but when it drew closer, a human female appeared at the lower part of the center, providing more perspective. Five times as tall as the girl, the floating, transparent ball settled into a glide at Fellina's left, just behind her wing.

"Exodus has risen!" Fellina called, her strokes seeming to take on new energy. "If the Starlighter is willing to help, our chances of success are much better."

"Who-eee!" Tibalt shouted. "We got us an angel! The Creator answered my prayers!"

Elyssa squinted at the girl hovering within the sphere. Colorful light flashed across her face, distorting her features, but her flowing blue cloak, flaming red hair, and vibrant green eyes shone through. "Koren?"

She nodded. "I will be with the three of you. I have seen the tales, so I know what has happened and what we must do. When we draw close to the grinding mill, I will give further instructions. Fellina, do not look my way, and close your ears to my words for now. If you watch or listen, you will likely be unable to fly."

A hundred other questions begged to be asked, but Elyssa swallowed back all but one. "What did you mean when you told me to release the whip?"

A girl, perhaps six years old, materialized in front of Elyssa, taking Tibalt's place. With her torso bare and her hands clinging to the spine, she twisted and looked into Elyssa's eyes. Three angry welts, red and oozing blood, marred her back. Tear tracks smudged her cheeks. Her face seemed familiar, like herself when she was that age. Then, just as quickly as the girl had appeared, she vanished.

Koren drifted forward over Fellina's passengers and then down until the edge of the sphere drew nearly within reach as it hovered in front of Tibalt. "You have seen the backs of the cattle children," Koren said, "and the stripes that prove the cruelty of their taskmasters. When you fell in the Zodiac's lower level, you gathered stripes of your own, allowing you to empathize with the plight of the children.

"Yet you are proving to be a cruel taskmaster yourself. You lacerate your soul with stripe after stripe, punishing yourself for crimes that are nothing more than inability to perform beyond your limitations. You whip yourself for lacking experience, for forgetting to pray, for not fully understanding the plight of the cattle children, and yet the Creator finds no fault in a single one of these mistakes.

"He fashioned you with a lack of knowledge and experience, and he delights in guiding you along this journey called life where you collect jewels of wisdom. Why do you punish yourself with every jewel you gather? Why are you ashamed when you learn, when the light of truth shines on your ignorance? It is not a sin to be ignorant unless you knowingly choose it, but now that you are enlightened, feeling shame in the midst of a shower of gems will darken your soul."

Heat from Exodus's radiance pulled sweat from Elyssa's pores. The whip of shame rose like a curling serpent, ready to slice her back once again—shame for feeling shame, a trap, an endless cycle. She clenched her eyes shut. No! She was human! She was no more guilty for being finite than those poor cattle children were for being slaves.

Koren continued, her tone hardening. "The guilty are those who see the light and shun it, cover it, imprison it. Because the light exposes their evil deeds, they lash out at those who carry the lanterns of enlightenment. The guilty snuff the lives of the lantern bearers along with the flames. Truth is a stench in their nostrils, and light-bringers sting their souls. They cannot bear the thought that someone basks in joy while they feel only pain. The only way they know to ease the pain is to extinguish the light."

"I recognize that from somewhere," Elyssa said. "Is it in the Code?"

Koren smiled. "More or less. I altered the words some- what to fit the situation."

Tibalt wavered from side to side. "Something's making me woozy."

Elyssa reached out and steadied him. "Don't listen! Close your eyes!"

"Will do." Tibalt hunkered low with his hands over his ears. "Go ahead. I can't hear. But that Exodus thing is as hot as a ball of lightning."

Elyssa released Tibalt and settled back, no longer gripping Fellina's spine. "What about me? Why am I not affected?"

"I don't know," Koren said, pursing her lips. "You seem to be quite gifted yourself, so maybe you're immune. Since I am now Starlight's primary source of history, per- haps I can find a tale that will provide more information, but until then I'm glad we can talk without any hypnotic effects."

"Sounds good," Elyssa said. "Since you're the his- tory expert, can you show me what's been happening to Jason?"

Koren spread out her cloak. "And I will also tell you a story about a certain dragon who guards those con- demned to the mill. She is a foul creature, yet she must be protected at all costs."

eight

Jason lay on his stomach at the rim of the basin. Covered by the branch he had cut, maybe no one would notice him. Two dragons had flown overhead during the hours he had watched and waited, but neither stopped to investigate. One might have been Fellina, but it seemed too risky to get up and check. A mistake could be costly.

The spot he had chosen appeared to be a good one. Directly below this point, the wall of the basin sloped toward the floor less severely than it did anywhere else. An agile human could scramble down, but climbing back up would be far more difficult, and both directions would be impossible considering who patrolled the floor.

Below, Julaz circled the grinding monolith for the hundredth time, pausing once to reignite the mounted torch with her breath. Her shuffling feet and tail had swept away every trace of footprints on the sandy bottom, and with no sign of human movements, there wasn't a way to find out who might still be alive. Yet Julaz continued her steady march. If the prisoners had all escaped or died, why would she be standing guard?

Jason looked at the holding cage in the wall's recess. Still no signs of prisoners—no hands clutching the matrix of wooden slats, no moans of pain.

Slowing her pace, Julaz yawned. Then, like a cat, she turned in a circle twice before settling to the ground.

Jason wriggled closer. *Yes! Go to sleep, you lazy beast. All I need is a few minutes.*

Sweat trickled from his forehead to his cheek. Jason brushed his arm across his face, but it didn't help much. His sleeveless undershirt lacked enough material to absorb sweat or protect him from the dirt or prickly heather. Scratches and smudges covered his bare arms from wrists to shoulders, uncomfortable but unavoidable annoyances.

After a few minutes, Julaz's body swelled and deflated in a steady rhythm. Jason glanced at the sky. Still no other dragons. Apparently these sisters weren't as vigilant as Fellina had said, at least when they were separated. Maybe they policed each other.

He pushed the branch aside, rose with it in his grip, and tightened his sword belt. Holding his breath, he stepped over the edge and set his foot on the slope. He then leaped into a run, holding the branch out to the side with one hand and his scabbard against his hip with the other. With each step, he sprang to the next, careful not to let his boots slide. When he reached bottom, he continued his run with several soft footfalls until his momentum eased.

He spun toward Julaz, twenty paces to his right. She slept at the base of the monolith, apparently undisturbed.

The cage lay thirty paces to his left. Would it be better to check for prisoners first or to slay the dragon in case she awakened? Hacking open the slats would be noisy. She wouldn't sleep through such a commotion.

Tiptoeing, Jason hurried to Julaz. Her body lay curled like a kidney bean, and her long neck snaked over her wing and flank. With her underbelly hidden, it would be impossible to deliver a fatal blow, and her thick armor meant that chopping her eyes or neck couldn't guarantee anything beyond sending her into a foul mood. So how could he open the prison without waking her?

At the corner of his eye, the torch's flame flickered. He glanced between it and the branch. Burning the door would probably be quieter than chopping it. It might be worth a try.

He pulled the torch from its bracket and skulked toward the cage, frequently checking the sky for Mallerin. When he arrived, he grasped one of the slats and peered inside. "Anyone in there?" he whispered.

"I am," a quiet voice responded. A shadow appeared, and the boy with the withered arm approached, a teenager with sinewy biceps but no meat on his ribs. "Who are you?"

"Jason. What's your name?"

"Basil. Are you —"

"I'm a friend, and I'm going to get you out of here."

Basil pointed at the sword on Jason's hip. "With that?"

"With this," Jason said, lifting the torch. "How many others are in there?"

"Just another boy my age and a man. The man's asleep, but I can wake him up."

Jason gripped the slat more tightly, digging the edge into his skin. The man who wrestled his father to the ground had likely turned the handle that crushed his bones. Taking a deep breath, Jason calmed his anger. The man had been forced to do it. It was still wrong, but cruel whips can drive men to commit evil acts. Survival, even in the midst of torture, is sometimes a sadistic motivator.

"Okay," Jason said. "Make sure they're both ready to leave quietly, then come back here. You're going to help me burn this gate."

Basil disappeared into the shadows for a moment before returning, breathless. "What do I do?"

After dropping the branch at the base of the gate, Jason held the torch in front of the cage. "Grab this. When I wave at you, light the branch."

Basil grasped the torch. "How will we get out of this pit?"

"I'm still working on that." Jason ran on the balls of his feet to the grinding stone, grabbed the ladder leading to the top, and carried it to the slope. He leaned the ladder against the loose soil and wedged it in place. The highest rung dug into the face of the wall about eight feet short of the top. A healthy adult could leap from that rung, grab the rim, and muscle up to solid ground, but the boys would need help.

A scuffling noise made Jason twist toward Julaz, his whole body tensing. She lifted her head and scratched behind her ear with a back claw, but her eyes stayed closed. Then, after lowering her head again, she resumed her rhythmic respiration.

Jason drew his sword. They had to hurry. Maybe he could stay low and battle the dragon if necessary, while the man climbed and pulled the boys to safety. Then he could help from below if anyone had trouble reaching the rim.

Taking another deep breath, Jason waved his sword. Basil set the torch against the branch and held it there. A column of gray smoke shot upward. Leaves crackled. The flames took hold and began to eat away at the lowest slats.

Jason scanned the sky. Still no patrolling dragon in sight, but if the fire got any noisier, this escape attempt would be snuffed out in a hurry.

A snort sounded, then a growl. Jason whipped around just as Julaz launched a ball of flames toward him. He ducked, rolled, and vaulted back to his feet. A sharp sting burned his left forearm, and smoke curled up from a black mark near his elbow.

Grimacing, Jason backpedaled toward the prison. Julaz beat her wings and gave chase. A loud clatter sounded behind him, but he couldn't look. He had to keep his eyes on the fire-breathing maw and hope for an opening to attack her underbelly.

Something on the ground caught his heel. He stumbled backwards and landed on his bottom. Julaz lunged, her mouth wide and her pointed teeth bared. Light surged from behind Jason, and flames leaped in front of him. A man thrust the burning branch into Julaz's mouth and shoved it deep into her throat.

Jason stared. *Father!* How could it be?

As Julaz reared up, backing away and screaming, Jason leaped to his feet and charged. He lunged past his father and drove the sword into Julaz's vulnerable spot, though not very deeply. He twisted the blade and yanked it back out. She screamed again and batted him with a wing, sending him flying. He landed on his side and slid, his sword between his body and the sandy ground. The blade sliced into his ribs, and the hilt jerked away from his hand. When he finally stopped, pain throttled his body. His vision blurring, he rose to all fours and crawled toward Julaz, groping for the sword.

Ahead, Edison attacked Julaz with a flaming slat. She crunched down on the branch and spat it out, then swung a wing, missing his head by mere inches. The boys threw burning shards at her, but they just bounced off her scales.

Jason struggled to his feet. Leading with his sword, he staggered toward the battle. He ducked under another salvo of flames and rammed the sword into the she-dragon again, deeper this time.

While Julaz toppled backwards, hot liquid gushed over Jason's feet, acidic and scalding. He leaped away, jumping from foot to foot to cool his stinging ankles. Julaz thudded to the ground in a choking cloud of dust, her belly skyward, her wound oozing steaming liquid.

Jason's father jerked his sword away and limped to Julaz's side, where her neck sprawled across the ground. He hacked near the base of her skull again and again. With each strike, Julaz's body shuddered. Finally, her head fell away. Her body continued to writhe, her tail curling in the sand and her wings jerking.

The two boys drew close to Jason, one on each side. Their mouths agape, they stared at the slain dragon.

With his back still toward Jason, Edison let his shoulders sag. Then, heaving a sigh, he turned and limped back, his feet landing heavily and the sword's tip dragging. Even in Jason's blurry vision, his father's barrel frame and wispy gray hair drew a beautiful portrait—the heroic warrior, Edison Masters.

Ignoring the pain, he dashed ahead and embraced him. "You're alive! I thought they put you through that grinder."

His father wrapped strong arms around Jason and pressed his cheek against his hair. "Julaz was angry with the other fellow for allowing me to get to the ladder. She grabbed him and threw him into the mill and ground him up herself."

He drew back and pushed the sword's hilt into Jason's hand, his face becoming grim. "Fortunately for us, his body got lodged too tightly in the grinder, so she was going to work on dislodging it when Mallerin returned."

"Speaking of Mallerin." Jason looked up. Apart from a few dark clouds hanging near the southern horizon, the sky remained clear. "We'd better get out of here before she shows up."

Edison touched Jason's side. "You're bleeding pretty badly. It's soaked through."

With the touch, pain roared back to Jason's ribs. Trying to hide a grimace, he lifted his shirt, peeling away the bloody material. A vertical gash in his side crossed every rib.

Basil whispered, "Ouch." The other boy nodded.

Edison shook his head. "If that hurts as bad as it looks—"

"It does, but we can't worry about that now. We have to get out of here. There's a forest nearby where we can find shelter. I left the girl there." With his lower legs still burning, Jason walked gingerly toward the ladder. Elyssa's pendant swayed with his unsteady gait, brushing against his chest. As he neared the ladder, an image of her battling from atop Xenith came to mind, her expression warrior-intense as she swung her sword. Had she escaped with Fellina? If so, where was she now? She wouldn't stand for hiding somewhere, waiting for him to show up. If she was able, she would be back.

He grasped a head-high rung and waited for the others to catch up. "Father, can you go first and help these two? I can push from down here." As sweat trickled into his wound, he winced. "And I might need help myself."

"Not a problem." While Jason steadied the ladder, Edison climbed up and stood on the top rung. He leaped and grabbed the rim with both hands, then swung his legs to the top. Now on knees and one hand, he reached the other hand down. "Basil, you first."

As Basil climbed, his crippled arm pressed against his stomach, the one-legged boy watched Basil's progress pensively, his ragtop head motionless and his sweaty torso smeared with dirt and soot.

"What's your name?" Jason asked.

He kept his stare in place. "Oliver."

"Pleased to meet you, Oliver. I'm—"

"Jason Masters. I know. Your father told us stories about you." Oliver turned and looked Jason in the eye.

"Thank you for saving us. You're as strong and brave as he said you are."

The heat in Jason's legs roared up his body and into his cheeks. "You're pretty brave, yourself. When you started throwing those—"

"Uh-oh." Oliver pointed at the sky. "Mallerin."

Jason spun. The huge she-dragon had just crested the ridge between them and the village and now swooped toward them, only seconds away. "Father!" he hissed. "Any ideas?"

"Just one. Give me your sword."

Jason gave the sword an underhanded toss. His father snatched it out of the air and rose to his full height. Waving his arms wildly, he shouted. "Mallerin! I chopped your sister's head off! Come and get me!" He ran along the perimeter of the basin toward a head-shaped boulder about one-hundred paces away, his limp hardly noticeable.

As Mallerin swung toward the boulder, Jason scrambled up the ladder. "Basil, wait at the top. Oliver, can you follow me?"

Oliver threw his walking stick to the side. "Just watch."

"Great!" Jason scrambled up the rungs. When he reached Basil, he pushed his head between the boy's legs and climbed to the top rung with him now safely on his shoulders. Basil grabbed the rim with his good arm and braced the elbow of his crippled arm. With help from Jason, he hoisted himself up, then turned and reached down. "Come on, Oliver. You can do it."

Jason turned and laid his back against the wall. "I'll help you climb over me."

Oliver grabbed Jason's belt and shoulder, using them as ladder rungs. His foot dug into Jason's waist, stretching his skin and widening the open wound.

Jason bit down hard on his lip. *Just hang on. He'll be up in a second.* With a quick glance, he found his father, slashing at the air from behind the boulder while Mallerin flew around, diving and shooting fire, then backing off and attacking again.

Once Basil pulled Oliver up, Jason leaped, grabbed the boys' outstretched hands, and rode their pull until he reached the top. He pointed at the trees where he had left Solace. "Basil, help Oliver run to the woods. I'll be there as soon as I can."

The boys took off. Jason dashed around the rim, clutching his side. Mallerin stood on top of the boulder. Her foreclaw wrenching his father's arm, she lifted him effortlessly and held him in front of her snout as if ready to roast him with a fiery snuff. Edison thrashed and squirmed but to no avail.

"Mallerin!" Jason shouted. "Let him go. *I* killed your sister!"

She turned and spat a wad of fire in his path, igniting a small blaze in the heather. "Come no closer, human!"

Jason leaped over the fire. No use negotiating with this monster. A quick strike was his only option. He spied his sword next to Mallerin's tail and lunged for it. A volley of flames flew toward him. He dove into a somersault, grabbed the hilt as he rolled to his feet, and leaped up to the dragon's tail. He ran along her backbone, sideswiping her protruding spines, and scrambled as far up her neck as he could. Grasping her with one arm, he hacked at her neck with all his might.

Mallerin jumped down from the boulder, threw Edison to the ground, and pinned him with a back claw. She then slung her neck back and forth, slamming Jason against the boulder. His wounded side struck first. A rib cracked. Blood flowed. His sword slipped out of his hand, and his vision darkened.

As she reared back to slam him again, a loud shout echoed all around.

"Mallerin! Stop!"

Jason struck the boulder again. Pain from the broken rib roared through his body. His grip around her neck loosened, and he fell, smacking the boulder once more. He slid to the ground and curled on his side, facing the dragon and the basin. His sword lay between him and the dragon's claw, not quite within reach.

Mallerin lifted her head. "Who speaks to me?"

Blinking away the fog, Jason found the source. A floating sphere, dazzling white, drifted down from the sky. It stopped and hovered over the basin, its closest point within ten feet of the rim. It radiated heat, soothing warmth that eased his horrible pain. It looked exactly like the star from the Northlands, but how could that be? Exodus was trapped, hopeless, begging to die.

Beyond the sphere, a dragon that looked like Fellina flew toward the forest, while yet another dragon headed in the same direction from a different angle. Maybe Fellina was hurrying to pick up the boys, trying to rescue them before a patrol dragon picked them up. Jason squinted. Fellina had no rider. Where could Elyssa be?

The voice returned, this time softer and more feminine. "Although you have hidden your identity for so long,
Mallerin, the Creator knows who you are, and Starlight
has told me your secret."

Mallerin wagged her head. "Away with you, sorceress.
You know nothing about me. If you continue this bedevil-
ment, I will crush this man into dust."

Jason pushed against the ground. He had to get up and
fight, forget the pain and save his father. He crawled on
hands and knees, grabbing his sword along the way. Only
ten paces separated him from the dragon's pinning claw.
Pain spiking in his ribcage, he gritted his teeth to hold
back a gasp.

"Look at me, Mallerin," the voice said. "Pay heed to my
call. I will tell you a tale of days gone by, days when you
were more than an executioner."

Clawing the ground as he crawled, Jason blinked at
the sphere. As in Exodus, a secondary light shone from
within, human shaped this time, but the dazzling radiance
and his blurred vision kept the image fuzzy and vague.
The human looked like a girl wearing a cloak, but it was
all so hazy. Dizziness swirled in his head, worsening with
every foot of ground he crossed.

"You were a queen, a member of nobility, the leading female among the Separators. Oh, how far you have
fallen! Now you are an executioner, grinding the flesh and
bones of what you consider human waste, a job so dis-
tasteful to other dragons, even the drones refuse to carry
it out."

Jason's arms trembled. He pushed his hands and
knees forward. His father, facedown under Mallerin's

crushing claw, lay only five feet away, but the swirling sensation made the entire world spin. Mallerin wobbled forward and back, but was she really swaying, or was her imbalance just part of his dizzied view?

"While a queen," the voice continued, "you referred to humans as chattel, as vile vermin, and you did so in a manner so degrading, you degraded yourself, proving yourself to be a pompous pig. You were so self-important, so condescending, everyone despised you. Although you provided the prophetic black egg, even your mate spurned you by banishing you from his royal court."

Jason drew within reach of Mallerin's claw. It lifted and then pressed down again, rocking as she wobbled. Bracing against the ground with his left arm, he raised the sword and aimed at her belly. He had to strike while she leaned back. Otherwise, she might press all her weight on his father. His arm trembled. His target wavered. Did he have enough strength to leap up and thrust the blade? A miss or a shallow plunge would mean death for him and his father.

A shadow appeared near the basin's rim, a black egg, semitransparent and as tall as a human child. Jason paused, again blinking. Where had it come from?

The sphere's voice grew louder, more passionate. "You are a mother, usurped by a fallen Starlighter, a human who now cares for your youngling, thinking she is more fit than you."

A ghostly apparition, slender and feminine, approached the egg and petted the shell. As she solidified, her identity became clear—Zena. The egg cracked, and a black dragon crawled into her arms. Stroking its head, Zena walked away, and the images disappeared.

"The Creator is displeased with your wickedness. Your cruelty is despicable in his sight. Yet he also knows that you have a seed of regret. Your current estate has brought you low, and you know not how to climb out of this pit. The Creator offers you an opportunity to make amends."

Mallerin rocked back and paused in that position, easing the pressure on her foreclaw. "What must I do?"

Jason flexed his muscles. It was now or never. He lunged toward Mallerin with his sword, but like a flash of lightning, another blade met his and blocked his thrust. The other sword-bearer wrapped both arms around him, and they toppled against Mallerin's underside. Their combined momentum sent her staggering backwards. She flopped to her side, her neck reeling out like a wild whip. It slapped Jason and his opponent to the ground, pinning them, and Mallerin's head thumped nearby.

The weight pressed down on Jason's cracked rib. Pain shot through every limb, every joint, every nerve. His ears rang. Darkness cascaded across his vision. Only a pair of green eyes pierced the veil, sparkling and lovely.

"Jason, are you all right?"

Jason blinked. Elyssa? Was she the other sword-bearer? He forced out a pain-streaked whisper. "No. I'm—"

A new voice interrupted. "Neither is your pappy. Both of you look like you were at the wrong end of a battering ram."

"Tibber?" Jason murmured.

"Yep. And I ain't a fibber about this. We have to get both of you to a hospital, if there is such a place around here."

"The Northlands." Jason licked his cracked lips. "Get the stardrop. Use the healing trees."

"Healing trees?" Tibalt said. "Son, I think someone twisted your necklace a hair too tight."

"Trouble him not, Tibalt. He is sane." The sphere's radiance drew closer. The girl within pushed back her cloak's hood, revealing red hair and a kind smile. "I know what he means. The stardrop is deadly when a person consumes it, but it heals when administered in the proper way."

"Koren?" Jason tried to focus on her, but her face stayed blurry. "The wolves. Taushin. What happened?"

"Fear not, brave warrior. All is well. No harm has come to me. I dwell within Exodus, and I will tell you my tale soon, but for now you must rest and allow others to bear your burdens."

Jason touched the pouch on his belt. This stardrop was for her. Maybe someone could scoop two more out of Exodus and put them with this one. "Koren." Every word seemed to drill a hole in his ribs. "Stardrop inside. For you. Must take."

"Peace, Jason. Just listen and rest." Koren lifted her arms and sang, and with each word, light poured out from the sphere at a point directly in front of her face. As thin as a rope, the radiance streamed toward him and enveloped him in a glowing embrace.

Rest, my brother, rest your mind.

Rest from battles, rest and find

That pain from wounds will fade away
As thoughts surrender, dreams hold sway.

Warmth caressed Jason's skin—soothing warmth that
dried his sweat. As he closed his eyes, the Exodus star,
Elyssa's worried face, and every other sensation fled away.

nine

With the rays of late afternoon filtering through the surrounding forest, Randall stood at the dungeon's back exit and gripped the gate's wooden bars. The two dragons locked within had stayed put. Even before spending all night and all day soaking up extane gas, they could have broken out at any time, but they had kept their word. So far.

Patting his pocket, he felt the outline of the crystalline peg Arxad provided as part of the deal to allow the dragons' escape from the portal chamber. At the time, it seemed like a bargain, but after learning that it provided only a one-way passage from Starlight to Major Four, it didn't seem quite as valuable. Still, if they ever returned to Starlight, keeping it handy would be a good idea.

He unlocked the gate and swung it open. Time to set the stage for his performance. Everything had to be in place, or else his audience wouldn't take the bait.

Inside the dungeon, a draft caught the edge of a sheet of parchment, weighed down by a stone, several steps from the gate. He entered and picked it up, reading it as he returned to the outside.

Randall,

I am working on gathering the troops we need for war on Starlight. Because of recent events that would exhaust my dwindling ink if I were to tell them, I was able to assemble a contingent of believers, but I will need more proof, or at least more leverage, if I hope to gather enough soldiers to do battle against the dragons. I will contact you in person soon so we can combine our efforts. Until then, I wish you well.

— M

Randall blinked at the partial signature. *M*? Who could M be? The only M around was Magnar, but he wouldn't have written this. The author had to be a soldier, someone who could assemble troops. And since the note had been placed well within the dungeon, that someone had access to the key.

Randall stuffed the note into his pocket. The existence of a mysterious ally wasn't exactly a comforting revelation. How many others now knew the secrets he had tried to keep? At least this ally would come to light soon. For now, he had to get back to his own plan.

Looking down at his clothes, he checked for any tell-tale sign of his hidden photo gun. Strapped to his thigh with a thin band, it seemed invisible beneath his baggy trousers.

He patted his belt where his scabbard should have been. Promising Orion he would leave his sword behind might have been a mistake, but it was the only way to get the coward to show up alone. Even then, the new governor likely wouldn't keep his promise. His archers would be somewhere nearby, bows strung and arrows ready.

Taking in a deep breath and holding it, Randall listened. Quiet footsteps sounded, someone of less-than-heavy build crunching evergreen needles nearby. Randall stepped away from the gate and looked at a path that led over a grassy hill and toward the palace. Orion approached. Although concealed by a long, hooded cloak, his tall, lanky body and constant glancing from side to side gave him away.

Randall sneered. Those who have earned no trust rarely trust anyone else. In spite of the archers' steady aim, Orion obviously feared an ambush. When he arrived at the dungeon gate, he pushed back his hood, revealing his hawkish eyes and nose. "What is your message?" he whispered.

"First," Randall said, gesturing with his eyes toward the forest, "send your archers away. You alone are experienced enough to understand the ramifications of"—he leaned closer—"a draconic presence in our world."

Their stares met. Randall firmed his jaw, matching Orion's stony expression. Playing this game meant striking a confident pose, assuming a stance of superior knowledge and position. He cocked his head and put on a half smirk. "Having dragon alliances puts one in control of any situation, don't you think?"

Orion's facial muscles relaxed. He nodded and walked a few paces down the path. "Archers!" he called. "Leave us! I am safe!"

Rustling noises erupted from the forest along with the tromping of feet. When all was quiet, Orion walked toward the dungeon, pushing a hand into a cloak pocket and withdrawing a photo gun. Stopping just out of reach, he aimed it at Randall. "While it is true that dragon allies are of great value on the battlefield, they are not so helpful when absent."

Randall forced himself not to blink. "What makes you think they're absent?"

"Shall I fire into the dungeon? That should blow up the only potential hiding place and likely disable any dragon allies who might be there."

Stepping aside, Randall spread an arm toward the open gate. "Feel free to shoot, but you and I both know how long it takes your gun to re-energize. I will be able to disarm you during that time." He faced Orion and spread out both arms. "Or you could just shoot me. The dragons will kill you before you fire another shot. You will never learn the secrets I hold, secrets that could give you control over not only Mesolantrum but also all of Major Four." He half closed one eye. "Think of it. Viktor Orion would have the power to extend his goodwill throughout the world, granting favor to those who deserve it, the faithful followers who believe in his sacred crusades. Not only that, the great governor could extend that beneficent hand through space, take the Lost Ones into his protective arms, and bring them home to the shouts and adulation of every man, woman, and child on both worlds."

Randall lifted his brow, signaling his desire for a response. He had practiced that speech for two hours, and it seemed perfect, but would Orion take the bait?

Orion lowered the gun, his expression willing, yet skeptical. "What do you want me to do?"

Randall clenched a fist. "Assemble our military forces. Every able man, whether active or retired, must be called to duty, including those in neighboring regions. There is a portal that will take us to a land in Dracon's northern climes, and we will be able to attack the dragon realm by surprise, rescue our people, and make sure no foul beast ever crosses to our world again."

"Why would dragons betray their own kind?"

Randall took a step forward. "A usurper has taken control there, and the deposed king wishes to restore his rule. If we help him, after we succeed, the high priest of that land will close every portal forever, and both worlds will live in peace."

Eyeing Randall carefully, Orion matched his forward step. Now within an arm's reach, Orion laid the gun in his palm and extended it toward Randall, but as he did, he whispered, "Take my weapon, Randall, so your dragon friends will believe that I am going along with your plan."

Randall glanced from Orion's eyes to the photo gun and back. Moving slowly, he slid his fingers under the gun and lifted it from Orion's palm. "Why are you doing this?"

"I am an expert in reading a man's heart, and I am certain of your good intentions. But hear me. You cannot trust these dragons. You lack the experience to consider all the possibilities. Have you thought of the ramifications of sending our entire military to Dracon? Not only will we be vulnerable for attack and takeover by the dragons, we could be marching into a trap that will kill every soldier we have."

Randall ached to look back at the dungeon, but he kept his stare fixed on Orion. He had a good point. Although Arxad seemed honest and reliable, Magnar was far from either. Maybe the bigger, stronger dragon had intentions beyond Arxad's knowledge. "Your reasoning is valid," he replied, his voice even quieter than Orion's. "What do you suggest?"

"Allow me to speak to your dragon friends so that I may propose sending a squadron to investigate. They will report their findings, and if they corroborate the dragons' claims, then we will send whatever forces are necessary."

"A test makes sense," Randall said, "but the dragons are nervous, too. They're taking the risk that you might conquer their world and not give it back to the deposed king. How can I convince them that you're trustworthy?"

"I brought a token of my goodwill, and I offer it without any conditions attached." Orion raised a hand and snapped his fingers.

A new rustling sounded from the forest. Randall took a step back, reaching for the sword that wasn't at his hip.

Orion half smiled. "Easy, boy. I sent my archers away, but I said nothing to my personal bodyguard. Do not fear."

Seconds later, a broad-shouldered man lumbered toward them, cradling a woman in his arms. Dressed in white silk, she appeared to be sleeping peacefully, but shadows hid her face.

"Lay her here," Orion said, "then go to your quarters. I will see myself home."

The man laid her gently on the path, then, clutching a sword hilt at his hip, bowed to Orion and marched away.

Orion swept an arm toward the woman. "I found your mother, and I now restore her to you."

"Mother!" Randall rushed to her, knelt at her side, and set a hand on her cheek. "Mother, wake up. It's me, Randall."

Orion curled a hand and looked at his fingernails. "We gave her a mild sedative to help her rest. She will awaken soon."

Randall shot him a hot glare. "If I find out you had anything to do with her imprisonment, I'll …" He let the threat die on his lips. He had to control his temper. His mother was safe, at least for now. Inhaling slowly, he rose. "How did you know you needed my mother as a bargaining tool?"

"Bargaining tool?" Orion chuckled. "My dear Randall, I have given her to you freely. My bodyguard merely held her in the forest until I was sure it was safe to bring her out. Lady Moulraine has been my friend since childhood, and I would never want to see any harm come to her. If you are looking for an enemy, I suggest you turn your attention to Drexel. When you told me about the note you found in his quarters, I conducted an investigation. My bodyguard found your mother bound and gagged in Bristol's quarters, and you know who held Bristol's leash. She was hungry and thirsty, but unharmed. I hope this gesture convinces you of my goodwill, at least enough to convey confidence to the dragons."

"I see your point." Randall slid his hands under his mother's body and lifted her as he rose. "I will talk to the dragons."

⊰⊱

Sitting near a fire in Taushin's quarters, Zena stirred the embers with a poker, giving the flames new life as they roasted a lamb on a rotating skewer. Taushin lay next to her with his head propped on her lap and his neck draped over her legs. His body stretched out to her side, shimmering black scales a stunning contrast against her silky white dress and the floor's ivory tiles.

She stroked his scales with Cassabrie's finger. It was such a delight to be able to see the details of the king's room — marble floors, velvet tapestries, and ornate carvings in the hardwood walls depicting exotic, long-tailed birds, sleek cats, and huge beasts with woolly coats and long tusks. Surely Taushin deserved this opulence far more than did Magnar.

With her lack of clear vision, it had taken hours to remove Magnar's personal belongings. She usually dared to use the finger only on rare occasions, believing the Starlighter's body to be a slow-acting poison to her own flesh, but Taushin had assured her that more frequent touches wouldn't bring great harm.

Now that she was able to see, one item caught her attention, a photograph of Magnar and Arxad hanging on the opposite wall, taken centuries ago when they were young and humans had such image-capturing equipment.

Sitting side by side, they each wore metal collars and chains. Magnar must have kept that photograph to remind him of the cruelty of his former slave masters.

Zena narrowed her eyes. It would be gone before the day was over. She would see to that.

Breathing a satisfied sigh, she crooned, "Your dinner will be ready in a few moments, my king. After you eat, I will make sure your rest is undisturbed. I assume such a dangerous flight has left you exhausted."

Taushin stretched out a wing and yawned. "I am tired, but there was little danger. The scent on Koren's boots worked perfectly." He laughed. "Even a blind dragon could follow it."

"But you are not blind now. I can see quite well, so your vision through me should be clear."

He turned his head, allowing Zena to rub the scales behind his ears. "Not as clear as when I look through Koren's eyes. Although you are a contemptibly inferior vessel, you will suit my purposes for now."

"For now?" Zena stilled her hands and forced down a lump in her throat. "What do you intend to do with me?"

Taushin's blue eyebeams drifted up her arm until they finally settled on her eyes and drilled into her mind. "Fear not," he said. "You will always be my servant. I cannot afford to sacrifice loyal slaves for no good reason. When I get Koren back as my surrogate eyes, you will serve us meals and clean our abodes. Koren and I will be too busy with other matters to attend to menial tasks."

"You mock me!" Zena jerked her head to the side, blocking his beams. "Why do you test my loyalty with insulting words? Why do you provoke jealousy between Koren and me?"

"It is quite simple, my companion in blindness. I want Koren to be your enemy. I want you to be ready to kill her at any moment if I deem it necessary."

"Why? She is pliable. She changes her mind constantly. She is not the insolent wench that Cassabrie was."

Taushin's beams found her eyes again. It seemed that his thoughts entered her mind at the same time he spoke, like a dull knife gouging her senses. "No, Koren is not Cassabrie, but she is still a Starlighter, and she is danger-ous. It is your right to hate her, for although she is no better than you and although she became my servant as you did, Alaph approved of her. This same Alaph rejected you, a servant of dragons, and allowed Cassabrie to strike you blind. The injustice is clear."

The horrid memory returned to Zena's mind— Cassabrie's vengeful, mocking verse as she cooked while attached to the Reflections Crystal. *This view of light will be her last; her eyes will darken, sight is past. Unless she holds my hand in faith, she staggers blind, a hopeless wraith.* Then Cassabrie transferred energy from the crystal and sent a blast from her eyes into Zena's, scald-ing them and crippling her vision. And for years Arxad and Magnar preserved that black-hearted demon's body behind her back, plotting against Taushin even as they protected him.

As she resumed her scratching, he leaned into her hands. "Have you decided what to do about Cassabrie's body?"

"That is another reason we need Koren," Taushin said. "Only she can go near Cassabrie's radiance without harm or hypnosis. I had hoped that since I was able to endure the presence of a stardrop in Koren's hand that I might be able to approach Cassabrie, but I tried only moments ago, and I could not draw close at all without being repulsed by her energy."

"It's not your fault, my king. I went in there again earlier today and tried to move her body, but the stardrops hold her there with great power. My eyesight while in her presence, however, was sharp, and I counted four stardrops in the floor and seven in the ceiling. It's no wonder that you are unable to approach. Even though I was there only a few moments, I nearly succumbed. I cannot imagine how difficult it would be for a dragon."

Taushin let out a long *hmmm* before replying. "It must be more than a mere stardrop mechanism that prevents us from coming near or taking her body. The tales Koren animates do not affect me because of my blindness, and I am able to influence her greatly when we are together, so there must be something about Cassabrie herself that makes a difference."

"Arxad likely anchored Cassabrie there in a way we haven't yet discovered. If she were to leave the chamber and the presence of the stardrops, maybe you would be able to influence her in the same way you influence Koren."

Taushin's ears perked up. "I think I understand. If we were to allow Cassabrie's spirit to take her own body, she would be more vulnerable. That is an excellent idea."

Trying to keep her hands from trembling, Zena smiled. "But there is great danger. What if Cassabrie indwells her body and you cannot control her?"

Taushin's tongue darted out and in. "It is risky, but it might be worth it. She is a cunning girl, so we will have to make a show of resistance. If she is able to take her body without opposition, she will be suspicious."

"Maybe we simply shouldn't tell the guard," Zena said. "Shrillet will be more than happy to provide opposition, and may the more powerful of the two survive. If Cassabrie recovers her body, all is well. If Shrillet kills Cassabrie, then perhaps the Starlighter is not as powerful and cunning as you believe."

Taushin nodded, though the gesture seemed half-hearted. "Your suggestion has merit. Yet I will hold out hope that Cassabrie is victorious. With her under my control, we will have no need of Koren. Cassabrie is the more powerful of the two, at least while Koren is still learning her gifts."

"But if Cassabrie doesn't turn, then—"

"Then we will kill her immediately. You have done it before; you can do it again. It should bring you great pleasure to get revenge on your old enemy." A grin spread across Taushin's face. "Again."

"Yes. Great pleasure. I could even get pleasure out of killing Koren if she proves to be a rebel. Yet as long as she is within Exodus, she will have great power, perhaps more than we can imagine. We cannot kill her. She is out of our reach."

A knowing smile crossed Taushin's face. "Not so, Zena. I found the spear."

Zena swung her head from side to side, searching the room. "Where is it?"

"Hidden. I will reveal it in due time."

"Where did you find it?"

"In Alaph's castle, at the bottom of a deep stairwell." He paused, frowning. "I also found Koren's boots and dress, so she has shed her outer garments. I will have no way of locating her again."

Zena looked through the opening in the ceiling. "Knowing Koren, she will make a public appearance soon. She will not be able to resist using her power now that she dwells within Exodus."

"My thoughts exactly. And when she does, she will learn what her people are really like. She imagines that they will gladly receive and apply the wisdom she bestows, but her wishful thinking will be deflated soon enough. She is in for a rude awakening."

Zena gripped the fire poker and threw it across the room. It struck the photograph, cracking the glass cover, its point embedded between Magnar and Arxad. "A very rude awakening, indeed."

⋇

Holding a bow over his shoulder, Randall propped open the dungeon gate. Arxad lowered his head and shuffled out into the open. Magnar followed, squeezing his muscular body through the narrow entrance. As both dragons emerged, they stretched their wings and limbs, their eyes flashing brightly and their scales shimmering in the evening moonlight. Even though they hadn't taken a meal since they arrived, the extane-rich air had obviously given them plenty of energy.

Randall nodded toward a dead stag on the path. A single arrow protruded from its chest. "I didn't have much time, so I have only this one. I hope it's enough."

"Thank you," Arxad said. "It will be sufficient."

Magnar stretched out his neck and looked Randall in the eye. "I heard some of your conversation with the new governor, but you intentionally kept your voices low during much of it. What were you hiding?"

"I kept my voice down for Orion's sake. I'll tell you everything I know."

While Magnar consumed the stag, Randall related the conversation. Although he had pondered Orion's conditions many times during his hunt, recalling them out loud gave the words more substance, as if spilling them into the open air in front of the dragons solidified them, transforming them from vaporous secrets to unavoidable realities. It made no sense to hide anything from either dragon. Orion's concerns were reasonable.

As soon as Randall finished, Magnar swallowed a huge mouthful. With blood dripping over his chin, he looked at Arxad, who hadn't eaten a bite. "You expected this offer," Magnar said. "Is your counsel unchanged?"

Arxad nodded. "Any leader would have the same concern Governor Orion has. I urge you to take this opportunity to make peace with Darksphere's rulers and fight our common enemy under these judicious terms. There is no reason to insist on your original plan."

"True. A scouting cadre of humans will report that we have told the truth. Yet surely Taushin realizes our plan by now. He could delay his ultimate weapon until he is certain all the forces against him have arrived."

"Hold on a minute," Randall said. "What ultimate weapon?"

While Magnar continued eating, Arxad kept his focus on Randall and spoke quietly. "As you might expect, we would not request an army unless we anticipated great danger. Taushin hopes to unleash a weapon that will kill every human on Starlight, including invading forces from Darksphere."

Randall rolled his fingers into a fist, forcing himself to maintain eye contact with Arxad. Catching glimpses of Magnar greedily crunching bones made this news all too believable. "What exactly is this weapon?"

"A hovering body of light we call Exodus. Taushin hopes to use Koren the Starlighter as its pilot to spread a disease that is always fatal to humans."

"Koren wouldn't do that," Randall said, shaking his head. "At least not intentionally. She's on our side."

Magnar swallowed again, scowling as a huge lump rode down his throat. "How little you know. Starlighters are unpredictable. Cassabrie and Zena proved that. Koren now wears the dark vestments and is doing Taushin's bidding. I knew this could happen. That is why I insisted on her execution, but Arxad, in his mercy, prevented me from averting this crisis."

"Why didn't you subdue Taushin?" Randall asked. "He's blind, right?"

"Arxad hoped to keep Taushin free because he alone knew how to seal a hole in Exodus and make it rise. Implementation of that knowledge would allow the star to fill the atmosphere with pheterone, the gas you call extane. With pheterone abundant, we could release the slaves and send them home. We hoped to learn the secret for resurrecting Exodus, work out a way to implement it without spreading the disease, and then subdue Taushin before he implemented it himself. That is why we are here."

"But you didn't have a way to get here until you found the portal peg. This plan could never have worked without it."

"*I* did not have a way to get here," Magnar said. "Because of a curse, I am unable to pass our barrier wall to the north or the mountains to the south. If we had been unable to find the crystal, Arxad would have guided the human army through a portal that emerges in our world in the Northlands."

Randall drew his head back. "A curse? What kind of curse?"

Arxad waited for Magnar to nod before explaining. "In our region of Starlight, we have constructed a wall on three sides, which the slaves believe to be a way to keep them in. That is true to a point, but the wall, combined with a mountain range on our southern border, creates a barrier that keeps something out, as well. These borders have been the site of many battles, so in order to establish peace, Magnar agreed to a mutual exile for the kings of the opposing sides, and a curse is the sealing enforcement. Our king, Magnar, is unable to cross the barriers, and in exchange, our opponents are unable to enter. Not only that, the curse sent our opponents to a place of captivity we know little about, and their king has been separated from them for as long as the curse is in effect. Because of this agreement, we live at peace."

"You have opponents that could threaten dragons?" Randall let out a whistle. "What kind of creatures are they? Another dragon species, or something else?"

Magnar thumped his tail on the ground. "Enough! We will talk no more of this. It is irrelevant to the matter before us."

"Okay, okay!" Randall stared at Magnar. This king he thought so cruel had made a sacrifice for his people. What kind of odd blend of goodness and evil could incite someone to cause so much harm while still being selfless in other ways?

Shaking off the thoughts, Randall nodded. "It's all coming together, except for one thing. How could a newly hatched dragon know a secret that no one else knew?"

"I wondered that for centuries," Arxad said. "We have a prophecy that foretold his ability, but we could only guess at how he would learn something no one else knew. Not even the king of the Northlands knew. He told me so himself."

Randall looked from one dragon to the other. "Do you know now?"

"We have a theory. Zena used another Starlighter's finger to communicate with Taushin while he was yet in the egg. That Starlighter, Cassabrie, was powerful, and even in death it is clear that her body radiates the mysteries of Starlight. Through a single finger, she might have communicated to Taushin the key to sealing Exodus."

Randall shuddered. "How do you know her body is powerful in death?"

Arxad and Magnar glanced at each other. With a sparks-filled sigh, Magnar nodded. "We have told him everything else."

"We also have an ultimate weapon," Arxad said. "We have preserved Cassabrie's body. If we could restore her spirit to her body, we would have the more powerful of the two Starlighters. Cassabrie would be a force Taushin could not overcome, even with Koren fully on his side."

"Even if Taushin unleashed the disease?" Randall asked. "Are Starlighters immune?"

"Koren wasn't immune, but ..." Arxad's voice trailed away.

"Wasn't immune?" Randall cocked his head. "How could you know that unless she contracted it? And if she contracted it, then how could it always be fatal?"

"Take care, Arxad," Magnar growled. "The human's questions will never end until he learns everything."

"This will be the last response." Arxad refocused on Randall. "She did contract the disease, and she died, but that story is one you need not hear. For now, we should—"

"Wait a minute! You can't spring that on me without explaining it. How could Koren have died? She's alive ..." Randall squinted. "Isn't she?"

"She is alive, but if I tell you that story ..." Arxad looked at Magnar.

"No," Magnar said. "I draw the line there. We cannot allow the humans to know. Not yet."

Randall pointed a finger at Magnar. "Listen. You're asking us to fight *your* battle, for *your* kingdom. Don't tell me—"

"For the lives of *your* people," Magnar barked. "And I will share *my* knowledge at *my* discretion. If lacking an answer to a question keeps you from a rescue attempt, then by all means stay here with your fellow soldiers, and we dragons will do what we must to save our planet. If the lives of human slaves are lost in the effort, then so be it. I will tell them that the people of Darksphere abandoned them because of their insatiable curiosity about tangential matters."

Randall grasped his bow and shook it. "Don't play me for a fool. I've watched my father's political maneuvering all my life, and I recognize a brow-beating dodge when I see one. You're the ones who kidnapped my people and enslaved them in the first place, so don't give me that verbal excrement about curiosity. You should be thanking us that Orion didn't order an immediate invasion to wipe out your species from the face of your planet."

Magnar spat out a ball of flames that sizzled past Randall. "You fool! If you knew the truth, you would drop down on your knees and beg for forgiveness! You are indebted to us for your life, especially to Arxad, so — "

"Stop!" Arxad spread out his wings, blocking the mouths of both combatants. "This is senseless."

Magnar used his own wing to knock Arxad's out of the way. "You and I both know that he is the senseless one. He barks at the howling wind, an ignorant mongrel who knows neither the source nor the direction of the breaths that gave him life." With a huff, he stalked back toward the dungeon gate. "If you can speak sense to him, then do so, but you may not tell him about his origins. You have said too much already." After squeezing again through the opening, he disappeared inside.

Arxad's wings sagged, uncovering Randall's mouth. He curled his neck and lowered his head, bringing his eyes level with Randall's. The two orbs lacked their earlier spark. "There is much you do not know, and you lack even the knowledge of why you do not know. Do not allow your curiosity to overcome your commitment. Trust me. Learning these secrets will not help you."

After a long moment, Randall nodded and loosened his grip on his bow. He hadn't wanted Magnar to win the verbal battle and set the agenda. Humans needed to be in charge, and with dragons in control of the knowledge department, it seemed impossible to gain the upper hand. He didn't need to know all the secrets, but the fact that Magnar wanted to keep them hidden was troubling. "There is one piece of information I'll need to know right away—the location of the other portal. If I am to lead Orion's scout team, I have to tell them how to prepare. A long march? Cold weather?"

Arxad's ears twitched. "Well, there is a problem. It has been so long since I passed through that portal myself, I am not certain I can find it again from this side. Forest growth has altered the landscape, so it is no longer familiar to me. In recent times, however, I sent an emissary who has informed me about the portal's location relative to landmarks you probably know."

"For example?"

"My emissary mentioned a gas pipeline's termination point in the forest. The portal is perhaps a ten-minute walk from there."

"Okay," Randall said. "I think I know where that is. We can get there in less than an hour. But what about the conditions where it comes out in your world?"

"Have the soldiers prepare for very cold weather, including ice and snow, then for a march of perhaps two days with a change to temperate conditions as their journey proceeds."

"That shouldn't be a problem. When should I tell Orion to have the men ready?"

"As soon as possible. Already the march from the Northlands might take more time than we have." Arxad turned toward the dungeon but, curling his neck, kept his focus on Randall. "Come for us when you are ready to depart."

"I will."

Arxad followed Magnar's path and faded into the dungeon's recesses.

As Randall closed the gate, a woman strode down the path, shadowed from the moonlight until she stopped within a few steps of Randall. "I heard you talking about having the men ready," she said. "Maybe you should ask a woman what to do."

Randall staggered back a step and studied the woman. With a hand touching the hilt of a sword, and toned arms pressing against her black sleeves, she resembled Marcelle, but her pasty complexion gave her a sickly appearance. Still, her auburn hair was tied back in typical Marcelle battle-ready fashion.

"Marcelle?" Randall leaned closer. "Are you all right?"

She waved a hand. "I'm fine. Just pay attention. I have been listening to your plans. This isn't the time to play games with Orion. This is life and death. Strike hard, and strike now."

Randall laughed under his breath. "I assume you have an idea to go along with that bravado."

"I do. Didn't you get my note?"

Randall touched his pocket. "Oh! So *you're* the M!"

"Of course." Marcelle set a hand on her hip. "Do you think any male soldier would have handwriting like that?"

"Well, I wasn't sure. It's possible that it was dictated to a female who just ran out of ink."

Randall winced. That sounded foolish. Marcelle's overpowering presence was making him feel like a little boy.

She rolled her eyes. "No, Randall. I just wanted to make sure no one else knows I'm here in Mesolantrum. I thought you had seen my handwriting enough times to know who wrote it."

"Okay, okay. I get the point." Randall tried to shake off Marcelle's verbal jabs. Her tongue was as sharp as ever. "You said you want more troops. What's your plan?"

"It's simple. We abandon the reconnaissance contingent idea, escort Orion directly to Starlight, and force him to order his armies to join us immediately."

"Kidnap him? Don't you know how many guards he has? Even his bodyguard has a bodyguard, and he has archers with him wherever he goes."

"Didn't you pay attention? He sent his archers and bodyguard away."

"Right. I saw that."

Marcelle let out a huff, but a wrinkle in her lips gave away a hint of mirth. "Follow me, my friend." She marched down the path into the forest shadows, a slight swagger in her gait.

Randall followed close behind. Soon she halted at a tree where a man stood bound to the trunk by vines, his cheeks puffed out as if something had been stuffed into his mouth. As he wriggled behind the vines, he grunted, red-faced, apparently trying to speak.

"He's enjoying a meal of socks." Grinning, Marcelle pointed at Orion's bare feet. "It's all I could find."

Randall sucked in a breath. "You kidnapped the governor?"

"Desperate times call for desperate measures." She winked. "Besides, have you ever known me to do things diplomatically?"

"Okay," Randall said, stretching out the word. "What's the next step? Authorization letters for our army? A call-to-arms appeal to the other governors?"

Marcelle pointed at herself with her thumb. "Leave both to me. We'll get the signatures now, and I'll fill in the verbiage. I already have the funds I need to get supplies for the troops. Now all we need to do is get Orion to Starlight right away so there'll be no chance for him to countermand the letters."

"If we can find the portal," Randall said. "We know its approximate location, but we still have to find it."

Marcelle picked up a long stick. "I know where it is. I'll draw a map."

Orion finally managed to spit out the socks. "Don't listen to her! She's a witch, I tell you. A witch!"

Like a cracking whip, Marcelle slid out her sword and pressed the point under his chin. "If you breathe another word, you will see your tongue skewered on this blade."

Orion's eyes grew wide and wild, but he kept silent.

Randall leaned over and picked up the socks, warm and damp. "Governor Orion, I thought you said your witch-hunting days were over." He then nodded at Marcelle. "Let him answer, as long as he does so quietly."

"I …" Orion swallowed, sweat beading on his forehead. "I did give up witch hunting, but look at her. She is practically a ghost. Feel her hands. They are icy. You will see."

Randall looked at Marcelle's hands, both locked into fists, one throttling the hilt of her sword. "Marcelle, do you have chills?"

Her jaw tightened. "We don't have time to do a medical diagnosis. Let's get on with the plan."

"Feel them," Orion said, nodding rapidly. "You cannot deny your own observations. I could tell you more of what I have seen, but you likely would not believe me."

"That's enough!" Marcelle grabbed the socks from Randall and began stuffing them back into Orion's mouth.

Randall looked at his fingers. For a brief moment, just as Marcelle jerked away the socks, a frigid breeze passed across his skin, and it faded as quickly as it had come.

"Marcelle?" Randall reached for her arm. "Something really is wrong with you. Let me feel your hand."

She shifted a step away, dodging his touch. "I told you I'm fine."

Randall looked at Marcelle. Avoiding his eyes, she stood with one arm across her chest, clutching the bicep of her sword arm.

"The things I don't know keep piling up," he said, "but at least we have a plan that should work. Let's get moving."

※

Magnar took in a deep draw of the pheterone-enriched air. "Take in all you can, my brother. Grow stronger. Our fellow dragons are counting on us to be their deliverance."

"I will be ready to sacrifice for them." Arxad scanned the dungeon. Only Magnar's shining red eyes pierced the darkness. "As if they deserve it."

"So speaks the humble priest, the dragon who seems to care more about the vermin than his own kind."

Arxad settled to his belly. Magnar's rebuke was a familiar one. Replying would only instigate an argument they had repeated a hundred times before. "Did you see the gun?"

"I did, but I detected no odor of gunpowder."

"Nor did I, but how can we be sure they have not discovered gunpowder on their own?"

"We cannot." Magnar blinked, temporarily darkening his eyes. "We have no choice but to continue with this plan."

"If they are too powerful for us to withstand, will you summon other help?"

"I know the idea that consumes your mind." Magnar's eyes swayed from side to side. "The Bloodless will stay where they are."

"Why do you continue to use that label? You know they have blood."

"Coursing along their scalelike skin, yes. With those red lines on the surface, anyone can see that they are not true dragons. They are Pariah's offspring, dark devils in a disguise of white. They are too dangerous to be released from their exile. Having one in our midst should be enough to prove that. Continue to call them the Benefile if you wish, but they will always be the Bloodless to me."

Arxad let out a *humph*. "A danger to you, perhaps, but if a human army threatens to overrun us, the rest of us would be glad of their help."

"You might get your wish. We still have no idea what will happen when I go through the portal."

Arxad kept his stare on Magnar's eyes. Darkness surrounded the red glow, hiding his expression, making it impossible to gauge his mood. With Magnar's curse still in place, what would his appearing in the North-lands bring about? Would it break the curse? If so, what would become of the other curses? Might the Benefile be released from their hated habitat? If so, what would they do? They might be outraged and ready to strike, and they could kill a large number of the soldiers before they had a chance to travel south. Would Alaph be able to control them? And what would become of the environment in the Northlands? Alaph's inability to pass the barrier wall wasn't part of the original curse. Would that limitation also be eliminated?

"I can feel your anxiety from here," Magnar said. "Settle your mind."

"I will try." Arxad laid his head on the ground. It was easy for Magnar to relax. After so many years confined in the Southlands, he wanted to break the curse, no matter what the Benefile might do. If they decided to become violent, the dragons of the South would need all the human soldiers they could muster, and he might have to break out the weapons he had stored in Alaph's castle. That, of course, would be their last resort.

ten

Koren stood in the midst of Exodus as she flew toward the dragon village. The glow from the Zodiac's spires and a lantern flame in the Basilica's belfry guided her way.

Earlier, Tibalt had escorted the hypnotized Mallerin to Fellina's home cave and secured her with chains in an inner room where no one could hear her screams. She had been compliant, but once Tibalt had finished binding her, her belligerence slowly returned.

During that process, Fellina hurried the two boys to Xenith at the family refuge, then returned to transport Elyssa and the injured warriors northward, an arduous task for any dragon, even the strongest males. Yet, when she flew away with Elyssa on her back and the warriors in her claws, she seemed up to the task, and with Jason's stardrop pouch secure in Elyssa's grasp, it seemed that all would be well.

It had been easy for Koren to hypnotize the barrier wall dragons, thereby allowing Fellina and company passage. In keeping with her Starlighter's purpose, she had also provided the dragons with a dose of wisdom, encouraging them to denounce slavery and cease their efforts to keep humans captive, though the words seemed to bounce off deaf ears.

As light flowed from her cloak and exited the sphere's membrane, Koren slowed. Now over the Zodiac, she faced south, the Basilica to her left and most of the places of business to her right. The grottoes lay farther to the right, and dots of light flickering in the distance proved that a few dragon residents had already ordered their slaves to set flame to their lanterns for the evening.

With Solarus gliding below the horizon, Exodus became the dominant light, spreading over the spires and casting a dozen spear-like shadows across the village's main street. The village still lay nearly deserted because of Taushin's orders, leaving only a few dragons out to patrol for wandering slaves who had ignored the ambiguous warnings. The humans had been sequestered for so long, many likely doubted the danger. Perhaps an amazing new phenomenon would be enough incentive to overcome their remaining fears. Now all she needed was a town crier to announce the news of her arrival.

Below, Tibalt crouched next to one of the Zodiac's columns. Light from Exodus exposed his hiding place, as well as the bald spot on top of his head. Koren waved. He stood and waved back, then rubbed his hands together as if summoning courage.

Koren slowly inhaled. She had stored these words for so long, they had to come out soon. Brinella had spewed fractured tales in a random fashion, for her wounded state had weakened her ability to assemble the words and control their flow. The poor girl. How long had she suffered? Hundreds of years? So lonely, feeling forsaken, unable to breathe the air of freedom. Yet now she lived with the Creator, her wound healed and her heart renewed.

Closing her eyes, Koren breathed deeply. Yes. Renewed. Abiding within Exodus was truly regenerating. Now she absorbed the Creator's bounty—wisdom, knowledge, eloquence—and with these gifts came the opportunity to deliver what she learned to those in need. What joy it would be to see their faces when they hear the good news! Still, a queasy sensation swirled in her stomach, along with a dull ache. It wasn't terrible, just annoying. Obviously she wasn't accustomed to all the flying around.

"Here I go!" Tibalt bolted from the column and ran along the middle of the street, waving his arms and shouting. "Hurry! Come out and see this! A star has fallen from the heavens! And wait till you see what she looks like!"

As he continued his cries, an adult human poked his head out of the seamstress shop window. Wide doors opened in the financial office, and two drones emerged along with their three human assistants—a young woman with a missing arm and two young men. All five looked up at Exodus, blinking.

Soon dozens of humans and several dragons streamed from their homes and lined the dusty cobblestone road, every head tilted upward. Buzzing whispers made them sound like a swarm of bees, and Tibalt's never-ending cries added to the chaos. Most of the humans shielded their eyes from the radiance, a few wincing as beads of sweat broke out on their foreheads. The dragons gawked wide-eyed, their necks swaying slightly as if dancing in time to an inner melody.

From the direction of Arxad's grotto, Madam Orley hurried as fast as her old legs would carry her, and she joined the swelling throng. After at least a hundred humans and fifteen dragons had gathered, a muscular middle-aged man pushed to the front. Holding up a hand to shield his eyes, he shouted, "Who are you, and why are you here?"

As Koren guided Exodus down, Brinella's warning about keeping the star away from humans came to mind. How close was too close? She never said. Maybe high enough to keep them from touching it would be safe.

When the star's lowest point hovered about twenty feet above the Zodiac's portico, she stopped her descent. From this angle, the man's face was difficult to see, especially with his hand lifted over his squinting scowl, but he looked like Yeager, the slave trader.

As she raised her hood over her head, she took another deep breath. "I am your Starlighter," she called loudly enough for everyone to hear. "I am the messenger who guides this star, and I have allowed myself to be imprisoned here for your sakes. Although this sphere was called Starlight during the years it watched over this world, it was later renamed Exodus. The last time Exodus visited the citizens of this world, more than five hundred years ago, no human here now was alive, and only the oldest dragons remember those days. They kept secrets. They whispered mysteries. They heard your questions but delivered no answers.

"Now in these days of prophetic convergence, I have come to reveal secrets, to unravel mysteries, to provide the answers you have sought for decades. All these years, you have been told lies, and you had no choice but to believe them. These lies have strengthened your chains and weakened your spirits. Yet that can change. If you will listen, you will learn the truth, and the truth will set you free."

Koren spread out her cloak and gave it a spin. "This world was once called Iris, for it was a world of color and beauty, unspoiled and brimming with life."

The cobblestones transformed into grassy turf. Flowers sprang up all around, dressing the newly formed meadow in dazzling multihued array. The Zodiac disappeared, replaced by a one-story wooden structure with a silvery tin roof, similar to a stable the livestock keepers used for sheep and goats, but the tall, wide door gave evidence that a much larger animal passed in and out of this abode.

"Now," Koren continued, "I will tell you a story about two men. We will meet Hiram first. The second man is called Bodner."

A ghostly man walked out of the stable carrying a small box in the palm of his hand and a long spear over his shoulder. A dragon with a collar fastened to his neck followed. Moaning with every shuffling step, the dragon shook his head as if trying to sling off the collar.

Hiram turned and jabbed one of the dragon's front legs. "Stop complaining!"

Several humans in the audience gasped, while the dragons continued to stare with mouths agape.

The servile dragon drew back his head as if to blow fire. Hiram dropped his spear and pressed a button on the box. The dragon began to shudder. From his snout to the end of his tail, he shook harder and harder. Finally, lifting his head, he cried, "Mercy, master! I will comply!"

"Comply? Lowbred, I think you were ready to fry me." Releasing the button for a moment, Hiram pointed the box at Lowbred. "You deserve a maximum jolt." Then, gritting his teeth, Hiram punched the button with his thumb and held it down.

The box let out a high-pitched squeal. Lowbred's long neck thrashed. His wings spread out and stiffened. Finally, he toppled to the side.

Hiram walked closer, still holding down the button. Lowbred writhed for a moment, then, after a shuddering convulsion, he lay motionless.

Like a wave, a chorus of new gasps passed across the onlookers.

Another man appeared next to the first. Wearing dirty trousers and a cap with a bill, he stared at the inert dragon. "Is he dead?" Bodner asked.

"Just paralyzed." Hiram released the button. "It's all under control."

Bodner shook his head slowly, letting out a tsking sound. "He has to die. We can't allow a dangerous dragon to live."

"True, but killing him now doesn't make sense. I don't want to haul his carcass to the grinding mill. I'll fly him there. He'll be flapping his wings toward his own death."

Bodner laughed. "Special delivery. From dragon to dog food."

"If the dogs will even eat this one. He's so tough I'll have to use the cannon to put him down."

"So when I hear the boom, I'll know it's done." Bodner picked up the spear and examined the bloodstained point. "I saw the new twins. When are you going to pick them up?"

"Later today. What genders did we get?"

Bodner gave Hiram the spear. "Two males."

"That's good. I need heavy lifters. Colors?"

"One's a sorrel," Bodner said. "The other's a palomino."

Hiram laughed. "Spoken like a true horse thief."

"Thief? You're the one who swindled that poor old widow out of those eggs."

"Swindled? I could have sent her packing. She was three months behind. I did her a favor."

"Whatever you say, Mr. Compassion." Bodner took off his cap and used it to fan his face. "It's a hot one, isn't it?"

Hiram flicked his head toward the sky. "No wonder. That fool star's coming this way."

"Again?" Bodner looked up at Exodus.

"Gentlemen!" Koren shouted. "Pay heed to me!"

"Sometimes I get the impression it really is trying to talk," Bodner said. "It's like I hear a mouse squeaking."

Hiram snorted. "That's all it is—noise. Nothing more, nothing less. As long as it doesn't interfere with our control box signals, let it squeal."

"Too bad your dragon's out of commission," Bodner said. "It's always interesting to hear dragons come up with their fanciful interpretations."

"If you want to hear a blithering idiot, go and listen to Cornwall. He was preaching in front of the tobacco shop this morning. If you hurry, he might still be there."

Koren spread out her arms. "Hiram! Bodner! You must hearken to me!"

"Seriously. Listen. That thing is clucking like a laying hen." Bodner nodded at Lowbred. "See if he's recovering. I could use a good laugh."

Hiram shoved Lowbred with his foot. "C'mon. I didn't hit you that hard. Get up and tell us what Starlight is saying."

With his head on the ground, Lowbred murmured. "Ask Cornwall. He will tell you."

Hiram delivered a savage kick to Lowbred's chin. "Do what I say, or you'll get another jolt!"

Heaving a deep sigh, Lowbred struggled to his haunches and gazed at Koren. "What do you wish to tell us, Starlighter?"

Koren checked her hood. It was still in place. "Here is my message. Compassion is the heartbeat of love. True compassion does not expect payment for the removal of a burden. Give freely to widows, to orphans, and to anyone less fortunate than yourselves. Masters of slaves, that includes those who serve you in bonds. As I have told you before, release them. Set them free. But you have not listened. Hear me now. A day will come when you will be enslaved yourselves, enduring lashes on your

196

own backs, lashes delivered by the species you so cruelly brutalize now."

While Lowbred relayed the message, Hiram and Bodner glanced at each other, smirking. Finally, Hiram let out a belly laugh. "Now *that's* a fanciful tale!"

"I did not make it up," Lowbred said. "I merely repeated her words."

"She? So now the star is a she?"

"I heard Cornwall say the same thing," Bodner said. "Claims that a blue-hooded redhead lives inside. I think he's been standing in the heat far too long."

"Let's see if we can find out." Lunging with his entire body, Hiram threw the spear. It sailed true, but when the point struck the membrane, the spear bounced back and fell. Sounding a thud, it embedded in the carpet of grass only a few steps away.

"You cannot harm the star," Lowbred said. "It is the guiding angel of Iris."

"Superstitious nonsense." Hiram yanked the spear from the ground and rubbed the shaft near the tip. "Maybe there is a way to deliver a bit more punch, but I'll have to use a different kind of metal and sharpen the point."

Bodner waved a dismissive hand at the star. "Let's just leave well enough alone."

"Why? You're the one who complained about the heat."

"I know. Everyone does, but—"

"Then it's time we did something about it. Having the star around makes the dragons arrogant, like they think they know something we don't. And there's nothing I hate more than an uppity dragon." Hiram poked Lowbred with the butt end of the spear. "I think fate has given you an extended life. We're going to pick up the new dragons. Then I want to pay a visit to a miner I know."

"What for?" Bodner asked.

"He's an explosives expert who knows how to rig a remote-controlled bomb. I want to end this guiding angel charade once and for all. We'll get rid of her heat and her sermonizing at the same time."

A few seconds later, the scene crumbled and blew away like dust.

Koren turned back to her audience. The dragons' eyes had glazed over, and most of the humans stood entranced. "Soon after, Hiram devised a sharper spear with an explosive much more powerful than your expanding gas capsules. Then one dark night, flying on a dragon to get within range, he plunged the spear into the star. White vapor surged from the wound, striking Hiram in the face. Blinded for a moment, he fumbled with his control box while the star zoomed away. Although he pushed the button with the same ferocity he employed against the dragon, the angel of Starlight had flown too far. Her light twinkled near the northern horizon, no brighter than the other stars that witnessed Hiram's foul deed."

Koren lowered her arms. "Dear friends, the guiding light has now been restored, and she is here to offer wisdom. If you will listen and heed my words, you can be set free from the chains that bind you."

"Wisdom?" Yeager asked, wearing a skeptical frown. "What is this wisdom?"

Koren eyed Yeager. Although every dragon and most humans had succumbed to her hypnotic power, a few showed signs of immunity, clearer eyes and impatient shifting of feet.

"Warriors have come from another world to liberate us," Koren said, "but they cannot do so alone. They will need you to rise up against the tyranny that has oppressed you for a hundred years. Only together will you be able to break the bonds and return to Darksphere, the planet from whence you were taken. And, dragons, I implore you to release—"

"Home planet?" Yeager nodded toward the area where the vision had taken place. "You showed humans living on this planet five hundred years ago, and now you're saying we came from Darksphere a hundred years ago. Which is it?"

"Both stories are true. Humans left this world and inhabited Darksphere, then came back as slaves."

"How? Why?" His questions slung out like spears.

Koren lowered her hood. "I don't know. Starlight hasn't given me the details."

Yeager pointed a finger at her. "I recognize you now. You're Koren, the girl who joined the dragons. You're one of them now."

A new murmur passed through the crowd, seemingly activated by a sea of bobbing heads.

Yeager looked back and nodded with them. "She's another Zena. You all saw. She was dressed in black then, and Taushin saw through her eyes. He's probably looking at us right now to see who'll stand up against him. I say we make a spear and send her back to the north. That will show Taushin that we won't listen to this foolish talk of rebellion."

"No!" Madam Orley shoved to the front and grasped Yeager's arm. "I saw Taushin torture Koren mercilessly. She is forced to obey him."

Several in the crowd murmured their agreement. One male voice rose above the others. "If she is a Starlighter, we should listen to her. You can see for yourself that she's not like Zena."

Koren found the speaker, a teenager near the back. She had met him a couple of times, one of the stone movers. Maybe he would embolden others to join him.

"I'm sure we all believe you," Yeager said, patting Madam's shoulder, "but we cannot allow anyone to listen to her. It would mean death."

"But don't punish her. She is just a slave like us. There is no need to talk about spears and sending her to the north."

"That's all well and good …" Furrowing his brow, he looked at Koren, again shielding his eyes. "If she stays out of sight and takes her heat with her."

Madam Orley set a hand above her eyes and stepped toward Koren. "Did you hear that? Everyone knows you're a slave, so no one will try to hurt you. Just go somewhere out of sight. The light you're shining is just too hot for some of us to take." She lowered her hand and squinted with her tired, old eyes. "You understand, right?"

"But I'm not a slave." Koren spread out her arms, opening the front of her cloak. "Look. I'm not wearing black. I can fly, and I am free to go wherever I choose."

Yeager cocked his head. "What did she say? She's mumbling."

"She's not a slave," Madam Orley said. "She's free to go anywhere."

A man piped up near the front. "No, she said she swears she'll be back, and she can lie to us whenever she chooses. I heard her."

Madam Orley shoved the man's shoulder. "Nonsense. Why would she admit to lying? A deceiver wouldn't do that. And I have known Koren for a long time. She is not a liar."

His face turning red, the man growled. "I know what I heard."

"No!" Koren shouted. "I said I am free to go wherever I choose, because I can fly."

"Now she is speaking gibberish," the man said. "She has gone mad."

Yeager nodded. "Even if she said she's free, the poor girl is addled. She's trapped inside that prison of light. She must be roasting in there."

"Addled?" Madam Orley pointed at the Zodiac. "You saw the story. We all did. Koren is a Starlighter, and you know the prophecy."

"Quiet!" Yeager barked. "You are not to speak of that prophecy. You know the punishment. You heard what happened to Cassabrie."

"Coward!" Madam set her hands on her hips, wagging her head as she spoke in singsong.

Starlighter, Starlighter, set us all free.

Break all our shackles, declare jubilee.

Light from above will reflect in each heart,
Burn away chaff, and true freedom impart.

Yeager pointed at his chest. "That freedom is in our hearts. We are humans, born to be slaves, and we will be slaves until we die. As long as we're free within, that's all that really matters."

She raised a stiff finger. "I used to believe that nonsense. I used to think I could be satisfied as a slave in Arxad's home. But I came to my senses. He is as cruel a tyrant as Magnar. No one in chains is really free."

As the argument between Yeager and Madam Orley continued, it seemed to spread throughout the crowd, creating pockets of verbal combat here and there. Obviously, the people had recovered from their daze. Even the dragons appeared to be more focused than before.

Koren gazed as them, a tear trickling down her cheek. These were her people, her friends. They were so blind! So deaf! Why wouldn't they listen?

Yeager pointed at Koren. "Well, I know a deceiver when I see one. She conjured that story she showed us. It never happened. Humans cannot enslave dragons. They are too powerful. It's impossible."

"Look!" the other man shouted. "She is no longer there. The star is empty. Maybe she was a phantasm, an evil spirit."

Madam Orley looked up at Exodus. "Ridiculous. I see her plain as day."

"Stop!" One of the dragons pushed the humans apart with his wings, shaking his head as if casting off a net. "I have heard too much talk of rebellion. Go back to your homes until Taushin gives us leave to emerge. I will deal with this Starlighter."

Koren leaned forward. It was Hyborn, one of the oldest dragons, the village's head financier and a slave master who had a reputation for cruelty.

With loud grumbles passing among the humans, the crowd dispersed. Dragons flew in low circles as if shepherding the masses, though some bobbed up and down in flight as they recovered their senses. Tibalt joined the stream of humans. He glanced at Koren, but only for a moment. His job was to blend in as a normal slave, taking Koren's place as one of Fellina's house servants. From there, he could go about freely and infiltrate, get a feel for what the others were thinking. Of course, his age might raise a few questions, but his story that he had been locked in the Basilica ever since before the days of Cassabrie could work. At least it might get the slaves to open up to him as they filled him in on the news.

Madam Orley backed away slowly, looking up at Koren. She spoke with her hands, using the signs Koren and Petra had invented to communicate silently.

"I believe you," her fingers spelled out. "I will try to help you." Then she turned and hurried down the path toward Arxad's cave.

When all had departed, Hyborn extended his neck, bringing his head within ten feet of Exodus. "Is it true? Is Taushin seeing through your eyes in order to root out opposition?"

Koren met Hyborn's gaze. It would be easy to say yes, easy to fool him into thinking she was still on Taushin's side. With her speaking gifts, he would be quick to believe and quick to leave her alone.

She tightened her hands into fists. Those were the old days and the old ways. She couldn't use her gifts to hypnotize a dragon and then leave him deceived. Dangerous or not, she had to tell the truth.

"I am no longer under Taushin's control." She extended her arms, baring her wrists. "My chains are gone. I have been set free. I will do all in my power to liberate my people." She softened her voice to a whisper. "And you, Hyborn, can help us. Can't you see how cruel slavery is? Didn't you see what Hiram and Bodner did to that poor dragon? Didn't that display turn your stomach? Doesn't it make you want to pledge to do everything within your power to end this madness?"

Hyborn spoke in an even tone. "Yes, I saw what those humans did to that poor dragon. Yes, it turned my stomach." He then switched to a deep growl. "But I pledge only to pay humans back for every demeaning insult, for every jab from that wicked spear, and for every shock from that cursed collar. For you see, I was that dragon."

"You ..." Koren gulped. "You were Hiram's dragon?"

"He called me Lowbred, but when Magnar set me free, I changed my name to Hyborn. And I was the dragon Hiram flew when he attacked the star. For that deed I am truly ashamed, but since I wore a dragon slave's collar, I had no choice."

"No choice? Really?"

"Other than death?" He shook his head. "I had to obey."

"Death is a better end than obeying evil." Koren straightened and folded her hands at her waist. "So what will you do, Hyborn? Are you loyal to Taushin or to Starlight?"

"Taushin *is* Starlight. You are the ultimate evidence. He said he would resurrect the star and restore pheterone, and the closer I draw to you, the more I can sense it. Perhaps breathing pheterone-endowed air is why I am not coming under your spell at this moment. Exodus is the source of our new life, and Taushin is the reason. He has brought Starlight back from the dead."

Koren spread out her arms. "Perhaps the Creator used Taushin as a catalyst, but the end result must be liberation for the humans. You no longer need slaves to mine for the gas. Isn't that so?"

"We no longer need them, true, and the prophecy said they would die. I will leave the timing of that execution to Taushin."

"What of Magnar?" Koren asked. "If he set you free in the first place, shouldn't you consult him?"

Hyborn's ears bent back. "First, he is not here to consult. Second, when you were wearing Zena's vestments, you showed us that he departed to places unknown. Some of us think he has gone to raise an army and will return to retake his throne. If he conquers Taushin, what will become of you? You are the symbol of Taushin's success. Considering how Magnar has treated Starlighters in the past, I cannot believe he will allow you or Exodus to remain. Then, our source of pheterone will again be the mesa mines, and humans will stay in captivity. I am certain you do not want that."

"Of course not, but most dragons have no intention of setting their slaves free. They want to slaughter them." Koren leaned closer and stared at him, hoping to draw him into her net. "Even now I can see this evil plan brewing in your mind. Your lust for revenge has lasted through all these years, and the newly enriched atmosphere has heightened your desire. Pheterone is not merely an energizer for you; it is an intoxicant, a lubricant for the violence in your mind. You have murder in your heart, and I can help you purge it."

Hyborn's voice sharpened. "It is not murder to terminate one's own property. It is my right. So say we all."

"All? What about Arxad? Would he agree with you? Even with his history of aiding humans, does anyone really question his loyalty to the dragon race?"

Hyborn backed away a step. "This is true. We all know Arxad has accompanied Magnar out of loyalty, probably to try to keep Magnar from a rash decision. If Arxad were to return and offer his counsel, I would listen."

Koren exhaled. Finally! An opening! "If I could show you proof that Arxad wants you to heed my words and distrust Taushin, would that be enough to change your mind?"

Hyborn's eyes shifted toward the Zodiac. "Perhaps. At least it would be enough for me to investigate further."

"Then let me see what I can find for you." Koren lifted her arms, spreading out her cloak. "Starlight, tell me—"

"Not now," Hyborn said. "I must check on my slaves. Return here tomorrow at dawn, and I will listen. In the meantime, I suggest that you stay well hidden. I think many of the slaves fear the punishment that will result if anyone heeds your words. You represent an unknown danger."

"I understand." Koren guided Exodus slowly higher. "I will return at dawn."

Hyborn bowed his head and shuffled back. "Until then, Starlighter."

Koren turned Exodus and glided swiftly toward the north, struggling to suppress the heartbreak welling in her soul. Her good news, her messages of freedom, had failed to penetrate. Like seeds on arid ground, they scattered with the wind.

A tear tracked down her cheek. What had happened? Hope lost. Freedom rejected. Fear chosen over courage. Instead of hundreds of slaves rallying together to rise up against their oppressors, most simply shrugged and turned aside. They were satisfied with their station, content with their chains. Slaves all their lives, they couldn't believe any human ever lived in freedom. How could anyone set them free from bondage to an idea? And with Hyborn being so resilient, how could she persuade the dragons to set the slaves free? Since he was one of the most revered dragons, all the others would listen to him, no matter how well she convinced them during their hypnotic trances.

"Creator!" she called as she drove Exodus forward. "I need wisdom!"

Koren arrived at the river and followed its northward course to the barrier wall. Now high in the air, her light illuminated the flat landscape to the north, far beyond the wall. Untold quantities of water flowed into the dragons' barricade of stones and mortar, but on the other side, no water emerged, not a drop. Where could it have gone? Underground?

She flew past the wall and over a flat grassy area. This time the wall's guardians didn't bother questioning her. They just looked up with slack-jawed stares as she glided by.

Soon she reached the end of the plain, marked by a stair-stepped slope. Water poured out from holes in the slope, forming streams that joined together after several hundred feet. Once merged, the river flowed on, north-ward, ever northward until it reached the waterfall she and Jason had seen not long ago.

Koren stopped over the restored river and looked back. At the wall, the water struck a barrier, an apparently impassable obstacle. Yet here it flowed on, unhindered by stone-burdened rafts, liberated to invigorate the meadow with its life-giving refreshment.

"It found a new path," Koren whispered. "It went underground and split up."

She let a smile emerge. A river cannot be stopped. The water has to go somewhere. It either piles up and overcomes, or it seeks another route. There are no other options. A river never gives up.

Koren lifted to her toes and spun in place, letting her cloak fan out. She laughed out loud, her smile so wide, her cheeks ached. "Thank you, dear Creator!" she shouted. "You have answered my prayer."

Finally, she stopped, her smile unabated as she tried to catch her breath. Now the answer was clear. Her fellow humans believed themselves to be without hope, born to live in slavery until they died. How could someone be set free from such an idea?

She clenched her fist. With another idea!

eleven

Elyssa slid down Fellina's side and dropped to the castle foyer's wooden floor. She clutched the pouch that held Jason's stardrop and shivered hard. Although the air was warmer inside the castle, the flight through the Northlands' frigid air had chilled her to the core.

She staggered toward the entryway, where Fellina had deposited Jason and his father, then dropped to her knees between their shivering bodies. "They're so co-cold!" she shouted. "Does the k-king have b-blankets?"

Flapping her wings, Fellina completed a running turn and stopped near Elyssa. "I will summon the king."

"Please hurry." Elyssa threw herself over Jason's curled body and wrapped her arms around him as tightly as she could. "I can't keep them b-both warm."

"You will keep no one warm. Your lips are blue, and you are shaking more violently than they are." Fellina stretched out her wings again. "Move aside. I will take them to the beds. I had to put you down here, because I cannot land in the healing chamber. After I take them, I must return to the Southlands to look for Arxad. Deference will lead you to Jason."

Elyssa scooted away on her knees. "Jason mentioned Deference. Where is she?"

"She will introduce herself soon." Fellina lifted into the air, circled the foyer once, and snatched Jason and his father with her rear claws. The two bodies dangling, she flew into a long, wide corridor and faded in the dimness.

Elyssa hugged herself, rubbing her upper arms as she rose. "Deference? Are you here?"

A shimmer of light appeared. Shaped like a teenaged girl, the light spread out a radiant skirt and curtsied. "I am Deference. Follow me. Quickly." The girl turned and ran into the corridor, an aura enveloping her and lighting the way.

Elyssa bolted after her. Her stiff legs felt like tree trunks, but after several steps, her knees loosened, and the chills eased. Soon she caught up with Deference and ran at her side. "Is it far?"

"Not far." Deference slowed and lowered her head. "Get down!"

Elyssa ducked. Coming from the opposite direction, a dragon flew by, passed a foot overhead, and zoomed toward the foyer. Fellina was obviously in a hurry.

Deference continued forward, her arms and legs appearing again as they moved. After a few seconds, she stopped at an open archway that led into another room.

Inside, the floor consisted of a network of tree roots, tangled and knotted. About ten steps within, a dragon sat on his haunches. It appeared to be gray or ivory, but in the dim light, it was impossible to tell for certain. His eyes, blue and shimmering, seemed foreboding, yet somehow inviting at the same time.

"Come in," the dragon said in a low tone.

Elyssa looked at Deference. She nodded, her radiance dimming once again. "He won't hurt you."

"Are you coming?"

"Soon." Deference set a hand on Elyssa's arm. The touch tickled. "Go on."

Elyssa stepped into the room on tiptoes, avoiding a hole just inside the doorway. The roots bent with her weight, crackling slightly, but they didn't break. With every step, the floor popped and bounced until she halted about a wing's length from the dragon. As her eyes adjusted to the dimness, she glanced around, not only to get a look at the room but also to avoid the dragon's piercing stare. A row of beds took shape on each side, but no one lay in the beds closest to her.

"What do you seek?" the dragon said.

Elyssa cleared her throat, hoping a new chill wouldn't shake her words. "A dragon named Fellina brought my friend Jason and his father in here." She opened the pouch and withdrew a glowing sac of skin. Using her fingernails, she ripped the sac open, plucked out the stardrop, and laid it on her palm, dropping the ruptured sac behind her. "We heard this might heal them somehow."

The dragon extended his neck and peered at the glowing white sphere. "Only one stardrop? There are two patients. When Fellina delivered them here, I put them in adjacent beds at the far end of this room. They are both badly injured, and I am sure they are bleeding internally. They will soon die without the aid of healing light. And now Exodus has risen, so we have no source for a second stardrop."

A new tremor shook her extended arm, and her voice quaked with it. "Can we split it in half?"

"Of course, but half will not heal either patient. With stardrops, it must be all or nothing."

Elyssa drew the stardrop closer. "Then I have to choose?"

"Yes, you must make a choice."

"But how? I can't decide whose life is more valuable. Only the Creator can do that."

"No life is more valuable than another, but that is not the choice you must make." The dragon took a step closer and set a wing tip on her shoulder. "Elyssa, it is time for you to take yet another step of courage."

Elyssa steeled herself. Not only did his touch send a tingling buzz across her skin, his words sounded like funeral gongs. And how did he know her name? Had Fellina told him?

"You have likely noticed that the stardrop once caused a dizzying effect," the dragon said. "Do you feel it now?"

Elyssa blinked at the stardrop. Although it had bothered her early in the journey, the effect had diminished, something she had attributed to the cold air. "No. I don't feel it now."

"And you will not as long as you are here." As the dragon took another step closer, his features clarified.

Thin red lines, like tiny blood vessels, drew a matrix across the pristine white background—scales that seemed flatter than those of other dragons. With the narrowest of gaps between them, they looked as much like human skin as they did dragon's. "There is only one hope for saving both humans. If you possess the proper gift, you will be able to ingest the stardrop and gain the power to distribute its healing energy."

She looked at the stardrop again. "What happens if I don't possess the proper gift?"

"Then you will die an excruciatingly painful death."

"How can that be? How could something deadly to one person be beneficial to another?"

"I did not say it would be beneficial to you, even if you do possess the gift. In fact, its power will likely cause you great pain in some ways, and that pain will continue the rest of your life."

Elyssa held the stardrop between her thumb and finger and drew it closer to her mouth. Warm to her fingers, it seemed fiery hot to her lips. She shifted her gaze to the white dragon. "How do I know you're telling the truth?"

The dragon's brow turned downward for a moment before rising again. "You do not, and I have no way to prove my words. You must decide based on what you know. If you decide that I am untrustworthy, then go your way. You cannot help Jason and his father. If you choose to swallow the stardrop and you survive, I will teach you how to use your power. If you take it and perish, I will see to a proper burial. But choose quickly. Their lights are waning."

Elyssa closed her eyes. Could she do it? Could she drop this flaming sphere into her mouth and swallow it?

Firming her chin, she nodded. For Jason. Yes, for Jason she could do it. She opened her mouth, tossed the stardrop as far back as she could, and swallowed. It merely tingled going down, warm but not burning.

She looked at the dragon. He stared back at her, his ears erect and his head tilted.

"Okay," she said. "That was easier than I—"

A shot of heat stabbed her insides. Sizzling fire erupted into her throat like a flood of burning bile, then surged deep into her belly, jabbing like a demon with a fire poker. Grasping her stomach, she fell to her knees and cried out loud and long.

She toppled to her side and curled to a fetal position on the roots. Hot gas belched through her lips as throaty words gushed like rhythmic bursts of a volcano. "Help! … Oh, help me! … Dear Creator, help me! … I'm dying."

More gas erupted, this time mixed with acid, burning her tongue and lips. She spat and coughed. Spasms twisted her stomach so cruelly it seemed that a saber-toothed beast gnawed her gut, shaking her intestines to tear them loose from her body. Would this kind of pain continue? For the rest of her life? No! It would be better to die!

Finally, the beast released her. The demon rested his poker. The acid settled to a simmer, and the gas pressure eased. She let her body go limp. Every muscle relaxed. Even her heart slowed to the beat of a death march. Then a sense of cold returned, as if her blood had turned to icy water and flowed to every part of her body. She shivered harder than ever. The end was near. As her curled frame quaked, she whispered. "I tried, Jason. I tried so hard. I'm sorry. I'm so, so sorry."

Tears flowed, cold tears that chilled her cheeks. Only a tiny core of heat remained, likely the stardrop itself burning a hole in the pit of her stomach. Like an overlooked ember after the dousing of a campfire, it sizzled on, radiating heat but no longer causing pain.

The core swelled, and its warmth spread, first coating her insides and loosening her stiff muscles. It radiated outward and thawed her frozen joints and skin. Yet no pain followed, only glorious relief.

She pushed against the floor and lifted her head, but her hair was tangled in the roots. Exhausted, she let her head flop back down.

The dragon snaked his neck toward her and set his eyes close to hers. "Try again. Jason and his father have very little time remaining."

Elyssa pushed, lifting her head a few inches, but her hair stayed entangled, too much to tear loose. With a surge of energy, she jerked against the flooring, but the roots wouldn't budge. "Cut my hair!" she shouted. "Or burn it with your breath! Just get me up off this floor!"

"I have no fire," the dragon said calmly, "but I can help." He lifted a foreleg and swiped a razor-sharp claw across her hair at the floor line. With the sudden release, she snapped upright and nearly toppled the other way.

Energy coursed through her body. Her muscles flexed. She leaped to her feet and scanned the room. "Where are they? What do I do?"

"First, I want you to know that my name is Alaph."

"Pleased to meet you." Elyssa cocked her head. "You look different now. Clearer. Brighter."

"For good reason. Look at your hands."

She lifted her hands. Her skin emanated a soft glow.

"Your face is glowing as well," Alaph said. "The light you see is your own."

"What happened? Did I die after all?"

"In a manner of speaking, but we can discuss that riddle later. For now, I will teach you how to use your gift, a gift you always had but now are able to use to its fullest."

With Deference following, Elyssa walked toward Jason's bed, keeping her footfalls soft on the roots. Just as Alaph had said, the roots, which he had called branches, led to humanlike trees, one standing behind each healing station.

When she stopped at the bedside, Deference joined her. "I call this tree Wisdom," Deference said, sparks from her mouth giving away her position. "Look at his face. Don't you think it looks wise?"

Elyssa let her gaze follow the trunk until she spotted a protruding knot, two recesses just above it, and a huge gall on each side. "I see a nose, ears, and eyes, but no mouth."

"Right. Most wise people I know don't say much, but they listen a lot."

"Good point." A branch from Wisdom protruded over Jason's bed. Like a human arm, the branch ended with an open hand, palm facing up, as if the tree reached out to ask for a trinket. She lifted to tiptoes and touched the palm with a fingertip. The bark absorbed her glow. Light filtered down and emerged at the back of the tree's hand, raining glittering sparks that fell to a sheet covering Jason's body.

Leaning over the bed, she set her palm on Jason's pale cheek. Her glow spread and coated his skin from chin to forehead. "Warm," she whispered. "High fever."

Deference nodded. "Infection?"

"Maybe."

With his mouth slightly open, Jason turned his head to the side and inhaled a gurgling breath. When he exhaled, a thin line of drool fell to the pillow, tinged with blood.

Elyssa cringed. "That can't be good."

"Probably bleeding into his lungs," Deference said. "In case you're wondering, my father was a doctor. He taught me a lot."

"Then I'm glad you're at my side. Keep telling me what you think." Elyssa pulled the sheet down to Jason's waist, exposing his undershirt-draped torso. Her pendant lay on his chest, the closed-hands side facing up.

Deference touched the pendant. "That might get in the way."

"I'll get it." Elyssa slid the chain over Jason's head and put it over her own, letting the pendant dangle. "Now for the shirt."

She pinched the shirt's hem at the side and lifted, peeling it from his skin slowly to keep the dried blood from pulling. As blood flaked away and rained to the bottom sheet, she peered at the wound. A bruise painted his skin purple and black from the bottom of his ribcage to just under his armpit, and a hole at the bruise's center revealed the jagged end of a bone, his broken rib. Blood dripped from the opening, slow but steady, as well as from a vertical gash that sliced across his ribs.

Deference pointed at a purple glow shining through Jason's skin over his pectoral muscle. "What's that?" she asked, pointing.

"A litmus finger. It's supposed to be a guide to finding a portal from our world to yours." Elyssa slowly lowered her hand to the wounds and set her palm over the bone. She closed her eyes and probed within. Two ribs had fractured. The other end of the protruding one was still attached to the rib cage, though barely. The second rib had been pushed inward, and the broken end scratched a lung, causing a quarter-inch tear. With every breath Jason took, the lung expanded and pressed against the bone. "I sense a pool of blood near a tear in his lung."

"That's what I was worried about," Deference said. "He can't survive for long in that condition."

"If not for this." Elyssa stood on tiptoes again and grasped the tree's hand as if greeting a friend. Her glow poured into the bark, sending veins of light toward the trunk. Seconds later, sparks rained from the tree hand's underside. Elyssa let go and cupped her hands under the glittering shower.

"Deference, do you have a bandage, a long, wide one I can use to bind Jason's ribs?"

"I'll see what I can find." Deference turned and ran across the roots.

When the sparks filled her hands, Elyssa poured them over Jason's wounds. Massaging gently with her fingers, she rubbed the energy into his skin while pushing some through the hole and the gash. He grimaced with every touch and groaned with every push.

Words flowed into her mind. "I'm sorry, Jason, but without pain there can be no healing. Without suffering there can be no renewal. Without sacrifice there can be no freedom. Seeds fall to the ground in every farmer's field, but unless they are buried and die, they never sprout to new life. Pain spawns growth. There is no other way."

As she continued the massage, her arms weakened, and dizziness swam through her head, but she continued scooping stray sparkles and gathering them over the wounds. The pendant glowed, growing hot enough to warm her skin through her shirt. The bone began to recede. Blood poured over her fingers. Jason's gurgles deepened.

Furrowing her brow, she infused passion into her voice. "Jason, hear me. I have told you many times that you are my warrior. You have rescued me from uncountable dangers, risking your life to save mine. I love you for that, of course, but I love you because of who you are. Even if you could never perform another heroic act, even if I had to care for you like this every day, I would still love you." Tears welled and began spilling to her cheeks. The pendant's glow brightened, and her strength continued to wane. "You're my hero, Jason Masters, because you never give up seeking to save the lost. Even in fields of thorns, you search for a rose. In darkness, you always find a light. And in the lowest level of a dungeon, in a cold cell forsaken by all, you found me in chains, in the midst of my own filth. Although you should have been repulsed at the sight of me, you looked upon me with eyes of love. And you set me free."

The flow of blood ebbed. The hole and gash began to close, and the bruise shrank. Breathing a sigh, she continued. "Do you know what else I learned, Jason? While the white dragon was teaching me how to use the healing tree, he told me I sprouted from a hybrid seed. As a Diviner, I have some Starlighter gifts. I am able to distribute Starlight's energy, which is what I am doing to you. As you absorb it, you will be healed, and your mind will be enabled to receive the wisdom of the ages. Alaph said that this wouldn't work on most people, only on those who have prepared themselves to receive it, those who long for light in the midst of darkness."

The hole sealed completely. The bruise shrank further, its color fading.

Elyssa lifted her hands—weak and feeble. Every spark had been absorbed, but it was likely enough. Her fingers dripping blood, she gazed at Jason's face. He breathed easily now, and color slowly returned to his cheeks.

She touched the pendant—still warm, though the glow had faded. She turned it to the side where two open hands had been carved and gazed at the escaping dove flying just above them. With tears flowing, she caressed the dove with a finger. "Freedom is the greatest gift of all."

Blood smeared the surface, but cleaning it would have to wait. It was time to go and care for another fallen warrior. As she turned, Deference arrived with a long stream of cloth trailing from her hand. "It took a long time," she said. "It's hard to carry things very far when you don't have a body."

"True." Elyssa laid a hand over Deference's dimming chest. "But you can do almost anything as long as you have a heart."

twelve

olding the map in one hand and a
flaming torch in the other, Randall
followed Miller's Creek as it wound
through a dense forest. Carrying a hefty backpack of
supplies and dressed in a heavy cloak, winter trousers,
two tunics, and thick boots, his march drew sweat from
his pores. Although autumn had come to Mesolantrum,
the air hadn't chilled enough to make this outfit comfortable. Promises of frigid winds on Dracon had prompted
a stealthy visit to Jason's home to grab extra clothing
for himself and Orion, and now a dose of frosty weather
would be a welcome blessing. Randall had also taken his
mother to Jason's commune, a safe refuge from the palace
conspirators.

Randall glanced at the map, hastily drawn by Marcelle
with a charcoal pencil that he kept in an inner-tunic pocket.
The portal lay at the center of a clearing just beyond the

boundary to the Forbidden Zone, but with the creek meandering close to several clearings, finding the right one near the midnight hour might be a challenge.

He marched on, reasonably unimpeded by foliage. Since Marcelle and a few others had been there not long ago, a narrow path cut a swath through the undergrowth, and recently hacked branches lay here and there. That helped. Maybe the path ended at the portal. Time would tell.

Still, finding the right clearing had its dangers. Marcelle said the portal should be open and that it would lead to a snow-blanketed forest. A person could walk through without any genetic key or crystalline peg, meaning he could stumble into Dracon without warning. Marcelle hadn't said that coming back to Major Four would be just as easy, so staying near the edge of each clearing made sense.

Randall imagined her marching next to him. Her experience would have been a boon, but staying behind to get the troops ready was more important. Since the army had no experience with dragons, they could benefit greatly from her confidence.

After squeezing between two bramble bushes, the path opened into a grassy circle. He drew the torch close to the map. This could be the one. Either way, it was time to signal the dragons.

Looking up at the sky, he waved the torch. Clouds veiled the moon and stars, a perfect night for getting two dragons from the dungeon to the outer limits of Mesolantrum without being seen. After some discussion, he and Marcelle had decided that it made more sense to keep the dragons' presence a secret. Not for fear for their

safety—who on Mesolantrum would attack a dragon?—
but because too many lives rode in the balance to risk
a panic. Marcelle's influence and the letter from Orion
should be enough to order the troops to the portal later.

Maybe.

He slid the backpack to the ground and waved the
torch again. The previous clearing, where the dragons
now hid, lay hundreds of feet back. No breeze passed
through the forest, and no sounds disturbed the silence.
With the circle of grass at least fifty feet wide, this clearing was big enough for them to land, but they would
have to be careful to stay near the clearing's boundary as
planned.

A loud crack sounded from above. Magnar crashed
through the branches at the edge of the clearing and flew
clumsily to the ground, dropping Orion as he leveled off
for a landing. While Arxad descended, Randall dashed to
Orion and helped him rise.

Orion brushed off his borrowed tunic and trousers,
both too large for his narrow frame. "Stupid beast! Why
are you so much clumsier than Arxad?"

Magnar stomped toward him, his head rearing back
like an adder ready to strike. "How dare you talk to me
that way, human! Now you will burn!"

"No!" Arxad beat his wings and shot between Orion
and Magnar. "Killing him is not wise."

"Why not? He has signed the letters. What further
need of him do we have?"

"You see?" Orion said, pointing at Magnar. "The dragons want nothing more than power. They plan to kill us
when they no longer need us." He brushed a lingering

twig from his shoulder. "That is exactly why I insulted him, to raise his ire. It was a test."

Randall glanced at his photo gun at one hip and his sword at the other. Either one would dispatch this sniveling liar and stop the bickering, but if Orion happened to be right, neither weapon would be enough against an extane-empowered dragon, and maybe two if Arxad decided to take Magnar's side. Maybe the right words would cool everyone down. "Orion, Magnar has been a slave master for longer than we've been alive. He's not used to humans insulting him. He just lost his temper. You saw Arxad flying to your defense. That should mean something, right?"

"Perhaps." Orion shook a finger at Magnar. "But we shouldn't turn our back on this one."

Arxad shoved Orion with a wing. "Do not take my protective ways as an excuse to be insolent. Since your signature is so powerful, you are still of value to us, so my protection might not be as benevolent as you imagine."

"Okay," Randall said, raising his voice, "I think we'd better get back to the task at hand." He held out the map. "According to this, it looks like we're in the right place, or at least pretty close. This clearing matches Marcelle's description."

All four turned toward the center of the grassy circle and stared, as if waiting for something to happen. Only a slight crackle from Randall's torch interrupted the eerie quiet. Moonlight broke through the cloud bank, illuminating a thin fog that crawled along the grass like a creeping ghost.

Randall stuffed the map into his trousers pocket and marched forward. Someone had to break the trance. "So do I just walk across the circle?"

"Wait!" Arxad called.

Randall halted. "What's wrong?"

Arxad took in a long draught of air, his tongue darting out and in. "I smell the Northlands' evergreens, so the portal is clearly open, but I sense something else, not an odor. More of a feeling, a familiar presence."

"Dragons can sense a presence?" Randall asked.

"Not usually. Because of certain duties I have as a priest, this is a presence only I would recognize. She has become an ally in some ways, though she is unpredictable."

"She?" Randall and Magnar said at the same time.

Arxad bobbed his head. "Perhaps it would be better to wait a moment."

The fog swept toward the center of the clearing. As it began a slow spin, it thickened and rose in a column. Streams of moonlight mixed into the misty cyclone, brightening and taking on the shape of a female human, though without facial details.

Magnar's ears flattened. "Could it be?"

Randall drew his sword and took a step closer. "Who is it?"

"No need for alarm," Arxad said. "She will not hurt you. Magnar, however, would do well to hide himself."

"I do not fear this apparition," Magnar growled. "You told me yourself that her power here is limited."

"Perhaps, but she knows this portal better than I do, and because you killed her, she will be less likely to help us if you are here."

Randall gave Arxad a quizzical look. *Killed her?*

Magnar grumbled something unintelligible, then added, "Very well. I will circle the area and return when she is gone. Then I will follow you through the portal." With a beat of his wings, he took off and faded into the darkness.

As soon as the breeze died away, Randall stepped closer to the spinning girl. Her rotations created a breeze of her own that wafted over his body. He shivered. "The Northlands air must really be cold to cut through what I'm wearing."

"It is not merely the air you feel," Arxad said. "You will see."

As the radiant ballerina continued, her toes drilled into the grass, drawing dirt into her vortex. Near the bottom, whiteness transformed into flesh tones. Two limbs and a pair of feet took shape. As the upwelling soil continued to churn, the particles seemed to stitch together a flowing white dress—a calf-length skirt, loose sleeves that reached just past her elbows, and a lacy neckline that lay across her collarbone. A cloak materialized, fanning out around her spinning body.

The dirt rose to her face and coated the shimmering fog with multicolored skin. Shining green eyes pierced the turbid mist, and as the particles settled a thin, alabaster face appeared. Finally, the spinning slowed, and the remaining dirt transformed into streaming red hair that draped her shoulders. When she stopped, her dress and cloak drew toward her body, accentuating her scant frame. She wobbled in place for a moment, then blinked at her audience.

"Witch," Orion whispered, barely audible.

Randall sheathed his sword and gave her a bow. "Greetings. My name is Randall."

"Yes, I know." She offered a graceful curtsy. "And my name is Cassabrie."

"Welcome to Mesolantrum."

"Thank you." Cassabrie walked toward him, tipping slightly.

Randall leaped forward and grabbed her forearm. "Let me help you." Cold shot through his body, tightening his muscles, but he managed to keep his hand from locking around her arm. As soon as she seemed stable, he let go and flexed his fingers, staring at her. Arxad said Magnar had killed her. Could it be true? He held the torch closer to Cassabrie's face. With her pale skin and gaunt cheeks, she certainly looked like a cadaver. But how could a dead girl speak and walk?

He drew the flame away, blinking as the memory of another corpse-like form resurrected. Marcelle had the same ghostly aspect and the same cold touch. What could it mean? Might she also be dead?

Cassabrie walked straight to Arxad and, with a grim countenance, addressed him in a formal tone. "I have news from Alaph."

"Then speak," Arxad said, giving her a nod. "His servant is listening."

"We are to go through the portal at once and close it behind us. When the troops arrive, I will open it again."

Arxad kept his stare focused on her. "I assume you are already aware of the consequences of such an action."

She nodded. "We must leave your brother behind."

"Leave him behind?" Randall shook his head. "We can't do that. Once the troops are gone, he'll take over the region, maybe the entire planet."

Orion pointed at Randall. "You see? I told you they were up to mischief. They planned all along to eliminate our defenses so they could rule our world. Sending Magnar away was merely posturing, and this creature's story is a fable, a way to get us to accept Magnar's abandonment here."

"Is that so?" Randall eyed Cassabrie. She seemed to delay her materialization until Magnar had left, as if knowing Arxad would suggest his departure. Everything this girl said and did seemed perfectly planned. Yet, Orion's logic still had a flaw. "If I were Cassabrie and wanted to secretly keep Magnar here, I wouldn't have told anyone ahead of time. I would have led everyone to the portal and then locked him out. Telling us her wishes beforehand proves her trustworthiness."

"I appreciate the vote of confidence," Cassabrie said, "but regardless of motive or trustworthiness, we cannot allow Magnar into Starlight. His presence in the Northlands will have disastrous consequences."

"I understand," Arxad said, nodding. "Is there a way he can return safely to the Southlands?"

"You could use the crystal for the mesa portal from the Starlight side." Cassabrie angled her head and looked at Arxad's underbelly. "Where is it? I thought it might be wedged between your scales somewhere."

"I have it." Randall touched his pocket. "I'll give it to Arxad when he needs it."

BrYaN DaViS

"How will Magnar and I coordinate our meeting there?" Arxad asked. "I will not be able to communicate with him."

"We can work on that later. For now, Alaph wishes for Magnar to stay here until he has served his purpose in this world." Cassabrie raised a hand. "The Creator as my witness, I received this command directly from his highest prophet."

"Another ploy," Orion said. "Perhaps it is Arxad she is manipulating. If he is an honest dragon, as you all insist, he is probably more easily duped than most of his species. An appeal to a heavenly authority is a common scheme when trying to influence a person of integrity."

Randall pointed at him. "As you should know. I've seen *you* do it enough times."

"Don't be a fool, boy!" Orion's growl matched his contorted face. "Whether or not you trust me is irrelevant. Do you trust the fate of our world to a dragon and a ... a dead girl? How can she be anything but a sorceress?"

A cold draft blew from Cassabrie's direction. "I am not a sorceress. I am a Starlighter."

"A Starlighter? Clearly a pretty label to disguise the beast within. Whatever she is, she cannot be holy."

Arxad looked up at the sky. "We have no time to argue. Magnar will soon wonder why we are delaying."

"How do you lock the portal?" Randall asked.

"In the same way the portal in the mine is locked." Cassabrie pointed at the ground and moved her finger as if drawing in the air. "There is a line of crystalline pegs. If you pull one out, the portal closes, and only one is loose enough to dislodge."

Randall touched his pocket again, feeling the peg Arxad had given him. "Let me pull it out. I want control of the portal."

"You already have the mesa portal crystal," Arxad said, his ears pinned back. "Do you demand control of every access? Your arrogance and distrust threatens our alliance."

Randall eyed the dragon. He was right. If the humans wouldn't trust the dragons, why should the dragons trust the humans? Sighing, he withdrew the mesa peg. "You take this one. You'll need it anyway to let Magnar back into Starlight. Just let me control who comes and goes here. Marcelle won't want a dragon deciding."

Cassabrie looked at Arxad. "It's a reasonable compromise, don't you think?"

"I agree. Put it between my scales, then let us depart."

Cassabrie took the peg and wedged it over the vulnerable spot on Arxad's underbelly. Once in place, she whispered into Arxad's ear. He replied, also whispering.

Randall eyed their facial expressions. They displayed no hint of stealth. Maybe Cassabrie was simply asking if the peg was comfortable.

As soon as the conversation ended, she hurried to the center of the clearing. "When you see me disappear, then walk through."

Randall nodded. "Proceed."

"What?" Orion squeaked. "Are you out of your—"

Randall slapped a hand over Orion's mouth, leaned close, and whispered, "If you don't shut your mouth, I am going to knock you out cold. Just trust me. I'll leave a message for Marcelle. She'll know what to do. Agreed?"

Orion's eyes darted around for a moment. Finally, he nodded.

"Then you'll be quiet?"

He nodded again.

Randall slowly released his grip. "Arxad, if you will escort Orion, I will go through last."

"Very well. You had better hurry. Magnar is not a patient dragon."

Now standing at the portal site, Cassabrie spread out her arms and closed her eyes. She lifted to tiptoes and began a slow rotation. Her aura returned, enveloping her again in radiant mist. Scales appeared on her forearms and lower legs, as if her skin had lost every drop of moisture. As her spin picked up speed, the scales peeled off and joined in the foggy cyclone. A new layer of scales formed, and it, too, flaked away. The process repeated until her entire body joined the flow. Soon, the mist scattered, and Cassabrie was gone.

Stretching out a wing, Arxad guided Orion toward the spot. Orion glanced once at Randall but said nothing as he and the dragon passed through the portal and disappeared.

Randall jammed the base of the torch into the ground, whipped out the pencil and the map, and smoothed out the parchment's wrinkles over his thigh. On the blank side, he wrote, *Marcelle! Beware! Magnar stayed behind.*

After rolling the map into a tube, he withdrew his sword, dug a hole near the clearing's boundary with the tip, and planted the map vertically, leaving half the parchment showing. Sighing, he whispered, "That'll have to do. I hope Magnar doesn't see it."

Sword in hand, he marched toward the portal. He forced his eyes wide open. The torch's flame flickered against the dark trees on the opposite side of the clearing. As he entered the cloud of gritty mist, the trees brightened and transformed into snow-laden evergreens.

"Human! Stop!"

Randall halted and turned. Magnar stormed down from the sky and landed in a run near the edge of the clearing. "It seems that I have arrived at precisely the right moment," Magnar said. "Where is Cassabrie?"

Randall nodded toward the Northlands forest. "She went in there." Now standing with one foot on Dracon and the other on his home planet, he glanced back and forth. Arxad and Orion stood at least thirty paces away, both gazing into the distance. Almost within reach, a line of crystalline pegs protruded from the snow-covered ground, but which one should he grab? If Magnar followed, he wouldn't have time to guess wrong and try again.

"Since the portal is open," Magnar said, "I assume she has helped us sufficiently. I will go through now."

The dragon, his head down as if anticipating a low clearance, stalked toward Randall.

Randall held up a hand. "Wait!"

"Wait for what?" Magnar stopped and swung his head from side to side. "Is there danger?"

Randall pointed at the torch several paces behind Magnar. "If that tips over, it could start a fire."

Magnar turned. "I will extinguish it."

Sucking in a breath, Randall leaped toward the pegs. He grasped one and pulled. It wouldn't budge. He slid to his right and grabbed another. It, too, stayed planted. He looked up. Magnar charged toward him, flames spewing from both nostrils.

Randall dove to the left, slid past the first peg, and snatched the next one. It jerked out, but his momentum sent him rolling sideways down a slope. He slammed into a tree, his back striking first. With pain streaking through his limbs, he blinked at the portal site. Clouds veiled the sun, and snow filtered gently through the trees, but no dragon plowed through the portal.

He opened his hand and looked at the peg—the key to returning whenever he wished. But how would he know when to let Marcelle and the troops in?

"Are you all right?"

Randall looked from side to side. There was no mistaking Cassabrie's voice. "Where are you?"

"I am kneeling in front of you. While on Starlight, I am but a spirit, but I can become visible if I move."

Randall searched the whiteness, but no ghostly girl appeared. He held out the crystal. "When should we open it for Marcelle?"

"Someone will have to stay here and return to your world from time to time. That's the only way to check, but I doubt that the army will be ready for quite a while. I think you would be more valuable if you were to travel south with Jason and Elyssa."

"Jason and Elyssa are here?"

"Yes." A hand appeared, its palm open. "For now, you can give the crystal to me. I have need of it, and my need is urgent. Arxad has told me what I must do with it. Trust me. You will not be lacking a crystal when you need it."

Randall searched the sea of white again. This time, a pair of green eyes shone, like two emeralds floating on a blank canvas. Her hand drew closer until it touched his cheek. Warmth flowed into his skin and coursed through his body, drawing new sweat from his pores.

"You can trust me, Randall. I am a Starlighter. What reasons could you possibly have for doubting the words I speak?"

A sense of dizziness flowed with the warmth. How could someone so gentle, so loving, so overflowing with peace possibly be untrustworthy? As her green eyes filled his vision, he whispered, "I can trust you."

"Lower the crystal into my hand." A shimmer appeared just above his waist, an appendage with four wispy fingers.

He set the peg gently on her palm. It sank for a moment, but with a spark-filled snap, she grasped it and slid it into an invisible pocket. "Wait here a moment."

In a stream of flashing moves, she vanished behind a tree, then reappeared in front of him. "Now, follow me." As she turned and floated away above the snow, her entire body became visible.

Grimacing, Randall climbed to his feet and watched her glowing outline glide across the ground. Lifting his legs high with each step, he tromped through the calf-deep snow. Cassabrie stopped behind Arxad and Orion and slowly faded, and Randall joined them at the edge of a slope that led into a valley. Far away, a range of mountains bordered the valley on the other side, their peaks reaching into the clouds. A castle lay nestled at the base of the tallest mountain. Mostly white except for three red turrets that almost reached the clouds, it appeared to be much larger than the governor's palace back home, but at this distance it seemed impossible to tell for certain.

"Jason is there," Cassabrie said. "A frozen river winds through the valley, making it treacherous to cross, and the castle has a hidden moat that swallows anyone traveling on foot, so Arxad will have to fly you there."

Randall glanced at Orion. It was good that Cassabrie hadn't mentioned Elyssa. Orion hadn't yet proven his claim that he had stopped his murderous hunt for Diviners. Calling Cassabrie a sorceress wasn't exactly a sign that his obsessions had changed.

"Okay," Randall said as he fastened his cloak's clasp. "I'm ready for a ride."

Arxad turned toward Cassabrie. "What are you going to do?"

"If I may, I would like to ride with you. After you drop these men off at the castle, could you transport me to the Southlands?"

"I trust that this is another command from on high."

"It is. From this point on, I cannot delay at any step. All of humanity depends on my haste."

꧁꧂

Xenith sat atop the hideaway stone, her head just below the treetops as she scanned the forest floor. Ever since Mother dropped off the two boys she had rescued from the mill and left again to take injured humans to the Northlands, all had been quiet through the night. Now dawn approached. Still, quiet or not, this wilderness was known to be home to many beasts that could harm humans, so this perch seemed to be a good place to watch for them.

Solace, Basil, and Oliver huddled at the base of the stone immediately below her. A cool wind had descended from the mountains, so they found warmth in closeness. Xenith smiled. Sometimes humans were so humorous. Even those who fought during the hottest days would forget their quarrels and sit close together during the coldest nights. It seemed that a desire for survival brought together the bitterest of enemies. Fortunately, these children were accustomed to enduring long periods of time without food, and exposure had also been a way of life. Yet, if Mother did not return soon, she would have to search for sustenance or at least hide them in the shelter so she could leave and learn what was delaying Mother.

A whistle sounded. Xenith jerked toward it. Could it have been the wind? Not likely. It was too sharp, too perfect.

A light shone in the midst of the trees, perhaps fifty human paces away from the stone. With a flap of her wings, Xenith descended and landed on the ground, facing the light. She kept her wings spread, shielding the younglings. If whatever lurked saw her first, it might decide a meal of human flesh was not worth the trouble of battling a dragon.

The light grew stronger. Soon a human shape emerged into the clearing, a female who seemed to be wrapped in a glow. As she walked, the trees she passed in front of stayed visible, as if she had no substance, and a cloak fanned out from her dress as if blown by an imperceptible wind. Completely white except for a sparkle of green in her eyes, she had to be one of the phantoms Father had talked about, the spirits of the dead who roamed the Northlands castle.

"Who are you?" Xenith asked. "Why are you here?"

The human stopped. "I am Cassabrie, a Starlighter from years gone by. It's good to see you, Xenith."

"How do you know me?"

"I know Arxad and Fellina very well. Surely your parents have spoken of me."

"They have spoken of phantoms from the Northlands such as yourself, but I do not remember them mentioning your name."

Cassabrie made a tsking sound. "Pity. Your father and I have discussed you a number of times. He has spoken with pride about your intelligence and your flight speed. He said you completed the hunter's regimen in less than an hour, a record for a dragon your age."

"This is true. I set a new standard." Xenith flattened her ears. "You did not answer my second question. Why are you here?"

Cassabrie glided a few steps closer. "To ask for your help in this time of great danger. Your parents are too busy with other vital matters, and my task is urgent. If I don't accomplish it, all of Starlight will likely fall under the dark wing of Taushin."

Xenith softened her tone. "What do you want me to do?"

"I need fast transport to the Northlands and then to your village."

"To the Northlands?" Xenith asked. "Have you not come from the Northlands?"

"I have, but my transport from there required haste, and now I must return to collect something I left behind. Since I cannot carry an object that far, I want to pick up a human rider who can carry it for me. She is a young female who should not be a burden to you." Cassabrie nodded toward the children behind Xenith. "She is not much bigger than that girl."

Xenith looked back at the younglings, who watched with wide eyes. "I suffered a bruised wing yesterday, but it is healing well, so I am sure I would be able to carry her. Yet I must stay here to protect these three until my mother returns."

"What if they could be placed under the care of another human? Would that allow you to go?"

Xenith shook her head. "Mother was quite clear. I must stay until she returns."

Cassabrie glided closer again. Her glow spread over Xenith's face. "Oh, but Xenith, her intent was to ensure the safety of these humans, not to keep you here. If you find an alternative way to protect them, you would be obeying the spirit of her command, and you would be free to help me save our world. Don't you think your mother would commend an act of sacrificial heroism? Just think what she would say if she learned that you turned down an opportunity to save Starlight simply because you had to strictly adhere to the letter of her command. Of course, she would never punish you for your rigid discipline, but she would also secretly realize that you lacked the maturity to make such an adult decision. Suppose something happened to her that prevented her from ever returning?

Would you stay here like a mindless drone until you all perished?"

A sudden sense of dizziness swam in Xenith's brain. "These thoughts had crossed my mind, and finding an alternative refuge is an option worth considering, but only if you are telling the truth. I learned long ago that humans will lie to obtain what they desire."

"I can prove that there is a refuge for these young humans as well as a vital reason for my journey."

"Without leaving this place?"

Cassabrie nodded. "Without leaving this place."

"Then bring forth your proof. This should be interesting."

Still no more than a shining spirit, Cassabrie raised a glowing hood over her head, spread out her arms, and gave her cloak a spin. "Not many days ago, a brave young warrior released the cattle children from the horrific cattle camp and took them into the wilderness."

"Yes, Elyssa told me about her adventure with Wallace. She has been worried—"

"Shhh." Cassabrie held a finger to her lips. "It is vital that you allow me to tell the tale without interruption, or it will not have the desired effect."

Xenith nodded. "Very well. I apologize."

"As you mentioned, Wallace and Elyssa worked together to guide the cattle children across the open mesa region, where they might easily be seen by patrolling dragons, and into the wilderness forest."

While Cassabrie spoke, Elyssa and Wallace appeared, pushing aside foliage as they entered the clearing. Yet, they, like Cassabrie, were phantoms. A host of semitransparent children trailed them, most half naked and bone thin. When the humans had all gathered, they began constructing several objects out of hewn branches and vines. As they worked, they faded in and out, and the objects grew rapidly, as if time sped beyond the normal rate.

"Elyssa trusted Wallace so much," Cassabrie continued, "she left the forty-one children in his care. She understood that a great journey lay in wait for her, and Wallace could handle this task. Not long after Elyssa departed, Wallace began searching for a different helper, an adult human by the name of Frederick who was also caring for young escapees from the cattle camp."

A building appeared. Constructed out of roughly cut logs cemented by thick mortar, it looked to be large enough to house ten to fifteen humans, depending on their size and how closely together they slept. An adult human stood near one corner of the building while several children watched a fire that blazed under the carcass of a small animal.

With a wave of her cloak, Cassabrie swept the scene away, leaving behind an empty clearing, the moss-covered stone, and three huddled, shivering human younglings.

Xenith blinked. The children seemed far away, as if she were looking at them through the wrong end of Father's sky scope. The clearing wobbled. Cassabrie's glow brightened as she spoke again, now with a voice that echoed throughout the forest. "If you will accept my request, I will make sure these little ones find this refuge. They will be warm and well-fed, cared for by humans. Here, they will be cold and hungry, and, although you are a noble and good dragon, they will not be as comfortable with you as they would be with their own kind."

Xenith shook her head hard. That helped clear her vision, at least a little bit. "The images you conjured are comforting, but I cannot be sure they reflect reality. I have heard that Zena was once able to do the same thing, and she convinced people of lies with her dark arts."

"Zena was a counterfeit Starlighter. A real Starlighter obtains power from the way the Creator fashioned her. For me, telling vivid tales is as natural as breathing. A counterfeit calls upon the forces of evil to mimic this gift, and it is a harsh, primitive copy that is motivated by the desires of fraudulent forces, not the desires of the Creator." Cassabrie pushed back her hood and walked closer. With each step, the green in her eyes brightened. "Arxad and Fellina will not come here soon. I know this to be true, because Arxad brought me to the village, and he and your mother are returning to the Northlands.

"I walked the rest of the way here. I plod along on foot. You fly faster than the eagles. I am but a breath of air, a spark of light that is blown about by the wind. You are the daughter of Arxad and Fellina, strong and capable, one of the few noble dragons remaining on Starlight."

Cassabrie stood so close, her radiance filled Xenith's vision. Her face shone with ivory light embedded with two brilliant emeralds. When her lips moved, her words came forth riding on sparkling jewels. "Xenith, without you, all could be lost. I cannot do this great work by myself. I beg you to help me."

Xenith stared at the lovely visage. Father had talked about heavenly angels, beings who could take the form of humans or dragons—radiant, resplendent, beautiful beyond description. Maybe Cassabrie was an angel. How could anyone object to fulfilling such a request?

"Very well," Xenith said, lowering her head close to the ground. "I will do as you ask."

thirteen

*J*ason opened his eyes. Covered with a linen
sheet, he lay on his back atop a bed, not
his own bed, yet strangely familiar. Above,
a dull gray backdrop spread across his field of vision,
making the room's size impossible to gauge. Light came
from somewhere, steady but dim, enough to give shape to
his surroundings but too little to make anything clear. An
object floated over his face, dark and vague, maybe close
enough to touch.

As he reached, a sharp pain stabbed his side. He let
his arm drop to the mattress. Whatever that thing was, it
would stay a mystery for now.

Moving slowly, he lifted the sheet. A bandage wrapped
his midsection underneath his inner shirt. Memories
flowed into his mind—the grinding mill, his father, battling the dragon, breaking his ribs. Koren.

Jason felt for his pouch. Gone! Had Koren taken it? Had she figured out what it was for?

Then a soft light emanated from somewhere close by, growing brighter. A human female form appeared far away, an aura surrounding her, like one of the servant girls in the Northlands castle.

Ah. Everything was coming together now. He lay in the tree room. The object above his head was an extended hand from one of the healing trees. But where was Father? Had he survived transport to his own healing tree? Maybe this girl would know.

Gathering his breath, he whispered, "Have you seen my father?"

"Jason!" The girl rushed toward him. "You're awake!"

Her voice blew the fog away. As her lovely, strangely radiant face filled his vision, he smiled. "Elyssa? Is that you?"

"Yes, Jason!" She grabbed his hand and clutched it tightly. "How are you feeling?"

"Not great, but I think I'll live." He tried to sit up. "Where is my father?"

"Don't worry. He's fine." She gently pushed him down. "He was pretty badly injured, but he's up and around now."

"Good." Jason breathed a sigh and let his body relax again.

"We were worried about you. You've been unconscious for a long time. Are you hungry?"

"Not really. Thirsty, though."

"The trauma probably spoiled your appetite." She stooped, then rose again with a mug in her hands. "Drink this. Deference left it here for when you woke up. It should quench your thirst and give you an energy boost. I had some, and it filled me right up."

As she helped Jason rise to a sitting position, he hooked his fingers around the mug's handle and inhaled the vapors. "Thanks. It smells good."

While he took a long drink, Elyssa reached up and touched the healing tree's extended hand. "These trees are amazing. With their help, I was able to use a stardrop to repair your ribs."

Jason searched his mind. He had dreamed about her rubbing sparks of light into his body. Did it really happen? After tipping the mug back and draining the last drop, he set it down at his side. "I remember. It hurt a lot, but most of the pain is gone now."

"That's good." Looking at her fingers, she touched the hem of his sheet, a shy smile appearing as she glanced at him without lifting her head. "Do you remember what I said while I was working on you?"

He thought for a moment. As the memory returned, Elyssa's gentle voice sent a jumble of phrases through his mind. *You're my hero, Jason Masters ... I love you because of who you are ... You set me free.*

As warmth spread across his cheeks, Jason gave her a weak smile. "I think so. I remember some words that felt really good."

Elyssa slid her hand into Jason's. "I meant every word."

A thin layer of radiance spread from her skin to his. Earlier he had assumed the strange lighting had distorted her appearance, but now the radiance seemed to emanate from within her. He withdrew his hand and touched the back of hers. "What's making you glow?"

Smiling, she studied her palm. "Remember the stardrops?"

"How could I forget? Those balls nearly burned holes through my hands."

"I swallowed one."

"What? How could you do that? Swallowing one killed Petra."

"I know." She laid a hand on her stomach and grimaced. "It burned so badly, I thought I was going to die, but the white dragon said I might survive, and it was my only hope of saving you and your father, so I took the chance."

He stared at her. "You took the chance? For my father ... for me?"

She nodded, her lips trembling. "How could I not?"

Jason looked into her softly glowing eyes. She had so much courage, so much love. She was amazing! He grasped her hand again and kissed her knuckles. "Thank you," he said, letting his gaze linger on her radiant face. "Thank you for my father, too."

"You're very welcome, Jason Masters." She smiled, her eyes now glistening.

"So ..." He released her hand. "How did you survive swallowing the stardrop?"

"I asked Alaph about that, but I'm not sure I understand his answer. He said I didn't survive, that I died and was brought back to life because I have some of the gifts of a Starlighter. Uriel Blackstone thinks Petra can also be resurrected. Her body has been preserved, and we're planning to test the theory. That's why I came down here. I hoped you'd be healthy enough to see the test."

"Sure, but what about the other girls? Deference and Resolute? Can they be brought back to life, too?"

Elyssa shook her head sadly. "They will have to await the Creator's great resurrection. Magnar and his friends ate their bodies."

"Ate their bodies!" As a wave of nausea churned Jason's stomach, he swallowed, forcing down bile. He spoke in a choked whisper. "Even Arxad?"

"No! He is not such a monster!" Elyssa covered her mouth with her fingers. "Sorry. That came out more forcefully than I intended. Alaph told me the stardrop might make me more passionate about things. Anyway, according to Alaph, Arxad never participated in the banquets. He has spoken out against them many times."

"Spoken," Jason muttered. "One dragon talked while other dragons crunched the bones of children."

"That's exactly what your father said."

Jason sat up again, this time more slowly, and threw the sheets toward his feet. Although his trousers were still dirty, his boots and undershirt were clean except for a blood smear over the bandage. "Where is my father?"

"He's helping Randall guard Governor Orion at the castle entrance."

"Orion is here? How?"

"Long story, but he doesn't know *I'm* here, so I'm staying out of sight for a while. You'll see your father soon. I promise. But I'd like you to come with me for now."

Jason pushed his legs over the side of the bed and, with Elyssa holding his arm, eased his weight to his feet.

The roots sagged, but only a little. A spasm tightened the muscles in his ribcage, but they soon relaxed.

"Are you okay?" she asked, still clutching his arm. "Can you walk?"

He looked into her compassion-filled eyes. "With you at my side, I'll be fine."

Smiling, Elyssa let go and gave him a light punch on the arm. "Now you're a charmer. That's not like you."

"I mean it. You risked your life to save mine. I'm not letting you out of my sight."

"Good! 'Cause you're stuck with me!" She wrapped her arms around him and pressed her cheek against his. "We're all together again—you, me, Randall, and your father. We're safe now."

"I remember seeing Koren when you and I kind of crossed swords. Have you heard anything from her lately?"

Elyssa drew back. "Oh, yes. Koren." Laughing nervously, she wiped a tear from her eye. "I guess I forgot about her."

Jason cocked his head. Why would she forget? "So ... any word?"

"Not since then, but I haven't asked anyone. She didn't come with us." She turned her head toward the doorway. "I suppose Alaph would know, but after my short talk with him, he didn't stay around. He makes himself scarce."

"Maybe we can find him again."

"Maybe so." Elyssa took Jason's hand and led him across the roots. "I have so much to tell you. Randall says there's an open portal here in the Northlands, and they used Orion to send for troops from Mesolantrum and a few nearby regions. When they arrive, we can go to the wilderness, find Wallace and the cattle children, and bring them here. Who knows? We might even find Frederick."

"And Adrian," Jason added.

"Right. And Adrian. This planet is filled with members of the Masters family. And that reminds me. Randall also spoke to your mother and told her you made it safely to Dracon, but he couldn't tell her everything, because the last time he saw you, you were in the clutches of a dragon. But for now she thinks you're safe."

"That's a relief. I wish we could get word to her that my father is safe, too."

As they walked along the left side of the corridor leading to the castle's main entrance, Elyssa slowed her pace and ran her fingers across a mural on the wall, a white dragon in flight. "It's around here somewhere."

Jason looked at the wall on the opposite side of the corridor. Another mural featured a black dragon, also in flight. It seemed to stare directly at him with shining blue eyes. "Is there a hidden door?"

"Something like that. Alaph said swallowing the star-drop gave me the ability to open it."

Her fingers tapped lightly on a colorful mural, each fingertip touching in turn. The corridor's ambient light, along with Elyssa's aura, provided enough illumination to see a few feet above her head, dimming to blackness as the wall reached toward an indiscernible ceiling. As Elyssa touched the white dragon, each tap of her finger raised a tiny white spark.

A blue spark jumped from the wall near the tip of the dragon's wing. "Here it is." Her fingers then tapped

several points around the first, each one raising a different colored spark. "It's like a code, and it changes every
time. The key is to find where the sequence starts, and
then I can sense the other touch points. The servants
here have no problem, because they don't have physical
bodies that veil their perceptions."

Finally, a spark as black as coal sizzled under Elyssa's
touch. It adhered to the wall and spread across the mural,
painting the white dragon in darker and darker shades.
Soon, the entire dragon's body had turned black, including a down-stroking wing that nearly reached the floor.

Elyssa lifted her foot and stepped into the wing, now a
hole in the wall. "Come on. It won't stay open long." She
walked through the hole and disappeared.

Jason followed, bracing himself on an intact portion of
the wall as he stepped through. With the Exodus chamber and the healing trees, the castle had already proven
itself to be a house of mysteries, but each new revelation
seemed more amazing than the previous one.

Inside, a narrow corridor led deep into the recesses of
the castle. About twenty feet ahead, a cylindrical capsule
with a semitransparent shell stood vertically, partially
obstructing the path. On Jason and Elyssa's side of the
capsule, a head-high rectangular opening allowed entry,
and a similar opening on the opposite side provided an
exit for anyone wanting to continue through the corridor.

Elyssa walked into the capsule and stood with her back
against the side and her arms lifted above her head. "Step
in here with me. There's not much room. Deference had
to take us up one at a time, but I think we can fit."

"Up?" Jason stepped across the corridor's marble tiles, touching the plaster walls on each side for balance. When he entered the capsule, he had to press close to Elyssa to fit. The pressure made his ribs ache horribly. Still, she smelled nice, a hint of lavender rising from her clean skin and hair.

"Tight squeeze," she said, smiling at him. "But it won't last long."

"Good," he grunted. "Not that I mind being close to you, but—"

"Cut the apologies. We're soldiers getting ready for war." She pointed her palms upward. The room levitated and began to rise, slowly but steadily.

Jason tightened his muscles. Would the wonders of this castle never end?

The corridor disappeared, replaced by open sky and the snow-covered landscape of the Northlands. A reddish tint coated the entire view, making the blue sky appear violet and the snow slightly pink.

When the cylinder stopped, a circular chamber appeared beyond the capsule's rear door. Tables and workbenches sat in various places on the floor's wood planks. An assortment of unidentifiable devices rested on the benches, and a sheet covered a lumpy object on one of the tables.

Uriel Blackstone stood at the side of a workbench at the far end, perhaps thirty paces away. With a quill in hand, he dipped the point into an inkwell and jotted something down on one of several parchments.

"Let's go!" Elyssa called as she hopped out and reached for Jason's hand.

Jason took her hand and stepped off the capsule's floor. With a *whoosh*, the hovering capsule fell through a circular hole. As it descended, it pulsed with light, dimming as the distance grew.

Still holding his hand, Elyssa helped Jason walk to the workbench. "We're here, Mr. Blackstone."

"Excellent." Uriel dropped his quill and held up a thin chain with a dangling pendant. "Now we can continue our tests."

Jason glanced down at his chest. Elyssa's chain and pendant were gone. "Is that Elyssa's?"

"It is, indeed." Uriel marched to the sheet and slid it gently off, revealing Petra lying on her back. "If it works, we will soon have a living, breathing Petra with us."

Jason walked slowly toward the table, barely able to breathe. Petra's body looked exactly as it had before, except that her hair was now clean and brushed. Her chest stayed motionless, and every muscle appeared to be limp. White manacles wrapped around her wrists, so cold they emanated frosty air that brushed his skin.

Another whoosh sounded. The hovering capsule reappeared, and a pair of female forms stepped into the room, radiant outlines that pulsed in and out of visibility as they moved and paused.

"Petra and Deference," Jason said. "It's getting easier to recognize the spirits around here."

As the two girls glided toward them, Uriel pointed at the manacles. "These are keeping her body preserved. I will remove them as soon as Elyssa is ready to revive her." He draped the chain over Elyssa's head and let it fall to her neck. "Remember to probe for the stardrop first."

Elyssa nodded. "I will."

"What will that do?" Jason asked. "What's so special about the pendant?"

"Do you remember when you slept against a tree shortly after the great storm?" Uriel asked.

"I remember."

"While you slept, I took the time to study the pendant. It sparked a memory from long ago, but my mind was still awash in fear and dread. Once I came here, the old sizzle returned. That pendant was carved from manna wood. Do you know what people in our world use it for?"

"We chew the bark to relieve the effects of extane. It slows metabolism."

"Correct, but the metabolism reducer is also effective as a sedative. If you burn it, inhaling the fumes will relax you, perhaps even put you to sleep. Back in my day, it was used to bring comfort to someone in great pain."

"Okay," Jason said. "That makes sense. Go on."

Uriel nodded at Elyssa. "If you would be so kind, please read it for him."

Elyssa lifted the pendant and set the edge close to her eyes. "The letters are tiny." She squinted, reading out loud while turning the pendant. "The halves are cleaved. Life has triumphed over death."

"What does that mean?" Jason asked.

"It's a dedication to someone who died," Elyssa said. "My mother gave the pendant to me. It was a gift from Marcelle, who carved it herself. When she was about fifteen years old, she watched the widow Halstead's execution, and it hit her hard. After everyone but the executioner was gone, she asked him for the stake the widow was tied to. She sliced out a section and carved the design and the inscription. The message that husband and wife would be together again gave her solace."

"Solace," Jason whispered.

Elyssa dropped the pendant to her chest. "Did you say something?"

"Just thinking out loud." He refocused on her. "Why would she give something so important to your mother?"

"When Orion started accusing me of being a Diviner, my mother went through a lot of turmoil, so Marcelle gave it to her, thinking it would bring her comfort."

"Did it?"

She shook her head. "Just the opposite. You see, the widow Halstead was a Diviner, so every time Mother looked at the pendant, she imagined me burning at the stake. She was going to give it back or throw it away, but I asked for it. Since you and I were both there when Orion had the widow burned at the stake, I thought the pendant might protect us. Kind of a silly, childish thing, but I believed it."

"Not really childish." Jason gazed at the pendant as it dangled in front of Elyssa's red vest. "I remember being there with you. We were both scared, especially when Orion personally lit the wood. The look on his face gave me nightmares."

"But I'll wager that he didn't gather the wood." Uriel raised a finger. "I know a man who was an executioner, a man named Porter. He once told me his predecessor added green wood to the pyre to make it burn more slowly and cause more suffering. Porter altered that practice and substituted manna wood for the stake and the kindling. It burns quickly and eases the victim's pain. I assume that became the common practice and continued through the widow Halstead's day."

"Probably," Jason said. "The wood did burn quickly."

"Our theory," Uriel continued, "is untested, but a good one, I think. Elyssa reported that while she was healing you, the pendant began to glow and grew warm to the touch. Perhaps it absorbed her metabolic energy and transferred it to you. My hope is that she can do the same for Petra."

"Energy to heal is one thing, but raising the dead?" Jason shook his head. "That's asking a lot from a piece of manna bark."

Elyssa lifted the pendant again. "It's not the bark. It's the Creator. He uses the bark to absorb energy from me. If I can seal the internal wounds, it could work."

"I suppose it's worth a try," Jason said, "unless it weakens you too much."

"I'm willing to take that risk." Elyssa reached out her hand. "Come, Petra. I'm ready."

A radiant outline of another hand appeared and clutched Elyssa's. Petra's spirit glided up to the top of the table and settled over her body. As she sank into her motionless shell, she slowly disappeared.

Deference jumped up and sat on the corner of the table. "If you don't mind, please let me know what you see inside her."

"Of course," Elyssa said. "I need your medical expertise."

Uriel touched one of the white manacles. "My concern is that Petra's body might deteriorate rapidly when I take these off, so if she doesn't respond, we must end the test immediately."

Elyssa nodded. "I understand."

Uriel squeezed one of the manacles, and a fastener under Petra's wrist popped open. After he pulled it off, he did the same to the other. "Now, Elyssa," he said, stepping back, "if you will proceed."

Standing with her waist pressed against the edge of the table, Elyssa slid her hand across Petra's abdomen, her fingers touching her shirt with a gentle caress. Her glow left a trail of dim radiance that faded as she moved.

Closing her eyes, she dipped her head. "The stardrop is embedded in her stomach lining. Light is flowing from it and up into her esophagus." Her hand glided from one spot to another. "I sense no perforations and no blood."

"She's been moved around a lot," Deference said, "so blood might have drained from her abdomen. It also could have clotted."

"That makes sense." Elyssa shifted her hand to Petra's sternum. "Her heart is motionless, as we expected. It looks like a normal heart, at least from pictures I've seen."

Deference slid closer, adding her aura's glow to Elyssa's. "Do you see any scalding? If the stardrop burns, it could have sealed her entire insides."

Elyssa shook her head. "The lining seems the same as Jason's, moist and smooth everywhere."

"Something must have killed her. If not bleeding or scalding, then what?"

"I don't know." Elyssa opened her eyes and looked at Deference. "I'm not a Starlighter. I can't recall history and watch it happen."

Jason stepped close to the table. "Elyssa, you have Starlighter gifts. You said so yourself."

"Not all of them. I'm not a storyteller."

"While we were walking to the dragon village, you said the story in the book came to life for you."

"Yes, but that was in the presence of a stardrop and that book I got in the Basilica. I could never replicate that."

Jason pointed at Petra's abdomen. "There's a stardrop in there."

"But no book. I think I would need some kind of historical record."

"Everything that happened is stored in her brain," Deference said. "It's better than a book."

"Maybe." A skeptical frown turned Elyssa's lips. "But how could her brain hold any memories? It's dead."

Deference touched Petra's head, setting it aglow. "Her spirit is inside her body. The memories are in there somewhere."

Closing her eyes again, Elyssa moved her hand back to Petra's stomach. "I'll follow the stardrop's energy and see what I can find." Her fingers glided up Petra's midsection, across her throat, and over her face until they rested on her forehead. "The light surrounds her brain, like a bath of radiance."

As Elyssa's pendant took on a reddish blush, something hot stung Jason's chest. He laid a hand over the spot where the litmus finger rested under his skin. It hadn't throbbed like this in a long time. What might it mean? A reminder that he had a piece of a Starlighter dwelling within? Maybe the infusion of stardrop crystals into his bloodstream had somehow stimulated it.

Elyssa's brow lifted. "I found something. I'm seeing lots of images, and I hear whispered voices, but they're coming so fast. They won't stop long enough for me to figure out what's going on."

Jason looked at Elyssa's glowing hand and imagined the rapid scenes and voices traveling from the point of contact up to her mind. It was like the whisperers that streamed from the star chamber and passed him by, leaving fractured messages he couldn't piece together. If Koren and Cassabrie pulled these messages out of the air and created visible tales with them, they could probably do the same thing with these memories.

"I have an idea," Jason said.

Elyssa kept her eyes closed. "What?"

He slid his hand into hers and pulled his shirt down at the collar. "Let's see what the Starlighter can show you now." The patch of skin over the litmus finger glowed, pulsing in time with the piercing stings. Still holding Elyssa's hand, he leaned over Petra. The light washed over Elyssa's fingers and Petra's forehead.

A new furrow etched Elyssa's brow. "The images are slowing down, and the voices aren't so quiet."

"Good." Jason stretched his collar further. The litmus finger stung worse than ever. "Let us know what you see."

"I see Koren and a dragon, a mean one. It looks like the room where they're keeping Cassabrie." Her eyelids quivered but stayed closed. "Yes. Yes, it is that room. I see her floating. The stardrop is on the floor. A hand reached out and grabbed it."

"I think you're seeing memories from physical vision," Deference said. "If you want to see what happened inside her body, maybe you should look for other input."

Elyssa moved her hand across Petra's scalp, combing through her hair with her fingers. "No, nothing there.... Not here either.... Ah! I might have something. I'm connected to some kind of recording. It's ... it's so strange. I feel like ... like ..." She moved her hand to Petra's mouth and let it glide down the outside of her throat. "Something weird is happening to me."

"What?" Jason asked. "Can you describe it?"

Elyssa gasped. "It burns! It burns so badly!" She slid her hand down Petra's chest. "Oh! Oh, help me!" Her own chest heaved. The pendant shone like Solarus, fiery orange. Lifting her head, she let out a wild scream.

"Elyssa!" Jason compressed her hand. "Are you all right? Should you break the connection?"

Her eyes clenching shut, she shook her head hard. Then, panting, she whispered, "Too hot. It's too hot. I cannot stay in this oven."

Like a rising mist, Petra's spirit lifted from her lifeless body, her face mimicking Elyssa's pain-streaked expression.

"The fire burns!" Elyssa shouted. "Oh, it burns! I must leave!"

"No!" Jason reached for Petra's spirit, but his hand passed right through. "You have to stay! Crawl back into your body. You have to stay there!"

As Petra sank back in, Elyssa panted. "I'm inside. I feel so hot, so very hot!"

Deference touched Petra's arm. "Her body is getting warmer."

"She has the energy now," Uriel said, "but she's not breathing."

"We have to start her heart." Deference laid her hands on Petra's chest, one on top of the other. "Jason, put your hands here and push in time with your own heartbeat."

Jason copied Deference's pose. "Like this?"

"Yes. Not too hard."

"How hard is not too hard?"

"Just don't break her rib cage."

Jason pushed, compressing Petra's chest and imagining his heartbeat as he repeated the action again and again, but with his own heart thumping so rapidly, might his rhythm be too fast?

"Help me!" Elyssa screamed. "Something is grabbing me! It's dragging me into a dark place! I'm being swallowed!"

Jason pulled back. "Is she all right?"

"That's better," Elyssa said. "I'm coming back out now."

"No!" Uriel pushed Jason's hands back in place. "Keep it up! You almost had her! Elyssa isn't telling the history; she is telling us what Petra feels now."

Jason compressed her chest again, trying to maintain the same rhythm. He closed his eyes and called out, "Tell me when to stop!"

"No!" Elyssa cried out. "It's sucking me back in!"

Uriel pumped his fist in time with Jason's pushes. "Don't listen to her! She's almost there!"

Petra's head jerked to the side. Her arms flailed. Her chest heaved, sucking in a deep breath.

"Now, Jason!" Uriel shouted. "Let her go!"

fourteen

ason leaped back. Petra's eyes shot open. She inhaled through her nose and looked around. For a moment, her eyes stayed wide, the muscles in her face tense, but as her breathing slowed, she relaxed. Looking at Elyssa, she lifted a hand and set it gently on hers.

Elyssa's face turned pale. Her legs buckled, and she collapsed.

"Elyssa!" Jason dropped to his knees and cradled her. "Can you hear me?"

Deference jumped from the table and joined him. "She's breathing."

"Energy transfer," Uriel said. "Her metabolic rate is likely below a level that can support consciousness, but since the drain has stopped, it's reasonable to hope she will stabilize."

Jason touched the pendant, still hot and glowing. This piece of manna wood had literally absorbed Elyssa's energy. Uriel was probably right about her recovery, but how long would it take?

Petra rose to a sitting position, then slid her body to the edge of the table.

"Wait," Uriel said as he grasped her arm. "Are you sure you can get up?"

She nodded and, with his help, lowered herself to the floor. She sat next to Jason and laid a hand on Elyssa's cheek, looking at Jason with forlorn eyes, as if Elyssa's condition might be her fault.

"It's okay," Jason said. "You're alive, and she'll be okay. It's worth it."

Uriel clapped his hands and rubbed them together. "Well, then, it seems that the stardrop did not harm Petra's body. It merely scorched the spiritual plane so thoroughly that Petra's spirit could not stay. She literally leaped out of the oven her body had become."

Jason looked into Petra's glistening eyes. They reflected a blend of joy and sadness. "That's probably what the Reflections Crystal does. When I was chained to it, it seemed like I was trying to jump out of my body, like being barefoot on hot sand."

"Yet the stardrop remains, so it is only the initial entry that purges the body. After that, it seems that the spirit is able to dwell there without a problem."

Petra grasped Jason's hand and clasped it in both of hers. She nodded at the clasp, her eyes wide. A weak glow surrounded her skin, making it shimmer.

"That's strange," Deference said. "Her skin looks like Elyssa's now."

"What?" Elyssa opened her eyes. "Did someone call me?"

Jason smiled and took her hand. "We were just talking about Petra and her new radiance."

"I remember falling. Did you catch me?"

"Not quite. You pretty much crumpled." Jason pushed her hair back from her forehead. "Do you want to try to stand?"

She smiled. "In a minute. I'm as dizzy as a spinning top."

Uriel crouched between Jason and Petra. "We have learned two important facts. First, although a stardrop is fatal, a person is able to be resurrected if his or her spirit stays in proximity. Second, Elyssa has the power to bring about that resurrection using the manna pendant. The process drains her, but she seems to be recovering quickly."

"Let's see how quickly." Elyssa reached out to Uriel. "Will you please help me up, kind sir?"

Uriel pulled Elyssa to her feet, then helped Jason to his.

Petra grasped Jason's sleeve and gestured with her fingers.

"She's using sign language." Jason looked into her eyes. "We don't understand. Can you write?"

Petra nodded.

"We have quill and parchment right over there," Uriel said, pointing at the workbench.

Jason led Petra to the bench, dipped the quill into the ink, and handed it to her. She wrote on a blank parchment in a neat, dark script, re-inking the quill with every few strokes.

As the words formed, Jason read them out loud. "I want to go back to the Southlands. I saw Koren fly away in Exodus, and I want to help her. I saw Taushin, the black dragon, take a long pole from the castle and fly away with it. It had a sharp point, so I think it is a weapon."

"It sounds like a spear." Jason tapped on the parchment. "Can you draw a picture?"

Again, Petra nodded. First, she drew long, delicate curves until she formed a circle, Then, after drawing a girl inside the circle, she made a man throwing a spear in her direction.

Deference drew close to the parchment. Her gesturing hand stayed visible as she spoke. "I told her this story. A long time ago, a man threw a spear at Exodus. The spear is stored down near the star chamber." As she paused, the hand disappeared. "Or it *was* stored down there."

Petra nodded and wrote more words, this time scratching them down quickly.

"I think Taushin took it," Jason read. "He is blind, but somehow he found it without Koren's eyes."

Deference glided back from the workbench. "That's no ordinary spear. Arxad told me some secrets about it."

Uriel crossed his arms over his chest. "You might as well tell us everything you know."

With her body fading in and out of visibility, Deference gestured again with her hands. "The tip is made of a metal that we no longer have in our world and one that you never had in yours. Arxad called it an alloy, and it was able to penetrate the star. Not only that, it had a tube attached near the point that was filled with a substance Arxad called gunpowder. It was used in powerful weapons hundreds of years ago. If it burns, it can destroy almost anything in a huge fireball."

"But it didn't destroy Exodus," Jason said. "Why not?"

"For some reason, the tube didn't burn. It's still attached to the spear."

"Why?" Elyssa asked. "It sounds too dangerous to leave lying around."

Shrugging, Deference said, "We consider it to be pretty secure that far under the castle. Arxad called the spear an antiquity, a reminder of the evils of the past. It's a mystery how a blind dragon could find it among all the other antiquities in the storage room. Not only that, it's a long way down those stairs, and it's too dangerous to fly blind."

Elyssa touched Petra's shoulder. "You said Koren wasn't there, but was anyone else with the dragon to guide him?"

Petra shook her head.

"At least no one she could see," Uriel said. "There are quite a number of invisible people here."

Deference appeared for a moment, a hurt expression on her face. "Mr. Blackstone, I'm sure the existence of invisible people is frightening, but you don't know them as well as I do. No one here would lead Taushin down the stairs."

Jason imagined an invisible spirit helping the black dragon find his way down the stairs. When he made the journey himself, he had two guides, Deference in front and Cassabrie inside. Between Deference's gentle manner and Cassabrie's comforting words, the downward part had been relatively easy. And Deference's denial that any castle resident would help Taushin rang true, but what about Cassabrie? Where was she now? Did anyone really know whose side she was on?

Breathing a sigh, he focused on the spot where Deference was seconds ago. "Can you check the storage room? I'm not saying Petra's wrong about seeing a spear, but maybe the one she saw isn't the one that pierced Exodus."

"I will," Deference said. "Now that Petra is alive, the rest of you should go to the main floor. Edison and Randall will want to hear the news."

Elyssa and Deference used the cylindrical capsule to transport Jason, Uriel, and Petra to the lower floor, where Deference opened the corridor wall with a wave of her hand. Apparently security wasn't as tight going through in the opposite direction.

When they arrived in the corridor, Deference led them to a table that abutted a wall at the side. At least a dozen mugs sat in a row near the table's edge. "Good," she said, gesturing toward the mugs. "Resolute has seen to your nourishment. Take your fill. We call it secret soup, because we have no way to taste it, but the king says it will supply your bodies for quite some time."

She gestured toward the main entrance. "Will someone go with me? That way I can hunt for the spear while someone else finds the others and guides them here."

Uriel picked up one of the mugs and bowed. "I will be glad to accompany you."

"Good. If they're not in the foyer, you can help me search for them outside."

Uriel and Deference walked down the corridor side by side. Like a glowing cape, her radiance trailed her body, taking most of the light with her.

While Jason, Elyssa, and Petra drank the warm, bland soup, a dim, ambient glow and Elyssa's faint aura provided enough light to see the white dragon mural, but the black dragon on the other side was no more than a vague shadow.

Petra walked to the opposite wall and laid a hand on the black dragon's wing.

"Is that the black dragon you saw?" Elyssa asked.

Petra nodded.

"Probably Taushin," Jason said, letting the word rest in the air for a moment. "Fellina called him a dark pretender."

"And he hatched from a black egg," Elyssa added. "Everything about him spells darkness. If he really has that spear, Koren's probably in big trouble."

While they waited, still drinking from the mugs, Petra taught Jason and Elyssa the basics of her sign language, including the letters of the alphabet. As she repeated them several times, Jason studied the finger positions. They were simple, but it would take him much longer than a few minutes to memorize them. Elyssa, on the other hand, picked them up quickly. While they practiced, Elyssa told Jason everything Randall had told her about his time in Mesolantrum, including Cassabrie's strange behavior at the portal site.

Soon, Uriel, Randall, Orion, and Jason's father joined them. As they approached, Orion's stare locked on Elyssa. She turned away and slid close to Jason, linking index fingers with him. "I'm not sure I'm ready to go into battle with him," she whispered.

"I know what you mean. Let's just stay calm and see what happens."

Jason let go of Elyssa's finger and embraced his father and Randall in turn. Elyssa gave both a hug as well, but when she came to Orion, she backed away and turned her head.

Giving Elyssa only a brief glance, Orion extended his hand toward Jason. "It's good to see you again. I hope there are no hard feelings about my remark at the invocation."

"If you mean the remark about sultry witches looking for a callow catch ..." Jason shook his head. "I haven't thought about it since that night."

Orion lowered his brow. "Yes ... I see."

As they exchanged stories, the newcomers drank their fill from the mugs. Elyssa said nothing, though she occasionally cast a suspicious glance Orion's way.

When the last story ended, Jason looked around at each tired and worried face. "We have a lot to do, but I have some questions. First, where is Arxad?"

Randall pointed toward the entry with his thumb. "He went to find Fellina, because we'll need more than one dragon to get us to the Southlands. He didn't say when he'd be back."

"Okay. How about Cassabrie? Where is she now?"

"No one has seen her since we came through the portal," Uriel said. "We discussed this earlier, and we have conflicting opinions concerning what her motivations might be."

Orion crossed his arms over his chest. "You know my opinion. She's a devil. She'll be our undoing if we don't watch out."

Randall snorted. "You think every unusual female is a devil."

"Mind your tongue, boy," Orion said, pointing at Randall with a rigid finger. "When a girl spins into existence in a swirl of dirt and feels as cold as a winter wind, you can't tell me there is no evil afoot. I learned the hard way."

"The hard way?" Jason asked. "Care to tell us?"

Orion turned toward the table and fingered one of the mugs. "I don't see why that's necessary. My past is inconsequential."

"Inconsequential?" Elyssa grabbed his sleeve and jerked him around. "Listen, after all the years of torturing my family with your rabid Diviner hunts, if you think I'm going to just forget about it and pretend nothing's wrong while I risk my life alongside you, then you're more demented than I thought."

His brow knitting, Orion glared at her, but after a short stare down, he let out a sigh. "Very well." He leaned back against the table, his hands gripping the edge. "When I was a boy of thirteen, I was lying in bed late at night and heard a bird that sang so beautifully I had to see it. I followed its song deep into the forest, and there I met a young woman. Although the dim moonlight prevented me from seeing her face clearly, I could tell that her skin was as pale as a cadaver's. Yet to me she was the most alluring creature I had ever seen — long hair that caressed the shoulders of a white gown and eyes that sparkled green in the moonlight. Like Cassabrie, she radiated cold, and I stood petrified as if frozen to the ground, so she sang a song that calmed my fears, trilling with a voice every bit as beautiful as that of the songbird. When she finished, she told me that she had led me into the forest to tell me something. She said that my parents and two sisters had been killed in a fire."

Orion's voice began to quaver. "I ran home as quickly as I could and found our house engulfed in flames. I threw bucket after bucket of water from our horse trough, but it wasn't enough. When our closest neighbor arrived, he broke through the flames and carried out my two sisters. They were dead, burned beyond recognition. Later, after the fire dwindled, my neighbor found a lantern with an insignia that was foreign to Mesolantrum. I concluded that the woman of the forest used the lantern to set the fire and called me away because she knew I was awake, and she didn't want me to douse the fire and rescue my family. I swore that day that I would find every sorceress in the land, whether Diviner or witch, and make them suffer in the flames that their kind inflicted on my family."

He finished with a sigh and picked up one of the mugs. Swirling the contents, he stared at it in silence.

Jason studied his posture. He seemed relieved to shed the burden of the horrible event. But was it all an act? Jason scanned the faces in the corridor. Uriel and Petra had glistening eyes, while those who knew Orion, especially Elyssa, displayed furrowed brows, though Randall's seemed more pensive than skeptical.

"So," Jason said, "do you think that girl was Cassabrie or someone else?"

Orion shook his head. "I can't be sure. I can pinpoint obvious similarities, but I was so young, so enthralled, I'm not sure the details are clear."

Jason nodded. If Orion were still fanatical, he would have answered with certainty and accused Cassabrie without question.

"You told me you ended your crusade," Randall said. "You invited Elyssa to come home without any further persecution. What changed?"

Orion glanced at Elyssa. "My perspective changed. I saw Marcelle quite some time before she captured me in the forest. I knew then she had become one of the same sort of devils I had seen that night in the forest long ago. Elyssa is not that type. She has strange abilities, to be sure, but she never exhibited an icy, corpse-like body. I decided it was foolish to chase and investigate every abnormal girl and instead focus on obvious witches like Marcelle and Cassabrie."

Elyssa linked index fingers with Jason again and whispered, "Are you believing this?"

"Not really. Don't worry. I won't let him hurt you."

She tightened her grip on his finger and said nothing more.

"Okay," Jason said, again addressing everyone, "so Cassabrie is a mystery. We'll just have to let her do what she will."

"It's not that simple." Randall shifted his weight from foot to foot. "She asked me to give her the crystal peg that opens the portal."

Jason's eyebrows shot up. "And you gave it to her?"

"Yeah. As much as I hate to say it, I think I'm starting to agree with Governor Orion. She kind of charmed me out of it. You know, the Starlighter gift."

Orion gave a firm nod but, to his credit, kept silent.

Edison clasped Randall's shoulder. "Don't worry. Cassabrie wants the troops to come, so she will likely return it. If not, we'll have to look for her. Someone has to open the portal for the troops."

"Arxad might have one," Elyssa said.

Jason looked at her. "What makes you say that?"

"If Arxad went to Major Four with Magnar, they must have gone through the Southlands portal. I seriously doubt that they would leave it open for anyone to pass through, so he must have taken the crystal with him."

Randall touched his stomach. "Arxad has it. Cassabrie wedged it between his scales."

Petra pulled on Jason's sleeve and spelled out a message.

Jason squinted. "Dragon coming?"

She nodded.

They turned toward the entry. Deep in the shadowed corridor, the form of a dragon took shape. Seconds later, Arxad wheeled around and called out, "Meet us at the foyer. We cannot land here."

As he flew back into the shadows, the breeze from his wings buffeted their bodies. Everyone jogged toward the entry. Jason began lagging, his side still aching, and Petra did as well, her body apparently not yet accustomed to exertion.

Elyssa dropped back with them. As the trio slowed to a quick walk, the group ahead also decreased their pace, but the distance between them kept Orion out of earshot.

"Maybe Arxad knows where Cassabrie is," Elyssa said.

"True, but we shouldn't ask him in front of Orion."

"Right. I hope Orion doesn't ask."

By the time they arrived at the foyer, Arxad and Fellina had already gathered the others—Orion, Uriel, Edison, and Randall—in a semicircle. Jason, Elyssa, and Petra joined the line at the far end from Orion.

Fellina's wings drooped low, and she let her body sag to the ground. She drew in deep, rapid breaths, but her eyes were clear as she stared at the humans, seemingly evaluating each one.

Arxad spoke in a low, even tone, without a hint of exhaustion. "It appears that events are coming to a climax in my village. Koren has flown there inside Exodus. Fortunately, she is no longer under Taushin's control, so she will likely try to use her influence over the humans to create a rebellion or perhaps convince the dragons to release them. In either case, I believe she will have to make many attempts before she is successful, so I think we can rest here for the time being. Since we flew much of the night, we should probably get some sleep as soon as possible."

"There's a problem," Jason said, raising his hand. "We think Taushin—"

Deference ran in from the stairway room, calling, "It's gone!"

"Correction," Jason continued. "We *know* Taushin has the spear that punctured Exodus. I assume he intends to use it in the same way."

Arxad's facial features sagged. "This is most troubling. We cannot rest. We have to leave as soon as possible."

"Right," Jason said. "Koren might be in big trouble, so—"

"Koren as well as every man, woman, and child on Starlight. Even if we leave now, it will likely be well past dawn by the time we arrive. I have had enough pheterone to allow me to travel without weariness, but Fellina does not have the same advantage, so we will have to go at a pace she can endure."

Fellina rose to her haunches. "For the sake of Star-light, I will do what I must."

Arxad smiled at her. "My mate is a most excellent trea-sure, but I think she downplays her fatigue." He turned back to the others. "I am not sure how we will pass the barrier wall guards with humans accompanying us, so we will have to face that obstacle when the time arrives. For now, we must decide who will be coming with us and who will be staying here."

Edison raised his hand. "I suggest that I stay here to conduct the army on the march southward. I have been there before, so I can find my way again."

"If you march quickly and rest only when necessary," Arxad said, "you will make it to the barrier wall in one day. Since your army is unacquainted with fighting drag-ons, it would be unwise to assume that you will be able to pass the wall easily. You will need whatever weapons your world can provide."

"I trust Marcelle will prepare them adequately."

"But how will we open the portal?" Randall asked. "Cassabrie took the crystal that controls it."

Arxad's brow lifted. "She did?"

Randall nodded. "She used her … uh … charms, I guess you might say."

"Interesting." Arxad looked at Fellina. She reflected his worried expression. "Opening the portal for the army is of no concern. I still have the crystal you returned to me."

Jason glanced at Arxad's underbelly. Indeed, it seemed that something sparkled in the midst of his scales.

"If they are interchangeable," Elyssa said, "why didn't Magnar demand that you bring one to him a long time ago?"

"Because he does not know they are interchangeable. And, in reality, they are not. A center peg is interchangeable with another center peg, but not with any of the others. Long ago, I brought one from the end of the Northlands portal line, but since the Southlands portal required a center peg, it did not work."

"So you deceived Magnar," Orion said. "You played the rebel's role instead of obeying your king."

Arxad swung his head and cast an angry stare at Orion. "To keep him out of your world, *Governor*. If you are displeased with my efforts to keep your world safe, then continue to question my actions. You might learn more about me than you really want to know."

Orion turned his head, his face flushed. "Very well. I grant your point."

Randall let his shoulders sag. "Well, at least we can open the portal. That's a relief."

"It is a relief regarding that problem," Arxad said, "but I am quite concerned about Cassabrie's activities. She is unpredictable. I provided her transport to the Southlands, but she did not have the crystal. In the spirit state, humans cannot handle objects for more than a few seconds."

"What could she use the crystal for if she had it?" Jason asked. "To open the portal at the mine?"

"Not likely. There is another lock the crystal can open, and if she knows about it, I am sure she will use it. Yet her movements puzzle me. Why would she obtain the crystal and then leave the Northlands without it? She would need a physical transport to get it to the Southlands."

Jason spread out his arms. "There's no one else here who can help her. We don't even know where it is."

"We have to assume that she believes she has a way. Otherwise, she would not have asked Randall for it."

"Arxad," Fellina said. "She is very aggressive and bold. Her courage knows no bounds. She will try to use the crystal on that lock."

Arxad brought his head close to Fellina's and looked at her eye to eye. "If she succeeds, everything will change."

"For the better," Fellina said, "or for the worse?"

"That depends on Cassabrie."

Fellina nodded. "And Taushin."

"True. If Taushin finds her, all could be lost."

"It is all well and good," Orion said, "for you good dragons to conduct a discussion in a covert manner. This is your world. But it seems to me that we humans have a large stake in these matters. Perhaps you would like to share your insights with us."

Arxad gave him another fiery stare. "No, I would not. As you indicated, this is our world. You are on Starlight, not Darksphere, and you will have to be satisfied with not being in control."

"Is that so?" Orion straightened his tunic. "We shall see about that, won't we?"

Arxad growled, sounding like an angry mountain bear. "If you think your army will be able to conquer Starlight, then you will be deeply disappointed if you try. They are coming to dispose of Taushin, and that is all. You have no idea what kind of power I can unleash on humans, so I advise you to erase all thoughts of taking control of this land. At this time, for the sake of your people, I suggest that you listen and obey."

Orion took a step back, but a cocksure expression remained on his face. "I surrender, Arxad. I await your orders."

Arxad shifted his head and scanned one end of the semicircle to the other. "Jason and Randall will ride on me to my village. Fellina will carry Elyssa. Edison and Orion will set up a shelter near the portal and await their army. I will give those two the crystal, take them to the portal, and then return for Jason and Randall. Deference, you will also ride with Fellina. If the worst happens, we will need your medical expertise. Everyone must be aware that there exists a high risk that everyone who travels to the Southlands could die. Do you all understand?"

Each traveler nodded. "I'm ready," Randall said. "I thought I was going to die several times on my way here. I'm already living on borrowed time."

Jason clasped Randall's shoulder. "We all decided before coming here that we would risk death, Arxad, but we appreciate the warning."

Petra clapped her hands, then spelled out *me* with her fingers.

As Arxad looked at Petra, a sympathetic smile crossed his face. "I am sure there is an interesting story that explains your presence here, but no one has taken the time to deliver it to me."

She again began to form words, but Arxad covered her hands with his wing. "Tell me later. For now, I want you to stay here. Resolute will see to your comfort."

Petra frowned and let her shoulders slump. She spelled out words so fast, Jason couldn't keep up.

"What did she say?" he asked Elyssa in a whisper.

"Something like, 'People with tongues often speak about courage and then won't let others live it.'"

"I feel bad for her," Jason said. "She seems like a brave girl."

"Yes, but she's better off here. Maybe she can help prepare supplies for your father."

Jason lifted his brow. "Would *you* be satisfied with that job?"

"No, but there isn't much we can do about it."

"I will gather sufficient weaponry for you," Arxad said. "Then when everyone has put on warm clothing, we will leave."

Petra signed, "I will get cloaks." Pumping her arms, she ran into the corridor leading to the healing chamber, angling toward the right. After about fifty paces, she grasped imperceptible handholds on the wall, scrambled up, and disappeared through a hole in the ceiling.

"Arxad," Fellina said, "Petra is small. I think I can carry her."

"You are already exhausted. We cannot risk any extra weight."

"But you are not tired; maybe you could take three."

"Simply flying with her is not the issue. It was easy to get past the barrier wall guardians without passengers, but it will not be so easy when we go south. If we have to employ avoidance tactics, any rider will be in danger. I will not risk Petra's life just to satisfy her desire to contribute."

Uriel cleared his throat. "Not that I have any death wish, but I also have a desire to contribute, and you did not mention a role for me."

"If Taushin uses that spear," Arxad said, "I will need you to work on a solution to the problem he will create. I have stored some research books deep under this castle, and I need you to study them right away. It will not take long for me to return with the most important volumes."

Uriel gave him a firm nod. "I look forward to the challenge."

"And what of Cassabrie?" Fellina asked.

"When we arrive at the village," Arxad said, "you should drop off Elyssa and Deference and check to see if Cassabrie is trying to do what we suspect. If so, you can ask her about her plans and motivations."

Fellina bobbed her head. "I understand."

As Arxad took wing and headed toward the stairway to the star chamber, Jason drew close to Elyssa and whispered, "What's all this talk about Cassabrie?"

"I was hoping you knew. The dragons are being very secretive."

"That's what worries me. Arxad says we're all going to face death, and he won't let us in on some of the risks. That's not exactly comforting."

Elyssa turned to him, linked her ring finger with his, and looked him in the eye. "Will you make a covenant with me?"

"A covenant?" He glanced at their fingers. Strange. She had switched from the usual index finger link. "What kind of covenant?"

"If I die ..." Her whispered voice began to crack. "If I die, don't leave me here on Starlight. Take my body home to my mother."

"Elyssa, I'm not going to let you d—"

"Promise me." Her lips quivered as she spoke. "Just promise."

Jason gazed into her tear-filled eyes. She was so sincere, so passionate. Of course he wouldn't leave her behind. "Okay, I promise, but—"

"No *but*s, Jason." Her voice steadied. "Let's be realistic. Death is a real possibility. We can't keep facing it and cheating it forever. Between you and me and Randall and Tibalt and Uriel, the odds are one of us isn't going to make it."

Jason nodded. "And my father."

"Right. So let's all promise each other that no one will be left behind. We'll do everything we can to take anyone's body home."

Jason gave their finger clasp a brief squeeze. "I'll spread the word."

"And one more thing." She leaned so close, her breath warmed his cheek. "And this one is just between you and me."

"Okay." As her eyes locked on his, he swallowed. "I'm ready."

"If I die, and you get married, will you wear my pendant at your wedding?"

He glanced down. The pendant dangled at her chest, the side with the clasped hands visible. "Uh … I suppose I could do that. Why?"

"Because when I was six years old, I vowed to be with you on your wedding day. If I can't walk down the aisle with you, I want to adorn you with love in the only way I'll have left." She lifted their link, kissed his finger, and walked away, her hands covering her face.

Jason took a step toward her, but a firm grip held him back. "Let her weep alone, son. There is nothing you can say."

Jason turned toward his father. "You heard what she said?"

"Every word. And she saw me listening. A covenant needs a witness, you know."

Jason looked at Elyssa again. She stood at the castle's entryway and stared out at the snowy landscape. "I didn't know she felt that way. I mean, we're good friends, but …" He couldn't find the words to continue.

"There's something about facing death that brings feelings to the surface. As a soldier getting ready to march into a dangerous battle, I have heard many men confessing their sins and making solemn oaths."

"You've told me that before. They make their vows because of fear, and if they survive, they don't live up to their promises."

"With rare exceptions." His father nodded toward Elyssa. "I'm pretty sure she is a rare exception. Her mother once told me Elyssa has been writing letters to you. She hoped to give them to you on your wedding night."

Dryness parched Jason's tongue. Elyssa was skipping steps even way back then, planning to marry someone who didn't have any idea he was supposed to be involved. "I never knew. Why didn't she—"

"Because it wasn't the time, and because she wants you to take the first step when you both are of age."

Tears welling in his eyes, Jason nodded. Elyssa's signature statement rang in his mind. *Lead the way, warrior.* Now it made more sense than ever.

His father tightened his hold on Jason's shoulder. "For now, I advise you not to say anything else about it. I think she didn't want to go to the grave without ever giving you a hint about the way she feels, but it would only further embarrass her if you bring it up again now. If you are of the same mind, you would have to wait a few years anyway. Just be the gallant warrior the Creator has called you to be, and all will be well."

"I understand." Jason looked at the finger she had kissed, the finger that might one day wear a ring, which would signify another covenant, the ultimate covenant between two people. Would he make that covenant with

Elyssa? Maybe. But for now he would honor the one he had just made, and he would do everything in his power to make sure it was unnecessary. If someone had to die to rescue the slaves, it would be Jason Masters.

fifteen

Xenith flew into the castle's entryway and landed on the wooden floor, scratching the surface as she ran to a stop. Not daring to take a breath, she looked around the spacious chamber. Father had mentioned this place, but only in the vaguest terms. He usually finished with "You would have to see it to understand." He was right. From the murals to the marble columns to the reflective floor in the corridor, the castle of the white dragon was magnificent.

"You seem frightened," Cassabrie said from her back.

"Awestruck." As Xenith took in the splendor, a breathy sound reached her ears, gentle sighs blended with quiet weeping. "Do you hear that?"

"I do." Cassabrie appeared in front of her as she pointed toward a dark corner of the room where a girl sat in a chair with her back to them. "Come. She is the one we're looking for. Starlight has told me her tale."

As Cassabrie hurried toward the girl, Xenith beat her wings to keep from shuffling across the wood. The quieter the better. Although the entry was wide open, the great white dragon might be angry at an unannounced visit.

Cassabrie glided to the other side of the chair and knelt in front of the girl. "Hello, Petra."

Xenith extended her neck, curling it so she could see Petra's face. Dressed in a heavy cloak open at the collar and thick trousers, she sat with slumped shoulders. Tear tracks stained her cheeks, and her eyes glistened.

"Why are you so sad?" Cassabrie asked.

Petra signed with her fingers, a language Xenith knew well from several months of having the kind girl in her parents' service. "They left me behind," her fingers said. "They think I can't do anything, just because I can't speak. But I can help."

Xenith opened her mouth to translate, but Cassabrie replied too quickly.

"Of course you can help. That's why I came here. I will take you to the Southlands, where you can help me do something so important it might very well save all of Starlight."

Petra's fingers spelled out her words more slowly this time. "Why would an angel want to use someone like me? Aren't you powerful enough to do it yourself?"

Smiling, Cassabrie glanced at Xenith as she replied. "As many times as I have visited you at night and told you otherwise, are you still convinced that I am an angel?"

Petra nodded. "I think I have figured it out," her fingers said. "I saw other angels here, so I think I died, and now I'm in heaven. I was just a ghost, and they put me back in my body. I don't understand that part, but I do understand that Arxad and the others left me, because they are waiting for the white dragon to tell me that I'm dead and can't leave heaven."

Cassabrie caressed Petra's arm. "If I take you to the Southlands, will you be convinced that you're not dead?"

Nodding again, Petra spelled out, "But not that you're not an angel."

"I was once called to be an angel. We'll see if I'll have another chance." Cassabrie laid a hand on Petra's chest. "To make things easier for both of us, I am going to enter your body. You will carry me with you, and I will be able to speak to you without anyone else hearing me, and you can answer with your hands. That will allow us to be silent as we converse. Do you understand?"

Petra nodded once more.

"Then will you grant me permission to enter? The process will be uncomfortable at first, but the feeling won't last long."

Petra spelled out, "Go ahead. I will always trust you."

Cassabrie glanced at Xenith again, the green in her ghostly eyes dimming. "I will do anything to keep that trust." Her glowing hand shifted to Petra's collar. Then, her body stretched out and poured in underneath Petra's tunic.

Petra stiffened. Her eyes grew wide. Her body trembled, as if assaulted by a bitter wind.

"Are you all right?" Xenith asked.

Shaking her head, Petra stood and pulled her cloak close to her body as she moaned softly.

"Maybe I can help." Xenith exhaled through mouth and nostrils. Spreading out her arms, Petra closed her eyes and let the warm air flow over her body. Her shivering eased. Then, her eyes opened wide again, and she stepped out of Xenith's jets. Sweat beaded on her forehead. She opened her cloak and flapped the material, drawing in cooler air. Finally, after nearly a minute, she settled and relaxed.

"Is she inside you?" Xenith asked.

Petra nodded and spelled out, "Now Cassabrie wants me to get the crystal and something else, some kind of box. She hid the crystal near the portal." She scurried to a dim corner of the room and picked up a black box, small enough to carry in her palm. "And here is the box."

Xenith stared. How could one human dwell inside another human? "Is Cassabrie speaking to your mind?"

Nodding again, Petra tucked the box under her arm and spoke with her fingers more quickly than ever. "She said we should hurry. The men you saw at the portal won't stay asleep for long."

"Then let us go." Xenith lowered herself to her belly. "Climb up and hold on tightly. I hope I can give you a smooth ride, but if the wall guardians try to stop me, hang on for dear life."

⇒⋅⇐

Koren guided Exodus southward past the barrier wall, her focus set on the Zodiac's twelve spires. They shone like gold against the purple backdrop, a sure sign that dawn approached. Trisarian hung low in the western sky, its lower arc brushing the treetops in the distance.

It had been a long, lonely night floating above the flower-speckled meadow, and the moons had been her only company. When Trisarian appeared at midnight on the eastern horizon, the great moon began its long journey across the entire sky, chasing the three lesser moons that sank out of sight soon after Trisarian rose. Dozens of shooting stars painted the heavenly canvas with white and yellow arcs, while nettle birds flew here and there, glowing green until the energy they had absorbed during their daytime slumber wore off. A vog had prowled the river's edge for hours, splashing in the water with its huge hairy paws as it tried to catch a fish it could crush with its powerful jaws and sharp teeth, unaware that a Starlighter watched its movements from a safe height, for even a vog's keen night vision could not detect a dark sphere hovering silently above.

Koren drove Exodus forward, wide awake in spite of not sleeping at all. At first, she had thought that her own light had kept her awake, but as she stayed quiet, Exodus dimmed, finally blinking out, taking away all light and heat. Still, although she stayed warm in her cloak, sleep never came.

Keeping the sphere dark with her silence, she floated over the spires and descended toward the Zodiac's portico. Trisarian's waning light revealed a woman wearing a skirt stealing across the cobblestones toward the Zodiac, a shawl covering her shoulders and head.

Koren lowered the star to within twenty feet of the road. Madam Orley? Yes! It was Madam Orley!

Madam stopped at one of the portico's columns and peered around it, as if hiding in wait. With one firm hand clutching a book, she didn't appear to be frightened, though the wrinkles in her brow revealed a good deal of worry.

Koren took in a deep breath. Speaking would probably light up the star and startle Madam, but it had to be done. "Madam Orley?" Exodus slowly brightened. "Madam Orley, it's me, Koren."

"I came here to see you." Madam emerged from her hiding place. "I overheard you talking to Hyborn about meeting here at dawn."

Koren floated closer but stayed about ten feet from the ground, still mindful of Brinella's warning to keep her distance. "What do you need?"

"First of all, thank you for sending Tibalt. He isn't much help with housework, but he knows a great deal about the Code." Madam gestured with the book. "It was supposed to go to Stephan, but since he died, I kept it."

"Yes," Koren said, "I remember."

"Tibalt pointed out this passage to me." Madam opened the book to a page near the end and began to read. " 'Like a guiding star, the Creator's word brings light to the soul. It ignites a flame within those who take it into their hearts. Like a refining fire, it burns away all that is impure. Those who seek cleansing will come to the light, and those who love darkness will try to extinguish the guiding star.' " She closed the book and slid it into her pocket. "Tibalt and I think you are shining that light, and some of our own people will try to destroy you. I have heard the grumbling already."

"Do you mean Yeager?"

She nodded. "But he isn't the only one. Some are old enough to remember Cassabrie, the first Starlighter. She didn't float around inside a sphere, but she did cause a lot of trouble. She wasn't shy about telling people what they ought to be doing, and most folks don't like that. It didn't take long before she had to go into hiding. Plenty of people were willing to turn her in to Magnar."

"So is that why you came? To warn me to be careful?"

"That, and …" She withdrew a folded parchment from her skirt pocket. "I was wondering if you could tell me what happened to my daughter, Agatha. Since you're a Starlighter, I thought you might be able to tell the tale."

Koren glanced at the parchment, but it was too far away to see any details.

A tear trickling down her cheek, Madam continued. "I now think that she has died, but I was hoping you could tell me. As I'm sure you remember, she was promoted just before you came to us, and"—she held up the parchment—"and I received a letter, but I wonder now if the letter is fraudulent."

As warmth flowed into Koren's body, a stream of words flooded her mind. "Oh, Madam, I do have a tale for you." She spread out her arms, fanning her cloak. "Agatha, precious daughter of Constance and Dominic Milton Orley, loved the sciences, especially those that revealed the mysteries of the human body."

A girl appeared next to Madam Orley. Sitting at a desk, she wrote in a huge book, a wavering candle near her elbow providing light. With dark hair and a blood-stained tunic and skirt, she appeared to be about fourteen years old.

"Agatha often worked in the butcher shop, which helped her learn about the internal organs and muscular and skeletal structures of animals. That study caused her to seek more knowledge from her father, who allowed her to watch surgeries. She then wrote down everything she learned and drew sketches of human anatomy."

Madam knelt next to Agatha's image, her hand trembling as she reached up and caressed the phantom girl's cheek.

"One evening during exam time," Koren continued, "Arxad visited the students, a rare event, for priests of the Zodiac are usually the ones who are visited by those in need, not the other way around."

The scene changed. Agatha, now wearing a clean skirt and tunic, sat upright in a chair. Arxad bobbed his head in front of her as if studying her eyes. "Her test scores are exactly what I had hoped," he said. "She will receive a Promotion."

Arxad led Agatha away, walking in place as if floating a few inches off the cobblestones. The book and pedestal from the Basilica theater room appeared, and Arxad halted next to them. "I chose this one for Promotion myself," he said in the dragon language. "She is proficient in medicine. Her teacher seemed curious as to why I would select a student with such high scores, but he did not verbalize his question."

Magnar shuffled into view, his eyes fiery. "Have you completed the preparations?"

"She has already had her time at the Reflections Crystal." Arxad presented a sheet of parchment in his clawed hand. "And here is her letter."

Magnar let out a snort of contempt. "What does it say? I always find these amusing."

Arxad drew the letter close to his eyes. "Dear Mother, I am happy in the Northlands with the great dragon king. Arxad told me I would learn more about medicine here, so I am looking forward to that. Papa will be proud of me when I discover the cure for the disease that now afflicts him. Please tell him that I will find it as soon as I can. I love you, Mama."

Magnar laughed. "She is as idealistic as you are."

"Perhaps we need more who embrace idealism." Arxad touched the top of Agatha's head. "This one is too pure and innocent to live among the corrupt."

"And are you the arbiter of worthiness to live? Congratulations, Arxad. You are now sitting in the Creator's judgment seat."

Arxad snorted a plume of smoke. "Spoken by the one who consumes the innocent."

"I am not the one who believes these vermin to be —"

"I know. I know. This is an old debate." Arxad pushed Agatha toward Magnar. "Take her. She is yours now." Agatha stumbled and fell in front of Magnar. Without another word, he snatched her with his claws and flew away.

Still on her knees, Madam Orley trembled, but she stayed quiet as she kept her stare locked where Agatha had fallen. A shining female form appeared, standing erect in that spot. Although composed of pure light instead of substance, she looked just like Agatha.

The surroundings altered from the Basilica theater room to the foyer at the Northlands castle. Arxad walked

close to Agatha, his claws biting into the wooden floor.
"Alaph will meet with you soon," he said. "He will want
you to choose a name that reflects your character. He has
a list of qualities from which you may make a selection."

"Just give me one that no one else wants." As Agatha
spoke, she faded, leaving only her lips visible. "I will be
glad to take it. I would never want to cause a disruption."

Arxad smiled. "There are several that fit you. Peace-
able? Deference? Goodness?"

"Then if it pleases you ..." She curtsied, bringing light
to her form again. "I will choose Deference."

Koren lowered her arms. The scene crumbled into
shards of radiance that evaporated in the dawning light.
"Agatha lives," Koren said, "but not in bodily form. Arxad
preserved her spirit, and now she serves the king of the
Northlands in that state. I have seen her myself, though
I didn't know at the time that she was your daughter.
She is happy and content, so I hope this news brings you
comfort."

Madam Orley rose to her feet and bowed her head.
Sniffling, she spoke in between sobbing spasms. "I am
... comforted ... but I am ... also confused ... Why would
Arxad ... take my precious little one ... to Magnar to be
..." Her final word came out in a wail. "Eaten?"

"I cannot answer for Arxad. We can only guess at his
reasons based on what we saw and heard."

During the ensuing silence, Madam composed herself. Then, her voice transformed into a spite-filled growl.
"Arxad is a dragon, so he does what is best for himself
and other dragons. When I next see him, he will answer
for taking my daughter from me." She then raised a

clenched fist. "We must rise up and fight. Maybe together we can break our bonds and escape to the Northlands."

"That is my hope," Koren said, "but it will require a united effort. Many of us will suffer, and some will die in the process."

"Then so be it. With you here to provide the truth about the dragons' cruelty, maybe people will listen. Maybe they will be willing to risk danger in order to find freedom."

"Enough of this talk!" A dragon flew at Koren and slapped Exodus with a wing as he passed. Exodus zoomed up, spinning wildly toward the Zodiac. Koren spun with it. Her cloak spread out, and light shot from her body, sending streams of energy through the outer membrane and all across the village.

Exodus struck one of the spires and bounced back, slowing its spin. Koren set her feet and halted the rotation. Then, gliding back over the street, she surveyed the brightening scene. Yeager now stood next to Madam Orley, wrenching her arms behind her back and tying them together with a rope. Hyborn flew to a landing and trotted up to them, his hot stare aimed at Koren. "So this is your plan!" Hyborn shouted. "You hope to incite a rebellion by twisting history to suit your purposes."

Koren inhaled deeply. It would be best to stay calm and just speak the truth. "I am not twisting history. I am showing exactly what occurred."

"When you show selected events out of context, you *are* twisting history. Yesterday in the presence of dragons, you displayed the overwhelming cruelty of humans, buying our favor with your hypnotizing rhetoric. Yet today you tried to ensnare this woman by telling of a singular act of cruelty by one dragon, and you hoped to ignite passions through emotional appeal." Extending his neck, Hyborn angled his head upward and looked at her nearly eye to eye. His voice lowered to a growling whisper. "Your power is great, Starlighter, and you have proven how dangerous you are."

Koren pulled her cloak closer to her body, trying to hide her trembling legs. Steeling herself, she kept her voice steady. "Is one act really out of context? That one act was committed by the dragon king who guides and represents you all, and it was not singular. Magnar has repeated his ravenous cruelty many times. What I have shown is enough to condemn the authority of those who enslave my people."

"It is true that Magnar has committed acts of cruelty," Hyborn said, "but that does not give you the right to stand in judgment of all dragons."

Squinting at her light, Yeager tightened Madam's binding knot with a hard jerk. "I knew you were a prideful princess when I sold you to Arxad, but now your lofty perch has swelled you into a high-and-mighty queen. You can't even walk or talk with us. How dare you try to get us to rise up against our masters! It is a hopeless dream and a foolish one."

Hyborn lowered his head and looked at Madam Orley. "In order to ensure that no humans heed this Starlighter's words, let us make an example of this woman. I will take her to the Basilica gate where she will be tied and left without food or water until she dies."

Koren balled her fists. "By whose authority? You can't take Arxad's housekeeper!"

"I spoke to Taushin about this matter earlier this morning. Since I am less susceptible to your charms than most, he gave me authority to quell any uprising through any means that I desire." Hyborn turned to Yeager. "Spread the news. The lockdown is over. Before going to their normal duties, everyone must pass by the Basilica and express their contempt for this rebel. Those who disobey will suffer the same fate."

"But I haven't done anything wrong," Madam Orley said as she twisted her hands and wrists at her back. "Is it a crime to want to be free from bondage?"

Hyborn slapped Madam with a wing, cutting her cheek. Blood poured from the wound and dripped to her shoulder. She cried out but quickly bit her lip.

"You will be silent," Hyborn shouted. "It *is* a crime to conspire with this Starlighter to incite rebellion."

"Leave her alone!" Koren drove Exodus downward, but Hyborn slapped the star again. As Koren flew upward in a wild spin, she dropped to hands and knees and looked through the sphere's floor. Below, Hyborn grabbed Madam Orley by the hair and dragged her toward the Basilica. "Go down!" Koren pounded the floor. "I have to help Madam!"

Exodus gradually leveled out, its spin easing. Then, as slow as a setting moon, it descended. "Faster!" she shouted, blinking away dizziness. "Why aren't you listening to me?"

Hyborn threw Madam toward the Basilica, slamming her head against the gate. Yeager wrapped the rope around her midsection and fastened her to the iron bars. "Now go," Hyborn said to Yeager. "Bring your fellow slaves. No one is exempt."

While Yeager ran toward the grottoes, Koren drew closer. She rose to her feet and whipped her cloak around. "Hyborn! Hear my words. You will regret this brutality."

"Is that so?" Hyborn laughed. "What will you do to me? Hurt my ears with your endless squeaking?"

She halted the lower part of Exodus just above Hyborn's eye level. "I call to witness every slave to whom you have been cruel!"

An old man hobbled toward Hyborn, bent at the waist as he leaned on a walking stick. A small girl followed, wearing short trousers. Red welts striped her exposed legs. At least twenty men, women, and children joined the procession. Each one bore a bruise, walked with a limp, or displayed whip marks.

As Hyborn watched them approach, his neck swayed from side to side. He blinked several times as if trying to ward off sleep. When the people drew near, they formed two lines that looped around him. As soon as the circle was complete, Koren called out. "You speak of singular events, yet each one of these slaves has borne witness to your cruelty multiple times. Shall I ask them to describe your crimes against them?"

Hyborn closed his eyes and wagged his head hard. "I will not stand here to be ridiculed by your phantasms!" He blew a stream of fire at the bent man, engulfing him in flames, then pivoted slowly in an arc, blasting the witnesses until they all disappeared. An errant burst of fire swept across Madam's legs. She cried out, shaking so violently the gate's bars vibrated.

Another old man ran toward the dragon. "Allow me to stand guard," he shouted. "I'll watch this cowardly rebel."

Koren clenched a fist. *Tibalt!*

"Who are you?" Hyborn asked. "I do not recognize you."

Tibalt bowed. "My name is Tibalt. I saw how you scorched those demons the Starlighter conjured." He swung a fist. "Whoo-hee! That'll teach that sorceress to mess with our masters!"

Madam Orley cried out. "Tibalt! Help me! I need water for my legs!"

"Do you know this woman?" Hyborn asked.

Tibalt squinted at Madam. "Met her last night. Been suspicious of her ever since. She said some crazy things about thinking we should be free. Imagine that! What would we do if dragons set us free? Why, we would probably starve and come back on our knees begging for our chains."

Koren cringed. *Careful, Tibalt. Don't pour it on too thick.*

Hyborn gave Tibalt a skeptical stare. "Do not think you can gain my favor with your fawning rhetoric. I have seen many deceivers in my time."

"And I have spent too many years in prison to want to go there again," Tibalt said, bowing.

"Magnar never told me about a human prisoner. Why did he detain you for so long?"

Tibalt pointed at himself. "Because I am the son of Uriel Blackstone, one of the original slaves. Magnar didn't want me spreading stories about how humans arrived here, but he also wanted to preserve me for, as he put it, a 'genetic resource.' Apparently, Magnar wasn't worried about me anymore, so he gave orders for my release."

"Yes," Hyborn said, still staring. "I see the resemblance."

Tibalt offered another quick bow. "Then you must know that I speak only the truth. The last thing I want to do is go back to that prison."

"Then stay here and guard her while I report to Taushin, but do not give her any water." Hyborn spread out his wings and spat a ball of fire near Tibalt's feet. "If you fail me, you will be the next fool I scorch. I can always capture her again."

Tibalt leaped back from the flames. "Don't worry. I'll watch that rebel like a guardian dragon."

Hyborn lifted into the air, swept past Exodus without a glance at Koren, and descended through an opening in the Basilica roof.

Tibalt looked all around before tiptoeing to Madam Orley. "Now try to stay quiet. I'll have you out of here before you can say, 'Magnar's a monkey.'"

As he worked to untie the knot, Madam Orley stared at Koren, her deeply etched face giving away her pain.

Tibalt muttered, "They must have knots here we don't have back home."

"You!" Yeager called, running toward them at a gallop. "What are you doing?"

"Nothing." Tibalt thrust his hands behind his back. "I was checking to see if her knots are secure."

Yeager slowed to a halt in front of Madam Orley. "Of course they're tight. I tied them myself."

"They are tight, indeed. Tight as a school marm's hair."

"School marm?" Yeager gave him a quizzical look. "What's a school marm?"

Koren pressed her fingers against her lips. *Careful, Tibalt.*

"It's a saying we had back when I was a young'un, way before your time."

"Madam Orley told me about you." Yeager checked the knots. Apparently satisfied, he turned back to Tibalt. "How many years have you seen, old man?"

"I lost count. More than ninety, I suppose. But since I just got out of prison, I don't know the folks here."

"Well, you'll have a chance to meet many of us. I gave the command to one of our tongue waggers, so it won't take long for word to get around."

While Tibalt and Yeager talked, Koren glanced around—from the Basilica gate to the hole in its roof to the Zodiac. She had to do something. But what? Maybe it would be best to wait for the other slaves to show up, then she could try to persuade them all at once. That might be the only way to get the proverbial river past the barrier wall, to communicate the new idea and create an unstoppable wave. At the very least, maybe someone would help Madam Orley.

After a few minutes, a line of slaves streamed up the slope and onto the street. Most appeared to be more tired than usual, perhaps weary at being summoned yet again to the village. Many gave Exodus a quick glance before turning away with a grimace. Children of all ages and sizes accompanied the adults, including infants carried in mothers' arms.

Koren lifted Exodus higher. Maybe if she stayed aloft until the right time, the people wouldn't be so annoyed when she began speaking. After ascending to at least five hundred feet, she looked down over the region the dragons called home. From this elevation, the area seemed small, like a ragged oval hemmed in by an incomplete wall and a range of forested mountains. Compared to the vast lands outside the barriers, the dragons' abode was no more than a …

Koren tapped her chin. An egg? Yes, that was it. It was a shelled-in habitat populated by creatures who knew little about the world beyond their boundaries. With the exception of the older dragons, they had no idea that other civilizations flourished, not only in their own world, but also on other planets. Their ignorance had led them to believe that their existence was the only one possible. Truly, humans and dragons alike were slaves, bound by their limited understanding, and since ignorance often breeds arrogance, they stubbornly insisted that those who delivered contrary ideas must be evil or else insane.

Koren sighed. Ignorance mixed with arrogance made such a foul stew, and those who brewed the concoction seemed unable to detect its rancid odor.

After a few minutes, Hyborn emerged from the Basilica and flew down to the street, apparently unaware that Koren watched from high above. As hundreds of slaves gathered, another dragon flew from the Basilica roof, a black dragon with a passenger dressed in white who carried a staff in her hands.

Koren guided Exodus downward. Taushin's appearance meant trouble. She might not get another chance to speak to all the people at once, so she couldn't let him spoil it.

Taushin landed next to Hyborn, and Zena slid off his back, still carrying the staff. A rope dangled from the staff's end and coiled over Zena's shoulder. As Koren descended, the people began lifting their hands to block her light. Some cringed. A few of the babies cried, while younger children hid behind their parents.

"Go back where you came from!" Yeager shouted. "We don't want you here!"

Koren allowed Exodus to hover about thirty feet above the Basilica's gate. She spread out her cloak and called, "Please give me an opportunity to speak. Surely you are kind and merciful enough to allow a girl such as I to plead for a moment of your time. You have the courage to bear with words. They cannot bring you harm."

Yeager pointed at her. "*Your* words can bring harm. You have the power to hypnotize, so stay quiet, or one of the dragons will slap you away again."

She avoided eye contact with him. "Listen, my friends. The dragons have imprisoned you for your entire lives. You know nothing beyond the barriers that surround you. There really is a Northlands and a true king of the dragons. I have been to his castle and have seen the wonders. From within that castle I resurrected Exodus, the star in which I now abide. Surely you must wonder where it came from."

"It came from the depths of evil," Yeager said. "It is scorching my skin, and I can already feel your words making me dizzy."

Taushin swished his tail back and forth, a sign of dragon amusement. "Let her speak," he said. "I am immune to her, so I will stay alert. I find her rhetoric entertaining."

Koren again kept her gaze on the people. "I am not here to entertain. I am here to tell you about another life. Like a river that has been blocked by a dam, you long for freedom to seek the valleys you were designed to refresh, but as you build up pressure to overcome the barrier, the dam builders bleed you. They kill those who oppose their rule. They torture children to bring you into submission. They instill fear in your hearts, telling you that beasts in the wilderness will tear your bodies to pieces. And although you have never beheld one of these beasts or witnessed such a slaughter, you embrace fear. You hold tightly to the security of things you have witnessed with your eyes. You see, the dragons know if you could travel beyond the wall and experience the beautiful valleys, you would realize this land of stunted trees, cacti, and arid plains is not where you belong. It is a land of deadness, a quarantined desolation. You would realize that lush foliage, unlike the legendary wilderness, does not hide wild beasts that wait to devour you."

Yeager shook his head as if throwing off a daze. "You cannot prove what you say."

"Oh, but I can." Koren spun her cloak and called out with a loud voice, "Fruit trees once lined this very street. Thick green grass lay across the ground upon which you stand. Flowers covered both the plain and the mesas where you now drill for pheterone, but who among you is old enough to remember those days?"

"I remember," Tibalt said. "Oh, what a beautiful sight!"

Koren gave him a brief smile. "But I will show you something even greater. Here is what the land looks like beyond the barrier wall." She thrust out her arms. The cobblestones vanished, leaving behind a carpet of dense grass. Flowers sprang up around the onlookers' feet, a dazzling medley of blues, reds, yellows, and purples. The Zodiac and the Basilica disappeared, leaving only the gate to which Madam Orley was tied. A tree erupted from the ground next to Taushin. In just a few seconds, it grew to seventy feet high, and its foliage cast a cooling shade over the people.

"In slavery you toil with backbreaking labors, and you sweat under a brutal sun. In a land of freedom, even during the hottest days, you could rest in shade like this and enjoy the fruits of your own labors instead of delivering them to the very taskmasters who scar your backs in exchange for the scrapings of the bones the dragons cared not to chew."

Koren took a breath. Hyborn and the rest of the dragons now seemed hypnotized. The humans, with the exception of Zena, had lowered their shielding hands and stared wide-eyed. Even Madam Orley seemed pain free as she watched with wonder.

While Taushin's blue eyebeams drilled into Zena's eyes, she stood straight and looked directly at Koren. "What will you do now, Starlighter?" Taushin asked.

"Everyone is under your influence. They await your command."

Koren nodded toward the north. "Open the barrier wall. I will take them to the Northlands."

"To the ice-covered desert? Will they grow food there?" Taushin laughed. "I think not. Unless you can conjure edible plants that can endure freezing temperatures."

"Then we will make a settlement in the valley in between. The land is fertile, and the climate is temperate."

Taushin extended a wing toward the crowd. "These people are incapable of planning a stable community. They are accustomed to being told what to do. And you are no different. You cannot teach that which you do not know."

Koren imagined herding the people into the colorful meadows. The scene sparkled with beauty, but what would happen when they had to learn to work the land without a leader to guide them and without whips to motivate their labors?

"As you can see," Taushin continued, "your fellow humans know nothing but slavery. They listen to you now, because you have put them in bonds. As surely as I shackled you with manacles and chains, you have shackled their minds with your hypnotic power. They will now follow you because of your power over them, not because they loved you beforehand, but rather because you forced them to love you. And this is exactly what I taught you.

"If you had stayed with me, you would have eventually learned to love me, but when I released you, you rebelled. The same will happen with these people. You will have to keep them under your spell for a long time before they follow you without compulsion. If you release them now, they will surely disavow any acquiescence to your authority. In fact, they are likely to denounce you and become aggressive toward you. Otherwise, in the unlikely event that you are able to maintain control, you will prove yourself to be the slave master that I am, a loving and benevolent leader who will do what is best for those who remain in bondage."

Koren scanned the sea of faces. Many stared with mouths agape, apparently unaware of their surroundings. Only the babies seemed immune as they squirmed in the arms that held them. If she could lead them to the fertile valley and keep them under her control, she could eventually get them to work together to make a new community. But at what cost? They would still be slaves, and she would be their chain holder.

Brinella's words came to mind. *A Starlighter must never leave her listeners in that state. If they come out of a trance on their own, they are susceptible to any influence that enters their minds. The Starlighter must command her visions to flee so her hearers can return to normal and decide whether or not to accept the wisdom she has provided. Otherwise, they are nothing more than ...*

"Slaves," Koren whispered. Although it would be better for them to have a truly benevolent mistress than a cruel dragon master, it would still be slavery. Without real freedom, every action would be in response to the rattle of a chain. Real love required real freedom.

"You cannot leave them standing here," Taushin said. "Do what you must. I said I would release the slaves, and

I will allow them to depart, but I will also do what I must to maintain my kingdom. Zena is an inferior surrogate. I need you for my eyes. I will make whatever sacrifice I deem necessary to bring you back into my embrace."

Zena scowled but stayed silent.

"What do you mean by sacrifice?" Koren asked.

"Sometimes chains are not enough. There are other means of persuasion at my disposal, and, should you continue your rebellion against me, my response will be bold and shocking." He lowered his voice to a menacing growl. "You have had your warning."

Koren glowered at him. No matter what this dark fiend had in mind, freedom was worth any sacrifice. It would be better to be dead than locked in chains again. Her role as a Starlighter would continue whether Taushin liked it or not, and the people would have the choice to follow her themselves.

She pulled her cloak in close and shouted, "Begone, visions! Fly away, phantoms! Release these people from your grasp!"

The flower-covered meadow melted, transforming into liquid color that seeped between the cobblestones. The village buildings returned, and the Zodiac's spires again cast their insufficient shade over the crowd.

As if awakened from slumber, the people began shaking their heads and blinking their eyes. Some even yawned, but they all once again raised hands to deflect Exodus's light.

Yeager jabbed a finger into the air. "She hypnotized us! She put impossible visions in our heads. She wants us to rebel against our masters, and we all know what will happen if we do that."

"They will slaughter our children," one woman said, holding her baby close.

"And us," a man added.

Hyborn raised his head high and broadcast his voice over the crowd. "She is a powerful sorceress, but if the people try to leave with her, she cannot stop us from killing the weak, sick, and slow of foot among you. The children will surely die."

"You must take courage," Koren said, lifting her hands again. "Even if some of us die, freedom is worth the price. I will do everything within my power to stop the dragons from hurting you. Since I resurrected Exodus, I am able to infuse the atmosphere with their precious pheterone. The mines can no longer produce, so they need me to stay alive and aloft, but they do not need slave labor to survive. Besides their arrogant pride, they will have no motivation for pursuing or destroying you, and when I hypnotize them, they will be rendered powerless."

"Hyborn," Taushin said, his voice calm. "Demonstrate to this Starlighter our willingness to maintain control of our kingdom. Burn the prisoner."

"As you wish." Hyborn blew a river of fire at Madam Orley. The flames covered her body, catching her clothes and hair.

"No!" Koren screamed. "You monsters! You murderers!"

Gasps erupted from the crowd, audible even over Madam's screams. Tibalt dashed out from among them and threw his body over Madam Orley. His momentum tore the charred rope, and they fell sideways to the street. He batted the flames with his hands, then rolled her over, snuffing the blaze.

"Shall I cook the old man?" Hyborn asked.

Taushin shook his head. "This is enough of a demonstration. If the woman survives, let her scars remind everyone that rebellion has severe consequences. The children will be next."

"Look at what you have done!" Yeager shouted, shaking his fist at Koren. "Madam Orley is a kind, gracious woman, and your rebellious words have brought about this … this carnage!"

As heat surged through her cheeks, Koren balled her fists. "I didn't blow fire on her. Hyborn did. Can't you see how cruel the dragons are? If we rise up as one, they won't be able to …" Smoke from Madam's burnt flesh streamed into view. Koren felt her mouth drop open, and her lips barely moved as she whispered, "Stop us."

"That's easy for you to say while up there in your protective bubble," Yeager said. "Come down here and repeat your treasonous words. Speak them while facing a dragon's flaming mouth like we have to. Then we'll believe you."

Weeping, Koren spread out her arms. "I can't. I'm … I'm trapped … trapped inside."

"By choice," Taushin said. "You entered by choice. You sealed the hole by choice. I told you beforehand that you would be trapped in there, that you should raise Exodus without sealing the wound, but you chose the prideful path, desiring to be a guiding angel, a prophetess who forever stands above her fellow humans, judging their actions and correcting their behavior."

Yeager waved a hand over the other humans. "Who made her a judge over us? She is just another slave, and a young girl at that. At least dragon masters have more experience than we do. The only time they ever discipline us is when we disobey. This girl is no more than a petulant busybody. You all know that. Because of her red hair and green eyes, she has always been favored by the dragons, and it has swelled her head. Now she thinks she is our judge."

Most of the people nodded. One man yelled, "Go away! You've caused enough heartache!" Others murmured about poor Constance Orley and how much she would have to suffer. Only one or two shouted in favor of Koren, including the stone mover who had seemed to support her the previous time they had gathered, but Yeager's supporters quickly drowned them out.

A woman who looked a few years older than Madam Orley pushed her way to the front and looked up at Koren, wincing at the radiance. "Listen, young lady," she said with a kind tone, "I knew your mother. Emma was a good woman, quiet and respectable, a real optimist, in spite of the fact that your father died before you were born."

Koren's throat caught. Died before she was born? The woman had to be mistaken. Memories of her father's good-night blessing still echoed, the same words she had heard replayed in the tale about another Koren and Orson. What could it all mean?

"Emma loved you dearly," the woman continued, "but if she saw what you are doing now, she would be ashamed. She believed no human has the right to judge another human. We give advice, to be sure, but we should never believe ourselves to be above everyone else. That's just common sense." She pointed at the ground. "If you'll just come down here and speak your mind like one friend to another, I'll listen, but I won't be talked down to."

Koren gazed at the woman's sincere face. It wouldn't do any good to explain Brinella's warning about keeping her distance from those with impure hearts. It would make her sound more self-righteous than ever. Yet she couldn't risk the closeness. Maybe an oblique explanation would work. "I can't. The star is too hot. You wouldn't be able to stand it. And since I can't leave, I have to stay up here."

"There is a solution," Taushin said. "Zena, show her."

Zena raised the shaft. It ended in a sharp point, and a short tube had been fastened near the barbed end.

Koren swallowed. A spear! It looked just like the one she had found near the star chamber.

"If we puncture Exodus," Taushin continued, "it will deflate, allowing you to descend, and then you will be able to exit and speak to your fellow slaves. I am sure Madam Orley will appreciate your help in Arxad's abode as she recovers."

Koren glanced at the spot where she had mended the wall. A thin scar still remained. "But when a spear made a wound last time, Exodus flew away to the Northlands."

"Which is why I attached this," Zena said, letting the coil of rope slide off her shoulder. "When the spear pierces Exodus, you can hold the shaft, and we will keep you from flying away."

"Then," Taushin added, "Exodus will remain grounded and still provide pheterone to our region. With no more need for human slaves, I will set them free. Dragons will even help them set up their own community. All you have to do is submit to me as before and become my eyes."

Yeager called out, "Did you hear that? Taushin promised us freedom! And we'll be free without a self-proclaimed angel telling us what to do."

A wave of nods crossed the sea of sweaty brows. Many people smiled in spite of the heat. The stone mover crossed his arms over his chest, shaking his head.

The young man's face finally registered. Scott was his name, a boy from the river crew.

While conversation continued buzzing through the crowd, Koren peered down at the Basilica gate. Madam Orley lay near the bars, smoke still rising from her scorched body. Propped on his knees, Tibalt straddled her, fanning her face with his hands. "How is she, Tibalt?"

He looked up at her, his face twisting in pain. "She's alive." The background noise nearly drowned out his words. "She wants to get up, but I won't let her, not in the mood she's in. She's ready to take on all the dragons by herself, but we can't let her get cooked again."

"Can you do anything to help her? Get some water, maybe?"

Tibalt nodded. "As soon as I see an opening, I'll look for some."

Yeager raised his hands, calming the crowd. "So let's get on with it. Puncture the star and bring her down to our level."

Zena lifted the spear and showed it to Koren. "Come as close as possible, my dear, so I can push it in gently. I don't want to hurt you."

"Hurt me?" Koren looked again at Madam Orley. If she allowed them to deflate Exodus, could she help her former mistress? The words spoken by Brinella's image returned to Koren's mind. *And you will learn that even the scrapings of the skin of Exodus can provide healing.*

"The scrapings of the skin," Koren murmured. Brinella must have meant that a stardrop could be used to heal someone, but as long as Madam lay down there and Exodus floated up here, no one could test the theory. And what good had she done as a guiding angel? Very few believed her. Taushin would likely turn his wrath on the children next. How could she allow them to burn while she floated above the suffering, simply because she didn't want to be Taushin's slave? She had to bring this madness to an end and stop those fiends. It seemed impossible to do anything more from her pedestal in the sky.

"Get off me!" Madam Orley shouted as she pushed Tibalt. "I need to talk to Koren."

After Tibalt helped her rise, she stood on wobbly legs, her face dark red and one sleeve burned away, exposing a blackened arm. She spoke with a stern tone, though her voice barely rose above a whisper. "You did the best you could, dear girl. I think it's time you came down so you can shine your light at our level. I will need your help." She then spelled out more words with her fingers: "You and I can plot against the dragons together."

As new tears emerged, Koren scooted Exodus closer to Zena. Her black eyes were clearer than usual, and as she stood in a white dress with her arm poised to throw the spear, her angular profile seemed surreal, like a celestial being ready to execute justice.

"A little closer," Zena crooned. "You're almost in range."

Koren gazed at the crowd. As if mesmerized again by her hypnotic charms, they stared with wide eyes and open mouths. They craved freedom. They ached for release from the toils, the threats, the intimidations, not only for themselves, but also for their children, both born and those yet to be born.

She had offered them freedom, and they refused. They didn't want to take the risk. They wanted freedom without cost, without sacrifice, without bowing to a higher authority.

"There," Zena said. "Hold the star right there. Let me know when you're ready."

Koren began weeping again. She pushed back her cloak, spread out her arms, and set her feet, balancing her body in case the star kicked away. "I'm ... I'm ready."

sixteen

ust as Zena drew the spear back, Taushin called out, "Wait! I hear something odd."

Zena kept her stare on Koren. "A beating of wings?"

"Yes. Wings. All dragon allies are either here or at assigned stations. You are my eyes, Zena. Search for the source."

"It's one of Koren's tricks," Yeager said. "She's pretending to give in, but she'll hypnotize us again. Spear the star!"

"Do not listen to that ignorant fool," Taushin said. "He has no idea of the danger that could come upon us if Magnar's curse has been broken."

While dozens of eyes scanned the sky, Koren looked at her outstretched arms. With her sleeves now up to her elbows, the red marks left by the manacles had come into view, as well as her slave's brand, eight black characters burned into her skin in the dragon language. Koren stared at them. What had just happened? Had Taushin's words hypnotized her? His speech was so seductive, and his threats had shaken her to the core, replacing thoughts of forever freedom with fear of immediate harm, the very fear she had warned her people about.

She bent her brow low. How could she submit to that cruel beast again? Even if it meant freedom for the other humans, how could she become a slave to evil? There had to be another way. The people had to swallow their pride and believe the Creator's guiding angel. If she couldn't convince the people of their need to change their hearts, she would have to wait for another opportunity.

A woman in the crowd pointed. "I see a dragon coming this way."

"Two dragons," a man said. "And isn't that odd? It looks like humans are riding on their backs."

Koren looked at the approaching dragons and their familiar flight styles. Arxad and Fellina! Maybe they had hoped for a stealthy approach, and maybe she could help them.

Letting Exodus drift back out of Zena's reach, she held up her arms. "Yes, it is odd, indeed. Watch them carefully, and listen to my words as you take in this unusual sight."

"No!" Yeager shouted. "We can't let her put us under a spell. Don't look, or you'll be caught in her trap."

As the people turned toward her again, she continued drifting away. "A spell? No, Yeager. I am merely telling the truth, which I have always told. Arxad and Fellina are coming this way. Train your eyes on them, and listen to me."

Yeager pointed at Koren. "Silence her! Throw the spear!"

Zena glanced at Taushin. "What is your bidding?"

"Throw it!" Taushin barked. "These dragons are not whom I feared."

Zena reared back again, but just as she lunged, Arxad dropped out of the sky and knocked her to the ground. The spear flew from her hands and rolled toward Madam Orley. Tibalt dove for it, but Yeager kicked him in the face, sending the old man sprawling backwards.

Madam Orley snatched up the spear and pointed it at Yeager. "Leave us, you coward!"

While Yeager backed away and blended into the crowd, Tibalt shook his head. "I ain't been kicked like that since old Juniper the mule planted her hoof right in my kisser."

Arxad landed in a flurry of wings. Two young men leaped from his back, their swords drawn.

Koren clapped her hands. *Jason! Randall!*

Jason pressed the point of his sword against Taushin's underbelly while Randall set the side of his blade against Zena's neck as she lay on the street. "Don't move," Randall ordered, "or my hand just might slip."

Arxad bumped into Hyborn. "You have heard what happened to Maximus, have you not?"

Hyborn nodded. "I have."

"Then heed my words. Trust me. Stay out of this conflict, and allow me to contend for our species."

"I will keep my peace for now," Hyborn said. "Yet if events transpire that threaten to topple dragon sovereignty, I will respond."

diviner

Koren glanced at Madam Orley. Still holding the spear, she crept closer to Arxad and Taushin. What did she have in mind? An attack would be madness. Someone had to stop her or at least distract her.

"What is happening?" Taushin asked. "I see a stranger with a sword, and I feel a sting in my abdomen."

"That's my sword," Jason said. "You will do as we say, or I will drive it through to your spine."

Fellina landed behind Arxad. As soon as Elyssa dismounted, Fellina took off again, appearing to head for the Zodiac.

"Elyssa!" Koren shouted. "Can you help Madam Orley? She has some terrible burns."

"I'm on my way." Elyssa rushed toward Madam. A glowing girl trailed her, her bare feet raising sparks as they made contact with the street.

"Deference?" Koren called. "Is that you?"

While Elyssa continued her dash toward Madam, Deference stopped and looked up, fading as she spoke. "Yes."

Koren glanced again at Madam Orley. Although she hadn't released her grip on the spear, she was allowing Elyssa to examine her charred arm. With Taushin and his allies temporarily stymied, it seemed that everyone focused on the minidrama taking place around Madam, as if awestruck by the ghostly girl with a glowing body who spoke like a normal human.

"Do you remember your real name, *Agatha*?" Koren asked.

As Deference nodded, her head appeared. "I remember. It wasn't so long ago."

BfYan Davis

"Agatha?" Madam Orley broke away from Elyssa. "Agatha, is that you?"

Deference turned toward her, cocking her head, apparently not recognizing the disfigured woman approaching her with a brandished spear. She backed away. "Who are you?"

Madam Orley halted. With her singed hair and clothes flapping in the breeze, and her skin darkened by soot, she looked like a scorched crow. *"Who am I?* I'm your mother, of course."

New whispers rustled through the crowd, but no one seemed brave enough to interrupt the eerie conversation.

Backing away another step, Deference shook her head. "I beg your pardon, but you're not my mother."

The spear trembled in her grasp. "Don't you remember me?"

"No, ma'am. I'm sorry."

"So the scoundrels drained your memory?" Madam turned toward Arxad and Taushin, her teeth clenched as she spoke with a threatening growl. "This is all your doing!"

Koren gasped. Taushin would see the attack coming through Zena's eyes, and he wouldn't care that Jason threatened with a sword. He would defend himself and kill Madam.

Running like a wounded bull, Madam charged with the spear. Koren pushed Exodus downward and knocked several people over as she blocked Madam's path. The spear plunged into Exodus's membrane and stuck there, half of its length now within the star.

Koren screamed. Such pain! It seemed that the spear had pierced her own body. She shot upward with Exodus. The rope dangled underneath, pulling slightly, adding to the torture.

"Koren!" Arxad shouted. "Stop!"

After halting Exodus at about thirty feet from the ground, she heaved in deep breaths, her brain dizzied by the quick moves. Below, Madam Orley wept on her knees, while Deference laid her glowing hands on her mother's shoulders.

"Is the star leaking?" Arxad asked.

Grimacing, Koren slid closer to the wound. It seemed that the spear plugged its own hole, and the star's membrane formed a seal around the shaft. "I don't think so."

Arxad waved a wing. "Stay where you are. We cannot allow the spear to be dislodged."

Jason sheathed his sword. "Randall, watch this dragon. I'm going to make sure no one touches that rope."

"No problem." Randall set his foot on Zena's arm and shifted the sword to Taushin, pressing the point into his gut. "Don't move, either one of you."

As soon as Jason grabbed the rope, Taushin let out a trumpeting wail, long and loud.

"He is calling for other dragons!" Arxad shouted.

"I'll put a stop to that." Randall drew his sword back, but just before he could strike Taushin, Zena swept her leg through his feet. He toppled backwards and slammed against the cobblestones. His head lolled to the side, and his eyes closed.

Jason tossed the rope to Elyssa, charged Taushin, and plowed into him, driving him to the ground. Tibalt staggered toward the battle, yelling, "I'm on my way!"

Belting out a scream, Zena leaped up and jumped on
Jason's back. She clawed his neck and cheek savagely.
Tibalt tore her away from Jason, but Zena threw Tibalt
to the ground and pounced on him like a wildcat. She
scratched the old man's face and drove a knee into his
stomach. He punched her in the nose, but she seemed to
register no pain.

Hyborn frowned, studying the battle as he glanced at
Arxad every few seconds. He seemed to be waiting to see
if the situation would get out of control.

"People of Starlight!" Koren shouted, pressing a hand
against her aching side. "Come to the aid of your fellow
humans! Now is the time to rise up. I know you have
never battled against your masters before, but if you want
to be free, you must fight now! If you capture Taushin and
Zena, you will be able to decide your own destiny!"

"Fight?" Yeager said. "You saw what Hyborn did to
Madam Orley. That was just a taste of what they would do
to our children." He thrust a finger toward the sky. "And
look. More dragons are coming. We wouldn't stand a
chance against so many."

A dragon descended from the direction of the Zodiac,
and another appeared, flying north from the mines. Soon
at least a dozen dragons approached from all directions.
When Zena turned to look, Tibalt grabbed her hair and
slung her away. Taushin clamped down on Jason's arm
with his jaws and slammed him to the ground.

Beating his wings, Arxad scooted toward them and
collided with Taushin. Taushin's teeth tore across Jason's
forearm, ripping his skin. With a back claw, Arxad

pinned Taushin to the ground, and, raising his head high, shouted, "Cease fighting!"

His voice rumbled like thunder. Everyone froze and stared at him. As he lifted his leg to allow Taushin to rise, several dragons landed, their wings pushing conflicting breezes through the crowd. Two stormed toward Arxad, mouths agape and teeth bared, knocking humans to the ground as they passed.

Arxad roared. "Stay where you are, fellow dragons! Taushin is unhurt. The slaves are not in rebellion."

Both dragons halted and looked around at the other dragons as if trying to decide what to do.

"There is no cause to react with violence," Arxad continued. "Let us have peace and discuss the reason for this assembly."

"I agree," Hyborn called. "Let us hear what Arxad has to say."

While the newly arriving dragons settled, Taushin rose to his haunches. Jason climbed to his feet, clutching his bleeding forearm. His sword lay on the ground, but he made no move to pick it up. He reached for Randall with his good arm and helped him to his feet. Randall blinked, as if in a daze. Tibalt stood in a stiff pose, like a soldier at attention, but he seemed ready to collapse at any moment.

Still holding the rope, Elyssa sat with Madam Orley. The two appeared to be whispering. Occasional sparks indicated that Deference sat with them as well. Madam held the Code in her lap, flipping through the pages. The edges were charred, but it seemed to be intact for the most part.

Koren released the pressure on her side and looked at her hand, reddened by sticky liquid. Blood? How could that be? The spear had punctured Exodus, not her body. Was she now connected to the star so completely that its wound had become her own?

And what should she do now? With so many dragons around, it was probably too late to fight. Their only chance was to capture and control Taushin, but Arxad seemed to have other ideas.

Koren looked out at Taushin. His eyebeams rested on Zena as she stared at Arxad. Blood spattered her dress, and her hair blew in disarray. "By what authority," Taushin said, "do you usurp control of this meeting? I am the king of the dragons."

"And I am high priest, so it is my duty to mediate conflicts. In that role, I supersede even the king. Perhaps you were unable to see that I ended the violence and a potential uprising. My role is that of a peacemaker."

"Very well. Say what you have to say. Then I will pronounce my judgment."

"When I arrived," Arxad said, "it was clear that Zena was about to plunge a spear into Exodus. The consequences of such an action are grave, so I had to stop it immediately. My passengers attempted to enforce my wishes in an aggressive manner, for which I apologize."

Taushin nodded. "I will take your apology into account."

Koren let Exodus drift lower. "Arxad," she said, trying to hide her pain, "Zena wasn't acting violently toward me. I was about to acquiesce to the spear, but I changed my mind at the last moment. That's when you arrived. Earlier,

Taushin promised to free the slaves if I would resurrect Exodus. I have fulfilled my part, and now pheterone is flooding the atmosphere. If Taushin has integrity, he will let my people go. If he would do what he promised, there would be no need for a revolt or any violence whatsoever. A good king keeps his word."

"A good king keeps his word," Taushin said, "according to the timetable he wishes to set. The cattle camp is empty, and the mining activities have ceased. I will let the people go when I believe dragonkind is able to adjust to life without servants and when humans have learned to take care of themselves. This is fair and reasonable for dragons and humans alike."

Koren surveyed the crowd. Taushin's words had a mollifying effect on everyone. They believed his rhetoric, even though he failed to specify a crucial element: the timetable. With those conditions, he could delay freeing the slaves for as long as he wished. In the meantime, he would never give up his attempts to get her back into his clutches. His tactics were clear—freedom for the slaves in exchange for her eyes. "To prove your words," she said, "you should set a firm date. I am sure we can agree on a reasonable time period."

Taushin shook his head. "Since such an adjustment has never occurred in the past, the time it will take is impossible to predict. Surely you can understand that we have to evaluate the humans' progress before we can let them go."

"It will never happen." Koren allowed Exodus to come within eight feet of the ground. "Dragons are addicted to human service, and humans are too accustomed to their chains. The only way to break these habits is for the humans to walk away from their chains, believing they can live without them."

"Nonsense. The change must be gradual. These people have been slaves all their lives." Taushin raised his voice. "What do you say, humans? Will you be able to defend yourselves against the wild beasts we dragons now chase away? Can you choose a leader who will govern you? Who among you is qualified to write your laws, police your activities, and render judgment when someone commits a crime? Can you build shelters in the colder climate when you have no craftsmen who have ever assembled anything more complex than a raft without the help of dragons?"

Murmurs rose from the crowd, peppered with a few clear statements. "He's right," and "I wouldn't want to be a leader," and "Hyborn chased a wolf away and saved my son."

"So you see," Taushin continued, "your own people realize that the faith you ask them to embrace is unreasonable. No one can make such a drastic change. It is impossible."

Koren glared at Taushin. He was crafty. His faithless rhetoric filtered into the ears of pitiful wretches who knew nothing other than cruel slavery. And those words brought nods of approval, nods of ignorance. How could someone who had never known freedom understand the reality of living without chains? Such a life seemed impossible, because they had never experienced it, nor seen anyone live it. Somehow, she had to show them the truth and expose Taushin for the liar he was.

Spreading out her cloak again, Koren called, "Jason! Elyssa! All who hail from Darksphere. Stand under me."

"No!" Taushin's ears rotated furiously. "You shall speak no more. You are too powerful for these good people and dragons to endure."

While Jason and the others from Darksphere gathered under Koren, Arxad lifted a wing toward Exodus. "Do you fear her influence? She speaks words, mere words. Allow us to decide whether to believe her or not."

"I appreciate your support, Arxad," Koren said as she spread out her cloak again, "but Taushin cannot silence me. No matter what happens, I must show these people what they cannot understand. Their slavery has blinded them, and they are deceived by those who are also blind. If I do not try everything possible to open their eyes, I would be a wicked sorceress indeed."

"She is a sorceress," Yeager said. "How else could a ghost be walking among us? She will hypnotize us again, and the dragons will retaliate against our children." He laid his hands over his ears. "If you want your little ones to live to see another day, don't listen to her."

Many others covered their ears, while some mothers covered the eyes of their children, especially those of the children who seemed to be trying to get a better look at Deference.

"I have an alternative idea." Taushin waved a wing. "Hyborn, select a child—a young female—and bring her to me. No man will rise up against us as long as we hold her."

With a quick snap of his neck, Hyborn snatched a female toddler with his teeth. He carried her to Taushin,

holding her by her tunic's collar. The girl wailed and
kicked, but Hyborn's grip stayed firm. A woman
screamed, "My daughter!" and tried to follow, but the
crowd held her back.

Hyborn set the girl down on her stomach in front of
Taushin and laid his tail over her struggling body. "This
one should be suitable," Hyborn said.

Arxad growled. "This is barbaric! Threats are no way
to control behavior. All you will do is prejudice their
thoughts against us and prove Koren's charge of cruelty."

"There will be no cruelty if the humans continue to
submit to my authority." Taushin nodded toward Koren.
"Say what you must, Starlighter. The people are aware of
the consequences if they heed your words."

Boiling inside, Koren spun her cloak around her legs.
"Hear me, you who live in chains, you who believe that
there is no life but slavery. You think you were born to
serve dragons and that there is no escape from your
labors, no avoiding their whips. I will show you otherwise. I will show you freedom. I will show you rest." She
lowered her hands to the floor of Exodus and, clutching
air, slowly raised her fists, as if pulling a heavy load from
below. Then she clapped her hands and spread them out
wide, shouting, "Behold!"

The village transformed again. A brown-grass meadow
stretched between the crowd and the Zodiac, and a shallow brook trickled over a bed of pebbles. Five children
and an old man danced at the edge, splashing each other
while laughing merrily. Three adults, two men and a
woman, sat to the right, one man with a long grass blade
in his mouth. Smiles abounded. The sound of singing

overwhelmed the babbling of the brook. In front of the
adults, a variety of breads and fruits covered a checkered
cloth of black and white.

One woman from the crowd padded slowly toward the
children, pointing. "That's Natalla! I'm sure of it!"

"And Tam," another woman said. "The man with the
grass in his mouth is Cowl, and Mark is sitting next to
him."

"And the man in the water is …" The first woman
walked through the grass to the edge of the brook. Then,
turning back, she shouted, "It's Micah! We thought they
were dead!"

Koren cried out again. "You are seeing the world we
have called Darksphere. The people standing under
me are the warriors who rescued Micah, Cowl, Mark,
and the girls. Now, instead of cringing under whips and
sweating through their toilsome labors, these former
captives play in a cool stream. You can see for yourselves
that there are no new stripes on their legs. Their eyes
are clear. Their faces are full. They exude joy. Slavery is
now a memory, a dark nightmare from which they have
awoken. This is the life that every child should live. Free.
Unshackled. Unburdened. Free to laugh, free to dance,
free to sing. Their chains are broken. Light has chased
away darkness. Love has conquered hate. Freedom has
triumphed over slavery."

Nearly every man, woman, and child watched the display, entranced, their shuffling feet drifting slowly toward
the joyous gathering. Yeager, his ears still covered,
glanced that way. His expression twisted into an angry
frown, but he stayed quiet.

"You fear for your children." Koren paused, wincing. The pain in her side was getting worse, and a deep gnawing in her gut seemed to grow, as if a rodent inside her stomach was trying to chew its way out. But she couldn't stop. Not now. "You fear that dragons will maim or kill them. It is true. They will. But is a moment of suffering worse than a lifetime of toil, decades of struggle, year upon year of lost joy? Will you sacrifice in order to provide the gift of freedom to future generations?"

A little boy broke away from the crowd and joined the circle of phantoms. He splashed with Micah and the others, his smile wider than any Koren had seen on a slave child. Several more children streamed toward them. Some looked back at the dragons, but when they saw their masters staring blankly, they turned and hurried to the dance.

Koren pressed a fist against her stomach, easing the pain enough to allow her to continue. "Taushin is a liar. He will never allow you to join these liberated souls. If you will only choose to believe my words, I will keep the dragons under my control. The few who can resist my power will not be able to stand against you."

"It's all true," Elyssa shouted. "I have been to that field myself."

"I took Micah and the others to that creek," Randall added. "I watched this celebration with my own eyes."

"I believe you!" one woman called.

An old man waved a gnarled hand. "It has to be true!"

While several more shouted their agreement, Exodus shifted lower. As its light made a halo around the Darksphere visitors, they moved out of the way.

Taushin shouted, "Koren cannot hold dragons under her spell forever. She will become weary, and when they break free, I will order them to kill every human who joins with her, as well as every child among you. There will be no exceptions."

A man with gray-speckled hair emerged from the crowd and looked up at Koren. "Will you really be able to keep the dragons under your spell?"

Koren studied the man's face. Although more wrinkled and scarred than the last time she saw him, he looked like Madam's brother, Samuel, one of the elder men. If he could be convinced, many would follow. "I will not lie to you, Samuel. My endurance is untested, and my strength could fail. Since I am merely a messenger, I think you will have to trust in the Creator rather than in me. The Creator is the one who calls you to freedom, and even if it requires the same agony your dear sister is suffering, we still must be willing to answer the call."

Looking down, Samuel shook his head. "Your words, the images of freed slaves, and your control over the dragons are temporary. They will soon fly away with the breeze. I think most of us need a better guarantee than that."

Koren moved her hand to her side and pressed against the wound. "Oh, Samuel, dear Samuel. Some might die. Some might suffer grave wounds. Even children might perish. Freedom cannot come without sacrifice. Joy for the many cannot come without the suffering of the few. I guarantee only that whatever suffering our people go through, the freedom the survivors find will be worth it."

"Survivors?" Yeager repeated loudly enough for everyone to hear. "So you don't guarantee anything."

A new round of murmurs buzzed through the crowd,
and expressions altered from smiles to frowns.

"If you turn against her," Taushin said, "all expressions
of rebellion will be forgiven, and you will be free to go
to your labors without punishment. And I will keep my
promise to grant your freedom as soon as possible, but
that cannot come without this rebellious girl's agreement
to submit to me."

Jason pointed a finger at Taushin. "What do you know
about freedom? You coerce with threats, sinking so low
that you hold a little girl hostage. Humans are consumed
by dragons, both in body and in spirit, and you grind the
leftovers into pulp to put out as bait for beasts. You are so
vile you call it a Promotion to be served as a dragon's dinner. You don't have a shred of decency, and no one here
should believe a word you say."

"You speak the venom of adders," Taushin yelled. "The
promoted slaves went to the Northlands. Arxad himself
will tell you that."

Arxad lowered his head. "I have nothing to say."

Fuming once again, Koren lifted her arms. "I didn't
want to show this orgy of carnage, but I must. I call upon
Starlight to give these people a view of Magnar's banquet
table. Parents, hide your children's eyes. This is a sight
they must not see."

The meadow disappeared. The brook evaporated. The
Starlight slave children ceased their dance, looking back
at the crowd with perplexed expressions. Several adults
waved their arms, urging them to return.

Magnar appeared where the meadow was before, sitting on his haunches. Agatha stood in front of him, wavering from side to side as if drugged.

"Arxad," Taushin said, "you must put a stop to this, or else I will tell them your role in this process."

Arxad's ears flattened. "I will not stop it. If the slaves hear about my participation, they will merely learn the truth. I am guilty of many crimes, and allowing this to happen is perhaps the worst crime of all. Let them judge me as they will."

Magnar grabbed Agatha's arm with a clawed hand. As he pulled her close to his open mouth, her eyes bulged, and her head bobbed like a rag doll's.

A woman screamed, then another. Children cried. A man covered a little girl's eyes and shouted, "How dare you show this to us? It's too gruesome!"

Yeager marched toward Elyssa. "I will put a stop to it!" He snatched the rope from her and jerked out the spear. The barbed point ripped a gash in the membrane, and the spear fell with a clank onto the ground.

Koren dropped to her knees, blood pouring from her side. Pain roared through her body. As she swayed back and forth, a gray cloud swept across her vision. It seemed that the ground drifted away, as if propelled by an unseen force.

Arxad's voice erupted. "Hurry! Throw the spear! We must keep Exodus from flying away!"

"I've got it!" Randall called. Seconds later, the spear again plunged through, this time making a hole above the first wound.

A new agony throttled Koren's body. More blood flowed. Something pulled the spear back through the hole, but the barb caught the membrane, holding it in place.

"Koren," Elyssa shouted. "Jason's on his way!"

Arxad's voice boomed. "Humans! Run for your lives! Hurry to your homes and wash yourselves thoroughly! The star is spreading a disease!"

More screams erupted, blended with the thunder of pounding footsteps. Each sound vibrated the spear, sending new shockwaves through Koren's body.

Blinking, she tried to look around. White gas spewed outward from the star's larger wound, and Exodus seemed to be pulling against the lodged spear. Randall and Tibalt stood below, holding the rope and keeping Exodus in place.

Jason climbed the Basilica gate's bars. Standing on top, he stretched toward Exodus, trying to grab the side opposite the wounds, but his fingers merely slipped across the smooth surface.

Fighting through the pain, Koren twisted to look at the spear. With tension on the rope constantly pulling, the barbed point tore at the membrane, ripping her own skin mercilessly. Fire crawled along the paper label around the explosive tube. It sparked and sizzled as if fueled by something more volatile than paper. She had to push the spear out or else risk getting her insides blown to pieces.

Clenching her teeth, Koren dropped to all fours and crawled toward the wound, but as spasms ripped through her muscles, she crumpled to a fetal position. A whispered prayer was all she could manage. "Oh, Creator ... have mercy ... Release me from this star."

Something snapped from around her head. The Starlighter's glowing crown floated upward, fading as it rose within Exodus. Gasping for breath, she watched the ground through the transparent floor.

Jason shouted from the top of the gate. "Elyssa! Throw me my sword!"

Elyssa scrambled for the sword and tossed it to him. He snatched the hilt out of the air and, with a wild swipe, sliced a gash in Exodus's wall and dropped the blade. He leaped and grabbed one side of the rip. As he hung there, a new stream of gas spewed over his hands and face. "I'm coming, Koren!" He sputtered and spat, but his determined expression never waned.

The pain in her side shredded her senses. The consuming beast in her stomach ravaged her insides. As a smoky curtain flooded her vision, dizziness spun the star into a wild frenzy.

The world above, below, and to every side blended into a whirlpool of colors, darkening every second, until everything turned black.

seventeen

As Petra slid down Xenith's back and set her feet on the floor of the incubator room, Cassabrie looked through Petra's eyes. The hole in the Basilica's ceiling provided plenty of light from the sun's early morning rays, illuminating the empty chamber.

She spoke to Petra's mind with a calm, even voice. "I see the passage that leads to the Zodiac. It's blocked by a stone. Do you see it?"

Petra lifted her hands in front of her eyes and spelled out, "Yes."

"You may nod for yes and shake your head for no. I will be able to detect those movements."

She nodded.

"Do you still have the crystal and the detonator? It was a pretty rough ride."

Petra reached under her cloak, patted a lump under her waistband, and nodded.

"Excellent. Now ask Xenith to stand guard here and wait for our return."

Petra spelled the command out quickly. Xenith nodded, her eyes exuding excitement. Earlier, as they crossed the barrier wall, one guard had flown to investigate, but with a series of brilliant, and frightening, maneuvers through the clouds, Xenith had eluded him. The journey had obviously stoked her adventurous spirit, and she took up her new post with vigor.

"You should be able to fit through a gap," Cassabrie said. "The obstacle was designed to keep dragons from passing through."

As Petra approached the passage, she said with her hands, "Dragons are strong enough to move a stone that size."

"Yes, if it were not anchored to the floor and wall. It seems that this was meant to be a permanent fixture."

After shedding her cloak, Petra lowered herself to her stomach and wriggled into a narrow opening between the base of the stone and the wall. Her shoulders wedged for a moment, but propelled by a sudden shove from the rear, she popped through.

Now on all fours, Petra looked back through the gap. Xenith's eyes appeared on the other side, twinkling with amusement.

"Just follow this tunnel, Petra," Cassabrie said. "I know it's dark, but the aura from the stardrop you swallowed should help you see."

Petra stood and laid a hand on a side wall. Letting her fingers slide, she tiptoed into the dark corridor. "Fear not the darkness," Cassabrie said. "Wallace told me about this place, and he is a noble young man. No matter how dark it gets, we can *know* that the ground is firm and no pitfalls await, because it has been tested by a trustworthy friend."

Petra's march gained speed. She looked down at her boots, barely visible in her glow. After a few seconds, they crunched grit underneath.

"Shhh," Cassabrie warned. "Slow your pace and try not to make a sound. Wallace didn't know if there would be a guard, but we have to assume so. Taushin is not one to leave this place unsecured."

Petra returned to walking on tiptoes. Ahead, a light came into view. Still looking through Petra's eyes, Cassabrie studied the path. Her many visits here in spirit form made the area a familiar one. She detected her body's presence long ago but never found a way to get to it. Now her chance had come.

The light grew brighter, signaling their closeness to the area where the sharp stakes lay under the Zodiac's entry corridor. The shadow of a long neck and head darkened the light before swinging out of view again.

"Stop," Cassabrie said. "Stay close to the wall."

Now in enough light to see, Petra flashed a finger message. "I saw a dragon."

"Me, too. It makes sense that it would be in that chamber instead of the next one. Most dragons wouldn't be able to stay around my body without losing their senses."

"What do we do now?" Petra spelled.

"We'll have to create a distraction. Let's see if we can draw close enough to get a look."

Petra tiptoed to the end of the tunnel and peered into the chamber. A bed of stakes took up most of the floor space, and a dragon stood to the right of the bed, its face pointing toward another tunnel on the opposite end of the chamber. Two lanterns on the wall, one near each tunnel opening, emanated strong, flickering light.

"A barrier wall guardian," Cassabrie said. "She will not be fooled easily."

Petra spelled out, "She is Shrillet. I have seen her before."

"I think only a dragon's voice will open the door. I will have to come out of your body for a short time so I can charm her into speaking the password for us. It will hurt again, so try not to groan."

Petra's fingers flew into action. "Not necessary. There is a hole in the door."

"Good, but we still have to get past Shrillet."

"If I run, maybe I can. If she chases me, she will become dizzy."

"She would be affected, but maybe not quickly enough. I could come out of you and try to hypno—"

A loud creaking noise interrupted. The chamber's ceiling opened. Two panels swung down, revealing a flying dragon dropping through.

"It's Fellina," Cassabrie said.

As Fellina landed, Shrillet swung toward her, her ears bent back and her eyes aflame. "Why are you here, mate of Arxad?"

"Taushin summoned all dragons to come to his aid," Fellina said, heaving deep breaths.

"I am excepted. My orders are to guard this area and allow no one to pass through."

Fellina thumped her tail, breaking one of the stakes. "And I am conveying the command of the king of the dragons. Are you refusing to obey?"

"Since when are you an emissary of Taushin? And since when does the high priest's mate take on such a menial task?"

"If you do not believe me, then follow and see. There is a great disturbance at the Basilica, and Taushin needs your aid."

"I have an idea," Petra spelled out.

"Okay," Cassabrie said. "Let's hear it."

"Too long to sign." Petra sprinted into the chamber.

"Wait! She will kill you!"

Shrillet roared at Petra. "What are you doing here?"

Petra, of course, didn't answer. She just kept running.

"You will die!" Shrillet reared her head back and launched a ball of flames. Fellina blocked it with a wing and flew at Shrillet, knocking her down.

As the two dragons fought, their tails whipped back and forth, Shrillet's on the floor and Fellina's in the air. Petra jumped over one tail, ducked under the other, and scurried into the tunnel leading to the sanctuary. She leaped through the hole in the door at the end of the tunnel and, once inside, halted.

Cassabrie gazed through Petra's eyes. Her body hovered over the floor, radiating silvery white light. With red hair, green eyes, and blue cloak, everything seemed intact, everything, that is, except two missing fingers.

Growls, roars, and shrieks pierced her reverie. The muscular guardian dragon would surely overcome Fellina soon. "Okay, Petra," Cassabrie said. "Let's find the hole for the crystal."

⋇

Clawing and pulling, Jason muscled into the sword-inflicted wound. He crawled across the floor of the deflating star, coming closer and closer to Koren's curled body as Exodus slowly sank.

Below, Randall let go of the rope and joined Elyssa. Positioned beneath the star, they extended their arms. "Jason!" Randall called. "Jump when you get her. Tibalt has the rope."

A sizzling sound and strange odor dragged Jason's attention from Koren's prone body to the spear jutting through the star's membrane nearby. "I have to check something." He scrambled past Koren and batted the sparks away from a tube attached to the spear. It stopped sizzling, at least for the moment. When he returned to Koren, he slid his arms under her body and lifted as he rose. The floor bent under their combined weights, and blood poured over his arms and dripped down to his trousers and shoes. "I've got you," he whispered. "We're only about eight feet off the ground now, so I'm going to walk to the opening and try to jump. Randall and Elyssa are down there ready to catch—"

The floor ripped away. Still cradling Koren, Jason dropped, bending his knees to brace for contact. Four arms broke his fall. As they steadied him, the arms guided him to his knees and Koren to the ground.

Elyssa swatted his shirt. "You're smoldering!"

"Thanks." Jason brushed Koren's hair from her eyes. She lay with her back on the ground and her hips turned to the right. Her cloak spread out underneath her body, catching blood in a pool next to her side.

Elyssa laid a hand on Koren's chest. "She's breathing, but I can't feel a heartbeat. She's losing a lot of blood."

"Where's Deference?"

"With her mother. She's coming."

"All dragons hear me!" Arxad shouted. "Go to your homes. Taushin has declared a new lockdown." The dragons took flight, some still wavering as they tried to shake off the effects of Koren's power.

Zena climbed aboard Taushin. As he lifted off the ground, he called out, "When the disease takes hold, you will need more than stardrops to cure their ills."

About ten paces from Koren, Exodus sat on the cobblestones, sputtering and sizzling. Its energy had collapsed into a ball of radiance, now no taller than a human adult. The spear lay next to it with the strange tube still attached.

While Tibalt and Randall gathered around, Deference knelt at Koren's side and reached her hand into the gaping wound. When she withdrew it, she looked at Jason and Elyssa in turn. "We can't just stitch the skin. She has internal damage that has to be repaired, or she'll die very soon. I'm surprised she isn't dead already."

Madam Orley joined them. She remained standing, her body stiff. "But we don't have a surgeon, Agatha. What can we do?"

"I think a stardrop's her only hope." Deference offered a weak smile and added, "Mother."

"But won't that just strip her spirit away?" Jason asked. "We didn't bring the manacles, so we don't have a way to preserve her body."

Arxad's head slid between Jason's and Elyssa's and hovered over Koren. "She is a Starlighter. Just as the stardrop did not kill Elyssa, it should not be fatal to Koren. Koren is likely even more immune than Elyssa was."

Jason looked at his palms. The pain from the last time he had scooped a stardrop was still a fresh memory, but that didn't matter. "I'll get one."

As he began to rise, Elyssa pushed him back down. "Stay put, hero. You've suffered enough." She hurried to the remains of Exodus, scooped out some of the radiance, and walked back slowly, compressing the light in her hand. "It'll be just a few seconds."

"Arxad, what's all this talk about a disease?" Jason asked.

As Arxad straightened, his head reeled back with his neck. "This is exactly what I feared. Very few know what happened the last time a human punctured Exodus. It released a disease that killed every human on Starlight. With the previous event, it merely sprayed the gas-born virus as it flew away. This time, Exodus stayed here and emptied every drop of its blight over the crowd."

"Had anyone come close to developing a cure?"

"Somewhat close," Arxad said. "At least we thought so. The most brilliant scientist I have ever known, Orson by name, worked tirelessly to find a cure. However, even though he was motivated by the impending death of his daughter, he was unable to complete his work before they both perished along with all of humanity. But he was able to salvage two uninfected human embryos, and we encased them in incubating eggs. I took them to Darksphere, cared for them until they hatched, and went back and forth between the worlds for the next thirty years, helping them learn how to survive. I provided some technology that the humans had here before the plague, including an understanding of genetics and light, but I tried to keep them from learning about advanced weaponry. All of this took place more than five hundred years ago. Only a few of us are old enough to remember those days—myself, Magnar, Hyborn, and our recently departed Tamminy."

"I've got it." Elyssa opened her palm. A dazzling stardrop rolled around in the center. "Now I have to get her to swallow it." She lowered herself to her knees, pushed the stardrop deep into Koren's mouth, and pressed her lips closed. Koren gagged and jerked her head, but her reflexes took over, and she swallowed the stardrop.

As Jason moved out of the way, Elyssa planted a knee on each side of Koren's body and dangled the pendant over her. She laid her palm on Koren's chest and, just as she had done with Petra, slid her hand toward Koren's stomach. "I found it. It just dropped out of her esophagus."

Koren lurched. Her arms flailed. She kicked wildly, but Elyssa sat fully on Koren's hips, pinning her.

Randall locked down one of Koren's arms, while Jason held the other. Koren's face glowed red. She wagged her head from side to side, groaning loudly.

Tilting her head upward, Elyssa cried out, "The pain! Oh! It's so horrible!" Her pendant seemed to catch on fire.

Turning redder than Koren's face, it sizzled as it swayed back and forth over Koren's abdomen.

Deference touched the wound on Koren's side. "It's not closing, but the bleeding is slowing down."

Koren's eyes snapped open, but they seemed crazed. She stared at Elyssa and cried out, "Can you see them? Look! You must help them!"

Koren's back arched, bucking Elyssa. Elyssa grabbed Koren's cloak and hung on, her eyes rolling wildly.

"I see them!" Elyssa cried out. "I see the people!"

As Koren settled, her whispers gurgled. "Dive ... dive into ... their pain. Say what I cannot. I will ... give you words."

Clutching Koren's cloak with shaking hands, Elyssa moaned as she spoke. "Their skin peels. Their flesh rots. The children crumble into pieces before a mother's crying eyes. Fathers mourn, lifting up arms with no hands as they beg for an end to the suffering. Common graves fill with limbless bodies, and no one sings a dirge. Who can weep when the reservoirs are drained?"

Elyssa pressed on Koren's stomach, her pendant still sizzling red as she spoke with a series of erratic gasps. "Some rot on the inside. With no loved ones to carry them, they must crawl to the grave and wait for death to come. Taking in a final breath, they curse the Creator and roll into the pit. There they join the forsaken, the forgotten, the foul masses who now carry the stench of souls who lived in the security of a shadow and carried it with them to eternal darkness."

Finally, Koren's eyes closed, and her breathing steadied.

BRYAN DAVIS

Elyssa blew out a long breath. She blinked and stared at her hand, still resting on Koren's stomach. "I can feel her heartbeat from here. It's strong and regular."

"The wound is still open on the surface," Deference said, "but the bleeding's stopped. I think she's going to be all right."

Jason patted Elyssa on the back. "You did it again! You're amazing!"

"I wish Orion could have seen you," Randall said. "If the light of goodness was ever in anyone, it's in you."

"Thank the Creator." Elyssa rose slowly. Her pendant's glow faded from red to dull orange, and its sizzling quieted. She set her palm under it and showed it to Arxad. "What about manna wood and the healing trees? Could you have used them to heal the infected people?"

Arxad brought his head close to the pendant, "We did not have the healing trees then, but they would not have helped. They are useful only for injuries. The trees consist of a variety of wood that is similar to your pendant, so they have similar limitations. Although they could mend some of the results of the infection, they cannot purge the disease."

"How long does it take for symptoms to show up?" Jason asked.

Arxad's eyes darted from Jason to Elyssa and back again. "It varies from human to human, but once the disease is contracted, it kills quickly, so you should assume that you have very little time. That is why I asked Uriel to begin studying the books I left for him, in case Exodus was perforated once again. They are Orson's notes."

Jason raised a finger. "Wait a minute. If this virus will infect every human, what about the army my father is leading down here from the Northlands?"

"Since Exodus stayed in our area, your army will likely not be affected unless they come near the humans who were exposed." Arxad curved his neck, making his head face northward. "And since it is an airborne virus, they should probably stay well north of the barrier wall. Any breeze could carry a deadly passenger."

"What good are the soldiers out there?" Randall pointed at the ground. "We need them here."

"But they'll just rot and die if they come here," Jason said. "Even if they were able to free every slave, where would they go? Back to Major Four to infect every human on our world?"

Arxad bent back and looked at Koren. "We should send word for them to wait in the meadow. When Koren fully recovers, perhaps we won't need them for battle. With a stardrop-empowered Starlighter, we might be able to set every slave free without an army."

Jason touched the edge of Koren's cloak. "You mean she'll become even more powerful than before?"

"It is only a theory, a theory based on what Cassabrie was able to do when energy from the Reflections Crystal poured into her. She emitted a destructive beam that left Zena blind."

"A photo gun wrapped in a girl's body," Tibalt said. "I needed that a little while ago."

Deference appeared, rising to a standing position. "I don't think you need me anymore. I would like to help my mother treat her burns."

"Of course," Elyssa said. "Take all the time you want."

"If you need us, we'll be at the butcher's shop. He'll have plenty of water." Deference and Madam Orley walked down the road, Madam hobbling on stiff legs.

Elyssa turned back to Arxad. "An energized Koren won't do any good if we all die. Even if I could use my pendant on every sick person, it would take weeks to help them all. It would be impossible to get to everyone in time."

Arxad's sigh left twin puffs of smoke in the air. "And futile. Treating symptoms instead of the cause brings only a temporary benefit. The infection would remain and continue its unrelenting damage. I witnessed its horror too many times to hope for a better result."

"Jason," Elyssa said, "weren't you exposed to the leak from Exodus when you were in the star chamber? You never got sick."

Jason scratched the back of his hand. "Actually, I did start feeling an itch on my skin, but it never developed into anything. Maybe when Cassabrie applied the star-drop particles to my hands to heal them, she healed the disease at the same time."

"Or," Elyssa said, touching Jason's shirt, "since Cassabrie was a Starlighter, maybe she was immune, and her genetic material inside you is like a vaccine that kept the disease from taking hold. That litmus finger might have saved your life."

Jason looked at Koren again. Her eyelids trembled but stayed closed. "What makes you think Cassabrie's immune? Just because she's a Starlighter?"

antn

"I'm not sure. It's a long story, but here's the short version. I met a ghostlike girl, who I now am certain was Cassabrie, weeks ago in my dungeon cell, and she told me if someone raised Exodus without sealing its wound, the disease would be unleashed again, and every member of the human race would die except for one. She said I was genetically protected, and only I could safely seal the wound."

"Whoa!" Tibalt said. "That's some whoppin' tale to be hiding from us all this time."

"I've been looking for chances to find Exodus, but other life-or-death emergencies got in the way. I didn't even think about it until recently. I thought back then it was a dream, or maybe I was going insane." Elyssa shrugged and gave a disarming smile. "Anyway, when I finally saw the star, it was already sealed, so I didn't mention it."

"Only one would survive?" Jason asked. "If Starlighters are immune, why would that be? Koren would survive, wouldn't she?"

"Maybe she meant besides me, you know, if I didn't come here to seal the wound." Elyssa rubbed her finger and thumb together. "When I used a stardrop to cure you, Jason, it burned off some of my skin cells, and they entered your body. That made me think that somehow the energy combines with the genetic code. Since you have part of Cassabrie already inside you, the same thing happened when Cassabrie healed your hands and cured the disease. If we can find the reason in our genetics, maybe Uriel could make a vaccine out of a combination of stardrop energy and the genetic code."

"There are many factors to consider," Arxad said. "Jason was in the star chamber in the Northlands. We have no idea how that might have affected the virus. Also, this disease killed Koren's genetic duplicate when she was a child. This is part of a much longer story, but I will provide a summary.

"After Cassabrie died, hoping to create a new Star-lighter, I used the genetic code I saved from the original Koren to create a new Koren. Her surrogate parents were not her original parents, but I named them Orson and Emma in case she had memories of those names. I say *memories* because I also preserved Koren's spirit in the Reflections Crystal, and that spirit, although very young, likely retained some vestiges of memory. Alaph showed me how to infuse her spirit into the embryo as I put it together. He explained that the Creator had blessed this procedure, but not being a prophet myself, I cannot verify his claim. It worked quite well, and now we have Koren."

Jason looked at Koren once more, this time staring. She had been preserved for centuries, the product of a complex plan to save both dragons and humans from extinction. "What did you do with Orson's genetics?"

"I used them long before Koren was reborn to create a scientist Alaph said we would need."

Jason looked toward the north. "Uriel?"

"Your deduction is excellent." Arxad's draconic lips bent into a wry smile. "As you might have noticed from your dealings with Uriel, his memory is selective and unpredictable. He seems to remember events as they are reintroduced to him, so my hope is that as he reads his own work, he will be able to resume his research without delay."

Jason nodded. "I noticed the memory problem. He met Koren, but he didn't seem to remember her."

"He remembers Koren as an infant. Perhaps her name creates a mental echo, but he has not yet been able to make the connection. Considering all the emotional ramifications, I think it would be unwise to reveal Koren's parentage to her until the crisis is over." Arxad let out a rumbling sigh. "In any case, to return to the topic, since Koren has the same genetics as her unfortunate predecessor, I do not see how she could be immune to the virus."

"Maybe she's not." Elyssa raised a hand. "Remember Cassabrie said that I'm the only one who can safely seal the wound. Since Cassabrie has no body, she knew I was the only immune *living* human. Maybe Cassabrie and I are the only ones who are immune."

"Interesting theory," Arxad said. "If it is true, I would like to know the source of her information."

Jason pushed a strand of hair back from Koren's forehead. "Then Koren's been exposed for quite a while. Why hasn't she shown any symptoms?"

"Maybe she has," Arxad said. "Her predecessor displayed none externally until hours before her death. Sometimes the disease killed from the inside out."

Elyssa walked back to the remains of Exodus, still a head-high ball of radiance, and scooped out another handful of energy. "So my theory," she said as she returned, "is if I use a stardrop and my pendant, I might be able to cure anyone who is infected if I slough off genetic material as I work."

"From what I saw when you healed Petra," Jason said, "the process is draining. There's no way you could heal that many people. How many are there? A thousand?"

Arxad nodded. "At least. Perhaps twelve hundred. And numbers are not the only issue to consider. Since the resistant genetic material is within you, it is likely in your bloodstream, so a topical application of stardrop material enhanced by manna bark and skin cells might not be enough."

Jason touched his chest. "If the litmus finger is like a vaccine for me, developing one on a larger scale is our only option."

"But if I go to the Northlands to give Uriel genetic material," Elyssa said, "I can't be here to counter the symptoms. Some people might die before a vaccine could be ready."

Jason lifted her tresses. "One of us could take some genetic material to Uriel. Back home, hair was enough to open genetic locks."

"Perhaps," Arxad said, "but we do not know if a genetic code will be sufficient for developing a vaccine. The finger inside you includes skin, bone, and blood. If the cure involves one of those components, sending hair will be a waste of valuable time."

Elyssa spread out her fingers. "I suppose I'll have to do it."

"Do what?" Jason asked.

"Give up a finger. If Uriel needs flesh, bone, and blood, it's the easiest way. If you chop a little finger with your sword—"

"No!" Jason said, wincing. "There's got to be a better way."

Elyssa raised her brow. "Do you have another idea?"

"I do," Arxad said. "We can have one immune human go to the Northlands while another stays here."

Jason glanced between Elyssa and Arxad. "Another? But Elyssa's the only one. Cassabrie's been dead for—"

"Maybe that is no longer true." Arxad spread out his wings. "Mount quickly. It is time to see what Fellina has learned about Cassabrie."

eighteen

While the battle between Fellina and Shrillet raged in the stakes chamber, piercing the air with shrieks and roars, Petra drew close to Cassabrie's floating body. Cassabrie studied the devices that held her in place—one glass disk embedded in the ceiling and one in the floor, each radiating stardrop energy. "I think I see where to put the crystal," she said into Petra's mind.

Petra signed, "Where?"

"The stardrops covered by the disks are arranged in a circle. You probably have to insert the peg right through the middle. But hurry. I don't think the dragon fight will last much longer."

Petra set the point of the crystalline peg on top of the floor disk and pushed, but it wouldn't penetrate. Her head swaying, she raised four fingers and pointed at the stardrops.

"I see what you mean," Cassabrie said. "Maybe since three are missing, the locking mechanism is broken."

The sounds of battle eased, replaced by heavy breathing.

Petra spelled out, "What now?"

"Look up for me! Quick!"

Petra slid the peg behind her waistband and looked up, giving Cassabrie a view of her body floating directly above. Beyond her head, the disk in the ceiling shone with seven untouched stardrops. "Are you too dizzy to climb?"

Without answering, Petra grabbed a handful of Cassabrie's cloak and a handful of her dress and pulled herself up. The body sank with her weight for a moment before rebounding. She set one foot on top of Cassabrie's and vaulted, setting her other foot in the crook of Cassabrie's arm. Finally, she set her knees on Cassabrie's shoulders.

"Wonderful, Petra. You're almost there. Fight my body's influence. Just concentrate."

The sound of breathing grew closer, punctuated by growls and grunts.

Balancing herself, Petra withdrew the crystal, set her free hand on Cassabrie's head, and shifted from her knees to her feet. Now fully standing, she reached the peg toward the ceiling disk. Cassabrie's body shifted and bobbed, but Petra compensated for every move.

A loud dragon cough sounded from the corridor. Petra wobbled. She rotated her arms, trying to keep her balance. Finally, she thrust herself up to tiptoes and pressed the pointed end of the crystalline peg against the center of the disk, bracing herself.

"It's not going through," Cassabrie said.

Petra shook her head, alternating between looking at the disk above and her precariously balanced feet below.

"Since you swallowed a stardrop," Cassabrie said, "I thought you might be able to push it through. At least that was my theory."

Petra spelled out "think fast" with her free hand.

"Let's see if I can give you a power boost." Cassabrie searched the energy fields. Radiance from four sources made their way into her mind—strong flows from the disk above and below, as well from as her lifeless body, and a weaker one from inside Petra. Extending her spirit's energy toward the source within Petra, she concentrated. Somehow she had to overcome the weakening effect her own body's radiance caused.

A panting, scratching sound drew near. Shrillet was probably only seconds away.

Pouring all her energy into Petra, Cassabrie cried out, "Now, Petra! Push as hard as you can!"

"Get down from there, you foul human!"

Petra gasped. With a leap, she thrust the peg as hard as she could. The point plunged through the center of the disk, and it embedded firmly within. Her feet slipped and slid down Cassabrie's chest. Petra threw her arms over Cassabrie's shoulders and hung on.

Blood oozing from one eye, Shrillet stomped toward them, a noticeable limp in her gait. "I told you to get down!"

Above, radiance flooded the implanted crystal. It shot a beam directly into Cassabrie's head and through her feet. In a brilliant flash of light, both disks shattered, and Cassabrie's body dropped to the floor in a mass of limp arms and legs. Petra landed on Cassabrie's chest, cushioning her fall.

"Now hang on," Cassabrie shouted. "I'm coming out of you and going into my body. Get one of the stardrops and make me swallow it. Shove it down my throat if you have to. I'll try to stimulate the muscles to force it into my stomach."

Petra wrapped one arm around Cassabrie's body and groped for the floor disk with the other.

"Oh, no, Petra! My body's on top of the disk!"

Shrillet whipped her spiny tail around and smacked Petra's cheek, but she hung on tightly.

"Let go immediately!" Shrillet teetered, still showing the effects of the energy that radiated throughout the room.

"Don't Petra. She'll roast you! The only reason she hasn't done it already is because you're hanging on to me. You'll have to drag my body off to get to a stardrop. She's hurt and losing control. She can't last much longer."

Petra dabbed her cheek and set her bloody fingers in front of her eyes.

"I'm sorry, Petra, I know it's dangerous—Get down!"

Petra ducked. Shrillet's tail whipped over her, brushing her scalp. Then Shrillet's teeth clamped down on her side, snagging her tunic and digging into her ribs. The dragon lifted, but Petra hung on to Cassabrie, moaning as she dragged the limp body along.

"Now, Petra! I'm transferring now! The disk is uncovered."

With a jerk of her head, Shrillet gave Petra a toss. She and Cassabrie's body flew several feet, then rolled completely over, leaving Petra on top again.

As the dragon advanced once more, Cassabrie poured out through Petra's chest and into her own. Petra moaned, louder this time. The transfer out was as painful as the entrance, but Cassabrie had no choice. The only way to save Petra from the dragon was to resurrect herself and fight.

"If you do not release her immediately," Shrillet said, her words now slurred, "I will sever your head from your body with a snap of my jaws."

Petra scrambled on all fours, jammed her hand into the floor disk's broken glass, and yanked out a stardrop. Shrillet blasted a stream of flames at her, but Petra lunged out of the way just in time. With the stardrop in her fist, she leaped back to Cassabrie, forced open her mouth, and pushed the shining sphere deep into her throat.

Shrillet snapped at Petra. She ducked again, but the dragon caught her hair, jerked her away from Cassabrie, and threw her against the wall, slamming her head on the stone surface. Petra slumped in a sitting position, her eyes closed.

Cassabrie pinpointed her energy on the throat muscles behind the stardrop. *Push it down! I have to revive and help Petra!*

"Now to dispose of this troublemaker!" Shrillet stomped toward Petra.

Cassabrie poked her head out of her body and screamed, "No! Wait!"

"What?" Shrillet pivoted, nearly toppling. "Who said that?"

"I did." Cassabrie ducked back down and watched the confused dragon through her body's open mouth.

Shrillet shuffled close and extended her neck. She set her snout over Cassabrie's face and sniffed. "There is no life in this human." Drawing back, she looked left and right. "Who is here? I heard you speak."

Cassabrie stimulated the throat muscle again. The stardrop moved down the esophagus slowly ... too slowly.

"If you do not answer, I will make a torch out of this girl."

Cassabrie called out through her body's mouth. "It is I, Cassabrie. Do not harm her."

"What? Impossible!" Shrillet drew close and sniffed again. "I detect something warm but no breathing."

The stardrop fell into Cassabrie's stomach. The energy field expanded, filtering through the stomach lining and then throughout the body. She spread her spirit, sending her arms, legs, and head into their proper places. Now if the attachment were to be made and Petra saved from the dragon, it was up to the Creator. There was nothing she could do but watch and wait.

"Someone is deceiving me." Shrillet marched back toward Petra, her gait still hobbled. "Whoever is here, you have until the count of five to show yourself before I kill this girl ... One!"

Cassabrie felt her body filling with energy, but it was so slow!

"Two!"

Her heart felt warmer, but it still wasn't beating. What might jolt it enough to get it started?

"Three!"

Heat filtered into her arms and legs, but they still wouldn't move. This was worse than any nightmare!

"Four!"

Her mind felt strange, like something was sucking it from her spirit. Could this be the attachment? Or might it mean the approach of final death—the journey to the afterlife? She had to shout, reveal herself, stop Shrillet! But she couldn't speak. Nothing seemed to work.

"Five!"

A blast of fire lit up the chamber. Cassabrie gasped. Her heart thumped. She shot to a sitting position and looked around. Flames covered Petra's clothes from her knees to her neck.

Cassabrie screamed, "Here I am, you monster!"

Shrillet turned. As she reared back to blast fire again, Arxad burst into the chamber and smashed into her. Jason followed. In a mad dash, he leaped for Petra and rolled her on the floor, desperately trying to smother the flames.

Arxad pinned Shrillet's head with a foreclaw. "Be still or die!"

"Human lover!" she snarled. "You have always favored the rats over your own species."

Randall hustled in, his sword drawn. "I'll watch this one," he said, pressing the point against Shrillet's underbelly. "You'd better find Deference. Fellina needs her."

With a beat of his wings, Arxad flew past Cassabrie, snatched a stardrop from the floor, and burst through the exit, creating a bigger hole than before.

Cassabrie struggled to her feet, her legs wobbly. As she staggered toward Jason and Petra, throbbing darkness veiled her vision.

Jason sat with Petra cradled in his arms. He looked up at Cassabrie, tears running down his sooty cheeks. "She's alive, but I don't know for how long. We need Elyssa and her pendant. She's with Fellina in the room with the stakes."

"I'll get her," Cassabrie said.

In a burst of movement, Shrillet jerked away from Randall's sword and slapped him with a wing. He fell to his backside and flipped into a somersault. Shrillet jumped to her feet and aimed her snout at Randall. "Human! How dare you threaten me with that puny weapon!"

Randall smacked her face with his sword, but it just bounced off her tough scales. Jason slid Petra out of his arms, shouting, "Randall! I'm coming!"

Shrillet swung her tail and smacked Randall's face with a spine, knocking him flat on his side. As the dragon drew in a breath, Cassabrie thrust out both arms and yelled, "Stop!" Like a wave of pure light, radiant energy burst from her hands and slammed into Shrillet. The force shoved the she-dragon to the wall and pressed her against it, keeping her pinned as new ripples pulsed from

Cassabrie's hands. "Jason! Strike her down! I can't do this for long."

Jason leaped to his feet and snatched up Randall's sword. Cassabrie lowered her arms, extinguishing the energy field. While Shrillet slumped to the floor, Jason drove the blade into her belly. His jaw clenched, he twisted the sword sharply and jerked it out, leaping away from the gushing fluids.

He grabbed Randall's hand and pulled him to his feet. "Are you all right?"

His cheek and chin dripping blood, Randall nodded. "I think so."

"You help him," Cassabrie said. "I'll help Petra." She grabbed a stardrop from the floor disk and scooped Petra into her arms. "Don't die, precious girl. I'll get you to Elyssa."

Her face as black as charcoal, Petra moaned and raised her burned hands. Slowly, painfully, she signed, "You're ... alive. You aren't an angel ... after all."

"No, dearest one." Cassabrie's voice quaked as she hurried through the tunnel. "I think when you see a real angel, you'll know it."

Petra's fingers began a reply, but they relaxed and dropped to her chest. Cassabrie ran faster, her heart pounding. Though the stardrops had kept her physical muscles from atrophy, it felt very strange to be fighting gravity after so many years.

When she reached the stakes chamber, she slowed to a halt, panting for breath. Elyssa knelt next to Fellina, who lay motionless on her side. Arxad sat on his haunches, his neck swaying with his head. He seemed to be sweeping his gaze from one end of Fellina's body to the other, apparently too nervous to stay still.

Elyssa's pendant glowed fiery red as it dangled below her neck. Koren sat against a wall with her knees pulled up to her chest and her hood raised over her head, shadowing her eyes. She appeared to be weeping.

"Koren!" Cassabrie called. "I have Petra! She's hurt!"

"Petra?" Her face twisting in pain, Koren struggled to her feet and limped toward them. "How did you get your body back?"

"Later." Cassabrie laid Petra close to Elyssa. "Can you try to heal her with the manna pendant? I have a stardrop in case hers is too weak."

Still kneeling, Elyssa looked up at Cassabrie. Tear tracks stained her cheeks. "It didn't work on Fellina, at least not very well."

Koren dropped to her knees and combed her fingers through Petra's hair. "Petra! Can you hear me?"

Petra made no sign, but her chest still rose and fell ... barely.

"Is Fellina dead?" Cassabrie asked.

Elyssa shook her head. "Close, though. According to Deference, Shrillet severed an important artery in Fellina's neck. Arxad can't move her, or she'll die for sure, and we have no surgeon. Deference is trying to repair the artery by stitching it with some of Koren's hair, but she can't hold on to things very well, and I can't get my hands between Fellina's scales to touch the artery."

"Do you have enough strength to try to save Petra?" Koren asked.

Elyssa clutched her pendant, her eyes weary but determined. "I'll do my best."

Cassabrie touched Koren's cloak. "Where is Exodus?"

"Near the Basilica," Koren said, pointing upward. "It's sitting on the ground, deteriorating."

Cassabrie knitted her brow. "You're no longer attached to it. It must have a Starlighter dwelling within, or it will dwindle down to nothing, and the world will forever be without a guiding light."

"Does it matter?" Arxad asked, his head now still and drooping. "Humans and dragons alike have rejected wisdom. We deserve to be without pheterone and without a guide. It is a lost cause."

"I don't believe in lost causes." Cassabrie set her fists on her hips. "And I'm not going to let Starlight perish into ultimate darkness."

Jason walked in, supporting Randall with a shoulder under his arm. "What can I do to help?"

"Water," Deference called, her glowing head appearing near Fellina's neck. "We need water for Petra's burns."

Cassabrie stepped in front of Arxad. "Is the fountain in the Zodiac still flowing?" she asked.

Arxad stared at her blankly. "It ran dry shortly after you perished. The butcher's barrel is likely full." He let his head droop again. "Every calamity has happened because I hesitated to oppose the evil around me. I assumed that patience rather than aggressive opposition would bring about the Creator's desired ends."

Cassabrie stamped her foot. "Don't play the despondent dragon. I know you too well. You have defended justice too many times to surrender now. If you want to lament about lacking aggression, then do it while making up for your passivity. Fellina is in the Creator's hands now, so it's time to show a little faith."

Jason joined them and slapped Arxad's flank. "It's time for action! Take me to the butcher's shop!"

"It is likely already too late for water, but ..." Arxad nuzzled Fellina's cheek, whispered something in her ear, then lowered his body. "Come. I will take you."

While Jason climbed on, Koren pushed her hood back, revealing her signature hair and eyes. "Is there anything I can do?"

"Yes." Cassabrie pushed the stardrop into Koren's hand. "You can do this as well as I can. I'll find a way to restore Exodus."

Koren closed her fingers around the stardrop. "We need to talk sometime."

"We will. I'm sure of it." Cassabrie stooped next to Petra and withdrew the control box from her scorched waistband.

"What's that?" Jason asked as Arxad rose from his belly.

Cassabrie quickly slid the box into her pocket. "Something that I must keep secret for now. I hope you will trust me."

"Sure. I trust you." Jason shrugged weakly. "I don't see why I shouldn't."

She looked at Jason's belt as he sat atop Arxad. Mounted as he was, with his sword hanging in a scabbard at his side, this young man she had dwelled within was an inspiring sight to behold. Yet, she couldn't tell him why she wanted Koren to exercise her gifts without a more experienced Starlighter around. He would ask too many questions. "Will you be my bodyguard, at least until I get to Exodus?"

"Of course." He reached down a hand. "I'll give you a lift. No use making Arxad get down again."

Riding Jason's pull, Cassabrie climbed up to Arxad's back and settled behind Jason, her hands braced on his hips. As Arxad reared on his haunches, she took in a deep breath. He jumped into the air and flapped his powerful wings, shooting upward so fast, her body pressed down on his scales. Soon he flew out the Zodiac's open double doors, through the portico, and into the air.

Exhaling, she luxuriated in the sunshine and cool breeze. Although it felt wonderful to move and breathe again, it seemed wrong to enjoy it. Petra lay back there in agony, close to death, and the fate of all the world rested on the skill of a Starlighter.

Cassabrie sighed. Years ago, she had refused to take Brinella's place as the guiding light, and her choice had cost everyone dearly. She wasn't about to make the same mistake again.

nineteen

"We'd better get started," Koren said. "Petra's barely breathing."

Elyssa touched Koren's head. "Can I get some more hair first? Deference prefers yours."

"Sure." Koren lowered her chin. "As much as you need."

Elyssa plucked several strands of Koren's hair and extended them toward Fellina's neck wound. "Here, Deference."

A glowing hand appeared and snatched the hair. "Thank you."

Elyssa hurried to Petra and crouched at her side. "Okay. Let's give it a try."

Koren opened her hand, revealing the shimmering stardrop.

"Who should swallow it?" Elyssa asked. "Me or her?"

"I have no idea."

Elyssa knelt over Petra, one knee on each side of her hips, and clutched her pendant. "Try to get Petra to swallow it."

Koren pushed the stardrop between Petra's charred lips, but as soon as the burning sphere touched her stub of a tongue, Petra bit down and spat half of it out. The stardrop fragment plinked on the floor and sizzled as it dwindled away. Her eyes clenching shut, she let out a gut-wrenching moan.

Elyssa reached for the stardrop, but Koren grabbed her wrist. "I don't think she'll let me try again. I'll just get her to swallow what's in her mouth."

"But she might need it all." Elyssa scooped up the now-tiny fragment. In seconds, it sizzled down to nothing. "This isn't good."

"It can't be helped. Let's do it."

Nodding, Elyssa laid her hand over Petra's dark lips while Koren massaged her scalded cheeks. "Come on, Petra," Koren whispered. "Swallow it."

As Petra's body trembled, Elyssa spoke in a soothing tone. "Settle down, sweetheart, and let me probe deep inside. I can feel the stardrop's energy near the back of your throat. It's stuck there, but it's healing the scar tissue." Elyssa looked at Koren. "I think she must have inhaled some of the flames."

"Looks like it. She might be burned all the way down to her lungs."

Using both hands, Elyssa ripped open Petra's tunic, peeling the fused material away from her melted flesh and revealing dark, oozing burns. "Oh, dear Creator! This is terrible!"

Koren grimaced. "Her skin looks like it's still burning."

Elyssa lowered her hand close to Petra's chest but jerked it back. "She's so hot! What should I do?"

"We need the water," Koren said, "but we can't wait."

"I think you're right." Elyssa eased her hand down onto the dripping sores, cringing as her fingers melded with the spongy, dark flesh. "I'm probing again. Pray for a miracle."

Koren drew her hood over her head and looked up. The ceiling was open, allowing her to see one of the murals in the Zodiac corridor, the painting of Cassabrie standing within the glowing sphere. Only moments ago, Koren had stood at the outer doorway studying the artwork while Arxad broke the stakes with his tail, allowing Jason and Randall to safely jump. Then, as she dropped down to their waiting arms, the idea of help coming from above never felt so real, but human help wasn't enough. They couldn't do this alone. "Creator of all," she said, her voice cracking, "hear my plea. Ease Petra's suffering. Cause the stardrops to do their work. Repair what is damaged and lift her to full healing. She is such a precious girl, an adopted sister I will always cherish. It is I who got her involved in all this trouble, and she bravely accepted every challenge. Bless her. Hold her. Let her know that you are pleased with her faith and courage."

"I sense a movement," Elyssa said. "It's not physical. Something is shifting at the very core of her being. When I healed you, I was able to connect myself with your thoughts and feelings, but this time I'm not finding the connection with Petra."

Koren licked her lips, trying not to cry. "Maybe it's because she's not a Starlighter."

"Or maybe it's because she's dying." Elyssa closed her eyes. "Wait. I think ... Yes, here she is."

Petra's body settled, and her eyes fluttered open. She lifted an arm and pointed toward the ceiling.

Koren looked. There was nothing but darkness.

"I ... I see him," Elyssa called. "He's coming this way."

Koren looked in the direction Petra stared. "Who?"

Elyssa's voice rang out with joy. "Cassabrie said I'd know an angel when I saw one. He is so beautiful!" Petra's mouth stayed closed, but her eyes seemed to communicate while Elyssa translated with spoken words. "He's holding out his hand."

Petra reached, straining and groaning.

"You're trying to touch the angel?" Koren asked.

Her own face twisting in pain, Elyssa nodded. "Take me there. I want to go to heaven. No one here believes in me."

"No!" Koren cried. "Don't die! Petra, my dear sister, don't leave me! I believe in you! I love you! I love you more than life!"

Petra's arm dropped to her side. She puffed fast, shallow breaths, her eyes now wild.

"Dear angel," Elyssa shouted, "please wait! I have one request before I go. I want to give Koren a message."

All three paused. As complete silence held sway, it seemed that time itself had stopped.

Petra took in a deep breath, then, with her eyes back to normal, she gazed at Koren. Lifting her hands, she began forming a message with her fingers, but they bent against each other, and the signs lost their shape. Finally, her arms fell limp at her sides, and she relaxed every muscle, her breath releasing in a long sigh.

"Petra!" Koren shouted. "I couldn't read your message! What are you trying to tell me?"

Blinking, Petra whispered, "I love you." Then her eyes closed, and her chest fell silent.

"Petra?" Koren brushed Petra's hair back again and again. "Petra! Sweet sister, can you hear me?"

Lying perfectly still, Petra made no sound.

Spasms rocked Koren's body. As she slid back on her knees, her words spat out in choking gasps. "Elyssa … did every word … you spoke … come from … Petra's mind?"

Her manner lethargic, yet calm, Elyssa peeled her hand away from Petra's skin. "Yes. Every word."

"Even … *I love you*?"

"No, I didn't say that." Elyssa nodded at Petra. "She did."

"But how? She has no—"

"I don't know how."

Her spasms easing, Koren touched Petra's gray lips. "Do you want me to look inside?"

"To see if she has a tongue?" Elyssa shook her head. "I don't want to know."

"Neither do I." Koren closed her eyes and again forced tortured words through her tightening throat. "She's gone, Elyssa. She suffered so much, and most of it was my fault."

Elyssa shifted away from Petra and crouched next to Koren. "How so?" Her voice sounded streaked with pain.

Koren shook her head. "I can't ... Not now." She leaned over and kissed Petra's forehead. "Good night, sweet sister. I'll see you again someday." She unclasped her cloak and draped it over Petra's body. As she rose to her feet, she wiped tears from both cheeks. After all they had gone through together, how could she just get up and leave Petra behind? But there was so much to do. With most of the population already exposed to the disease, she had to spread the word and give everyone hope for a cure.

Randall limped over to Elyssa and Koren. "I'm so sorry! I wish I could've helped, but I didn't know—"

"There was nothing you could have done," Elyssa said. "Thank you for standing guard."

"Well, I don't want to sound callous or anything, but I have a question."

"Let's hear it." Elyssa wiped her hand on her shirt as she rose. "I don't promise any answers."

"How did Petra get here?" Randall asked. "We left her in the Northlands."

"I'm finished," Deference called.

All three turned toward her. "Will the stitches hold?" Elyssa asked.

The shining spirit emerged from Fellina's body. "They should for a while, but we need to find something stronger than hair."

"The butcher sometimes does surgery," Koren said. "Most humans either heal on their own, or they die, so he doesn't get much practice. I saw him stitch up a boy once. He uses string made from the gut of a sheep."

Deference nodded. "I was just thinking that."

Randall regripped his sword. "Then we should pay this butcher a visit and get some."

"But he doesn't keep it in his shop," Koren said. "He said it was hard to make, and since he doesn't want people wasting it, he hides it in a safe place."

"Then maybe Arxad can force him to give us some."

Koren shook her head. "I don't think humans are going to be in any mood to give a dragon anything right now, especially with the threat of a deadly disease hanging over everyone. The butcher is sure to be fresh out of it, if you know what I mean."

"Tibalt would be perfect for that job," Elyssa said. "He probably has wounds that need stitching."

Koren looked up at the open ceiling. Without a healthy dragon, there was no way to get to the Zodiac's exit. "I'll tell him, but I'll have to go through the tunnel to the Basilica."

"Wait a minute," Randall said. "Didn't anyone at least think about my question? How did Petra get here? I'm guessing it had to be a dragon, but Arxad and Fellina were with us."

Elyssa tapped her chin with a finger. "Of the dragons that would cooperate, that leaves only Xenith. She's fast. I should know. I rode her on a wild escape."

"Okay," Koren said, "if Xenith brought her, that means she must have dropped her off in the Basilica. She might still be there making sure no one followed Petra."

"Or she might be waiting for Petra to return." Elyssa leaned over and stroked Fellina's wing. "Since Arxad will want to stay with Fellina, Xenith is the best option for transport to the Northlands. Someone with immune genetics has to get there."

"Right, the disease. But who will go? You or Cassabrie?"

"I don't know yet, but if I go with Xenith right away, I'll need someone to tell Arxad."

Koren pointed at herself. "Then I should come with you. I'll wait to see what happens to you before I look for Tibalt."

"I think that should work." Elyssa clasped Randall's arm. "Will you stay and guard Fellina and Deference while Koren and I look for Xenith?"

"Of course, but who will guard you and Koren?"

"You are such a chivalrous knight," Elyssa said, patting his cheek.

Koren smiled in spite of her pain. "He certainly is."

"We'd better get going." Elyssa marched toward the tunnel. Koren followed, looking back at Randall.

With one hand on the hilt of his sword, he called after them, "Wait! You didn't answer my question."

"I know!" Elyssa entered the tunnel and began a slow jog.

Pressing a hand on her wounded side, Koren tried to keep pace. Randall's voice faded behind her. "Why won't people answer my questions?"

⋙⋘

The moment Arxad landed in front of the Zodiac, Jason slid down and helped Cassabrie dismount. He ran to a large bucket Arxad had placed gently on the ground just before he landed. Grabbing the handle and an attached rope, he lugged the water to the open doorway. Stopping at the threshold, he looked down into the lower level. Randall stood next to Fellina, his sword drawn.

"How is she?" Jason called.

"Better. She tried to talk, so I told her about the neck injury. She's staying still."

Arxad flew over Jason's head and zoomed into the lower chamber. He landed with a thump, pulled in his wings, and nuzzled Fellina.

Jason held up the bucket. "I got the water for Petra. Arxad didn't want to try to land with it down there. He thought it would spill. I have a rope, so I can—"

Randall slid his sword away. "It's too late, Jason." A sigh nearly overwhelmed his voice as he looked at the floor. "She's dead. Elyssa and Koren just left for the Basilica."

Jason dropped the bucket. As water poured to the lower level, he leaned in to get a better look at the chamber. Near the left edge of his view, a blue cloak covered a motionless body.

He swallowed down a lump. Poor Petra. She of all people didn't deserve to die. So much death. So much suffering. Would this slaughter of innocents ever stop?

After clearing his throat, Jason nodded at Randall. "I'm going to see if I can help Cassabrie." He turned and kicked the bucket off the threshold, sending it tumbling through the portico, down the stairs, and out to the street.

He met Cassabrie at the bottom of the stairs. Using the edge of her cloak, she dabbed tears from her eyes.

"You heard?" he asked.

She nodded and looped her arm through his. As they walked toward the Basilica, she leaned her head against his shoulder. "What I am about to do," she said, her voice quavering, "will finally set everyone free."

Jason angled his head to watch her as they continued. Her expression seemed resolute, unchangeable. "What about the disease?" he asked. "We don't have a vaccine yet."

"If this works, we won't need one, at least for those who are willing to apply the treatment. But you had better go ahead with the vaccine plans, just in case."

Jason refocused ahead. Cassabrie spoke in riddles, apparently unwilling to reveal her plans, but it couldn't hurt to ask. "What are you going to do?"

"I can't tell you, and please don't ask me why."

"Okay, but I know you're going to try to raise Exodus again. Are the holes sealed?"

"Before Koren resurrected Exodus, I had hoped that Elyssa could seal the wound and stop Taushin's scheme to infect everyone. You see, another Starlighter once dwelt in the star, and Elyssa, being a Diviner, could have sealed the membrane from the outside using her healing gifts and without contracting the disease, but things didn't quite work out that way. So, after Koren took the other Starlighter's place, we discovered that Taushin had stolen the spear. It wasn't hard to guess what he might do, so I had to come up with my alternate plan."

"Is it dangerous?"

"Not for others."

"That means it *is* dangerous, doesn't it?" He stopped and grasped Cassabrie's arm. "Could you die doing this?"

As she stared at him with her piercing green eyes, a breeze blew back her cloak. Her skin glowed with a thin, delicate aura, as if painted with phosphorescence. "Jason," she said with a solemn tone, "don't ask me to reveal what I am not willing to reveal."

He waved his hand toward the grottoes. "I just don't want you to sacrifice yourself for these … these … Oh, I don't know what to call them."

Her eyes seem to boil like green storm clouds. "Human beings? Miserable wretches who are too frightened to know what to do? Slaves in chains who are blinded by their cruel captivity, fearful that any rebellion would cause their children to suffer torture or death?" She pointed toward the south. "Jason, you've seen the cattle camp. You've seen the grinding mill. These monsters have ripped the hearts out of the women and stripped the backbones out of the men. Cruelty does that."

Jason shoved a hand into his pocket. "Okay, I'm sorry for thinking like that. I know they're valuable no matter what. I learned that the hard way. I'm just trying to protect you."

Cassabrie backed away a step and let her cloak flow freely. "Jason, I am a Starlighter, born to sacrifice. I am not yours to protect."

"Listen …" Jason dragged a toe across the ground before looking at her again. "I don't understand what a Starlighter is supposed to do, but why can't Alaph do something? He's powerful, isn't he?"

Her answer echoed like rolling thunder. "What I must do, only a Starlighter can do. There is no other option."

Jason looked around. How could she have done that with her voice? If she was trying to hypnotize him, he had to shake off the effect. Too much was at stake. "Okay, back to you and Exodus. How do you know if the wounds are sealed now? And how are you going to get inside it?"

"I think when it collapsed on itself, everything sealed." Cassabrie began walking toward the Basilica again. "I just have to expand it. It might not be as big as it was before, but that's okay. I don't need much room for my experiment."

Jason hustled to catch up. "Experiment? You mean what you're planning has never been done before?"

"Never. Based on some things Alaph told me, it should work, but I think it really depends on the people."

He reached over and touched her pocket. "Does the experiment have something to do with that thing you took from Petra?"

She laid a hand over her pocket's opening. "That's all I'm going to say about it. I have said too much already."

When they arrived at the Basilica gate, they found Tibalt leaning back against the bars, a sword in hand. Exodus sat on the cobblestones about fifteen paces away, still shining and sizzling, only slightly smaller than before. The spear that had punctured it lay close by. He squinted at Cassabrie. "I see red hair, but that ain't Koren, unless someone altered Koren's face and cut off two of her fingers."

Cassabrie raised a hand and looked at the gap with a sigh. "No. I'm not Koren."

"Tibalt," Jason said, "this is Cassabrie. She's going to try to save Exodus."

"Aha! The other Starlighter." Tibalt pointed at Exodus with his sword. "I've been guarding it and the spear, but no one's come around at all. I can't say I blame them. With all the talk of disease, no one would want to mess with a superheated ball of fire. Not that they'd want to anyway, but—"

"Listen, Tibalt," Jason said, "I have some bad news. Petra is dead. A dragon burned her."

Tibalt's head drooped. "Oh … That's terrible. The poor girl."

"And Fellina's hurt, so with a disease about to strike, things aren't looking good at all."

"I get it, young'un. Time to be serious."

Cassabrie walked toward Exodus and picked up the spear. "Maybe I can change our fortunes soon." She ripped the explosive tube from the point-end of the shaft, then lifted a leg, snapped the spear over her knee, and threw the two halves to the ground. "This spear will never puncture Exodus again."

"Jason!" a draconic voice called.

Jason looked up. Xenith dropped from the sky, barely catching herself with a flurry of wings as she landed in a run.

"Have you seen my father?" she asked as she scooted toward him. "There is trouble in the Basilica."

"What kind of trouble?"

"I was waiting in a room that has a passageway that leads to the Zodiac."

"The incubator room." Jason nodded. "Go on."

"I had taken Petra and Cassabrie there and was waiting for them to return. I heard voices, so I flew up to the ceiling hole and perched there to see who was coming. Taushin flew in from a lower level carrying Zena. Then Hyborn joined them. I heard Taushin say that they were going to wait for someone to come out of the passageway. They said something about capturing Cassabrie and killing anyone who was with her. Of course, I wanted to warn Cassabrie, but Hyborn and Taushin would certainly have stopped me. When I saw you down here, I thought it best to seek your aid."

Jason pictured the scene in his mind. The ceiling was high, but maybe not too high to jump from if something on the floor could provide a cushion. "Your father is in the Zodiac's lower level with your mother. She's hurt."

"Mother is hurt?" Xenith unfurled her wings again and turned toward the Zodiac. "I must go to her."

"And tell your father what you told me. We'll need his help." Jason pointed toward the Basilica's roof. "But first, can you take me up to that hole?"

"Yes, I will be glad to."

"Can two ride?" Tibalt asked.

Xenith looked up at the roof of the Basilica. "It is a short flight. I can take two."

"Tibalt, you don't have to—"

"Of course I have to. I'm not doing any good babysitting this spitting star, and it sounds like there's some big trouble brewing." He tapped himself on the chest. "You need a sidekick with a keen eye and sharp mind. I ain't got either one, but I'll do my best."

Jason laughed. "I'm sure you will." He glanced at Cassabrie. She gave him a nod. "Okay," he said. "Let's go."

Xenith lowered her body, allowing them to mount. Jason sat at the base of her neck, while Tibalt straddled her about two feet back, leaving a protruding spine between them. He reached around the spine and swatted Jason's arm. "Let's see what that evil critter is up to."

Jason patted Xenith's neck. "We're ready."

As Xenith ascended in a wide circle, Jason looked around. Arxad flew out of the Zodiac in a hurry, banked hard, and headed away from the village. Whatever the priestly dragon's errand might be, it meant he and Tibalt might not get any help with Taushin and company for quite a while. Still, it could be that nothing would happen during that time.

Below, Cassabrie stood next to Exodus, her hood covering her head and shading her eyes. With the explosive tube tucked under her arm, she inserted her hands deep into the radiance and, as if sweeping curtains of light open, forced a wide gap in the membrane. She then lifted her foot, stepped inside, and melded with the sizzling star. The opening snapped closed behind her in an eruption of sparks, leaving just a ball of radiance wobbling on the cobblestone street.

After a few seconds, Exodus began to expand, and the outer wall grew more transparent. Inside, Cassabrie's frame came into view, a shadow in the midst of brilliance. With her arms spread and her cloak fanned out, she appeared to be speaking or perhaps singing. Then, as if awakened from slumber, Exodus began to rise.

Jason shifted his gaze straight ahead. Xenith fluttered her wings, ready to land on top of the Basilica. It was time to pay attention to his role, not Cassabrie's. He had to make sure Elyssa returned to the Northlands safely. Nearly every human life on Starlight depended on it.

twenty

As they ran side by side through the tunnel leading to the Basilica, Elyssa glanced at Koren. Her hair and skin glowed far brighter than did her own. She was a real Starlighter, not a hybrid Diviner. With shining red hair and brilliant green eyes, she was truly beautiful. And dressed in ragged trousers and thin tunic, she seemed vulnerable, needy, dependent. No wonder she entranced dragons and humans so easily, and no wonder Jason seemed so …

She took in a quick breath. *Stop it, Elyssa. Don't be an idiot.*

As they neared the end, Koren faltered, holding a hand against her side. Elyssa stopped and wrapped an arm around her shoulders. "Can you make it?"

Koren raised her hand into her glow. Blood smeared her fingers. "It's not bleeding much. Nothing like it did earlier."

Frowning, Elyssa lifted the edge of Koren's tunic and peered at the wound. *"You're* the one who needs stitches."

"I can't take the time to get stitches. I have to make sure you're safely on your way to the Northlands."

Elyssa guided Koren to the wall where she could lean and rest. "It won't help matters if you bleed to death. I'll do my part, and you do yours. You need to keep telling people to have courage and be ready to escape."

"I did." Koren turned her head, her expression morose. "They wouldn't listen to me. I failed."

Elyssa laid her hands on Koren's cheeks and looked her in the eye. "I saw you up there in that star. Telling people what they need to hear when they don't want to hear it is courageous. If people refuse to listen, it's not your fault. And it doesn't mean they won't listen the next time, or the next time. You just have to keep trying."

Koren's sparkling eyes locked on Elyssa's. "It's a lot easier to talk about it than it is to do it, but I think I'm gaining a new power that might help."

"Really?" Elyssa lowered her hands. "What power?"

Koren shifted her eyes lower. "Take a look."

A new glimmer appeared from below Elyssa's neck. Her pendant glowed, first orange, then red, almost as brightly as it had when she tried to heal Petra. "Are you doing that?"

Koren nodded. "Cassabrie once shot beams from her eyes that blinded Zena. She was bound to the Reflections Crystal then, so that's where she probably got the power, but I think the stardrop is giving me the same kind of energy. It's hard to control, but I'm working on it. Maybe this new power will give me more courage."

"Well, I'm sure the stardrop helps, but watching Jason taught me an important lesson. Courage is generated by love. Since you love your people so much, let that reenergize your courage."

Koren spread out her arms. "But what should I say? I don't have Exodus anymore, so I'll have to try to convince them one person at a time, and I won't have a platform or a powerful presence to let people know I'm speaking the Creator's words."

Elyssa raised a mental photograph of Koren standing high above the crowd as she delivered her message. With hands blocking the heat, most of the people had no desire to take in a single word. "You know, I think it might be better this way."

"How so?"

"For some, platform and presence mean nothing. They're stubborn and won't respond. For people like that, sometimes we should just ask questions and let them ponder. All we can do is give them the key to unlocking their chains. If they won't use it, there is simply nothing you can do, no matter how much love and courage you have. Some people are comfortable in their chains. They want to be slaves because they don't have the courage to live in freedom."

Koren averted her eyes. A glow emanated from them, strong at first, but it quickly faded. "Have you ever lived in freedom, Elyssa? Do you really know what it's like to be completely unshackled?"

Elyssa tilted her head. "What do you mean?"

"Never mind. We've lost enough time already." Koren walked toward the stone at the end of the tunnel, now visible in her glow.

"Wait a minute!" Elyssa marched after her. "How can you spear me with a question like that and just walk away?"

Koren stopped and knelt at the gap between the tunnel exit and the blocking stone. "I'm just practicing what you told me."

"You mean asking questions? Do you think I'm stubborn?"

"Yes, I do." Koren slid her hand into Elyssa's. "Your stubborn determination to fight for freedom, to help others less fortunate than yourself, and to sacrifice your life to save our people is a beautiful sight to behold. Yet, I think focusing on how terrible the slavery is here on Starlight has blinded you to your own slavery on Darksphere. At least here we know we're slaves, and that's the first step to seeking freedom." She lowered herself to her stomach and belly-crawled into the gap.

Elyssa stooped and watched. In the dim light, it seemed that manacles wrapped around her own wrists, chains dangling to the floor. The air smelled like the dungeon where she had spent too many dark and lonely nights—fetid and dank. The Starlighter's influence was at work.

As soon as Koren's feet disappeared through the gap, she let out a muffled grunt.

"Koren?" Elyssa called. "Did you hurt yourself?" She dropped down and peeked through the gap. Shadows skittered here and there on the Basilica's floor tiles, but no other sign of Koren appeared.

"Koren?" Elyssa's heart raced. Something was wrong, but should she follow and expose herself to the same

danger? That would be brave, but stupid. She pushed her
head a little farther in, closed her eyes, and probed. As
her mind crept into the incubator room, a sense of guilt
weighed her down. Why hadn't she done this earlier
instead of fussing about Koren's remarks? It was stupid to
get so distracted when —

Stop it! You're getting distracted again! Release the whip!

After taking a deep breath, she continued the probe.
Her mind drifted across the room. Warm bodies stood
here and there. Anger in one of them. Fear in another.
Both human. Two dragons stood there as well. There
was no way she could win a confrontation with them,
especially if her only ally was a wounded and captured
Starlighter. It would be wiser to go back and get Randall —

Something grabbed her hair and pulled. "Randall!" she
screamed. "Help me!"

As her body squeezed into the gap, she groped for
a handhold. Her fingers clutched the side of the tunnel
entrance, but the force from the Basilica room jerked her
so hard, her neck felt ready to snap. She let go. Her chest
and stomach scraped against the tunnel's rough floor
before sliding out onto smooth tiles.

When the pressure released, Elyssa jumped to her
feet. Her head pounded so hard, darkness pulsed in her
vision. Hyborn sat within reach, holding several strands
of hair in his clawed hand.

Taushin and Zena stood near the center of the room,
and Koren knelt in front of them facing Elyssa, her mouth
gagged and her hands tied behind her. Blood streamed
from a wound near her eye, trickled down her cheek, and

dripped from her jaw to the floor. She heaved shallow breaths but kept her stare fixed on Elyssa.

Zena stooped behind Koren, brandishing a dagger in her pale, bony hand. She rolled up her ivory sleeve and held the blade against Koren's throat. "Elyssa, you will be silent, or I will slay this Starlighter."

Elyssa rolled her hands into fists. The cowards! She glanced around the room for Xenith, but she was nowhere in sight.

Taushin flashed his eyebeams on Zena. "By my count, there are four humans remaining in the Zodiac — Cassabrie, Jason, Randall, and the girl."

"Petra," Zena said. "But I heard Elyssa call for Randall. If Jason were still in the Zodiac, she would have called for him. She has a great fondness for Jason."

Taushin nodded. "An excellent point. However, it is also possible that Shrillet killed him. The tear tracks on Elyssa's cheeks indicate that possibility. My bigger concern is Cassabrie. We cannot wait long to see what has become of her. If she has reanimated her body, we must capture her as soon as possible."

Elyssa sneaked a glance at the hole in the ceiling. If Xenith was here earlier, maybe she left because she saw Taushin and his companions coming, but surely she would have tried to warn someone. Maybe Xenith would return with Arxad ... and maybe not. She couldn't risk waiting. She had to do something to protect Randall, and getting the dragons out of here had to be the first step.

"You're right about one thing," Elyssa said. "The longer you wait here, the more energy Cassabrie will build up. The power she's generating while you wait will be of such magnitude, nothing will be able to stop her from destroying you."

Koren glared at her. The copper flames in her eyes sent a strong message. *Don't tell him!*

Elyssa concealed a swallow. Maybe Koren already had something planned. So what now? The only reasonable option was to keep talking so Randall could hear her, but would Zena really slit Koren's throat? Probably not. She was too valuable to them.

"Anyway," she added, "you have no idea what you're up against."

Taushin chuckled. "What kind of fool do you take me for? If that were true, you would not warn us in advance. Cassabrie is not attached to the Reflections Crystal, so she has no energy source. Not only that, she will be hesitant to act as long as I have a hostage. Hyborn could separate a head from a human's body in the time it takes a Starlighter to draw a breath. I have no concerns about what she can do to me."

"Hyborn," Zena said, "encourage Elyssa to come and kneel with Koren."

Hyborn gave Elyssa a shove from behind, clawing her back.

"I'm going!" She grimaced at the pain but quickly shifted to a smirk. Touching a finger to her chest, she marched toward them with a confident gait. "What about me? Did you know that I have Starlighter powers as well?"

Taushin's blue beams strengthened, striking Zena's eyes. "Even with Zena's pitiful vision, I can see that you are not a Starlighter. Your eyes are green, but you lack the fiery red hair."

Elyssa stopped and pinched her hair. "It means nothing. Haven't you heard of hair dye on this world?"

"My spies have watched you," Taushin said with a dismissive wave of his wing, "and there have been no reports of phantoms appearing while you speak. And as Zena said, you display a great fondness for Jason. When we capture him, which will be soon, you will do whatever we say."

"Oh, really? You have spies? It seems that we have a problem with loyalty in our ranks." She glanced at her pendant. It glowed orange again. With another quick glance, she caught a glimpse of Koren nodding at her. Was it a signal that her power reserves had returned? Even as these thoughts raced through her mind, words poured in, full sentences that formed without forethought. Could this be part of her Starlighter-like gifts, or was Koren providing these thoughts from where she knelt?

"Actually," Elyssa said as she knelt next to Koren, "you're right. I do like Jason. In fact, I suppose *love* is an appropriate term." She jabbed a finger at Taushin and let the inflowing words spill out. "But let me tell you this, you monster, our love for the slaves of this world, for the Creator who made them, for the blessings of freedom that are the Creator's to give and not yours to steal — that love is enough to drive us to sacrifice anything to snatch the souls of Starlight away from your wicked grasp. If the Starlighters really could do something with their powers to break free and stop your madness, they would do so without care for my life or Jason's life, because we would rather die than live in chains."

"Elyssa?"

She flinched. That was Randall's voice calling through the gap.

"Elyssa, is that you in there?"

"Don't answer," Zena whispered, "or Koren is dead."

Hyborn shuffled close to the passage and reached a claw toward the gap.

A shadow made Elyssa glance up. The ceiling hole directly above led to bright sky, but there seemed to be nothing there to cause the shadow. Closing her eyes, she probed the area. Two humans stood atop the Basilica, both showing signs of aggression. Could Jason be one of them? If they were here to help, she had to make sure they had a safe place to land.

"Randall!" Elyssa shouted. "Stay in the tunnel! Hyborn's here ready to catch you!" She grabbed Zena's arm with both hands and pushed the dagger away. Koren shot to her feet, turned, and locked her stare on Zena's face. Twin shafts of light, pale and faint, radiated from Koren's eyes to Zena's.

Sizzling smoke erupted from Zena's sockets. She screamed. "No! Not again!"

"Hyborn!" Taushin's eyebeams swept wildly across the room. "Come and stop this fighting."

While Zena writhed on the floor, Hyborn stomped toward Elyssa and Koren. Elyssa snatched up the dagger and cut through Koren's gag and bonds. "Don't run," Elyssa whispered. "Just back away slowly."

"Should I hypnotize him?" Koren asked.

"When he gets to where we're standing right now." They slid their feet slowly backwards. Elyssa looked up again. Jason and Tibalt stood on opposite sides of the ceiling hole. Jason gave her a nod.

Down on floor level, Randall's head and torso came into sight, wriggling through the gap behind the stone. He appeared to be stuck, but he made no sound.

The moment Hyborn reached the center of the room, Koren raised her hands. "Halt! Hear my voice!"

Hyborn stopped. "It will take more than a few words to control me, Starlighter. I told you I am more immune than other dragons." He looked at Taushin. "What do you want me to do with them?"

Taushin's beams settled on Hyborn's face. "Kill Elyssa and capture the Starlighter for me. After that, dispose of Zena. She is no longer of any use to me."

Jason dropped from the ceiling hole, his sword drawn. He landed on Hyborn's back, toppled over, and slid down his scales. As soon as he hit the floor, he scrambled to his feet and lunged with his sword. Hyborn batted him to the side with a foreleg, sending Jason staggering backwards, then reared his head, ready to blast fire.

"Hyborn!" Koren called, wincing as she pressed a hand against her side. "I command you to hear my voice."

Hyborn's ears turned toward her, but he kept his stare fixed on Jason. "No, Starlighter. Your friend will feel my fire."

"Hey! Sparky!" Tibalt waved from the ceiling. "Do you hear *my* voice?"

"What?" Hyborn reared up and looked at him. "Who are you?"

"You'll find out." Tibalt leaped, waving his arms like a madman as he shouted, "Catch me if you can!"

Jason lunged and rammed his blade into Hyborn's underbelly, but it penetrated only a few inches between his rigid scales and stuck there. Hyborn slapped him with a foreleg, sending him sliding on his back.

Tibalt crashed onto the dragon's neck. A spine pierced his shoulder and exited through his back. He wrapped both arms around Hyborn's neck and cried out, "Finish this lizard off!"

Wagging his neck, Hyborn slung Tibalt back and forth.

"Hurry!" Tibalt called, his voice faltering. "This isn't ... as easy ... as it looks."

Jason leaped up and charged, but Hyborn's tail swiped so close, a spine almost stabbed his leg. He jumped clear and backed away.

Elyssa ran to Jason's side. "What do we do?"

Jason braced his legs as if ready to charge again. "I'll have to jump in and grab the sword, but he's thrashing like a flopping fish."

She glanced at the passageway. Randall had just crawled out and was rising with his sword. "You'll have help in a minute."

"We don't have a minute." Jason lunged, but Hyborn slapped him with a wing, slinging him across the room. He hurtled toward the passage, colliding with Randall, and the two slammed into the stone.

Hyborn shot a ball of fire in Jason's wake, but Randall threw himself and Jason out of the way just before the ball splashed on the stone. In a fluid motion, they rolled up to their feet and faced the dragon again.

Hyborn's mouth erupted with a river of flames that swept the floor. Elyssa hopped over the expanding carpet of fire and kept hopping as the torrent continued. Jason, Randall, and Koren jumped as well, but Koren slowed her bounces, panting as she braced her side. The flames covered Zena, catching her clothes on fire.

Jason dashed over to Koren, scooped her into his arms, and began hopping from foot to foot. "Stop this madness! Can't you see you're killing your own?"

"Hyborn!" Koren shouted. "Stop the fire, spare my friends, and I will go willingly!"

Taushin nodded. "We accept."

Hyborn extinguished the jet, breathing heavily as he growled through his words, "Come to me, Starlighter."

"Give me one minute." Koren wiggled down from Jason, then ran to Zena and beat out the flames with her hands.

Elyssa joined her, clutching her pendant. "Do you think we should try to heal her?"

Koren nodded. "She's a slave who needs release. One of us could get a stardrop from—"

"No!" Zena rose to a sitting position, her dress so scorched, it flaked away from her blackened shoulders. She braced herself with her hands and climbed to her feet, her face a twisted mass of melted flesh. "I will not accept your pathetic mercy!"

As Elyssa and Koren stepped back, Zena batted her eyelids, briefly halting the smoke still rising from her sockets. "I cannot see at all now, my prince, but I am here to serve you in whatever way I can."

Taushin snorted. "What good are you to me now? You are blind, crippled, worthless."

"Allow me to show you that I can still do something worthwhile." She dipped her knee into the shallowest of curtsies. "If it pleases you."

"She can help me pull this sword out," Hyborn said. "It is wedged between two scales. Then she can get this fool of a human off my neck."

Taushin heaved an impatient sigh. "Let us get on with it."

"I will try to hurry." Zena extended an arm as she staggered.

Koren rushed to her side and grasped her other arm. "Let me help you."

Zena scowled at her. With dark blood oozing from her eyes and hideous welts forming on her chin and cheeks, she looked like a risen corpse. "Why do you care, you annoying pest? I am your enemy."

"Because there's still a chance for you to change," Koren said. "Appeal to Arxad. He is forgiving. He will—"

"Silence!" Zena pressed something into Koren's hand. "Use your Starlighter gifts on someone else. There is no hope for me." She jerked away and continued her staggering march.

"This way," Hyborn said. "Another five paces."

Zena groped for the sword until she grasped the hilt with both hands. "Are you ready?"

"I am ready. It will take a great deal of strength."

"I think I have enough remaining." Zena rammed the sword into his belly.

Hyborn roared in pain. His legs trembling, he lunged backwards, making Zena slide on the floor as he pulled her along. Then, her teeth clenched, she twisted the blade and jerked it out. "There. I have done what you asked."

As fluid poured from Hyborn's wound, he teetered from side to side. "You ... you traitor!"

"Yes, Hyborn. I am a traitor." Zena turned toward Taushin with a whisper so soft, Elyssa could barely hear it. "And I chose the wrong master."

As Hyborn toppled to the side and crashed to the floor, Zena marched toward Taushin, the sword in hand. "Speak to me, my prince. Guide me to your presence."

Taushin began shuffling backwards. "Come no closer. I cannot see you, but I can hear you. Beware of my flames."

"I fear no flames." With the sword raised, Zena ran toward Taushin in a stumbling, zigzagging path. Taushin blasted her with a ball of fire and set her entire body aflame.

Jason rushed to Hyborn. "Randall! Help me with Tibalt!"

"Cut the spine!" Elyssa called. "Then pull him off!"

Koren ran again to Zena, but the sorceress's scorched body crumbled into ashes. Koren stopped and fell to her knees, weeping.

"What is happening?" Taushin asked, his eyebeams again sweeping the chamber. "Hyborn? Are you there?"

Elyssa pressed a finger to her lips and grabbed Randall's sword. She skulked toward Taushin. Behind her, grunts and groans from Tibalt and the others concealed the sound of her padding steps.

Taushin backed away again. "I smell you, filthy human." He beat his wings and flew into the air, his snout high as he circled the room.

"He's sniffing for the exit," Koren said.

After a few seconds, Taushin found the hole and zipped through it.

Elyssa rushed back to Jason and Randall as they laid Tibalt gently on his side. They had already sliced away his shirt, exposing his pale, leathery skin. Blood trickled from near his collarbone down into a nest of gray chest hair. Like a curved dagger, the spine protruded several inches on both sides.

She touched his back near the point it exited. "That looks awful."

"Well," Tibalt said, his voice gravelly, "are you gonna get me one of those little fireballs or what? I like spicy food, and I have a hankerin' for some right now."

Elyssa handed the sword to Randall. "I'll get it."

"I don't think there are any in the floor," Jason said as he crouched at Tibalt's side. "There are still some in the ceiling, but I don't think you can reach."

"Then I'll need a boost."

"Xenith should be there with her parents by now. Maybe she can help you and then fly you back."

Randall sheathed his sword and jogged toward the passage. "I can't let you go. There might still be trouble brewing there."

"It'll burn your hands," Jason said.

Randall stopped at the stone and looked back. "If you can handle it, I can handle it."

While Randall crawled through the gap, Koren sidled up to Elyssa and whispered, "You don't have to go to the Northlands."

Elyssa looked at her. "Why not?"

Koren showed Elyssa her fist, then slowly opened it. In her palm lay a finger, complete with two knuckles and sealed by thick stitches on one end.

Elyssa touched the middle section. The skin seemed pliable, not as stiff as she expected. "Is this what Zena gave you?"

Koren nodded. "It's Cassabrie's. If we can get this to Uriel, you'll be able to stay here and heal as many people as you can."

"Or at least stall the infection."

"So we'll get this finger to Arxad and ..." Koren's voice trailed off.

Elyssa cocked her head. "What's wrong?"

"The string!" Koren's voice spiked with energy. "We're supposed to get the stitching string for Deference and Fellina!"

"Don't worry about it." Jason rose and joined them. "I saw Arxad flying out of the Zodiac like a lightning bolt. Deference probably told him she needed the string."

Elyssa pushed her hair off her forehead. "Whew! That's a relief."

"Right. Cassabrie and I were walking to the Basilica, and ..."

While Jason told the story, Elyssa tuned out the details. There was so much to talk about but so little time. Soon, they would all face death again together. They could tell stories to their hearts' content later.

"So," he continued, "Arxad flew out—"

"Jason." Elyssa pinched his sleeve. "Will you sit with me for a minute?"

He glanced at Tibalt, who lay quietly on his side. "I guess he'll be all right."

"Go ahead," Koren said as she knelt close to Tibalt. "I'll stay here with him."

Elyssa kept her hold on Jason's sleeve and led him to the stone. She slid down its face and sat cross-legged in front of it. Jason joined her and copied her pose, his hands folded. With blood smears on his cheek and forehead, rips in his shirt and trousers, and a bruise painting his jaw purple, he looked like he had lost a fight with a bull. And who could tell how many more wounds ached under his clothes?

"So," Jason said. "Did you want to talk about something?"

She touched his bruised jaw. "Are you in pain?"

"Quite a bit, but I'm trying to ignore it." He gave her a dubious stare. "Is that what you wanted to talk about?"

"Not really." She leaned against the stone. "Back home when we sat behind the roots of that fallen tree, if someone told you we would go through all this pain, what would you have done?"

He shrugged. "I don't know. I'd have to think about it."

"Well, you probably have about three minutes to think and then three minutes to tell me."

Jason pulled up his knees and rested his chin, staring straight ahead. Elyssa did the same. From where they sat, the incubator room spread out before them — Tibalt and Koren halfway between the center of the room and the right-hand wall, Zena's ashes closer to the center, and a shaft of sunlight drawing a circle where Jason had landed on Hyborn. The dead dragon lay in a twisted heap a few steps from that spot.

"Petra's dead," she whispered. "Randall's father, too. A terrible disease is about to strike every human on

Starlight, and we think we have an army from Major Four marching toward us soon. If we can get word to them to stop so they can avoid the disease, the slaves won't ever be set free, and everything we've done will be a waste. And even if they don't come all the way here, they might get infected anyway. If they do come, they'll be infected for sure, and when they go home, they'll infect everyone on our world. That means every human on both planets will probably die."

Pressing his lips together, Jason nodded. "That's the most pessimistic outlook, but it's a real possibility."

Elyssa touched the floor. "Or else everyone could stay here and die, leaving Major Four untouched. That's the other option."

"So what's the point? Why are you going over all the darkest scenarios?"

She waved her finger between them. "You and I might be the only two humans left in both worlds. We're both immune. At least we think you are now because of the litmus finger … Well, and Cassabrie. That makes three of us."

"Okay," Jason said, nodding. "I'm getting the picture. No matter what happens, you and I have to survive."

"Or you and Cassabrie."

Jason shifted forward, his gaze far away. "I don't think Cassabrie will be around."

Elyssa leaned closer, trying to gauge his expression. He seemed ready to cry. "What do you mean?"

As he turned toward her, his features sagged. "If you could've seen her …" His voice cracked, and he took a long breath as if to steady his emotions. "I think she's going to resurrect Exodus or die trying. She'll either be trapped inside or dead."

Elyssa gazed into his sparkling eyes. The Starlighters really meant a lot to him. No wonder. They were amazing girls. But what did his love for them mean for the future, for the hopes of a Diviner who loved a conflicted warrior so much? Swallowing down her own emotions, she breathed a quiet, "I think I understand."

After a few seconds of silence, Elyssa patted Jason's knee. "So, back to my question. If you knew then what you know now, would you still have come to Starlight?"

"Without a doubt."

"Why?"

Jason pointed at Koren. "For her. For Cassabrie. For Solace, Oliver, and Basil."

"And Wallace."

"And Wallace and every slave on this world." He shifted toward her, passion creeping into his voice. "When I sat under that fallen tree, I wanted to go to the dragon world because I was being hunted as a murderer and because Frederick was there. Sure, I thought it'd be great to bring the Lost Ones home. I wanted to be a hero. But I learned it's not about me. It's not about anyone being a hero." He settled back against the stone. "It's about freedom."

Elyssa let his declaration sink in. Freedom. She and others had thrown that word around so many times, it seemed to have lost its meaning. She touched his knee again. "Do we really know what freedom's all about?"

Jason looked straight ahead. "Well, we're not free in Mesolantrum. Orion chases you like a cat after a canary.

My family lives in a commune working their fingers raw, and for what? So the fat nobles can have more padding in their posteriors. Yet the nobles are slaves, too—slaves to their appetites, to their social status, and to their own self-image."

Again she let his words settle. "You've been thinking about this for a while, haven't you?"

He nodded but stayed quiet.

"Then, if even the nobles are slaves, how can anyone have real freedom?"

Jason pointed at Koren. She sat next to Tibalt, combing her fingers through his stringy hair and singing a quiet song. As she sang, blood trickled down the side of her tunic.

"Like that," he whispered.

"So to be free from slavery ..."

"You have to be willing to die for others. Fear of death is the final slave master. Most people will do anything to avoid death, including letting others suffer or die. They're just as enslaved as Petra was, but now she's free, and they're not."

Elyssa pressed her fingers against her lips, trying not to cry. "Then ... then we *do* know what freedom is like."

"Yes, we do." Jason climbed to his feet and reached out his hand. "And now it's time to unlock more chains. I hear Randall coming."

"From the tunnel?" She rode his pull up to her feet.

"No, from the air." He nodded toward the ceiling. "Dragon wings."

Xenith flew through the opening, carrying Randall on her back. As he held to Xenith with one hand, a tight grimace twisted his face.

When the young dragon landed, Elyssa ran to them, holding out her cupped hands. "Do you have it?"

"Yes!" Randall jumped down and rolled a stardrop into her palms. "And good riddance!" He blew on his skin. "Jason carried that thing how far?"

Jason smiled. "Don't worry about it. You did it. That's all that matters."

"Follow me," Elyssa said. "I'll need your help to get that spine out." She hurried to Tibalt and knelt at his side. "It's your turn, my dear friend. Open up for some spicy food."

As she drew the stardrop close to his mouth, Tibalt looked at it cross-eyed. "Got any water to go with that?"

twenty-one

Cassabrie guided Exodus into a slow descent. Below lay a blanket of snow that spread out from the Northlands' southern border to a range of mountains that stood behind the castle like huge dragons with white beards and hoary heads. Evergreens huddled on a ridge to the left as if gathering to shelter each other from the bitter cold. A hefty breeze shook the branches, breaking accumulated ice and powder from the needle clusters. The crystals rained on the mounds of white underneath, a miniature snowstorm that swirled in sparkling eddies and swept down to the valley.

Far over the trees, dark clouds rolled in and blocked Solarus, dimming the landscape. A few wind-driven snowflakes decorated the sky, not enough to veil her view, but they might be a sign of more snow to come.

After stopping Exodus directly over the ice-covered river, she glanced between the forest to her left and the castle to her right. At the top of the wooded ridge, the portal's line of crystals lay in sight, making her perch the perfect spot to watch for the coming army. Two men waited there. The heftier of the pair stood facing the portal, while the other paced between him and a canvas tent, plowing a path through knee-deep snow with his long legs. Plumes of vapor rose from their lips before dispersing in the breeze.

Cassabrie studied the pair. Edison set the peg into the hole, walked forward a few steps, and disappeared, only to reappear a moment later, shrugging his shoulders. He picked up the peg and paced with Orion.

Cassabrie nodded. The troops weren't there yet, but it probably wouldn't be much longer. If Randall's account of Marcelle's passionate entreaties proved to be true, her prompting, combined with Orion's signature on military marching orders, would surely bring the army without a problem.

She gazed at the portal clearing. The soldiers had to come. They just had to. If Magnar incited fear in the populace as she and Alaph had hoped, the soldiers might delay, choosing to stay in their world to combat the new menace. Still, Magnar yearned to come to the Northlands and break his curse, so maybe he stayed hidden. If so, the soldiers might walk through the invisible door at any moment. Even if Orion's orders and Marcelle's pleas failed, the innate passion in fathers and husbands to protect their precious ones from a dragon invasion would set their feet to marching.

She let her gaze wander around the glowing star's inner membrane. As Alaph had told her, the sensation of being attached to Exodus sent ripples of delight through-out her body. Tales poured into her mind, and during her journey to the Northlands, she had repeated them and sent them out as wiggling streams of light that dispersed in the air. Now it was time to be silent, watch, and listen. The time for telling tales would come again soon enough.

Earlier, one strange phenomenon occurred that Alaph hadn't mentioned. As soon as she had inflated Exodus, a shining dome appeared, floating head high. Since it looked like a crown, she ducked under it, and it adhered to her head. Immediately the tales began to flow, proving that the dome was, indeed, the guiding angel's crown.

Outside, one of the eddies danced down the ridge's slope and paused over the river's blue-tinted ice. The snowflakes in the vortex thickened, making it look like a laundered sheet twirling in the wind. After a few seconds, the rotation slowed. Wings emerged from the sheet, and a long tail grew as if generated by the spin. Finally, in a flurry of wings, a white dragon shook away the remaining flakes and flew up to Cassabrie's level. As he glided around her in a slow orbit, his blue eyes trained on her, and the wake his body and wings created made her spin at the same speed, keeping her facing him at all times.

Cassabrie held her breath. What would Alaph say? Her own efforts to resurrect Exodus hadn't been part of his plan. But how could it have been? Even he probably hadn't known that the star would collapse.

Emitting ice crystals as he spoke, Alaph continued his orbit. "Have you come to see if I approve of your chosen abode?"

Cassabrie dipped into a curtsy, staggering slightly as the star continued its slow spin. "No, Alaph, but I do hope you will approve of my heart."

"Your heart is spotless. Your motivation is pure." Alaph's ears bent back. "Yet I am concerned about the path you have chosen."

"Then do you know what I intend to do?"

"It is not difficult to discern."

The star spun faster. While the snowfall thickened, the castle and the forest zipped past in rapid succession. Now dizzy, Cassabrie spread her feet to stay erect. "Am I making the right decision?"

Alaph continued beating his wings, orbiting Exodus again and again. "What do you think, Starlighter? What would make this choice of yours the right decision?"

"If it works. If it saves the people."

"I see." The blue light in his eyes stretched out into a line, like the tail of a meteor in the night sky. "So does a good result always justify the means a person chooses in order to attain that result?"

As the dizzying sensation worsened, Cassabrie lowered herself to her knees. "No, Alaph, but aren't love and sacrifice always justified?"

"Only if all involved understand the costs and are willing to pay them. Otherwise it is neither love nor sacrifice."

Cassabrie kept her eyes focused on the blue line. It seemed to be the only constant in the spinning world. "I think everyone knew the costs."

"Is that so?" Alaph's eyes flashed like burning sulfur. "In case you are unaware, Petra did not recover from her burns. Did she realize the potential cost before she agreed to help you resurrect your body?"

As a wave of sorrow washed over Cassabrie's mind, her throat tightened. "Well ..." Her voice pitched into a barely audible squeak. "No. I knew I could die, and I was willing to risk it, but I didn't know Petra would."

"Yet you knew she *could*."

"I suppose so. I'm not sure." Cassabrie closed her eyes and laid her hands over her ears. Although her throat loosened, the heat of shame surged into her cheeks. "I'm so dizzy! I can't think straight. I suppose I knew, but I wasn't really thinking ..." The thought died on her lips. There was no avoiding the awful truth, no excuse for the fact that she hadn't bothered to learn if Petra understood the risks. Obviously the poor girl was willing to help in every way she could, but she needed to consider the potential cost, every cost. It wasn't fair to settle for anything less than full disclosure.

In her mind's eye, the castle and forest slowed, and her dizziness ebbed. Visions of recent events blended in—Petra climbing to get a stardrop, Shrillet setting her ablaze, Petra's final words as she breathed her last. "I love you."

Although her brain had stopped spinning, Cassabrie kept her eyes closed. How could she know Petra's last words? She wasn't there to hear them. Yet the vision in her mind was as clear as if she had witnessed it herself. A girl without a tongue whispered an impossible farewell, a peaceful good-bye bathed in contentment.

She reopened her eyes. Exodus sat still, hovering only a few feet above the river. Snow fell heavily now, most of it undisturbed by any wind. Alaph sat on the snow-covered ground to her left, the evergreen forest beyond him, veiled by the curtain of falling flakes. With his head high on his outstretched neck, his eyes drew level with hers, and his stare seemed to delve deeper than before.

"Starlighter, your silence is profound. Share your thoughts with me."

She swallowed before answering. "I … I made a terrible mistake, but it won't happen again. What I have planned won't risk any life except my own."

"Are you certain? Earlier you said you were dizzy and could not think straight."

"When I closed my eyes, the dizziness went away. Then everything became clear."

"Interesting. I wonder if those whom you influence feel the same way."

Cassabrie tried to read his expression, but his brow stayed smooth, and his ears perked high. He gave no sign of anger or disappointment. "What do you mean?"

"When you speak as a Starlighter, your hearers report a sense of dizziness. When do they think clearly? Is it when you are speaking, or is it when you are silent?"

Cassabrie let his words sink in. While it was true that dragons and humans seemed influenced by a Starlighter's wisdom, the effect rarely lasted. Most reverted to the way they were before, believing the lies she had tried to counter. No matter how hard she had tried, her hearers, for the most part, returned to acting on impulses that drove them as fiercely as did the whips of dragons. Neither she, nor Brinella, nor Koren penetrated past their ears. The influence was temporary. A Starlighter's words didn't change their hearts.

"You need not answer, Starlighter. I can read your face well enough to see that you understand."

Cassabrie clutched the edge of her cloak. It seemed so useless now, nothing more than a silly disguise. "What do I do with this information?"

"Keep it tucked away for future use. Perhaps when you carry out your plan, all will see the light that brings about real change."

Cassabrie reached into her dress's pocket and felt the explosive tube and control box. The plan she had in mind didn't seem to relate to Alaph's lesson at all. Maybe it would become clear eventually.

A shout sounded from the forest ridge, deadened by the falling snow. Edison and Orion stood together at the crest, waving at her.

"It is time," Alaph said. "Your desire to become a guiding angel is about to be fulfilled. May the Creator grant you the courage you need to perform all that is in your heart."

With a beat of his wings, Alaph leaped into a spin and transformed again into a snow-filled vortex. The cyclone skipped across the river and blended in with the storm until everything appeared to be as it was before.

A grinding noise made Cassabrie look down. Cracks had formed in the river's ice, and water now trickled over and around the floes. Rain mixed in with the snow, sizzling as it pelted the star's shell.

She lifted Exodus higher and hurried toward the forest. Rain in the Northlands? That had never happened while she had been around. And why would such thick ice break apart so quickly? The star couldn't be that hot.

Ahead on the ridge, Edison waved his sword, and his shouts grew clearer as she approached. "An army detachment is coming!"

After hurrying through the precipitation, now all snow once again, Cassabrie halted about thirty feet in front of Edison and Orion. "Is the portal open?" she asked.

"It was open a moment ago." Edison withdrew a crystalline peg from his pocket. "I closed it for now. I didn't want our good governor to run in there alone."

"I assume," Cassabrie said, suppressing a grin, "that you are protecting him from Magnar. That is a wise and noble act."

"Well, that's not exactly what I had in mind, but we did hear dragon wings on the other side not long ago. Magnar is close by." Edison sheathed his sword. "Marcelle showed up at the portal with three scouts, and the scouts returned to their detachment to lead the rest of them here. They could arrive at any moment, and I wanted them to see proof that there are dragons and human slaves here."

"Ah! You want me to tell a convincing tale so they'll be motivated to march in these cruel conditions."

Edison bowed his head. "That was my hope."

"Then get ready to open the portal," Cassabrie said, spreading out her arms. "I will set this forest stage with actors and actresses they will not soon forget."

⋊⋉

Jason stood on the village street, Elyssa on one side, Koren on the other. High above, Arxad and Xenith flew north. Arxad planned to escort his daughter past the barrier wall and then let her fly to the Northlands on her own, Cassabrie's finger in a pouch tied to her neck. He would be back soon to care for his mate, who now lay quietly on the Zodiac's lower level, fully stitched with the butcher's string and guarded by Randall.

Deference, with Elyssa's help, had been able to stitch Koren and Tibalt as well, and now Tibalt sat in the Zodiac with Deference, Randall, and Fellina, telling them stories about dungeon life and giving them hints on how best to raise a rat.

A short time ago, Jason and Randall had buried Petra near a spring she loved, and Koren sang a beautiful song about freedom, finishing with lines none of them would ever forget:

And she who spoke the fewest words
Gave love in deeds, in blood, in flame,
And now she sings Creator's songs,
Her tongue unleashed to praise his name.

Letting out a sigh, Jason turned to Koren. "Have you had enough time to recover? I think we need to hear a tale."

Koren spread out her cloak and curtsied. "Yes, young man. What tale would you like to hear?"

"Is it too soon to tell us where Taushin went and what he's up to?"

"Maybe. Maybe not. Let's find out."

Jason raised a finger. "And how about what's happening up north? Can you check on my father and the troops?"

"We shall see. Maybe we will also learn where Cassabrie went with Exodus. If not for her being inside the star, I wouldn't be able to tell any tales at all." Koren pulled her hood over her head and fanned out her cloak again. Her green eyes glittering, she looked up at the sky. "Starlight, wounded planet, grieving world, I ask to see mysteries of the recent past. The foul beast who fashions himself a king is likely plotting against your people, and those who live in fear of dragon whips will suffer if we delay in stopping him."

With a spin of her cloak, Koren backed away from Jason and Elyssa, taking dramatic steps as she scanned the street as if searching for a lost coin. "Taushin cannot see, so he must find eyes, eyes he can trust. Zena is dead. Hyborn, too. And his captive Starlighter has flown to freedom." She stopped and gasped, her eyes wide. "Dragons! He has found them, gathered them, convinced them to follow his kingly rule. Pheterone is plentiful, so they are appeased."

Taushin appeared next to her, pacing back and forth on the street. In front of him sat at least forty semi-transparent dragons, some of them huge guardians. A hefty she-dragon sat in the front row: Mallerin. As Taushin paced, he frequently aimed his eyebeams at the hefty she-dragon. Apparently he had found his surrogate eyesight—his mother's.

A human knelt between Taushin and his audience, shivering as he faced the watching dragons. Sores marked his forehead and both arms, some so close together they appeared to be one long abrasion. They oozed yellowish fluid, but the man didn't bother to wipe it.

Jason nudged Elyssa. "That man looks like Yeager."

"It is Yeager," she whispered. "He doesn't look so bold now, does he?"

Koren whipped her cloak around again. "Starlight, give us sound so we may hear their schemes."

Taushin's voice rode the air, warped at first, but the words and cadence soon matched his moving jaws. "Even now a host of humans from Darksphere approaches. They plan to invade and destroy us. Such is their passion for freeing their fellow humans."

"Then let them go free," one of the guardians said. "We have no need of them any longer."

Taushin shook his head. "That will not stop the invasion. They believe we will return to steal them away again, so they want to get rid of us once and for all. Our only choice is to attack and kill them first."

One of the drones raised a wing. "If their army is such as you described, then we will be slaughtered. We should fly to a refuge until they take their vermin home."

Taushin began pacing again. "Oh, yes. We will fly to a refuge, but first we will attack them in a way they cannot withstand." He waved a wing at Yeager. "That is why I brought this human here. He is infected with the disease that Exodus unleashed, and the virus spread quickly through his body. One of us will take him to a place where the advancing army can see him. Since he is extremely contagious, he will be their downfall."

"But will he not simply shout for them to stay away?" the drone asked.

Taushin laughed. "We have already taken care of that problem. The pitiful man lost his tongue only a few moments ago. I do not think anyone else will mourn that loss. He used it too frequently." He stopped his pacing again. "I need a volunteer to take him to the human army. It will be dangerous. You must get him as close to the marching front line as possible. When you return, I will make you my personal bodyguard, and you will enjoy the fruits of that position."

The guardian again spoke up. "And what are those fruits?"

"There are two immune humans. When all the others die, these two will be easy to pluck from the ground when we return from our refuge. The volunteer is free to do whatever he wishes with them, and I am sure you know what I mean."

Several of the older dragons looked at each other and laughed. "A Magnar-style banquet," one of them said. "But what of Cassabrie? I saw her fly to the north in Exodus. She is dangerous, and I assume she will return."

Taushin nodded. "She is dangerous, and she will return. I am preparing a surprise for her. When it is finished, I will let you all know what it is. Do not fear. She will not be a threat to us much longer."

"I will take the human," the guardian said. "The rewards outweigh the risks."

"Good. Go quickly. Cassabrie's greatest threat to us is in revealing our plans to Koren." He turned toward Koren and cast his eyebeams on her face. "And if you are listening, Starlighter, remember that you are telling a tale from the past, so we have already undertaken this plan. It is too late to stop us, and you have very little time before you join Petra and Yeager."

Koren swept the cloak over her face, blocking the eye-beams. Taushin disappeared first, then the other dragons, and finally Yeager.

She turned toward Elyssa and Jason and shuffled their way. Her shoulders low and her head drooping, she seemed to be exhausted.

"What's wrong?" Elyssa asked. "Are you sick?"

Keeping her stare downturned, she nodded.

"The disease?"

Koren drew her cloak back from her arm, revealing a line of sores from her wrist to her elbow. "They popped up a short time ago. I've been feeling sick deep inside for a while, but these are the first sores."

"Oh, Koren!" Elyssa embraced her and whispered into her ear. "Go to Deference. Maybe she knows of something that will slow it down." As she drew back, she gave Koren an encouraging smile. "Maybe Uriel has already figured out something, and all he needs is the genetic material."

"Yes." Koren's head drooped again. "Maybe."

Elyssa hooked her arm around Jason's. "Are you ready? Or am I skipping steps?"

"No need to explain." He drew his sword from his hip scabbard and checked the blade. "There's no time to lose."

"Are you feeling well enough to march?"

425

"Even if I had to walk barefoot on broken glass." After sliding his sword back in place, Jason lifted Koren's wrist and kissed her hand. "I'll be back as soon as I can."

Elyssa tightened her hold on his arm. "You mean *we'll* be back."

"We?"

"Of course. Did you seriously think I was going to let you go without me?"

Smiling, he shook his head. "I guess that was pretty—"

"Chivalrous." Elyssa pulled back and wagged a finger at him. "And you'd better stay chivalrous, or I'll tell your father what you said to me at Miller's Creek when we were six years old."

"Six years old? I don't remember that. What did I say?"

Half closing her eyes, Elyssa crossed her arms over her chest. "Just keep being a gentleman, and no one will ever know."

Koren hooked Jason's other elbow. "Will you take me, too?"

"But you're sick," he said. "You should—"

"Elyssa's the healer, so I need to stay close to her." Her bright smile lit up her face. "Besides, maybe I'll be able to sneak a look into a certain event that happened at Miller's Creek. I'm terrible at keeping secrets, you know."

Jason tightened the elbow hold. "Okay, that settles it. Koren's coming, too."

Elyssa locked gazes with Koren. For a moment, it seemed that they probed each other, each gifted young woman searching for a light, a connection, a meeting of the minds.

Finally, Koren smiled. Elyssa smiled back and slid her hand into Jason's. "That sounds good to me." She nodded toward the north. "Lead the way, warrior."

Check out this sample chapter from Liberator, book four in the Dragons of Starlight series

one

Jason steadied himself on the stone-movers' raft and scanned the sky from horizon to horizon. Elyssa had said dragons lurked in the area. Her Diviner's gift of detecting a presence in the air or hidden in the shadows seemed as sharp as ever. The fire-breathers were out there ... somewhere.

As he, Elyssa, and Koren floated northward on the river's slow current, clouds hovered low to the east, drifting closer with a freshening breeze. The western view held a forest beyond the opposite riverbank—peaceful and quiet. No scaly, winged beasts sailed or shuffled anywhere in sight. That was good, especially since Randall and Tibalt were marching through the forest in search of Wallace and the cattle-camp children. Maybe they would find the refugees in time to warn them about the deadly disease spreading through Starlight, a hard-enough task even without dragon interference. Since the disease was so contagious, and since Randall and Tibalt had both been exposed, providing a warning while staying at a safe distance would require more than a little ingenuity.

Turning to the front of the raft, Jason looked straight ahead. The first obstacle to their journey stood due north; the great barrier wall separating the Southlands region from the rest of Starlight, the same barrier that imprisoned hundreds of slaves and kept them from escaping the confines of the dragon kingdom. Now he and his friends had to break out and travel beyond the forbidden boundary.

Less than an hour earlier, Arxad had assured them that the wall was clear of guardian dragons when he passed by. He had escorted his daughter, Xenith, part of the way to the Northlands as she ferried Cassabrie's finger to Uriel Blackstone. They hoped Uriel could use the girl's genetic material to find a cure for the disease the punctured Exodus star had unleashed on the world.

Arxad then returned to the dragon village to care for his injured mate, Fellina. He offered the humans no direct transport, only a brief description about how to get past the wall—vague advice based on what he had been told. With the ability to fly over the wall, Arxad had never tried the alternative entrance himself. Still, if his advice proved reliable, easy passage would help them avoid a delay they couldn't afford. With the army from Jason's home planet of Major Four marching southward from the Northlands, and Taushin, the new dragon king, planning to send a diseased human into their ranks in order to infect the soldiers, someone had to warn the troops to stay away from the contagion. Since Elyssa was immune to the disease, she was the only one who could do it safely, making her transport vital.

Jason settled to a sitting position. The raft, built for moving stones from the mining pits to the barrier wall, seemed quite steady, easily carrying its three riders—he and Elyssa near the front, and Koren closer to the back—as well as two gunny sacks filled with food and extra clothing, each sack about the size of a small child. During the first part of their journey, Elyssa had been chatty, providing updates on sensations she felt as they procured the raft and provisions. Lately, however, she had grown quiet and somber.

Koren, sitting cross-legged with her hood pulled over her head, had hardly uttered a word—just a thank-you whenever he helped her move from place to place. With the Exodus disease now ravaging her body, she seemed to be getting more feeble by the hour. Although her face had turned pale, her hair, poking out around the edges of her hood, was still as fiery red as ever, and her green eyes sparkled. The physical traits of a Starlighter, a girl who could gather tales of the past out of the air, were still evident.

Less than a quarter mile away, the wall loomed. The uneven stones, cobbled together with pebbly mortar, seemed to rise as the raft drew closer, drifting on the placid current at a walking pace. They would arrive in a few moments.

Leaning close to Elyssa, Jason whispered, "Do you sense anything?"

"I still sense dragons, if that's what you mean, but they're not close." She rubbed her thumb and finger together. Her eyes, not quite as green as Koren's, gleamed in the sunlight. "I sense a change, the way the air feels after a bolt of lightning strikes nearby."

Jason searched the sky again. Even though no storm clouds loomed, it was wise to heed Elyssa's gifts of perception. Her auburn hair didn't match the striking red hue of Koren's, making her appear to be a Starlighter's shadowed reflection, but she possessed equally remarkable gifts, only subtler, more hidden. "I don't see any storms," he said. "I heard that it hardly ever rains around here at all."

"No storms," Elyssa said, her brow wrinkling, "but I sense something odd, too odd to describe."

Talk It Up!

Want free books?
First looks at the best new fiction?
Awesome exclusive merchandise?

We want to hear from you!

Give us your opinions on titles, covers, and stories.
Join the Z Street Team.

Email us at zstreetteam@zondervan.com
to sign up today!

Also—Friend us on Facebook!

www.facebook.com/goodteenreads

- Video Trailers
- Connect with your favorite authors
- Sneak peeks at new releases
- Giveaways
- Fun discussions
- And much more!